PRIMEVAL ORIGINS

LIGHT OF HONOR

BAVonsik
22 Mar 2017

BRETT VONSIK

CELESTIAL FURY
PUBLISHING

This is a work of fiction. The events and characters described herein are imaginary and are not intended to refer to specific places or living persons. The opinions expressed in this manuscript are solely the opinions of the author and do not represent the opinions or thoughts of the publisher. The author has represented and warranted full ownership and/or legal right to publish all the materials in this book.

Primeval Origins
Light of Honor
All Rights Reserved.
Copyright © 2016 Brett Vonsik
v4.0

Cover Art by Daniel Eskridge and Brett Vonsik

This book may not be reproduced, transmitted, or stored in whole or in part by any means, including graphic, electronic, or mechanical without the express written consent of the publisher except in the case of brief quotations embodied in critical articles and reviews.

Celestial Fury Publishing

Paperback ISBN: 978-0-578-17255-2
Hardback ISBN: 978-0-578-17256-9

Library of Congress Control Number: 2015910844

Web site with Primeval Origins Lexicon and Encyclopedia: www.primevalorigins.com

PRINTED IN THE UNITED STATES OF AMERICA

Primeval Origins

By Brett Vonsik

Paths of Anguish
Light of Honor

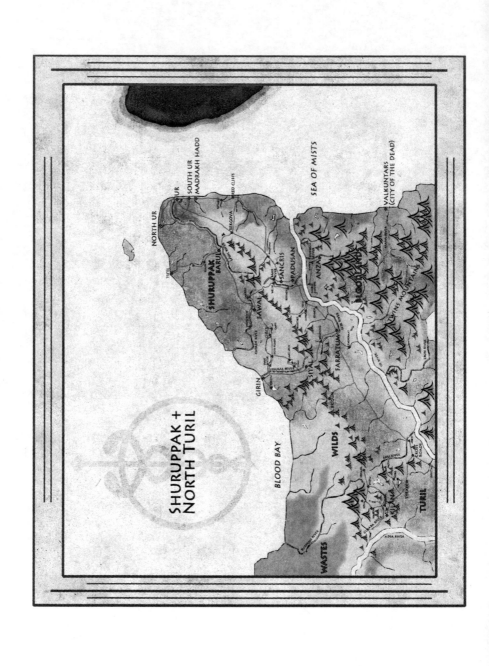

SHURUPPAK +
NORTH TURIL

Morality . . . Creation's precious gift to mortal life, alive within the Spark of Spirit; the bedrock sustaining fellowships, nourishing trust, and the principles of governance uplifting humanity from the beasts. For life, absent Morality, is existence as lowly animals driven in compelling purpose by the primal imperatives of survival, possession, and dominance, never heeding to ethical Principles, Virtues, and Righteousness.

Honor wielded . . . the sword of Morality rejects corruption and tyranny, the immortal enemies of the Light. Honor shields the Light from the devourer of virtues and righteous deeds . . . temptation, as disease consumes mortal flesh, leaving what Light remains twisted and defiled; tis the Honor within Light, the authority of strength and courage to resist . . . fight . . . repel . . . and push back corruption of self and governance with piercing sight, able to see purposeful illusions of collective imperatives and deceptions that incrementally lay the nets of slavery and tyranny over the unaware.

Morality absent Honor leads not to the benevolent nor the trusting nor the compassionate, but to selfishness, self-corruption, and the tyrannical heart, all acting in righteous guises and caring proclamations casting illusions to the unaware. Shadows of truth allowing lies to be embraced with nary a wary glance, and the immoral without merit; Morality without Honor dims the Light, defiling with a corrupting taint making the Light . . . selfish . . . dark . . . evil . . . unworthy in Judgment.

Morality embraced in Honor . . . highly sought by Creation; for without both guiding the creature man, no trust can be given as no trust is earned; no agreements hold, no oaths bind, no laws stand, no governances endure, no civilizations survive. Free Will binds by mortal choices in each Light's journey toward Righteousness or immorality. Creation's purpose declared in Commandments fixing Righteousness from the immoral, sets the path to virtuous life, and measure affirming or denying each Light in Judgment.

Endless are the canards and challenges to Morality and Honor . . . For the intent of the immoral, from lowliest governed to loftiest pronouncing rule, is redefinition of the high-sought bedrock. A redefinition born of self-weakness seeking securities, comforts, pleasures, and dominion over others, all with purpose satisfying selfish desires and wants cloaked as needs and rights; though none hold firm justifications in such ill-formed covets, only Creation's standard endures weigh and measure as Morality embraced in Honor held firm within the Light is Creation's vanguard against all that is foul, all that is evil in the cosmos.

The Harbinger of Judgments

Vanquisher

The gray-colored, nonslip-coated deck under Nikki's feet and the belly-high composite rail she tightly gripped rose and fell with the rolling swells of an anxious sea in the late afternoon's fading orange-hued sky. The fresh-scented ocean spray periodically filled her nose as the ninety-meter exploration yacht cruised the unsettled Atlantic waters somewhere in the Caribbean. How fast . . . She guessed fifteen knots, maybe more? This was all new to her. The strangely configured yacht was stable and durable . . . built for research in the most hostile places around the globe, as she was told by one of the crew. It had few comforts one would consider luxury, though the ship's stabilizers combined with its design kept the decks mostly level as the bow cut through the agitated sea kicked up by a retreating storm to the southwest. Nikki needed medication to keep herself upright and not lose her stomach despite the ship's advanced features. The downside to the medication, when added to the unrelenting high-speed cruising of the past four days, allowed Nikki little sleep. She would have protested to the ship's captain commanding their continuous high speeds causing an unrelenting pounding to the ship and crew . . . if it had not been needed to evade United Nations ships and aircraft hunting them. Nikki still had a difficult time believing the U.N. hunted them. She didn't understand their motives if doing so, but the crew was convinced; so Nikki quietly endured. When she lay in her bunk resting, she did so in a semi-meditative way. She felt tired, fatigued . . . out of "go juice." Though, as bad as Nikki felt, Anders looked worse standing next to her . . . pale-green skin color, bloodshot eyes, congestion sounding to be in his sinuses and upper chest. Fortunately, he wasn't running a fever she knew of or Nikki would see him bunk-ridden. Anders insisted on "staying vertical," as he put it . . . and not in his bunk, despite his walking around the ship sometimes as if drunk. He insisted on being awake for any new findings from the medical lab where their unconscious "friends" were being examined by Doctor Dunkle for the past four days.

"You should be resting," Nikki nagged at Shawn Anders again. He leaned into the safety rail of the starboard observation nest, a half-moon platform extending out from the bow side of starboard deck five. Anders, dressed in his now washed dark khaki field shirt and even darker pants and field boots, looked as if he was about to lose his dinner. Nikki cringed in sympathy.

"I'm not going to be wrapped in a blanket when the most significant discovery made by mankind *ever* is meters away being examined," Anders shot back defiantly and angrily. "I should be in there! And so should you! They won't even give us PDAs or remote monitors to let us watch what they're doing. '*Operational security,*' they say! '*Anyone could listen in,*' they say! How is anyone to function beyond remote dig sites these days without PDAs or PIMs?"

"The captain and crew treat us as if we're in their way." Nikki felt wounded at the thought of being considered so. She continued complaining, "Doctor Dunkle shoos me away when I get close to the med-lab. He says the sensors he's using on them 'go weird' when I'm near."

"How can that be?" Anders asked skeptically, then stared at the passing wake below as if expecting something to emerge from the waves, or for him to give something back to the sea. He swallowed hard, then continued. "Us . . . in the way of the crew of the *Wind Runner* . . . as if they're experts in the fields of paleontology and archeology? And what's with naming this ship *Wind Runner*? It doesn't even have sails!"

Frustration and anger filled Nikki too at being treated as insignificant. After a few moments of stewing, she decided it wasn't healthy or helpful to do so and thought on Ander's last question, trivia . . . a distraction. It was a curiosity, the ship's naming . . . and it nagged at her, and she didn't know why. Then it came to her. An ancient name she learned from her dreams. "It means 'Im'Kas.'"

"What the hell does *that* mean?" Anders snapped back, then swallowed hard as he turned a slightly different shade of green.

"It's the name of a powerful warrior from a time long ago . . . creation myth stuff," Nikki answered as if reciting an excerpt from a history book. "The language is Antaalin, a very ancient precursor to the Sumerian language of 3,000 BC, as well as several other lost languages, to us, even older than Sumerian."

"Never heard of it," Anders barked. His mood was argumentative, but Nikki let it pass. "Where did you learn these unknown tidbits you keep zinging at me?"

Nikki looked out over the roiling ocean with wave crest-to-trough heights of four- to six-feet while she searched her memory trying to think if she had read this particular "tidbit" anywhere. *Nothing.* "I don't know how I know it. I just do."

"Are you making this stuff up . . . to keep me mentally occupied?" Anders asked with a hint of a smile.

"No," Nikki answered flatly, honestly. "I've told you I feel like I know them."

"Our *friends* in the medical lab?" Anders sought to confirm her meaning.

"Yes," Nikki replied a little cautiously. Anders was skeptical of her assertion that she knew them. "I told you I feel like I can sense . . . feel their moods, almost know their thoughts. It's all confusing. I get flashes of things . . . sometimes I understand . . . Most other times, it's confusing."

"Well, I don't subscribe to telepathy or ESP," Anders dismissively stated his position on the matter as he stood tall, then immediately went to hunching over the railing as he concentrated a little while on something unseen to Nikki.

"I didn't say . . ." Nikki didn't get to finish her protest.

The sky suddenly turned a shade darker as an electrical hum filled the air. Nikki and Anders looked around seeking to understand what had just happened. A deathly still quiet fell over the ship, except for the wind and that electrical hum. A crew member, the thick-bodied Cuban dressed in the crew uniform of light khaki pants and short-sleeved shirt, came bounding down the steps from the upper decks forward of their observation nest. He ran up to them with an air of urgency. Nikki wished she could remember his name as he approached.

"You two need to be in the med-lab," the Cuban demanded in his Spanish accent.

"What's happening?" Nikki asked.

"No time to talk." The Cuban was insistent. "Get going!"

"But Doctor Dunkle doesn't want me in the med-lab," Nikki protested as the Cuban pushed them along aft past a set of stairs going to the deck above and into the protected corridor running the starboard side of the ship. They scurried along where the ship's hull extended upward on their left and the transparent walls separating them from the inner ship on their right. To Nikki's surprise, the walls were no longer transparent, allowing her to see into the forward crew lounge . . . All the walls were now a subdued gray metal texture.

"Captain's orders," the Cuban announced as he insisted they keep moving. "The captain turned on the array covering the upper deck. In a couple of minutes we'll all get cooked if we stay out here."

"What . . . cooked?" Anders managed to get the words out in between noxious belches.

"How——" Nikki started to ask another question as the Cuban touched an access pad on the gray wall to the inner compartments, then pushed them through into the interior of the ship when the vacuum sealed pocket-door hissed, sliding open. The thick-bodied Cuban didn't follow as the door slid closed, then hissed again before the vacuum seal was remade.

"Damn pushy guy," Anders complained with a hint of disdain.

The room where they stood was the starboard-side vestibule of the forward crew lounge. The open space to their right faced the bow providing an open panoramic view through semitransparent exterior walls that many of the crew desired when not working. Nikki pondered at the surprises of this ship. There were more than a few. These exterior walls were possible with nanotechnology, as she was told, though Nikki wasn't clear how the thing worked. The lounge was the only place on the ship Nikki knew of with better than Spartan-style seating, having large cushioned chairs and a couch with a low entertainment table, in addition to stools at several wall-mounted counters, and a kitchenette that was out of view. A large holowall projection system at the bow-side of the room displayed an empty image instead of the unsettling news of unrest and riots from around the world of the past few days. A hint of buttered popcorn lingered in the air, teasing Nikki's nose. Her stomach grumbled as a spike of hunger struck her. Anders groaned as he swallowed hard and changed into another shade of pale-green. Nikki worried he would make a mess of things at any moment. She looked about the room for anything that might act as a bucket. There were several garbage baskets, if needed.

Another pocket-door just to their left whooshed open, revealing the medical lab, or what some of the crew called "Sickbay." The tall, dark-haired Doctor Dunkle, dressed in a white lab coat over khaki pants and a black button-down shirt, stood between two biobeds in the middle of the lab, both occupied by Nikki and Anders's "friends." Nikki gave the doctor a nervous smile. He returned a solemn look before motioning them to enter. The pocket-door whooshed closed once they stepped into the forbidden grounds of the lab. The lab had a distinct scent of cleanliness, to the point of sterile. Nikki welcomed the smell.

Doctor Dunkle looked at the bio-readings of his two *patients* immediately upon Nikki and Anders's entrance. Nikki felt the doctor considered his *patients* more *specimens* by the way he spoke of, poked, and prodded them. It unsettled and angered her. Some of that came out the last time Nikki and the doctor were in the lab together. She begrudgingly admitted to herself that her being forbidden from this place was due partly because of her protests. She sought to control her "p's" and "q's" now that she again tread in Doctor Dunkle's domain.

"Don't move," Doctor Dunkle demanded of Nikki with a finger of his left hand pointed directly at her. He almost ignored her otherwise while he silently monitored readings from both biobeds while wearing an intense expression. Only audio beeps of heartbeats filled the room.

In addition to the slight rising and falling of the deck that Nikki had gotten used to and compensated for while walking and standing, the ship suddenly started listing right, causing Nikki to shift her weight to keep her balance. Glancing at Anders with concern for his condition, she found him with his hand against the wall on their left, near another pocket-door to the outside deck. He looked to need the wall to keep himself steady.

"Use that medical waste can next to you, if you must." Doctor Dunkle had no sympathy in his voice for Anders.

Nikki kept her eyes on Anders in case he needed help. Somehow, the man continued to defy his body's urges. Before she knew what was happening, the doctor had stepped over to her, placing a biosensor on her forehead. Nikki jerked her head away from him as she stepped backward.

"What are you doing?" Nikki demanded as she reached up to remove something stuck to her forehead.

"Leave it," the doctor demanded. "I need to see if you are interacting."

"What? Interacting? You're making no sense," Nikki protested.

The doctor kept on with his intense scrutiny of numerous bio-readings from his two subjects on his handheld ePaper flexi-display. He absently spoke, "These two are full of surprises. Their blood types are unknown, but high in antibiotic properties. Subject Two has an immune system rivaling crocodilians. Subject One . . . well, he could be dunked in the worst bacteria festering swamp known, and I suspect he'd just walk out of it wanting nothing more than a good shower. Their tissue density is much higher than any of us . . . 36 percent for Subject Two and 48 percent for Subject One. They have additional muscle strands, tendons, and colored fibers throughout their bodies . . . as if out of control Morgellons cases."

"That's not possible, unless . . ." Anders fought back being sick in midthought. "Unless they've been genetically modified . . . a lot."

Doctor Dunkle dismissively sniffed at Anders's comment.

"Isn't Morgellons terribly painful?" Nikki asked.

"Readings changed . . . Subject One's Alpha is modulating . . . hypergamma waves, at 161 hertz, have spiked and remain elevated with modulation." Doctor Dunkle talked more to himself as if taking notes than trying to explain what he was doing. "I'm detecting a new hypergamma wave pattern from Subject Three, Ms. Ricks . . . at an unsteady 161 hertz. Its low in amplitude, but confirmed present and . . . almost matching in wave pattern with Subject One's pattern. Subject One's lambda wave patterns detected as new, some . . . twenty-three minutes ago, is unchanged. The synchronized lambda patterns coming from an unknown source continue to grow in strength, but is not originating from Subject Three."

A slight trembling quality in the doctor's voice combined with a hint of congestion and several forced breaths while dictating made Nikki curious if the doctor was also sick. Anders looked about to fall over with that pale-green coloring, and now looking closer at Doctor Dunkle, Nikki saw hints of a similar complexion. She wondered if she was next at catching something. She decided to not worry about it. If an illness was running around the ship she would get it too. Nikki thought it strange the calmness in which she felt over getting ill. Stranger yet, she felt calm . . . safe, but she didn't know why.

"I can't stand the pathetic sight of you any longer," Doctor Dunkle announced as he stepped close to Anders in a way that Nikki couldn't see what he was doing. A short hissing sound filled the room before the doctor turned to Nikki giving her a visual once-over. "Your coloring is good. You don't appear ill. Do you feel ill?"

"No," Nikki answered calmly . . . matter-of-factly. She felt good, she realized with a smile.

"Our subjects have infected everyone except you." The doctor continued while looking over Nikki closer, particularly her face. He placed the back of his hand to her forehead. Nikki allowed him to with little concern over his intentions or if he planned to give her a shot of whatever he gave Anders. "Makes no sense. You've been closest to the subjects and you appear healthy . . . when the facts of the situation tell me without my antibiotics or immune booster cocktail you should be lying on the floor next to your colleague with the same terrible complexion he's sporting."

Nikki felt an inner calmness while smiling back at the doctor. She felt . . . safe. Hugged in a warm blanket of safe, in fact. The doctor saw something in her face or demeanor that spiked his curiosity, bringing on an even closer inspection of her with his old-school exam methods; taking her pulse, physically touching her face and neck, checking for anything indicating illness or something out of the ordinary. He smelled her breath which she took no offense to.

"You're too healthy . . ." the doctor finally announced. "And happy. You appear drunk, but I don't detect any alcohol on your breath. Are you on meds I don't know about? Did you pick up a little of the local pharma while in South America?"

Nikki calmly answered "No" to his questions. She realized she did feel happy . . . and safe. She smiled to herself despite getting a solid whiff of the doctor's "xactlee's breath"; where his breath smelled exactly like his butt. Nikki snickered happily to herself at her silent joke.

Realization filled Doctor Dunkle's eyes just before he whirled about returning to the biobeds to look at sensor readings of his "subjects" on his ePaper flexi-display. He tapped the paper-thin flexi-plate several times before putting on that "Aha!" look. "I'll be . . . there it is at almost the exact same 161 hertz, but a different modulation. Computer . . . continue recording."

Doctor Dunkle then spoke in that dictation voice of his, "Subject Three appears to be sharing . . . no something more than that. She appears to be linked in some manner to Subject One via shared hypergamma brain wave frequencies . . . at 161 hertz. Subject Three appears inebriated . . . almost euphoric at this time. Her condition appears to have manifested itself very quickly after entering the same room as Subject One. Her bio-readings are all in the highly healthy range and continue to get stronger . . . stronger as her brain waves become closer to being synchronized in modulation with Subject One's pattern. What the hell? This can't be. The patterns are starting to look like . . . the patterns I took of Mr. H . . . years ago. Interesting is an understatement. Subject One's lambda brain wave pattern appears to have synchronized with a second lambda pattern from the unknown origin."

It was difficult for Nikki to follow Doctor Dunkle's comments on his observations and his reasoning . . . speculations. Facts. Facts. Facts. She needed facts. Her professors demanded it. Nikki frowned at the latter thought, then smiled big at no one in particular.

"What are you stupidly smiling at, Nikki?" Anders asked with an edge in his tone. He now stood with his butt to the wall and hands on thighs supporting himself. His coloring still looked terrible, but he seemed to have more energy now, after that shot the doctor gave him.

"Stupidly?" Nikki replied. She smiled broader. "He knows. It knows."

"What are you talking about?" Anders asked with a frustrated grimace.

"Yes. What are you talking about, Ms. Ricks?" Doctor Dunkle asked with an intense interest.

The white lighting in the room suddenly dimmed as red lights brightened until the entire room was bathed in red. An annoying alarm sounded. Nikki felt multiple resounding shudders within the ship.

"The captain just placed the ship into a defensive posture," Doctor Dunkle informed Anders and Nikki. The doctor sounded startled and a little confused as he tapped away at his ePaper. With a wave of his left hand over his flexi-display, in a sweeping gesture toward the workstations to Nikki's right, a desktop holo-display lit up with a visual image of what looked to be a control room, maybe the bridge, with an overlay of digital data Nikki didn't understand. The scene moved about erratically, left and right, then focused on another ePaper flexi-display in the scene held by someone with big hands. The doctor stood mesmerized watching the desktop holo-display. The scene flowed from digital maps with moving icons and vectored lines on the in-scene ePaper and displays around the bridge. None of what she saw meant anything to Nikki. The view swept upward to a view of out of the window from what she was now certain was the bridge of the *Wind Runner*. Another tapping at his ePaper by Doctor Dunkle silenced the alarm, though the med-lab remained bathed in red.

"What are we looking at?" Anders asked.

Doctor Dunkle shot a hot glare at Anders. "The captain's vid-eyes."

Anders and Nikki looked at the doctor with no idea what he was talking about. Doctor Dunkle showed visible frustration as a contemptuous expression formed on his face, then disappeared almost as fast. "The captain and key others aboard have vid-eyes. Artificial lenses that are video cameras . . . with informational overlays and sound capture. Mr. H insists on senior crew using the things. The captain doesn't know I can tap into them, so keep this quiet. It's the only way I know what's going on around here."

"So, what's going on?" Anders asked.

"We're being pursued by an unknown ship that just launched UCAVs at us . . . that are now approaching our stern," Doctor Dunkle answered while keeping his eyes glued to the holo-display. He tapped his ePaper again, activating the sound from the bridge. Multiple people were talking rapidly in an acronym soup that Nikki didn't understand. The video feed now saw the captain looking at a thermal image of the closing UCAVs on his ePaper. Five triangular-shaped things all with black bodies almost undetectable on the thermal, three were carrying what looked to be cylinder-shaped objects slung underneath them.

"What are they carrying?" Nikki asked, worried the UCAVs were bringing bombs.

"I'm not sure . . ." Doctor Dunkle kept his attention fixed on the holo-display. "S.C., identify approaching aircraft and payloads."

A few moments passed before a hauntingly familiar male voice Nikki felt she should know announced, "Five Xanthium Class Twelve UCAVs approach. Three UCAVs are configured with drop pods, each capable of deploying a wide range of ordinance or a single assault soldier."

"Huh . . .," Doctor Dunkle thought for a moment before speaking his conclusion. "I'll bet they're soldiers. They mean to board us! S.C., secure all existing med-lab files, data, and ongoing data collection with Level Three access."

"Level Three Security Protocols executed for med-lab," the S.C. voice replied almost immediately. The male voice of the ship's computer nagged at Nikki. It was familiar somehow.

Another voice announced over the holo-display feed, "Thirty seconds out. Captain . . . engage them?"

The radio on the bridge crackled with a Western Asia accent. "Vessel *Wind Runner*, this is the United Nations frigate *Watchman*. You are ordered to lie to."

The bridge crew froze. Nobody spoke as they watched the captain scan the bridge.

"Affirmative, Mr. Beckmire," the captain replied calmly in his singsong accent. Nikki misidentified him as European the first time she heard him speak with those rising and falling inflections in his cadence. Later, she learned his accent was common to those from where he lived most of his life, Trinidad. "Power up the EM shields and weapons. Blast those UCAV buggers out of the sky."

"Hard to port!" The captain commanded without warning. "The *Watchman*'s using the wireless trying to distract us from those UCAVs. I mean not to let them drop those pods on us."

"Are they bombs?" Another voice asked from the bridge.

"Either that or Action Men meaning to board us," the captain answered in his singsong inflections as the ship listed right as the *Wind Runner* made its sharp left turn to port.

"Hard to starboard!" The captain commanded sternly again, without warning. "Keep at the evasive maneuvers. Make it a challenge for the UCAVs to target Him. Launch the minis. Find their mother."

The holo-display video of the bridge swung to the rear of the compartment looking at a dark-haired crewman dressed in khaki pants and short-sleeved shirt pulling weapons from a built-in wall locker. The captain's vid-eyes overlay identified him as Robert Gomez, *Wind Runner* Security Office. Nikki felt proud of herself as she was starting to understand how the vid-eyes worked. The weapons he passed out to the bridge crew looked like military rifles and shotguns of some types, but Nikki wasn't certain which. After all, she didn't like the things any more than her government, who continuously distributed safety announcements demanding the reporting of anyone with an unlicensed weapon . . . which meant all weapons. The *Wind Runner* listed left as the ship turned starboard.

"Mr. Gomez," the captain sternly spoke with flat emotions, his rising and falling inflections muted, "pair up the watch and station them on all decks. They are to cut down any intruders. Report status over internal ship blowers . . . keep off the mobiles and wireless. These fellows will be monitoring anything not a hardline."

Gomez tossed several more weapons to unseen crewmen, then exited the rear door of the bridge with a weapon in hand and another slung over his shoulder. The captain's eyes returned to the holo-display at the front of the bridge command console that now showed a three-dimensional tactical display of what Nikki concluded was their situation. The UCAVs easily maneuvered behind the *Wind Runner* as it listed right again, turning port. The UCAVs made a pass at the ship, but had trouble lining up a drop of their pods. Nikki heard and felt firing of some type of large guns followed by what sounded like a rocket launching aft of the med-lab.

Nikki looked at Doctor Dunkle for answers, yet didn't voice her question out of concern that the answer would make her feel unsafe. The doctor watched a tactical display on his ePaper. He spoke without looking at Nikki or Anders. "Those are .50 caliber railguns and antiaircraft missiles."

On the bridge, the captain continued issuing orders in his stern, singsong tone, "Find her, gentlemen. We know she's not American, so we have freedoms, and thankfully, she's not Chinese or we would be sunk by now. Find her. I don't want to get a hammering by that heavy railgun she carries."

The radio crackled again. "Vessel *Wind Runner*, this is the United Nations frigate *Watchman*. You are ordered to cease-fire and lie to. Prepare to be boarded."

More railgun fire and another missile launch rattled the med-lab. Nikki knew she should be feeling fear . . . a lot of it, but she did not. *Strange*, she thought, but didn't know why. Voices from the bridge drew her attention back to the holo-display. The captain darted his eyes between the bridge's tactical situation display and the thermal sensor. Using information from both displays, it looked like a missile from the *Wind Runner* shot down one of the UCAVs as the other four made another pass at them. Nikki felt the ship take several hits as the captain watched on the tactical display two of the UCAVs drop their pods on the far stern section of the main deck, aft of the helicopter pad, as another black triangle fell to a railgun's antiaircraft fire.

On the med-lab's holo-display, a big finger touched the PA button on an ePaper flexi-display held by the captain. Over the loudspeakers outside of the med-lab, the captain's voice projected loudly ordering his crew to engage all intruders with deadly force.

"Are they going to board us, Captain?" Another unfamiliar, unseen voice to Nikki on the bridge questioned.

"They have already, Mr. Miller," the captain answered flatly. Looking to his ePaper, the captain tapped Secure Comm followed by Personal-Range selections. His ePaper display and vid-eyes overlay matched lists of crew within range. "Mr. Gomez, report . . . on a hardline, if you can."

Only the muffled exchange between the bridge crew could be heard as the *Wind Runner* listed left. Another burst of railgun fire from the aft deck ended abruptly with an explosion shaking the med-lab.

"What was that?" Nikki asked with a growing concern for their safety.

"One of the railguns is offline." Doctor Dunkle answered as he tapped his flexi-plate. "Something took out the aft gun."

A scratchy voice over the holo-display caught Nikki's attention. "Gomez from the quarterdeck. I've got movement near the helipad. Two black-suited intruders. One blew away the aft railgun. We're engaging them."

Nikki heard an extended rumbling of gunfire and unintelligible yelling from multiple places low and high around the med-lab. On the holo-display, the captain's vid-eyes followed the tactical display and onboard ship cameras. The crew battled two soldiers in dark-colored armor advancing forward on the main deck from the helicopter pad. Nikki grew concerned with the ease they advanced through the resisting crew despite taking numerous small arms hits. A UCAV flew over the aft deck dropping a third pod. It broke apart almost the instant it was released from the UCAV. Another armored soldier fell free from the twirling pod shells, landing in a crouch with a charged electrical display on the EM array aft of the quarterdeck. The soldier carried a hefty gun. Directly in front of the soldier, Gomez and another crewman fired on the dark-armored intruder with everything they had. Guns blazed as bullets riddled the armor, but all deflected off . . . some throwing sparks.

"S.C., identify armored intruders," Doctor Dunkle commanded the ship's computer.

The S.C. answered in that male voice as Nikki watched in horror as Gomez and his fellow crewman were knocked down in a hail of bullets from that hefty gun. She feared them dead. "Intruders are identified as *Tyr Soldiers*, wearing United Nations Mark IV battle suits."

"Doctor, are we safe in here?" Anders asked with thick skepticism in his voice.

"Next to the mini-fusion reactor room, this deck is the heaviest armored," Doctor Dunkle answered with a less-than-confident tone.

The sense of being safe waned from Nikki. Anxiety started to fill her as she struggled not to panic. A beeping tone from his ePaper flexi-plate drew Doctor Dunkle's attention to the bio-readings and brain wave activities he was monitoring. "Everything just went out of synchronization . . . The readings are all over the place, except for the lambda waves."

Doctor Dunkle appeared frustrated as he begrudgingly considered something before opening a compartment to the left of the holo-display where he retrieved several handguns. He waved Nikki and Anders close, then handed a gun to each of them. "These are a last resort. Aim at the face shields of the Tyr Soldiers. Every other round is armor piercing followed by an explosive."

"Do you really expect these little things to work on that armor after what we just saw?" Anders protested.

"They will have some effect," Doctor Dunkle replied with a pragmatic tone of hope, "though I can't guarantee anything at this moment."

The captain's vid-eyes now followed the ship's cameras on his ePaper as the Tyr Soldier who downed Gomez jumped to the quarterdeck just aft of the bridge. The captain ordered his bridge crew to abandon their stations for the auxiliary bridge below as he moved out of the direct line of the aft door. Nikki heard the rapid footfalls and chaotic yells of the bridge crew as an explosion blew the aft door apart, sending a concussion wave and shrapnel everywhere. The captain was knocked to the deck in the explosion. Darkness filled the holo-display. When the captain's vid-eyes started transmitting again and he was able to focus his eyes, a Tyr Soldier stood in the doorway, his gun rapidly firing, sending shockwaves, not bullets, throughout the bridge. The captain raised his weapon as he lay on his back. It looked like a big gun to Nikki. Another explosion, originating at the Tyr Soldier, filled the bridge when the captain fired. Again, a few long moments of static and darkness on the holo-display. The captain's vid-eyes started transmitting short moments later when he reopened his eyes. Continuous groans of pain came from him. He was in bad shape if Nikki read his vitals correctly on the vid-eyes overlay. The Tyr Soldier was slumped over the twisted wreckage of the bridge door. His armor heavily damaged, though it appeared to be reforming . . . regenerating.

Doctor Dunkle's attention was drawn again to his ePaper by another series of beeping tones. His face took on a confounded expression. "I don't understand . . . lambda, hypergamma, and epsilon waves are all spiking in Subject One, but from what? His brain hemispheres have been out of synchronization, but now are starting to match up to each other as the lambda patterns strengthen."

"Really, Doctor?" Nikki was incredulous. "Worrying over bio-readings when the ship is being attacked?"

"I second that," Anders added with more vigor than Nikki expected given his sickly condition.

Without warning Nikki didn't feel well. Dizziness and a feeling of being disconnected from her surroundings grew intense. Then a seizure hit her. Nikki felt it, was aware of the seizure and what it was doing to her, the painful spasms everywhere and her inability to control her body. Time no longer mattered, nor could she measure it. Only the spasms mattered . . . painful and intense. Then it all subsided. Relief washed over her as she realized she now slumped over one of the beds. She hoped it was Rogaan's, then chastised herself for the selfish thought. Anders and Doctor Dunkle lifted her up from under her arms back to her feet where her shaky legs were almost unable to keep the rest of her upright, forcing her to keep hands clamped to the edge of the bed. She realized she no longer held a gun in her hands. Where it was she didn't know. A mix of contemptuous and guilty feelings washed over her concerning the weapon as she realized which bed she leaned against. *It's Aren's bed.* Nikki felt disappointed.

"Dunkle, evacuate the precious cargo," the captain ordered over the med-lab's intercom. Pain filled the man's shaky voice, his singsong inflection almost nonexistent.

Doctor Dunkle tapped his ePaper to acknowledge he understood his orders when bullets riddled the starboard door, leaving indentations in an almost horizontal line across the door. A second burst of fire from outside the lab made indentations at the upper edge of the door where one of the locking lugs secured the door. A third burst left indentations at the lower edge of the door where the second set of lugs locked the door in place.

"Ah . . . Doctor, what do we do?" Nikki almost cried her words as fear and panic gripped her hard. She looked to Anders for answers, who now stood with a much-improved complexion, but he looked as dumbfounded as she felt.

"Emergency in med-lab," Doctor Dunkle called out to what Nikki assumed was the ship's intercom. "Enemy soldiers attempting to breach laboratory exterior doors starboard—"

Boom! A stunning and deafening explosion knocked Nikki to the floor. She lay on the cool surface for what seemed a long time. An acrid smell filled her nose causing her to choke. Her ears rang loud, and her head throbbed in pain. Nikki sucked in a breath that brought on intense choking as acrid air filled and stung her lungs. She regretted taking the breath even after the intense coughing subsided. She vaguely remained aware of the doctor and Anders by their pain-filled groaning. The screeching sound of metal being bent pierced the ringing in her head. Nikki struggled to open her eyes . . . clear her head. *Who would think opening one's eyes would require so much effort?* Again, she tried. Blurry spots of light dominated her vision. She blinked hard several times before regaining enough of her sight to see the fuzzy outline of a Tyr Soldier peel back the lab's starboard-side sliding door.

Gunfire rang out just above her, causing the ringing in her ears to hurt as projectiles struck the Tyr Soldier's upper chest and shoulder, careening off the black armor into the surrounding walls or exploding on contact. The small explosions caused the dark-armored soldier to reel back some. Nikki hoped they punched through the armor somehow and hurt him. Her hope evaporated away when she saw the Tyr Soldier's left arm raise and fire a pair of dartlike projectiles over her. She heard the trembling voice of Doctor Dunkle above her before he collapsed partly on top of her. The weight of his body across her legs made it difficult for her to move . . . to get up and run.

Anders, lying on the floor between Nikki and the Tyr Soldier, raised his gun with a trembling hand and fired repeatedly. Projectiles careened off the dark armor, then ripped holes in the walls and ceiling. The exploding projectiles peppered the black armor in several places and walls beyond. Before Nikki realized what was happening, the Tyr Soldier cleared the mangled lab door, grabbed Anders by the neck and shoulder yanking him from the floor, then bull-rushed him into the wall on the opposite side of the lab with a loud thud. Nikki feared Anders to be broken and killed by the impact. She rolled over trying to see him better with the hope he still lived. Anders struggled against his overpowering foe and still held his gun. He then fired it several more times at point-blank range into the armored chest of his tormentor. Anders cried out in pain as the first projectile ricocheted off the armor, striking himself in the shoulder, the second projectile exploded abdomen high. Anders dropped his gun to grab at his chest and stomach with twitching movements betraying the terrible pain he felt.

He's dying! Nikki feared for Anders. *He's killing him!* She pulled herself out from under the barely moving doctor and looked for something to hit the Tyr Soldier with. She could not allow the Tyr Soldier to kill Anders. She found the doctor's gun lying by her feet. Her emotions swirled in conflict. She never thought of shooting a gun, let alone actually shooting someone. Anders yelled out in agony. She decided. It was an easier choice than she thought. Picking up the gun with both hands, she pointed it at the soldier's back. Her hands trembled, visibly shook. She fired. Nikki didn't know how many times she pulled the trigger or if she hit her target. The next thing she knew, the Tyr Soldier had her in his grasp, tossing her into the wall next to where Anders lay on the floor with his back propped up against the wall. She felt weightless when tossed, then the painful impact of the wall jarring her back, shoulders, neck, and head, then the thud of her body on the floor. The impact with the floor shot pains through her hips and legs as her head landed on Ander's thighs. A horrid synthetic voice hissed, sending a wave of chills through Nikki. "How dare you defy the Tyr!"

The Tyr Soldier grabbed both Nikki and Anders by the necks and lifted them up with their backs against the lab's outer wall, such their feet no longer touched the floor, then stated, "Your punishments—Death."

Pain racked Nikki as her neck stretched. She gripped the armored left gauntlet of the soldier with both of her hands, trying to keep her neck from breaking. She did her best to pry one of the fingers from her throat. Nikki choked. The Tyr Soldier was too strong. She couldn't breathe. *I'm going to die.* Nikki feared dying. She wasn't ready to die. Panic took her over, and she kicked wildly at the dark armor in front of her. Nothing. Nikki's vision started turning gray. Her struggles slowed, and she struck with less force as her energy to fight off her killer waned. *I'm dead.* Nikki begrudgingly accepted her fate. She looked away from the black face shield of the Tyr Soldier in front of her where she could see her reflection. She didn't want to watch herself die. She wasn't ready for this. An erratic melody of beeps drew her attention to the biobeds over the left shoulder of her would-be killer where two strangers . . . no, they were more than strangers—lay oblivious to what was happening. They would also die this day, and she could do nothing about it. The erratic tones were from Rogaan's heart rate and brain wave EEG rhythms displayed on the bio-monitors above his head, showing increases in both along with unsynchronized brain patterns. The world darkened for her. A surge of panic welled up inside her at the thought of her last breath. Her heart raced as anxiety filled her every emotion. She felt it as much as she felt anything before in her life. Calm. A soothing calm suddenly fell over her. With harmonious tones, the monitor above Rogaan's head displayed all of his brain waves and brain hemisphere locked in synchronization. His heart rate strong and steady. Nikki looked back into the black face shield of the Tyr Soldier where her reflection stared back at her. She smiled. The Tyr Soldier tilted his head, confused at and pondering Nikki's reaction to her imminent death.

Nikki knew it was coming before she saw the thick, muscular arm with its metallic forearm guard come crashing down on the left arm of the Tyr Soldier. She felt the release of the armored hand from her throat and her short fall to the floor where she crumpled in a slumped kneeling position gasping for air. Looking up, she saw the Tyr Soldier stunned by the blow with his arm dangling down. He released Anders from his right gauntlet, allowing his limp body to fall to the floor with a thud before turning toward a foe he hadn't anticipated. Facing the Tyr Soldier was the muscular build of a white-robed six-foot figure standing ready in a relaxed fight stance. His unkempt hair obscured much of his face, but Nikki knew what it looked like . . . knew how he set his jaw when readying himself for battle. She felt his confidence . . . his determination. She smiled. The Tyr Soldier swung a right-handed haymaker at his foe with the obvious intent to end this battle in one shot. Rogaan easily ducked the sweeping attack with surprising speed, then hit his armored foe in the chest with a right-handed palm strike complete with rotation of his upper body and hips. The Tyr Soldier flew backward, slamming into the locked port-side pocket-door leading to the crew lounge. The metal door was left with an indentation of the Tyr Soldier as the dark-armored warrior landed on his boots in a slouched stance. It appeared he was stunned by the blow. His left arm snapped toward Rogaan, then fired a pair of what Nikki now knew as TASER darts. Rogaan deflected them away with his dark blue forearm guards. Rogaan's arms moved in a blur, further surprising both Nikki and the dark-armored U.N. warrior. The Tyr Soldier raised his right arm at Rogaan firing a burst of projectiles. In a blur, Rogaan rotated his upper body and used his forearm guards to deflect most of the projectiles. Several hit Rogaan's left hand and unguarded wrist, passing completely through and destroying a secondary monitor below the main one to the biobed he slept in a moment before. The other projectiles deflected by the metallic guards ricocheted around the room. Rogaan's demeanor turned dark . . . angry . . . enraged. He launched himself at the Tyr Soldier with a quickness catching Nikki by surprise. Rogaan landed in front of the dark-armored Tyr Soldier, striking him with a straight right-hand punch to the head that he held for a long moment with his foe's helmet pinned to the dented door. The Tyr Soldier's body slumped limp. When Rogaan withdrew his punch, the dark-armored U.N. warrior fell to the floor in a heap . . . lifeless. Nikki, surprisingly, realized the shape of Rogaan's right forearm guard changed, reformed with an added spikelike blade extending from his fist. A vertical slot was left in the dented pocket-door where the helmet of the dead Tyr Soldier had been pinned. Rogaan had completely driven his blade through helmet and door. Blood slowly dripped onto the floor of the lab from the vertical slots in the black helmet.

Rogaan stood up as he examined the unmoving body of his foe with eyes practiced at the task. When satisfied that what he set out to do was done, he turned his attention to Nikki and Anders. He looked her over briefly, then moved to Anders without a change of expression. Nikki wondered at what Rogaan saw when he "examined" her. On Anders, Rogaan immediately found wounds on his shoulder and side. Rogaan's forearm guards, his *Ra'Sakti*, reshaped itself as if liquid metal crawling over his skin to his hands where it conformed with dark blue metallic tendrils over his palms and fingers. Placing his hands on Anders's wounds, Rogaan concentrated for a few moments before Anders started twitching wildly, then fell still. Without ceremony, Rogaan rose, leaving the still and unconscious Anders on the floor. Then, Rogaan's attention turned to Aren. He stepped to a spot in-between the two biobeds. Staring at the biobed monitor displaying Aren's erratic bio-readings, Rogaan appeared to understand what he looked at. Aren's bio-signs were weak and getting worse, as if Aren was dying. Nikki wondered at that. *How could Rogaan know or understand the English displays?* Rogaan then passed his hands over Aren's body in what appeared to be a quick examination of his friend. As he did with Anders, Rogaan placed his hands over a growing red spot on Aren's side, then concentrated for a few moments. Aren did not stir. Leaning over his friend, Rogaan spoke to Aren, "*Negeltu, ga dusa.*"

Nikki understood Rogaan's words though she knew he didn't speak them in English or any language known . . . "*Awake, my friend.*" A look of concern grew on Rogaan's face when Aren didn't respond. He then started looking around Aren's bed for something, inspecting shelves and opening compartments. Frustrated is how Nikki interpreted Rogaan once his search ended with hands on hips.

"*Mese me Aren's Agni zagin duruna?*" Rogaan asked Nikki.

Nikki sat shocked as Rogaan addressed her directly. Until now, his presence felt like a living dream, and for the first time he became real to her instead of a manifestation of her mind. "*Where is Aren's Agni stone placed?*" Nikki stammered trying to answer him, but not knowing what facts to answer with made her attempt at meaningful communication sound incoherent, ending in Nikki feeling red-faced; stupid.

"*Aren's Agni zagin?*" Rogaan asked again with raised brows. "*Aren me itti namhul ma aste shu Agni kalag shu lirum.*"

"I don't know where Aren's Agni is," Nikki answered Rogaan's request for his friend's crystal stone. He wanted it to use on his friend to regain health and physical strength.

"How in the hell do you understand him?" Anders groaned out his question.

Nikki jumped nervously to a crouch at Anders's words and tone. She thought Anders unconscious, or worse. Looking at him, Nikki found Anders rousing from the floor with more vigor than she thought possible. He was close to death a few moments ago. Now . . . ? She decided she better answer him or find herself on the annoyance end of his questions. "I just do. Remember, I told you . . . Antaalin."

"I never heard of Antaalin," Anders argued as he raised himself to a sitting position against the wall. "Where are you getting this from? It doesn't exist."

"Antaalin is the more complex ancient root language of Sumerian," Nikki replied with conviction. "Rogaan's sort of speaking Sumerian when he speaks Antaalin."

"Sort of speaking what . . . this Antaalin or Sumerian?" Anders cynically asked.

"Antaalin . . . Sumerian is a simplified form of it," Nikki replied honestly.

"Aren needs his Agni stone!" Rogaan spoke slowly as if to get the words right, but his forceful tone made it clear he expected to be listened to.

Nikki looked at Rogaan with mouth slung open in astonishment as she stood up. *He spoke English.* She shook her head to wake herself. "How . . . How do you know how to speak English?"

"Not difficult . . ." Rogaan replied having to think of the words as he spoke. "*Ni estugar ima udi.* I listen in rest."

"This is remarkable . . . beyond remarkable." Excited, Nikki looked to Anders wanting to share this extraordinary moment with the only other person conscious that could appreciate the discovery. "Do you know what this means? Rogaan learned English without any training. He learned in his *rest* . . . when he was unconscious with us hauling him around South America—"

Bursts of gunfire rattled and unintelligible yelling came from several directions outside the med-lab . . . on the same level and aft and also from above.

"Agni stone?" Rogaan spoke with a calm, yet impatient tone.

"I don't know where his Agni stone is . . ." Nikki told Rogaan a second time before pointing at Doctor Dunkle. "But he might."

Rogaan stood motionless for a few moments, then stepped to the unconscious doctor and dropped to one knee. He placed his hands to either side of Doctor Dunkle's head. Those dark blue metallic tendrils crawled out across his palms and fingers again. Nikki shivered as the flowing metal crawled over Rogaan's hands. Rogaan seemed to command it, and it appeared to obey him. Still, she feared it, but didn't know why. Rogaan concentrated a few moments before Doctor Dunkle's limp body started to twitch and spasm. The doctor suddenly opened his eyes with a wild fearful stare.

"Calm . . ." Rogaan instructed the doctor in an even tone.

Doctor Dunkle focused his eyes on Rogaan. "What the hell was that?"

"*Kalag zu zumru,*" Rogaan answered the confused doctor, then continued, slowly speaking. "Mending your body. *Sanu we mese Aren's Agni zagin me duruna?*"

"What are you talking about?" Doctor Dunkle asked Rogaan with a shaky voice while his body shivered terribly. Rolling over to look at Anders, Doctor Dunkle asked again with a trembling voice, "What's Subject One asking?"

"I don't know," Anders answered before pointing an unsteady finger at Nikki. "She's the one that seems to speak his language."

Doctor Dunkle appeared more confused looking between Anders and Nikki. A stout hand grabbed the doctor by the back of the neck and another at his left shoulder. Surprise exploded on the doctor's face, then turned to fear as he was easily yanked to his feet. Shaking, Doctor Dunkle slowly turned to face Subject One once Rogaan released his grip.

"He's asking for his friend's Agni stone, Doctor Dunkle," Nikki translated.

"I don't know what that is," Doctor Dunkle replied while keeping his eyes fixed on Subject One. "Tell Subject One, I don't know what he's asking."

"It's the gemstone Aren had," Nikki clarified. "The one you told me looked odd for a mineral."

"Subject Two's *gemstone* is in the lab safe," Doctor Dunkle answered with an uncertain quality in his voice. "Tell Subject One that . . . what I said."

"His name is Roga of the House An, or Rogaan in common speech," Nikki corrected the doctor. "And you might want to get that gemstone. It seems to be important for *Aren* to heal."

Doctor Dunkle stood on unsteady legs while wearing a face of indecision. He looked to Anders, then Nikki, before nervously returning his gaze to Subject O . . . Rogaan. The doctor took a fearful step back at Rogaan's glare. With those eyes and his muscular build, Subject . . . Roga of . . . the House An . . . , Rogaan, carried himself in an intimidating way. With a shaky voice, the doctor spoke as he pointed to the floor in front of the holo-display. "It's there. I'll open the safe and get it for you . . . for Subject Tw . . . Aren . . ."

Doctor Dunkle kneeled, then waved his hand just above the floor three time before a green illuminated keypad revealed itself on the floor plate. Nikki moved closer. Her curiosity won out over her cautiousness. The doctor attempted to input a five-digit code several times with his shaking hand. The keypad turned red, then green after the first attempt, then red along with a harsh warning beep on the second attempt before disappearing. Doctor Dunkle looked nervously at Rogaan. "I'm sorry. Let me try again."

Rogaan grabbed the doctor, impatiently pulling him away from the safe. The dark blue metal guard on Rogaan's right arm flowed over his hand, then projected a short blade from his knuckles. In a quick motion, Rogaan hammered his fist into the floor just to the right of the display with a resonating clang. The floor buckled slightly under his fist. Rogaan remained still for a moment, then started to pull at the floor. He braced his left foot over the now unusable keypad, crouched again while grabbing his fisted gauntlet with his left hand and then with a strain, peeled the door of the safe back in a screech of protesting metal. Rogaan indifferently discarded the door in the direction of Nikki, causing her to sidestep the twisted hunk of metal. Anders, now on his unsteady feet, grabbed at Nikki's shoulders for support as he maneuvered around the discarded door, forcing Nikki around Rogaan, close to the ripped open side door. At first, Nikki was irritated at Anders's presumptive touch, then softened her emotions after looking at him with his "a little green around his gill" appearance.

Looking back at Rogaan, she found him rummaging through the safe's contents . . . sheathed dark daggers, a sheathed blue sword that look oddly familiar, a red and black leathery hide carry case almost the length of her arm and as thick as Rogaan's, and a leathery brown belt with attached pouches of what she knew not. Rogaan stopped his searching when he placed his hands on a small black metallic box. He carefully opened it, revealing a set of different colored gemstones carefully placed in a foam inset. Rogaan selected a black gemstone, removing it from its box before closing it. He immediately made his way to his unconscious friend and placed the gemstone high on Aren's chest near his throat while speaking in his native tongue, "*Kalag ga dusa. Negeltu ma erim we.*"

"*Mend, my friend. Awake and join me.*" That was what Nikki heard Rogaan say to his friend before Aren's limp body twitched and shook as the air around the black gemstone became wavy, as if looking at heat rising from a hot road in the middle of the day. Rogaan inspected Aren's wounds after tearing open the red-soaked spots of the biosensor robe. The wounds were from ricocheting projectiles from the Tyr Soldier, Nikki realized. Rogaan nodded as if satisfied, then returned his attention to Aren's bio-monitor. Aren's vitals and EEG looked erratic on his bio-monitor, but no long worsened. After a minute, his vitals stabilized. Rogaan appeared satisfied as Nikki breathed a sigh of relief. She hadn't realized how attached she felt to Aren too, until now. She wondered at the strong bond between them . . . her, Rogaan, and Aren. *Why is it? How did it happen?*

A whistle of darts passing her head caught Nikki by surprise, making her involuntarily jump. The darts found Rogaan's ribs and the electrical current flowing over the TASER's wireless link now caused his body to quiver and legs shake. Aware of Rogaan's pain, Nikki stepped toward Rogaan with the intent to help before thinking that the current harming him would also hurt her. She turned to find the source to try stopping it there. Nikki sucked her breath in at what confronted her. In front of her stood another Tyr Soldier. This one bigger than the last.

Nikki suddenly felt sick . . . anxious . . . unsteady on her feet . . . unsafe. Her breathing became labored . . . restricted, and she was getting light-headed. Confused about what to do, she turned back to Rogaan hoping for answers . . . for him to help her. Instead, despair filled her. Rogaan still stood, but struggled to do so. His muscles convulsed from the TASERing, and it appeared he had little command of his body. It was taking everything for him to stay upright. The bio-monitor behind and above Rogaan displayed crazy readings. At the top of the monitor, a red warning banner flashed in synchronization with an irritating beeping. It read what Nikki thought were the elements of electrical current—0.2 amps and 2,000 volts at 19 pulses per second. Then, the warning banner began flashing quicker as did the beeping while the numbers drastically climbed—0.3 amps and 102,000 volts at 19 pps. Rogaan groaned through gritted teeth as he collapsed to one knee and both hands on the floor, still trying to hold himself up. He fought. She was aware of his pain now . . . It stung her, making her legs wobbly. Nikki wondered at Rogaan's strength of will . . . his defiance against challenges. The warning banner changed—the electrical current fell to 2,000 volts, then climbed again to a sustained 3,000 volts. What was the Tyr Soldier doing to him? Nikki wanted to know so she could stop it. Her awareness of his pain felt excruciating and made her light-headed, feel about to pass out. A growl from Rogaan drew her attention from herself. Still down on his left knee, but holding onto the Aren's bed to keep from completely collapsing,

Rogaan fought through his pain and unresponsive muscles, took hold of the darts with his left hand, and yanked them from his side. The red flashing warning banner on Rogaan's bio-monitor disappeared, along with that irritating beeping. Relief washed over Nikki as pain fell away. She no longer felt as sick as she did a few moments before.

In a quick move, Rogaan threw the darts back at the Tyr Soldier, both whistling by Nikki's head making her flinch and duck. Nikki looked back at the dark-clad U.N. soldier to see if the TASER darts had struck him. One dart found the wall behind the Tyr Soldier. The other was embedded in the upper area of his left chest . . . between chest and shoulder plates. Nothing. The Tyr Soldier appeared unaffected by the dart.

Raw emotions hit Nikki, staggering her. Not knowing what happened to her, she turned to Rogaan, suspecting and fearful somehow she was feeling what he was experiencing. What she saw scared her. Rogaan filled with rage as he stood up to face the Tyr Soldier. Nikki could feel it . . . see it . . . It was in his eyes and on his face and in the way he moved . . . He intended to kill and make a mess of it.

Suddenly, a dark-armored arm crossed over Nikki's left shoulder and chest taking her attention from Rogaan. She felt herself being pulled backward until she became painfully pinned to a hard surface. She was stuck against the body of the Tyr Soldier. His strength was incredible and hurting Nikki such that she yelped.

"Let her go!" Demanded Anders who stood on shaky legs at the opposite side of the room. The brief hope his demand gave Nikki faded away when she realized Anders was in no condition to help her and that Doctor Dunkle was nowhere to be seen.

In a jerking motion, the Tyr Soldier hauled Nikki back through the peeled away door and onto the main deck's outer walkway. In desperation, Nikki struck repeatedly at the armored arm with her fists, then tried to kick and stomp his armored feet . . . She did her best trying to break free. Nothing. It was as if the Tyr Soldier didn't even notice her struggles. Backward she went, dragged toward the aft deck where the helipad loomed over the walkway. Nikki hoped for Rogaan to rescue her, but he was not to be seen. He did not follow and now, she no longer felt his emotions. A surge of panic welled up within her. *Where is he taking me? What is he going to do to me?* The Tyr Soldier stopped just short of the helipad overhang. Moments passed. Nothing happened except for the whining noise of those invisible UCAVs passing overhead, sporadic gunfire, and the occasional voices of men in pain or fearful for their lives. Worry started blending with panic, gripping Nikki so hard she had trouble getting a breath as she again struggled against her captor. This time the U.N. soldier squeezed her in a crushing grip until she settled down. When the pressure lessened on her chest, she sucked in a gulp of air that reduced the flashing lights now filling her sight. A few more gulps of air and some blinking cleared her vision. When she looked up she saw the ship's island superstructure housing the bridge, the medical bay, and other vital functions for the first time since the attack. She noticed the array was damaged in several places on the deck above and above that as if struck by an explosion . . . a missile or something like it. The flat superstructure between the island superstructure and the helipad housing what Nikki now understood to be cargo and weapons bore scorched marks and some holes. Otherwise, it was intact with all of the access door on this deck sealed. An exterior set of ladder hand- and footholds mounted to the superstructure was just to her . . . *their* left. A duplicate set was at the other end of the open air superstructure some twenty meters forward of them. A glance to her right showed her the ocean had settled some from the last time she saw it. Nikki realized the ship slowed and was now almost at a stop.

A sinking feeling in the pit of her gut gave her shivers all over. Nobody was going to rescue her. She plunged into a chasm of despair that sent tears streaming down her cheeks. Then, Nikki felt it . . . determination. No longer the anger, the rage, or hatred. Simple determination guided by controlled intent. She looked up and found Rogaan striding confidently toward them on the deck's outer walkway. In his left hand, he carried his bow. His blue metallic bow. Still dressed in the white biosensor tunic, he now wore a wide strap over his shoulder and chest with a dark sheathed dagger attached to it . . . likely his *shunir'ra* case. A leathery wrapped handle and blue metal pommel were visible just over his right shoulder . . . Nikki suspected it was his sword from the safe. She felt a ray of hope rise inside of her. She smiled just before she felt herself lowered, fast, like she was falling, then vaulted upward. The painful grip of the Tyr Soldier never leaving her even as they landed, standing upright, on top of the superstructure just forward of the helipad. She feared her captor was not going to let her living body go. Before them were two parallel marked walkways going forward in between three elongated hatches now opened. The center one had three rows of vertical tubes . . . twenty-one in all, most were sealed, with six having scorch marks and broken seals. The two hatches open on either side of the center one had mangled machinery mounted on rotating turrets. *Must have been the mini-railguns the crew was so proud of.* The guns stood destroyed. Fifteen and some meters forward, a large horizontal cargo hatch was in its up and sealed position. Beyond, the damaged superstructure with its twisted and burnt array and walls gave testament to the lethality of their attackers. A wave of fear swept through Nikki. For the first time she considered they would not win this battle. The events of the evening started to sink into her thoughts. UCAVs, Tyr Soldiers, and a mother ship . . . a U.N. frigate, likely with bigger guns and an attitude, all hell-bent on stopping them. It was overwhelming. Frightening.

Rogaan landed on top of the Spartan outfitted superstructure just forward of the cargo door. He moved quickly. Nikki didn't see him until he jumped from the ladder holds. Rogaan immediately settled into that casual fighting stance he demonstrated in the medical bay. Confident or cocky . . . Nikki wasn't certain which. Truthfully, she didn't care. She felt better with him standing in front of them with his attention focused in her direction. Her fear faded, replaced with a renewed hope.

"*Wussuru inaa seher,*" Rogaan demanded in Antaalin, firm and confident.

"Not understanding," the Tyr Soldier replied in that eerie synthesized voice.

"He said . . . release the youngling—me, you idiot," Nikki translated before she thought about what she was saying. A nervous pause filled the dusk air atop the superstructure of the *Wind Runner.* Nikki didn't intend to insult her captor . . . It just slipped out.

Rogaan spoke in English, slowly. "Release the youngling . . . immediately."

"Now, I hear you," the Tyr Soldier mocked Rogaan. "Won't comply. Drop your weapons and surrender or suffer justice."

"Justice is birthright not suffered," Rogaan instructed in English after a moment of thinking the translation. "Suffering is from the unjust, the unclean."

A mix of emotions swirled in Nikki. She was having trouble knowing which were hers and which were Rogaan's thoughts. *How is this possible, anyway?* Movement high above caught Nikki's eye. Another Tyr Soldier, with arms raised and hands balled into fists, leapt from the quarterdeck three levels up and looked to be dropping right on top of Rogaan. Nikki opened her mouth to warn Rogaan of the danger, but he seemed to sense it. *He knows.* Just before the Tyr Soldier landed on him, Rogaan stepped forward slightly while raising a fully gauntleted blue metallic fist straight up. The gauntleted fist and the chin of the Tyr Soldier met with an audible clang and thud, sending the dark-armored soldier sprawling on his back into the superstructure behind Rogaan, unmoving. Nikki looked on surprised and shocked at Rogaan's action and of the ease with which he did it.

A moment passed with Nikki holding her mouth slack-jaw open before she felt the tightening hold of the Tyr Soldier close behind her. Something bad was about to happen, and she feared it was going to doom her. In a blur, Rogaan raised his bow, aiming it at Nikki, and drew without an arrow. Nikki barely had the time to flinch when she heard, and felt, the passing of something just above her head. The sensation of an electrical charge causing her hair to stand on end immediately followed. The hold of the Tyr Soldier lessened, then fell away just before she heard a clunk behind her. *What just happened?* She asked herself as she cautiously turned to look at her captor. He lay on his back, also unmoving, with blood pooling under his helmet. *He's dead,* she realized. She stared at the body for an unknown amount of time, then looked at Rogaan. He approached her with a confident stride. As he did, he lifted his right hand head high as something that looked like a rotating metal disk flew directly into his gauntlet where it disappeared . . . absorbed, if Nikki's eyes weren't playing tricks on her.

"*Za silim?*" Rogaan asked her in Antaalin.

"I think so . . . I'm unharmed." Nikki answered, still not certain what all just happened. "Are they . . . dead?"

"*Anna,*" Rogaan confirmed her suspicion, still in Antaalin. Then, Rogaan spoke more slowly in English. "You have obligation to tell me of these attackers and why . . ."

Rogaan's words trailed off as he looked east into the darkening sky above an almost undiscernible ocean. He stared into the distance without speaking. A worried expression fell upon him while searching the darkness.

"What is it?" Nikki asked as the ship rolled mildly on the ocean. They were at a full stop, drifting on a now almost calmed water. The whining hum of a UCAV passed somewhere overhead, causing Nikki to look up, but she could not see it despite it sounding close.

"Danger unknown to me," Rogaan answered Nikki while keeping his eyes set on the dark horizon.

Nikki followed Rogaan's gaze looking out into the darkening void. A flash, just at the edge of her ability to see it, off in the distance, just at what Nikki could make out as the ocean's horizon. Rogaan stiffened. He looked left and right so fast, Nikki thought she imaged it. Then, without warning, Rogaan grabbed Nikki and threw her forward toward the ship's island superstructure. She felt herself lofted in the air above the ship's deck as the world moved in slow motion. Frightened and confused, she kept her eyes on Rogaan wondering why he threw her. A dim glowing reddish light trailing something unseen streaked left to right, passing through the superstructure underneath where Rogaan stood looking up at her. The rear of the ship exploded under Rogaan in a ball of fire and shrapnel, sending him tumbling skyward. A hot wall of pressure struck Nikki hard, propelling her faster though the air until she hit something, plunging her into darkness.

Chapter 1

Dangerous Trails

The sun sank slowly toward the tall treetops sitting on the high ridges behind their fast-moving line of sarigs. The afternoon temperatures remained comfortable as it had the past few days, made so by the cool breeze from the north coming off the Spine Mountains. Rogaan still sat behind Ruumoor on their shared sarig, trotting to keep their place in line with the rest of their companions. Kardul kept true to his word, pushing them and their steeds all through the afternoon without rest except for moments when he allowed them all to slow or stop for someone to relieve themselves, usually Suhd, or to ensure his direction was true and to cautiously avoid a growing number of tanniyn herds and predator packs. Longwalkers mostly blocked their way and threatened to trample them. The huge animals, with uncurious natures, but very protective of their young, gave Rogaan a new sense of what large was. Surprisingly, the immense beasts appeared out of nowhere without the slightest hint of song or a trembling of the ground. They gave no warning they were near. Rogaan found this amazing. When their group came upon the longnecks gobbling up the forest, the *Kiuri'Ner* leading them instantly decided a course of action, navigating everyone around the massive animals skirting the edge of the herd, keeping an eye on the dominate bull who gave them chase until they were downwind and clear of the herd. The heavy rank odor of the herd's dung hung with them for a time as they quickly covered ground through the remainder of the afternoon. Flying biters and bloodsuckers proved to be worse than tanniyns in making their travels uncomfortable, even painful. Rogaan welcomed the offer of those purpled flowers the *Sharurs* somehow found along the way. He crushed the flowers in his hands, then rubbed the pungent-smelling remains on his exposed skin. The flowers really kept the biters and bloodsuckers away. Rogaan thanked the Ancients for the invention. With the buzzing and biting reduced and at a distance, Rogaan found himself getting more comfortable riding his sarig instead of simply hanging on and hoping not to fall off.

Rolling hills gave way to flatter lands allowing easier going for a time as the forest grew increasingly difficult to travel except for established game trails made by tanniyn, which Kardul was forced into using. The forest was too dense for fast travel, and they had to get ahead of the jailers' wagons. Rogaan learned enough over the last few days that fresh game trails meant danger, and the larger the game trail the greater the danger, whether from bite or foot or tail. And, it seemed the buzz of biters and bloodsuckers formed dense clouds wherever fresh dung lay in piles. Thankfully, the purple flower salve with its pungent smell, refreshed by the companions several times so far this day, kept the buzzing clouds at bay. At some point in the afternoon, Rogaan no longer wrinkled his nose at the odor and forgot he wore the salve until another cloud of pain attempted to descend on him. Then, he thanked the Ancients and the last *Sharur* who had given him more of the flowers.

Kardul had them hustle down a wide game trail marked with fresh tracks and droppings looking and smelling to be from longnecks and maybe a trailing pair of ravers followed by leapers. Rogaan felt proud of himself for being able to read the tracks and dung signs. Broken and felled trees were all about them, lining the pathway. In-between, the buzz of biters and bloodsuckers were ever present. Rogaan tried swiveling his head every which way, hoping not to see teeth and claws. It made him dizzy and nauseated, forcing him to scan the forest with more thought and discipline. Still, it was unnerving and exhausting. Kardul and his men seemed alert . . . on edge, if Rogaan read them right. They actively scrutinized the forest as they went, each member of the team with their part of the wilds to keep watch over. They worked as a team. That did not give rise to a sense of comfort for Rogaan; instead, making him even more nervous that they were so on edge. Looking ahead, Suhd seemed to be fighting sleep with her head bobbing up and down and her swaying in the saddle a little side to side. Falling off the sarig now would be bad at best and maybe deadly. Rogaan wanted to help Suhd . . . keep her from falling and was about to yell out to her when Trundiir gave her a gentle elbow. Rogaan felt that jealousy roil again in his chest. He chastised himself for feeling this way, but was not able to shake the thought of Trundiir getting to touch her where he could not. Rogaan sought something else to fill his thoughts with. Pax looked alert and nervously scanning the forest, as well. He seemed more helpful than troublesome to the *Sharurs*. An interesting turn. Everyone appeared to be nervous of their surroundings, except Suhd, who still looked tired. Rogaan's heart ached for her. He wished for her arms to be around him and his around her.

Broken trees, tracks, and fresh droppings continued marking the recently used trail by a number of large and dangerous animals. The scent of the wilderness had a pungent yet sweet smell to it as the odor from fresh dung mixed with new growths of colorful and aromatic flowers. Rogaan did not know whether he should wrinkle his nose or sneeze at the barrage of smells hitting him. At this point in their travels, the wide game trail was the only passable way through this wilderness; the rest of the forest loomed thick with dark stands of tall trees mingling with dense underbrush and tangle bush where the sun penetrated. This pattern of foliage kept on for marches before the trail forked. The main trail with the fresh animal signs forked left, and a smaller, less-used trail by the far reduced evidence of tracks and dung, went right. The *Kiuri'Ner* led them right. Rogaan felt relieved. *Less chance of meeting a hungry animal with teeth and claws*, he tried to convince himself. No longer feeling as much on edge, he spied Suhd riding behind Trundiir. He stole looks at her as often as he could, both so he could feel recharged at seeing her again and again, and to make sure all hands were where they should be. Rogaan could no longer deny he was jealous of Trundiir having Suhd on his sarig when she should be with him. Jealously roared inside Rogaan, nearing a rage, each time Suhd placed a hand on Trundiir's arm or shoulder as she shifted in her saddle to get more comfortable. He did not like these uncontrolled feelings, but did not know what to do about them. Looking for another distraction, he found Pax and Adul looking all the bit at odds with each other atop the sarig they shared. Adul, wide awake and alert, scanning his surroundings, and Pax now appearing as if trying to sleep in the saddle by the way his chin frequently rested on his chest and body swayed. Only an occasional stiffening of his back, as if suddenly waking enough to catch himself from falling out of the saddle, made Pax look aware of his surroundings. Adul seemed annoyed by his saddle mate's lack of interest in staying alive and jabbed him with an occasional elbow to add to the times Pax's back stiffened. Pax then pretended to look about for a few moments before repeating the cycle. It was amusing watching the two. Rogaan chuckled to himself. This was more like the Pax he knew. Ruumoor glanced back at Rogaan with a confused scrunch of the eyes until the *Sharur* realized what Rogaan was looking at, then chuckled a little himself.

Kardul pressed on, down game trails, and then through light forest thickets when the trails were undiscernible. Not long after plunging into the aromatic flower-filled thickets, Kardul signaled for all to stop in the late-afternoon sunlight, his right fist snapped into the air as he reigned up his sarig. Rogaan had drifted off, mostly daydreaming about pleasant things . . . Suhd's embrace, when his sarig came to an abrupt halt. He immediately went fully awake and at alert looking around for the danger. The forest looked vibrant with significant contrasts between the greens and browns of the underbrush, the browns, grays, and yellows of the trees, and the mixed colors of their steeds and his companions. His surroundings looked somehow . . . unnatural. The scent of sarig and flowers filled his nose so powerfully he almost could not suppress a sneeze. Even the scent of Ruumoor now offended him so much he wrinkled his nose. Rogaan wondered if the *Sharur* practiced any sense of hygiene. Looking around, Rogaan wondered what forced Kardul to bring their line to a halt. He could see little with the brush and small trees level to his eyes, but his ears located heavy footsteps on dirt, breaking branches . . . and logs, toppling the small trees, and low grunts of what Rogaan took for large animals ahead and to their left. Kardul redirected their line of sarigs to the right, then moved deeper into the thickets at a cautious pace. It appeared Kardul picked a path that would take them away from the unseen danger and split two thick stands of tall pine trees off in the distance. Kardul's and Adul's heads were on swivels, looking left and right in urgency. With such limited visibility, travel through these sweet-smelling thickets felt unnerving to Rogaan. Kardul and his sarig suddenly side-stepped left as Adul pulled up short his sarig. A low, rumbling bellow reverberated through the air that Rogaan more felt than heard. Adul kicked his and Pax's sarig into a gallop off to the left following Kardul. Trundiir, with Suhd now fully awake and clinging to the *Sharur's* back, did the same as Ruumoor followed suit, with Rogaan hanging on to his saddle. As they passed the spot Kardul and sarig jumped, Rogaan came eye level with a huge bulk of sinew and bone, a dark yellowish and red-brown shieldback. The animal seemed alarmed . . . almost panicked slightly crouching in a defensive posture. The beast bellowed, then grunted as Ruumoor and Rogaan passed within several strides of it, its body a muscular wall of danger filling Rogaan's vision and nearly bringing his heart to a stop.

"No . . ." Ruumoor moaned as he kicked hard into their sarig's flanks. Rogaan strained to hold onto the saddle and stay seated as the sarig lurched and sped forward. At first, Rogaan heard the breaking of bush and small trees making up the thickets, all coming at him, then he saw the shadow of the massive tail, with boney blades edge on, sweeping toward him. Rogaan ducked as quickly as he could, pulling himself down flat behind Ruumoor. Plant debris slammed into his right shoulder, arm, and leg, and the sarig under him as the shieldback's tail passed right atop of him with frightening speed. He felt the glancing strike of the tail brush his neck and shoulders, heavy enough to almost unseat him. Looking back, Rogaan found the shieldback enraged and bellowing and stomping, turned in the opposite direction with its tail sweeping back toward Ishmu and his sarig, who were following them in an unsettled trot. Ishmu urged his steed into a gallop, but was too late. The shieldback's bone-bladed tail struck the sarig under Ishmu, launching both steed and rider into the air. The sarig flew over Rogaan broken and twisted in odd ways, landing in a mix of thrown brush and dust just to his left. Its body unrecognizable as a sarig. Ishmu launched high into the air with him, letting out a long, wavering yell until he hit hard onto the ground a half-dozen strides behind Rogaan and Ruumoor. Rogaan yelled to Ruumoor to stop, but the *Sharur* did not hear him and kept their sarig moving at a fast pace. Rogaan thought to jump from the steed and go back to help Ishmu, but Ruumoor kept their sarig twisting and turning through the thickets, not allowing him to dismount without getting injured. In a short time, they emerged from the thickets, making the tree line where the rest of their companions pulled up their steeds.

"Where's Ishmu?" Adul asked with a concerned tone.

"He fell when the shieldback killed his sarig," Rogaan answered honestly.

"Why didn't you aid him?" Kardul accused Rogaan and Ruumoor with his eyes.

"I had no knowledge of him falling," Ruumoor answered as he twisted to glare at Rogaan.

"Stay here." Kardul commanded with a frustrated expression as he urged his sarig back into the thickets.

Bellows and grunts from the shieldback herd filled the thickets between the stand of tall pine trees now looming over the companions and the far stands of trees they came from. Kardul was nowhere to be seen or heard. His voice may have been lost in the bellows, and they would never know he yelled out. While waiting for Kardul and, hopefully, Ishmu to return, Adul chewed on Ruumoor for not stopping and aiding their fellow *Sharur*. Ruumoor argued back before falling silent and accepting the rebuke. Then Adul started chewing on Rogaan for not telling Ruumoor of their fallen companion. Rogaan too started arguing back that he had tried alerting his saddle-mate when Kardul and Ishmu emerged from the thickets mounted on a single steed. Ishmu looked in pain, but sat upright, holding onto the saddle and Kardul. Kardul did not bother to stop. He kept his sarig moving at a quick walking pace.

"Let's remove ourselves from these wilds before nightfall," Kardul growled as he passed the six of them seated on three of the four remaining steeds they started off with on this journey.

Trundiir stolidly kept his eyes focused forward and to the ground as he lightly kicked his sarig into moving out. Adul glared at Ruumoor and Rogaan as he urged his steed to follow Trundiir and Suhd. Pax wore the look of an uncaring observer as his and Adul's steed carried them off in-between the stands of pines after Kardul and Ishmu. Ruumoor turned back to glare at Rogaan one more time before spurring their sarig to the rear of the line of companions.

"What?" Rogaan felt he needed to defend himself before getting cut off. "I tried to—"

"I'm not hearing any of your lies," Ruumoor spoke with a vicious tone. "You've been enough trouble. I'll be glad when you're taken care of."

Rogaan did not know what to make of Ruumoor's comments. *What does he mean 'taken care of'?* He wanted to ask, but knew he would get just more non-answers; instead, Rogaan settled into his saddle for the rest of their afternoon travels. Kardul continued leading them at a hard pace, on lesser traveled trails and through more thickets. As the sunlight started fading in the late afternoon, Rogaan felt the sarig under him and Ruumoor laboring with each step, and did not know if it would survive much more of this pace. Ruumoor sensed the animal struggling as well, and started talking to the steed while patting its shoulders and neck. Rogaan hoped Ruumoor's encouragement would keep the sarig upright. Nightfall approached quickly and they were not yet clear of the forest. In truth, Rogaan had no idea where they were or how far it was to the *di'tij* Kardul and his men spoke of . . . the *Last Stop*. He was totally dependent on the *Kiuri'Ner* and his *Sharurs*, and he realized he did not like it. Worse, he did not know how far to trust anyone. It seemed everyone, Kardul included, had plans for him that he did not understand. Rogaan decided he did not like that, either. He just wanted his father free from his Farratum captors . . . and Pax and Suhd's parents too. But he felt not a bit in control of this "rescue," and it started to grate on him as they closed on what Kardul described as their ambush location.

At the gloomy hour of dusk, the feet of their sarigs struck the hard-packed dirt of a road. Relief washed over Rogaan and, from what he could tell, everyone else at the sight of the wide dirt road running through the forest wilds. They were alone on the road in the final light of the day.

Kardul surveyed their surroundings and seemed satisfied. "We're just a few marches to the *Last Stop*. Keep moving or our steeds might not get us there."

Again, they pressed on, their sarigs sounding exhausted by the labored breathing of the animals. Kardul kept their pace slow and steady to what Rogaan thought they could walk. He guessed Kardul did not feel so much in danger as they were while in the forest and that their steeds just could not survive anything faster. Rogaan nodded silently in agreement, yet worried his sarig might fall over with its next step. Looking to his friends, Rogaan saw Pax and Suhd with smiles as they looked around in the failing light. Rogaan too felt relieved to be out of the forest and onto a piece of civilization. He never thought before how vulnerable folks were out in the wilds and just how important *Kiuri'Ner* were to their safe travels and their very lives outside the safety of stone and timber walls of Brigum. There was more to being a *Kiuri'Ner* than filling meat racks and making stories for others to embellish . . . a difficult and enormous responsibility protecting the folks they serve.

The hard-packed dirt road took them north and east for a short time in almost complete darkness before the moon rose above the trees and bathed everything in an eerie blue. Unsettled by the pitch-black darkness they traveled in, Rogaan started his practiced and controlled breathing used for calming himself before a long or difficult bow shot. Ruumoor looked back at him with an expression he could not read, but a disapproving grunt from the *Sharur* told Rogaan his saddle-mate was not impressed. Rogaan's eyes adjusted to the new light, allowing him to see colorless details almost as sharp as if in daylight, but only for short distances before all blurred and faded into shadows. His improved sight helped calm his fear of the unseen and unknown, but only a little in truth. The rest that kept Rogaan from jumping out of his skin at every screech, howl, or growl was Ruumoor and the others sharing his experience, though none of them seemed to share his angst. A short time traveling on the road after the moon rose brought them in sight of what appeared to be lights in the distance. Kardul kept them at the slow and steady pace as the sarigs still suffered labored breathing, and Rogaan continued anticipating the animal under him to collapse with each and every step. As they closed on the light points, Rogaan found the torches lit along a stoutly built bridge of wood timbers. It spanned a break in the land more than a stone throw wide. Beyond, the road led to a torch-lit citadel Rogaan hoped was the *di'tij*. Kardul kept them at the slow and steady pace onto the well-kept bridge, the sarig foot pads nearly silent on the wood. The only sounds telling of their presence beyond breathing of the steeds was the creaking and groaning of the bridge under the weight of four sarigs and the eight companions. *Kiuri'Ner* and *Sharur* showed little interest at what lay below the bridge as they crossed, but Pax and Suhd were like curious younglings trying to look over the edge of the structure into the below where Rogaan heard splashing, hissing, and deep growling. Looking with the aid of moonlight, Rogaan made out a river flowing with objects moving against the current causing ripples and splashes of notice. In places, the forms of snapjaws he could make out both on the banks and in the water, some larger than seven or eight strides. A chill ran through him at seeing so many flesh-eating animals in one place and wondered if anyone or anything could survive a river crossing here without the bridge. After passing over the bridge, they came to a halt in between two sets of stone walls guarding each side of the road and forming the outer boundary of the compounds inside. Almost-still flags flew atop both walls. The top baring the lightning bolt crest of Shuruppak above another baring the crossed spears and towers crest of the city Farratum. On their left, a mortared stone wall stood eight strides tall and almost two hundred strides long. Wooden watchtowers sat at the corners of the rectangular-shaped structure. In them, watchmen armed with spears and bows warily observed their approach. To their right, a ten-stride high wall of mortared stone stood at the south side of the road. A manned stone watchtower at the corner closest to their approach extended the height of the wall to almost eighteen strides high. The wall also ran some two hundred strides in both directions, along the road and parallel to the river. A handful of wood watchtowers sat atop each wall at near evenly spaced intervals. A growing number of watchmen, also armed with spears and bows, observed their approach. Entering the road channel the walls formed, Kardul led them to a spot halfway along the stone and mortar where timbered gates stood astride the road, one in each wall facing each other.

"Hail to the Keeper of the Watch," Kardul spoke loudly and deeply after he signaled the line of sarigs to come to a stop. "We seek shelter within the walls of the *Last Stop*."

Rogaan felt himself falling to the left. Both he and Ruumoor cursed in surprise as their sarig toppled. Rogaan suffered a jarring impact as the sarig struck the ground bouncing him upward and to the side of the road where he came to a painful stop face down in the dirt. Rogaan's left shoulder and ribs ached, and his head throbbed. A bit disoriented at first, he shook off a light-headed sensation as he stumbled to his feet . . . all the while spitting dirt and what he suspected was dried bits of dung from his mouth. Ruumoor stood near Rogaan simply looking at their sarig with what Rogaan thought

was a sorrowful expression. The animal had been pushed past its limits
bringing them to the safety of this place. If an animal could have honor, this
beast of burden demonstrated it . . . to its last breath. Rogaan too felt sorrow
at its passing.

"Dinner!" a voice bellowed from somewhere above on the torch-lit
ramparts. "Open the gate!"

At first, Rogaan was uncertain if the pronouncement of an evening meal
was meant as a general call or that their fallen sarig was to be feasted upon.
When Kardul and his *Sharur* showed no reactions to the gate to the north
compound creaking open, he confirmed with assuredness it was the sarig they
meant to carve up and put over a spit. Rogaan caught a glimpse of Pax smiling
at all the blunt talk. Suhd seeming not to understand the subtle banter looked
blankly at the two of them.

Nine guardsmen clad in *Tusaa'Ner* blue hide armor with red belt sashes
emerged from the open gate and set themselves in a well-practiced arrow tip
formation pointing their spears directly at Kardul. Rogaan felt his heart sink at
the sight of the *Tusaa'Ner*. More *Tusaa'Ner* and a number of indistinctly liveried
crossbowmen loomed over the tops of both walls and watchtowers. He was
doomed . . . they were doomed. He thought to flee, but flee where? This was
not Brigum where he had familiarity, it was out in the wilds . . . away from
home. He was so far from home. Despair started to wrap its arms around him.

"Announce yourselves," demanded a thin Baraan with graying hair and
dressed in a Farratum *Tusaa'Ner* blue tunic and red belt sash. The Baraan set
himself in the middle of the formation the nine guardsmen formed.

"We travel to Farratum from the estates of Isin," Kardul replied more
formally than Rogaan expected. The Baraan did not flinch a bit speaking a
lie.

"State your purpose," the thin *Tusaa'Ner* "greeter" continued, almost as if
reading his words and applying a formality to them.

"We escort the children of Isin to the Shield City on family matters,"
Kardul replied. He lied expertly, Rogaan concluded.

The thin Baraan regarded all of them in a practiced manner before
speaking. "Place your names in the Traveler's Record. Do you need aid of a
healer?"

"Your hospitality is generous, kind sir," Kardul replied formally. "Of course, we will record our names. We may need a healer once we look after ourselves. May we call upon such service when needed?"

"As you wish," the thin Baraan replied. He dispersed the guardsmen and the archers at a wave of his hand. "The attendant inside will guide you to the stable master to see after your steeds and will assign you quarters."

Rogaan stood shocked he was not getting arrested by the *Tusaa'Ner* here. He wondered at it. He assumed he was marked for capture from one end of Shuruppak to the other. A swarm of men and a few women dressed in slightly soiled tunics and carrying torches came trotting from the open gate and surrounded the fallen sarig quickly. Ruumoor protested their intentions until Kardul gave him a look, "the look." A dejected expression washed over Ruumoor, head to toe. He grumbled as he started removing his gear from the *lightless* steed. "Not another sarig. Get your belongings, youngling, before these scavengers cook them too."

Kardul and his *Sharur* dismounted, stretching their legs, arms, and midsections. Pax and Suhd did the same, though Pax quickly gathered his bottom pack and some other items Rogaan was uncertain of what they were, greeted his sister with a short embrace, and then led her by the hand to Rogaan.

"I no like it," Pax started from under his wide-brimmed hat while shifting his bottom pack to a more comfortable position. "Too many red-sashes, and they be lookin' for ya."

"What would you have us do?" Rogaan asked honestly.

"Not be knowin'," Pax struggled with an answer. "I be just sayin' . . . I no be likin' bein' here."

"Neither do I," Rogaan agreed.

"We can't go nowhere else," Suhd broke in, her eyes wide. Was it fear Rogaan saw in her beautiful eyes. "Not after nightfall. Not out there. Kardul has brought us this far. We have to trust him."

Pax gave Rogaan a sharp look when Suhd spoke of trusting Kardul. They silently agreed with nods that they were not as certain of Kardul as she, but neither of them spoke of it. They kept their doubts and fears between themselves as Kardul's *Sharur* collected them up and guided them toward the *di'tij* gate.

Chapter 2

The Last Stop

With some urgency, the *Sharur* ushered them into the *di'tij*, almost pushing Rogaan along and not giving him much opportunity to collect his things. The heavy scent of burnt wood filled the air as they approached the gate . . . cook fires or fires to warm and push back the cool night air, Rogaan presumed. Once inside the protective walls of the citadel, Rogaan saw it was a place clearly built with minimal defenses, more focused on tending to travelers and keeping animals out than protection from war bands. Ahead of them, Kardul was deep in discussion with who Rogaan assumed was the attendant, a thin, dark-haired Baraan in a clean gray tunic and sandals carrying a small clay writing tablet. Rogaan suspected they were arguing over the arrangements and payment for their stay. It looked as if the attendant was having none of what Kardul insisted upon. While their verbal jousting continued, all of their steeds were led into the citadel by younglings half Rogaan's age. The younglings placed their steeds into a wood fenced pen off to Rogaan's left that made up most of the west side of the compound except for a stable work area on the far west wall and a long building on the north side of the pen that looked like a general store . . . of sorts. Some fifty strides to his north, directly in front of Rogaan, stood a rough-looking wood-planked building with a slanted roof, a tavern named the Long Journey by the sign hanging above its door. The east side of the compound was filled with four rows of small barracks. At first, Rogaan thought they were for the *di'tij's* guardsmen, but women and youngling clothing hung on suspended ropes between the buildings for drying. Several small ones were running around their mothers who were still tending to wash or other chores. This clearly spoke of a living space for local workers as well as passing travelers. Simple wood watchtowers with slanted tiled roofs stood in each corner of the citadel . . . at least, this side of the *di'tij*. Atop the stone and mortared wall, a wood-planked defensive wall half the height of a person protected the watch guardsmen from dangers outside, but was otherwise open to all those inside the citadel.

"Take that as payment!" Kardul growled loudly to the attendant while pointing to the quartered remains of the sarig Rogaan and Ruumoor had ridden in on, now being carried in parts past them by the tunic-dressed workers on their way to the tavern. A pang of regret struck Rogaan. The sarig had been a good steed.

"Eeeuuw . . ." Suhd grimaced and scrunched up her nose as she looked away from the bloody parts being carried. "They won't be make us eat it . . . will they? I mean, it carried you here."

No one answered her question. Some gave her stares as if she said something stupid. Suhd shrunk a little bit, withdrawing from those stares, while stepping toward Rogaan. "Just no proper way to treat it, I be sayin'."

"Agreed," the attendant answered Kardul loudly, then added, "Though, no longer than four days."

Kardul begrudgingly nodded in agreement to the attendant before turning to his *Sharur* and pointing to the second row of buildings from the tavern. "We have these two bunk houses."

The *Sharur* immediately started off for the bunk houses casually talking to each other about things Rogaan did not understand, their words more unclear with each of their steps. He stood watching them until Trundiir looked back to him and made a motion . . . an overemphasized motion of his fingers tapping on the elongated black and tan hide case holding Rogaan's *shunir'ra*. *Trundiir still carries my shunir'ra!* Rogaan realized with a warming of his cheeks and a tightening of his chest. Panic and anger quickly followed with his instinct to go fetch his *shunir'ra* back. But the touch of Suhd's hands holding his arm kept his feet planted where he was. Looking at her, Rogaan stood torn . . . hoping she would let go so he could retrieve his property, returning it to its rightful owner, and hoping she would not let go or stop holding onto him for a long time. Suhd held him a little more tightly while looking up at him. Feelings roiled and spun within him. He realized, *I could never ask her to let go*.

"I need a chamber pot," she stated with a little color in her cheeks. Suhd charmingly looked up at Rogaan with those wide pleading blue eyes and with a calm expectation he would save her from her uncomfortable situation. *Wildflowers*.

Her request surprised Rogaan, caught him off guard. He looked at her blankly for a few moments before Pax slapped him on the shoulder while wearing his sly, knowing smile. Pax announced, "Welcome to me family."

Rogaan did not understand his friend. Some sort of trick was playing out with him the target. Then he realized Suhd's request must happen often . . . needing a chamber pot. A question formed in his mind . . . *Then, how did she hold her water for so long on the sarig?*

"Rogaan . . . please." Suhd was gazing up at him with now suffering wide radiant blue eyes. Rogaan melted. He looked about for where one might be. He thought of the bunk houses, but suspected the *Sharur* would be there, and he did not want their eyes watching Suhd. Then he looked to the torch-lit entrance of the tavern, the Long Journey.

"Yes, this will work," Rogaan said to the cool night air and to himself. *There must be a pot in there, and hopefully, someone to point us to it.* He took Suhd's hand and led her to the tavern. Pax followed close behind smiling to himself as they briskly walked.

The Long Journey looked every bit worn down with warped graying planks of old wood covering the exterior of the wood-framed structure. The entranceway porch was covered by a small overhanging roof to keep rain away from the large single graying wood door. The stained splintering wood boards of the porch deck had a worn arc scraped into them from years of the door swinging open and close. A waft of cooking spices and other things unknown to him touched Rogaan's nose as he reached for the iron door handle. Rogaan thought of home as his stomach rumbled. The pleasant smells made him hungrier than he already felt. The place was run-down . . . true. Rogaan thought he was being kind with his assessment of the place and wondered what kind of establishment could look so shabby yet smell so good?

"Rogaan . . ." Suhd now bounced a little on her feet.

He opened the door to an empty room that looked to fill the whole building. Unoccupied hardwood benches surrounding small square tables filled the floor. A raised counter populated with empty drinking mugs and dishes spanned the far wall. A brown brick hearth with a low flame sat in the far right corner. It illuminated that part of the tavern. A large candle chandelier hung from the tall ceiling centered above the room, illuminating most everything else except where wall lanterns were needed around the serving room. Rogaan stepped into the tavern with Suhd quickly pressing in behind him, followed by Pax wearing a wide smile.

"Greetings . . ." Rogaan spoke out loudly. After a few moments of silence Rogaan called out again. His hopes of being Suhd's hero, no matter how small, began to fade away. "Is anyone here?"

"Rogaan," Pax pointed to a tall bronze pot off to their left with a top opening the size of two of his fists. "What do ya think?"

"Did not expect a chamber pot out here," Rogaan answered innocently.

Pax gave him a confused look, then a wider smile. "It be for spittin', no . . . ya know. Either in it or on the floor by the looks of it . . . me sister."

Suhd pushed past them in a hurry with her green knee-length dress hiked up slightly. She reached the pot and looked in before scrunching up her nose. "This smells terrible. You no expect me to—"

"Suhd," Pax cut her short, "not much of choices."

"Turn around . . . both of ya," Suhd demanded. She impatiently wiggled about waiting for them to turn away. Rogaan and Pax gave each other a grin, then complied with her demand.

"Ya know," Pax spoke casually crossing his arms as he did and still smiling ear to ear, "she snores somethin' when she be real tired. And I just have ta warn ya she—"

"Stop tellin' lies, Pax," Suhd insisted as the ringing of her water in the pot filled the room.

"I have an obligation ta me friend," Pax played with his sister.

"What of me?" Suhd asked of her brother.

Rogaan could not believe this was happening. His cheeks felt very warm, and he did not know what to say. His best friend and the girl he cared for arguing while she relieved herself in a spitting pot in the main serving room of a strange tavern . . . far from home.

"What in the name of the forsaken Ancients are ya doin'?" Boomed a deep voice that echoed throughout the entire tavern.

Rogaan nearly jumped out of his skin at the reverberating voice. He spun around to see who was in the room with them. As he did, he caught a glimpse of Suhd's upper thighs as she jumped from the pot before her dress fell down her beautiful legs. Rogaan thought his heart stopped . . . for a moment. Pax too looked surprised and a bit embarrassed at his sister's display, if that was possible. A big Baraan, almost twice as wide as Rogaan, though not a finger taller, stood in the far doorway dressed in a gray shirt and breeches with bloodstains on a short white apron covering his belly and under gut. He stood with his arms folded across a broad chest, blocking the way to the back rooms. The Baraan was not fat, simply big . . . wide, and his arms were larger than Rogaan's by no small amount. The big Baraan stood looking at them with his short-cut black hair mussed and a scruffy black beard that tried hiding a wide scarred face. He was chewing on something while waiting for their answer.

"My apologies," Suhd offered in a shaky voice. "I could no hold me water another moment, and I——"

"The sitter is out back, youngling," the big Baraan growled. "I told all of ya to stay gone until the bell got rung. Can't do everything at the same time. Got me a fresh sarig to carve up. Yawl be eatin' good for the next nights."

Pax quickly took up a spot next to Suhd. Rogaan too, flanking her other side, to protect her. Pax spoke, "We mean no disrespect——"

"What do ya call dropping water in my spittoon to be?" The big Baraan barked back. "A man's got to spittin' in there."

"Oh, Kalal, worse been put in that pot." An equally wide and almost as tall Baraan woman with brown hair pulled back in a tail to her midback chided her fellow as she pushed past him into the room. "You know that, big cuddles. What have we here . . . ?"

The stout woman stood there in her ankle-length green dress and stained yellow apron. She was handsome with kind, but *don't dare cross me* eyes. She stood as proudly as Lady Eriskla ever made to. Yes, she was in charge of this place, or at least thought so.

She looked back to the big Baraan with a disapproving frown. "You should see better. These young ones are lost in their travels and need a warm meal."

"Shimil, they——" the big Baraan started, but was cut off.

"Kalal, have Isiki prepare three stews," Shimil instructed her husband, then turned her attention back to her young patrons. She pointed to a large wash basin and drying cloths near the entrance. "Wash up, then get cozy by the fire. Kalal, stoke those coals some before they think us wildly."

Shimil had her daughter, Isiki, a young, plump, brown-haired girl with pimples, wearing a plain gray dress, bring out three bowls of stew and some flat bread for them to eat. Rogaan, like Pax and Suhd, attacked the stew, devouring their meals. It was only when they were almost done did they look up, realizing their manners were completely lacking. Rogaan felt his cheeks warm and Suhd's became visibly red. Pax seemed unabashed and kept shoveling. Shimil just smiled and proceeded to show them motherly kindness while gliding in and out of the room serving them food, water, and spice wine. She made them comfortable, so much so that Rogaan felt as if he were home for a time and found he forgot his problems for a while before speaking of them openly. Shimil demonstrated her deftness at making small talk, drawing out information you never meant to give, like Suhd letting it out that their parents were arrested, and Pax speaking of the jail wagons set to arrive at the *di'tij* tomorrow, and Rogaan slipping and confirming both. After revealing what he thought was too much, Rogaan fretted. *Will the keeper tell the Tusaa'Ner of us?* He feared she would, but something of her ways . . . her motherly ways, gave Rogaan hope she would keep their words to herself.

"We have mouths with loose tongues." Rogaan scolded Pax and Suhd and himself for their carelessness talk. He was careful to speak of this in-between serving sessions by the keeper and her daughter, who engaged them in friendly conversation with each new serving. Shimil and her daughter orchestrated the bringing out of meats and biscuits and cheese and drinks while keeping the friendly conversation going. The hearth smelled of flamed hardwood and a strange scent of flowers wafted in the air. Rogaan did not recognize the flowers, but found their scent very pleasant. Small flames and coals in the hearth bathed them in a comforting warmth while Shimil and her daughter kept working at loosening their tongues. Rogaan found it strange that they never asked for coin. "We need to take better care who we tell what to."

Worse, their loose tongues and carelessness with information made Rogaan realize . . . They did not have a plan. They had not thought through how to free Father or Pax and Suhd's parents. He chillingly realized they were not prepared and despair gripped him. Events had swept them up since the day he and Pax returned to Brigum, not leaving much of a chance to breathe or think and certainly not to plan. Now in position ahead of the jailer caravan, he put his head in his hands at the overwhelming realization that they were a small number against an army. Dread filled him as he leaned forward, hitting his head on the table.

"Rogaan . . . What be wrong?" Suhd asked, still caught up in the comfortable atmosphere the keeper had made for them.

"Ya thinkin' what I be thinkin'?" Pax asked Rogaan in a sober tone while looking about to see if Shimil or her daughter were in earshot. Satisfied they could speak . . . privately, he continued. "How do ya plan ta get our ma and fathers free?"

Rogaan looked up at his friend with a blank face. "I have nothing. No idea how to get our folks free and get away from here. We do not even know how many guards are in the caravan, how many wagons and prisoners they have, or how many *Tusaa'Ner* and loyal men are in this place that will try to stop us."

Pax replied with a serious expression. "Two jail wagons, two troop wagons, three supply carts all be pulled by niisku. Near abouts forty Farratum *Tusaa'Ner* and maybe a couple hands full of those black-hearted *Sakes*. Four prisoners. Our parents and a Baraan as tall as me father. And here . . . I thinkin' no guard will be likin' what we have ta do."

Rogaan stared at his friend with his mouth agape. He saw the whole affair at the Hall of Laws just as Pax, but failed to remember anything near these details except for those in black uniforms shoving his father into a jailer wagon. Suhd sat smiling as if she expected her brother to know such details. Pax gave her a wink.

"We have da night ta watch da guards here," Pax continued, forming a plan. "We be needin' sarigs ta get away and keep ahead of da *Sakes* and *Tusaa'Ner*."

"Where will we go?" Suhd asked. "Won't tanniyn be a danger traveling?"

Rogaan looked at them as if he had never seen either of them before. He was surprised at their attention to details . . . and scheming, or at least Pax's, and Suhd's confidence in her brother's scheming. He shook his head in a satisfied, yet thankfully disbelieving way, then answered Suhd. "My mother's family. Their estate is large, and it provides trails to the mountains and their mine deep in the wilds. We get our parents free and run and keep running from here . . . on steeds. It will take us less than two days to be in Isin lands. Meaning . . . We need to get rest tonight and the following, if this is going to work. As for the beasts in the wilds, they move around a lot during the day, looking for food and water. Tanniyn quiet down at night. Most of them have poor sight after the sun sets, making travel safest then, except for the leapers and some others. They have better night sight than us. They will be our greatest fear traveling when the sun goes down. Ravers and other longtooths will add to our problem by days. We learned this from Kardul and some others on the hunt."

"Kardul will help us too." Suhd spoke with certainty. Pax and Rogaan shared a less confident look between them. Suhd scrunched her brows in confusion, "What . . . ?"

"Suhd, Kardul and his companions will no be tellin' us how ta save our parents," Pax spoke up first.

"I do not know what to believe of Kardul and his band of *Sharur*," Rogaan added. "Kardul said they would help us free our parents, but his *Sharur* seem less concerned of our parents than with us. I have seen the way they look at all of us. I do not know if they can be trusted to free our parents."

"Maybe Kardul and Trundiir—" Suhd started to defend them before getting cut off.

"Kardul be no friend of me or ya." Pax made to set his sister straight. "He sayin' so much on da trail. But he has his eye on Rogaan."

Rogaan gave Pax a concerned look, worried at what his friend was insinuating about the *Kiuri'Ner's* intentions for him. Pax returned an exasperated look at Rogaan. "He be havin' plans for ya. Me and Suhd be in da way . . . I think."

"Well, maybe Trundiir can be . . . maybe," Rogaan spoke of the one *Sharur* who seemed different than the others. "I think . . . Maybe he might help. And . . . Kardul seems a little too easy to kill a fellow and that fight with Im'Kas . . . the Dark Ax. I just do not know. Seems everyone has plans for me that I do not know of."

"Ya just givin' Trundiir a chance because he be Tellen," Pax accused. "I say we no trust 'em all. We need ta be ready ta break our parents free without Kardul and his band. We do this. We can be doin' this."

"Maybe you are right," Rogaan agreed, hesitantly. "But I have to get my *shunir'ra* back from Trundiir before we start."

"Let that ta Pax," Suhd spoke with pride for her brother. "We know how important it be ta you. He can snatch anything from anyone."

"Trust me, Rogaan." Pax asked for his friend's unconditional trust.

Rogaan nodded in agreement. "If he will not return it to me freely, then I will trust in your *snatching*."

The warmth of the hearth bathed them as they continued talking details of what needed preparing. Suhd moved to share Rogaan's bench while they plotted. At first, Rogaan was unnerved and did not know how to act with Suhd so near. He stammered much as he was distracted from his thoughts. Then, as their conversation progressed, he stopped thinking about how he should act around her and just conducted himself as he would with Pax. She warmed to him, taking his hand shyly and hugging him several times when she approved of pieces of the plan. It was impossible for Pax to hide his grin. Suhd obviously ignored the smell of sarig and the purple flower ointment on him. He was ripe with the scent of the beast. She too smelled of steeds and ointment despite their washing of hands and faces prior to the meal, but as pungent the scent of sarig hung in the air, she smelled of wildflowers . . . sweet wildflowers. Her scent intoxicated him. He felt more than willing to ignore the unimportant smells to be close to her and her wildflowers. Rogaan found himself being drawn to Suhd more deeply as the moments passed. To look into those beautiful blue eyes of hers was to lose himself into . . . well, he just could not describe it, even to himself. Suhd wore joyful smiles at Rogaan's delighted heart with each of her touches and in the way she looked at him. He wanted this to last forever.

Chapter 3
Treachery

A group of four guardsmen dressed in the blue hide armor of the *Tusaa'Ner* noisily entered the establishment and sat themselves at a table in the middle of the room. They were followed by other guardsmen until almost every table filled. Over twenty guardsmen took seats in the place and all were hungry, wanting the fresh sarig Shimil had on the cook fires. The tavern was plunged in rowdiness and impatience.

Rogaan grew angry at their presence, more specifically, their interruption on his moment with Suhd. Not only did they intrude on his and Suhd's sharing of talk and touch, but they brought with them unpleasant odors and foul talk. Rogaan wondered if any of them bathed in days and by their wrinkled noses, Suhd and Pax agreed with him. More guardsmen pushed into the tavern until only standing places along the walls remained. The pleasant scent of wildflowers fled Rogaan's wanting nose as more came filling the Long Journey. A bad mood settled on Rogaan as his head started to hurt. He wanted to yell . . . lash out at the guardsmen for making noise, fouling the air, and sharing his time with Suhd.

Shimil and family served them all an evening meal of sarig and tatters and spice wine with speed and efficiency Rogaan found surprising and pleasing. Some of the men eyed Shimil's young daughter as she came and went with hungry looks they should be ashamed of. When Shimil's venomous stare caught their eyes, their faces darkened and only managed frequent sly glances at the aware youngling, who seemed to take joy in the guardsmen's attentions. Rogaan, Pax, and Suhd had long since stopped talking of their plans due to so many ears being so near and talked of safe topics such as Brigum's affairs or some unknown details of their family life they wished to talk of. As the meal went on, many of the guardsmen turned their attentions to Suhd with, at first, their occasional glances . . . turning more and more to long lust-filled stares. Isiki was almost completely forgotten by the crowd as Suhd looked to be uncomfortably mortified at the unwelcomed attention. Rogaan fought his protective instincts . . . and jealousy at every one of their looks. He knew to get into a fight with a room full of *Tusaa'Ner* guardsmen was a losing act for them and their parents. One rough-looking fellow with a poor keeping of his uniform kept eyeing Suhd lewdly in a way that infuriated Rogaan. The Baraan eyed at her like a leaper looking at a wounded meal and was giving her none of the honor and respect she deserved. Rogaan stared back at the guardsman who seemed amused at his attempt at intimidation. The fellow kept his hungry eye on Suhd even when Pax joined Rogaan staring back at him to make it clear his gaze was unwelcomed. The fellow appeared to be pleased with himself in making three younglings uncomfortable. Rogaan's fury built, but he held it in check . . . for a time. Just when Rogaan felt he would explode, the rough and tough guardsman rose from his table with his companions, his eyes still on Suhd while wearing an expecting grin. The big guardsman, maybe a little taller than Rogaan, strode to their table to a spot off Suhd's left. Pax followed the fellow with heated eyes, but kept his seat instead of challenging him. Rogaan did not watch the guardsman approach as he was fighting with himself not to meet the cad on the floor and pound him.

"How 'bouts a little dance, lass?" The brown-haired, scruffy-bearded Baraan *Tusaa'Ner* guardsman more demanded than asked in a tone lacking respect or politeness.

Rogaan almost jumped up from his bench as did Pax. With a mature poise, Suhd held up her hand keeping them both from committing rash actions. Her eyes focused forward away from the guardsman. "No interest."

"No interest in a little dance and having a fella?" He asked in a snide way, playing up his question so his companions could hear.

Pax rose from his seat half a blink quicker than Rogaan, both confronting the guardsman with heated demeanors and blazing stares. Immediately, the guardsman lost his snide and arrogant grin, replaced with a mix of surprise and caution on his face as he looked past them to the tavern's front door. Rogaan and Pax shared confused looks . . . Who knew it would be so easy?

"The *lass* made herself known," Trundiir rumbled before leaning out from behind the guardsman, his white beard sticking out from this hooded cloak. *How did he sneak up on the guardsman without me seeing him?* Rogaan wondered. Rogaan caught sight of Trundiir's hand under the fella's blue tunic. A shocked smile came to his face as he realized Trundiir must have the guardsman's prize possessions in hand . . . and likely twisting them from the look of discomfort on the Baraan's face. When the fella did not respond to Trundiir, his expression turned painful. Trundiir was not being gentle. "Leave the youngling be or I'll remove what I hold of."

The guardsman quickly nodded in agreement. A stolid look of satisfaction came to Trundiir with the unspoken answer. Then, with a little more of a twist and tug that forced a yelp from the Baraan, he staggered back to his companions holding his crotch. Trundiir watched the angry Baraan with a casual disregard, as if he did not matter, but also not closing his eyes to catching any rash actions. Trundiir made to ask Suhd a question, but the metallic ringing of swords being drawn filled the room. Trundiir kept a calm face, but shook his head slightly in disbelief before turning to confront the entire tavern full of *Tusaa'Ner* guardsmen.

"Bad plan!" Kardul's voice boomed from the tavern entrance. The room full of guardsmen looked to Kardul, questioning him with their eyes. Kardul remained calm as he took several steps into the room with his *Sharur* following him. "Not for my friend or the younglings. The Tellen would kill half of you before you organize yourselves. Now . . . if a one dares to cut as little as a lock of hair from them, I'll skin him alive."

"That's Kardul . . . isn't it?" A guardsman in back asked his companions. The room of tough-acting guardsmen started looking to each other, not so certain of themselves any longer. A murmur rose, then settled down as swords were sheathed and guardsmen rejoined their companions at tables and immediately started acting as if nothing happened. The offending guardsman who had started the confrontation waddled gingerly back to his table, keeping his eyes to the floor. He sat with a grimace as his companions snickered at him. But no eye in the tavern was taken from Kardul and his *Sharurs*.

Rogaan felt a heavy burden lift from him as his anger subsided. As much as Suhd's honor had to be protected, fighting a room of seasoned guardsmen was foolhardy, if not deadly. Still, he was ready to take them on to keep Suhd's honor and reputation pure. Rogaan looked to Trundiir. "My gratitude."

"Mine too." Suhd stood and kissed Trundiir on his white-bearded cheek. She looked relived. Trundiir appeared to blush, though his face remained stolid.

Rogaan felt his heart sink, and his jealousy boil at her kiss of the Tellen. He realized immediately his feelings were uncalled for and felt embarrassed for them. He hoped his face was not as red as it felt, though by the way Pax glanced at him, his face could be glowing red as his father's smithing fires.

"Mine also," Pax added, though not as enthusiastically as his sister.

"Makes me all warm watching you four," Kardul interrupted with a hint of insincerity. Rogaan caught Trundiir's stolid demeanor breaking just for a moment as he shot an unwelcomed glance at Kardul. Kardul either did not notice Trundiir's display or did not care for it. He looked about to see if anyone was near enough to listen to their words. Not satisfied with all the ears around, he nodded toward to tavern door to the citadel grounds. "Need to talk. Walk with me."

Kardul led Rogaan from the tavern without ceremony. They left Suhd sitting at the table looking after them with concerned eyes, as much for herself as for Rogaan. Pax sat at the table as well, flashing a look of panic before determined anger washed across his face. Rogaan guessed his anger was likely at being left out of this discussion. Trundiir plopped himself down at their table before Kardul ushered Rogaan out of the tavern, who felt guilty leaving Pax and especially Suhd in the tavern without him, but Trundiir's presence made him feel confident they would be kept from more unsavory advances by the guardsmen. Pax and Suhd had as much at stake as him, and he felt a bit wrong talking plans with Kardul without them. Still, he had little choice. Kardul had the experience in these matters, and he wanted to understand what Kardul had planned to help free their parents. Stepping outside into the windless, cool air of the night, only a few buzzing biters hovered about him. They did not bite thankfully, due to the purple flower ointment Rogaan wiped on himself while riding through the forest. The scent of dung hung sour in the air, wafting from the fenced stable yard to his right where their steeds now mingled and rested with other sarigs and smaller animals. Lanterns hanging from poles near the barn at the opposite end of the stable yard cast eerie shadows over the animals. Rogaan shivered a moment, not from the cool air, but from the uncomfortable and dark atmosphere hanging over the *di'tij*. From the bunk houses an unfamiliar tune, played from a windpipe, sounded pleasant to him, if a little rough. Kardul strolled toward the main gate with Rogaan at his side with little talk. A small group of Baraan dressed in dirty tunics and complaining to each other tended to a small sarig in front of the barn. They seemed oblivious to everything except what they were doing. The *di'tij* walls stood over the inner citadel with thinning ranks of guards. Rogaan guessed many were taking their evening meal or tending to other duties. Those still on watch were mostly keeping an eye on him and Kardul. Rogaan thought that strange. *Should they not be looking into the wilds?*

Behind and to the right, nestled up to the same *di'tij* wall as the tavern, a long wood building having the look of a general store collected a mix of guardsmen and livered workers, the bunch carousing under its lantern-lit covered porch overlooking the corralled steeds. Several cook fires danced low in front of the four rows of wood barracks on his left. Barefooted womenfolk, dressed in worn tunics, huddled over pots stirring what Rogaan assumed to be stews. A hand of little ones ran wildly between the barracks, annoying their mothers and frequently getting swatted for it.

"Thought of how to see your father free?" Kardul asked.

"Well . . . I . . . We hoped you had ideas," Rogaan lied. He, Pax, and Suhd had schemed a plan they believed would free their parents and allow them to escape. It was simple, filled with uncertain risks, but it was a plan. Once free of his jailers and away from the *di'tij*, Rogaan did not speak to his friends of where he figured his father would take them. Pax would jump out of his skin. Suhd would likely end up in tears and wails. The Ebon Circle temple. The attacks on his home and on his mother's carriage with Suhd proved the name Isin was not enough to deter those with motivations to hunt them down. So far, it seemed just about everyone had their eyes on him and his family for reasons still to be revealed. It all made little sense . . . the law and assassins after him and his family had to have different motives for wanting them . . . temple and end-of-the-world zealots, Brigum's leadership and *Tusaa'Ner*, Farratum's *Tusaa'Ner*, the Ebon Circle itself, and that unknown traveler Rogaan wanted to believe had helped him. But how could he be sure of anything? His head hurt with all the possibilities. The Ebon Circle was the only place Rogaan could think that was beyond the reach of most of those after them . . . and for some reason beyond him his father thought the dark temple to be the safest place.

Kardul scrubbed his unshaven chin while looking off distantly. He kept in deep thought for a short time before scanning the walls and main gate with that predatory gaze of his. "It will be difficult."

"We are ready for difficult," Rogaan puffed out in bravado.

Kardul sniffed loudly as he looked to the main gate again. "Difficult means people can, and likely will, get hurt . . . maybe *lightless*. Your father will be a target and by doing this, so will you."

"I understand," Rogaan replied without bluster. "Father is doomed if we do not act."

Kardul stood for a time pondering, occasionally glancing at the main gate and walls. He sighed deeply, then spoke. "Youngling, I, as many do in and around Brigum, owe much to your father. What you want may not be possible. It will depend on many things yet unknown if we can free him in this *di'tij*. Worse, we might have to wait until the jailers leave this place for Farratum to free him. If to be successful here, we'll use the moment when the caravan first arrives as the *Tusaa'Ner* guardsmen will be looking for a meal and rest. The local guard are likely to reinforce them. We may be able to find weakness in their wagon protection then . . . before they figure how to work with each other. If the *Tusaa'Ner* wagon protection is light, we look for weakness and opportunity to free your father. If heavy, we wait until they leave before making to free him."

"Wait?" The word burst loudly from Rogaan before he realized he spoke. Kardul seemed surprised with his raised brows at the outburst. He quickly glanced to the walls and main gate, then back to Rogaan.

"We must be careful," Kardul explained in an even voice. "And you and your friends need to stay hidden while the caravan is here."

Rogaan gave Kardul a confused look. "Why?"

"The *Tusaa'Ner* in the approaching caravan know your face," Kardul explained. "They'll toss you into that jailer wagon the moment you're spotted."

The Tusaa'Ner was rather insistent at putting me in irons, Rogaan reflected.

And . . . he, Pax, and Suhd had not planned for the added *di'tij Tusaa'Ner* guarding the wagons. They in the caravan did know of him . . . they and the whole town seemed to be after him and Pax. His ability to move freely about the *di'tij* here will be hindered after they arrive. Their plotting to free their parents had holes and just became more difficult than they planned. Rogaan looked to Kardul, who was looking to the main gate as if he was expecting to see someone. "Will you tell me more of your plan? How we would free our parents if we wait for the jailer wagons to return to the road toward Farratum?"

It struck Rogaan then, that they need not wait until the jailer caravan arrives and departs this *di'tij*. They could stage their parents' escape late tomorrow when they were rested with fresh sarigs and the caravan approaching this *di'tij*, with their folks and guardsmen tired and worn down from the day's travel. It was as near a perfect opportunity as they could hope if they could figure a way to free their parents from those wagons without getting caught or killed. They would disappear into the wilds retracing their trail with Kardul and his *Sharurs* in the lead. With this new revelation and much excitement, Rogaan asked Kardul, "What if we—"

A half-dozen *Tusaa'Ner* guardsmen pushed the main gate open and entered from the road. Clad in dark blue armor and helms, red waist sashes, short swords drawn, they looked ready for a fight. Intently they scanned the *di'tij* for someone of something. Their eyes fixed on Kardul and Rogaan. The red-caped *Tusaa'Ner* motioned for his men to follow as he stepped purposely toward him and Kardul. Kardul showed no emotion . . . no panic or even a concern as they approached. He stood, patiently watching them close the thirty-stride distance between them. A wave of panic welled up inside Rogaan. *They are coming for me!*

"No good." Pax spoke in a pained voice from just behind Rogaan.

Rogaan nearly jumped out of his boots at Pax's words, being surprised his friend got so close without him noticing. Kardul snapped his head around, his face a mix of surprise and annoyance. It was obvious Pax had surprised him, as well. Kardul's eyes shot up from Pax, looking beyond him toward the Long Journey. The *Kiuri'Ner's* eyes flashed what Rogaan thought was uncertainty or indecision for a moment before his jaw set in anger.

Following Kardul's stare, Rogaan found a fretful Suhd trotting toward them, followed by a walking Trundiir. His teeth now grinding and eyes narrowed, Kardul looked unhappy at all the added company.

"You there!" An accusing voice resonated deeply.

Rogaan's innards turned to water as he spun around. Standing before him were six *Tusaa'Ner*, all with arms outstretched and their sword tips pointing at his chest.

"Is it him?" One of the guardsmen asked nervously. The *Tusaa'Ner* looked young, in fact, younger than Rogaan himself, by the hairless chin under the helm, Rogaan guessed.

"Tellen fits the description sent from Brigum," the red-caped guardsman answered. The *Tusaa'Ner* leader looked at Kardul with uncertain eyes . . . No, more like questioning eyes, Rogaan caught in the moment before the guardsman set his jaw firm and stare turned stern. "Arrest him."

Kardul stepped between the *Tusaa'Ner* and Rogaan. The *Tusaa'Ner* leader exchanged a questioning stare with Kardul. Rogaan was not sure what was happening; he stood looking on at the surreal scene playing out before him. Pax tugged on his wrist trying to drag Rogaan from what looked to be a brewing fight. Kardul calmly announced, "Nobody's getting arrested."

"I have my orders," the *Tusaa'Ner* leader stated in his young, stern voice.

"I have mine," Kardul countered. "You'll make no arrest here."

"I insist," the *Tusaa'Ner* leader countered back with defiance that seemed to surprise him. "You have no authority here, Kardul. Yours is on the roads and in the forest. Not within these *guarded* walls."

Kardul's *Sharurs* stepped from the shadows all around them, making their presence known. The *Tusaa'Ner* commander took in the attempt at intimidation. He hesitated, but only for a moment before raising his fist. More than a dozen archers, crossbowmen and longbow men alike, immediately raised their weapons with nocked bolts and arrows, pointing them at Kardul and Rogaan. Kardul remained calm, how . . . Rogaan did not know. His own insides felt as if they were about to explode, and his gut cramping was so tight it would double him over if this kept up for long. Kardul stood silent and motionless for a time. It felt forever to Rogaan. Even Pax had stopped tugging at his left wrist. Suhd made her way to his side, wrapping her arms around his right bicep and snuggling up close with eyes wide with fear. She felt wonderful against him, but this was a dangerous moment that could go out of control in a flinch. He needed to get her away from him so she would be safe.

"Do it your way," Kardul held the *Tusaa'Ner* leader's eyes in a level stare. With a wave of Kardul's left hand, the *Sharur* melted back into the shadows. The red-caped *Tusaa'Ner* nodded in satisfaction, then motioned for his men to take Rogaan.

"Nooooo!" Suhd resisted Rogaan trying to peel her from him.

"You must," Rogaan told her in his gentlest voice while looking into her frightened, pained eyes. Pax stepped back as the guardsmen grabbed Rogaan, while Suhd had to be forced by one of the guardsmen by grabbing her wrist and pulling her away. Rogaan's blood boiled at the Baraan touching her and being rough enough that she grimaced.

"Take the other younglings too," the caped *Tusaa'Ner* commanded.

"No!" Rogaan growled. "You want me, *not* them. I will go quietly. Just leave them be."

"Yes, you will go quietly, *stoner*," the young *Tusaa'Ner* leader agreed maliciously.

Two blue-clad guardsmen grabbed his arms tightly, restraining him. Two more did their best to take hold of Pax, but he was too fast for them, spinning and rolling and weaving until he was lost to the shadows near the barracks. Another guardsman grabbed a handful of Suhd's long black hair and pulled her head back, causing her pain enough that she yelled out. The guardsman grinned and seemed to enjoy his domination of her. Rogaan's blood could be no hotter. Without warning, his world slowed. Rogaan quickly realized everyone seemed to move half his speed. The sickening feel in his innards and head that usually came with this strange perception was pushed aside easily by him this time. Instead of fighting this sensation, as he did previously, Rogaan instead embraced his heightened senses and new physical self. Jerking free of the *Tusaa'Ner* holding his arms, Rogaan charged the guardsman taking his amusement with Suhd's suffering. He closed the five-stride distance in what seemed to him to be a bound before slamming his fist and forearm into the helmed face of the guardsman. The *Tusaa'Ner* went crumpling to the ground after Rogaan struck the Baraan's head as hard as he could. The Baraan bounced off the ground, then slid a stride into a stable yard fence post where he lay unmoving. Rogaan looked to Suhd who appeared as shocked as relieved not having her hair being used as a restraint and that the guardsman went down so easily. She reached out to him and touched his left forearm. When Rogaan looked into her eyes, his world slowed and he heard her words of thanks. Rogaan's heart skipped a beat, and his hands trembled as he took hers. Just as he calmed and started to lose himself in her eyes and touch, fear filled those radiant blue moons as she looked past Rogaan. He turned as fast as he could, placing Suhd behind him to shield her from whatever danger she saw. Two sword pommels filled his vision just before the world went dark.

Chapter 4

Liberty's End

A clatter of metal on stone echoed in the darkness. Rogaan's head felt like it would explode from the noise. Ringing in his head brought his eyes to a painful wince as he tried to look after the noise, but found the darkness he was in too deep. *Where am I?* He asked himself as his heartbeat quickened a little. His thinking felt sluggish, a struggle to form thoughts and hold focus on them. *What is wrong with me?* A flash of panic struck him, remembering the pair of pommels in his face. He fought back the panic by controlling his breathing . . . slow . . . even. The old method taught to archers and others needing focus, calm to do what they do. He wanted to hold onto his reason and clear his head enough to learn what happened to him. Retreating footfalls echoed, boots he thought, accompanied by an unintelligible mumbling of words that sounded like gravel poured in a pile and a snide chuckle made him feel as if he was not among friends. An iron door squealed closed on unoiled hinges, and a heavy swing latch set in place confirmed his fears.

"Ya be awake?" An urgent, but familiar soft voice made Rogaan's heart jump. "Rogaan . . ."

"I am," Rogaan replied. He realized he lay on his back on a cool stone surface. "Everything is dark. I cannot see."

Silence filled the air. Rogaan worried he was dreaming Suhd was near. He tried to raise himself, but felt as if a tanniyn sat on him. He could not move, not his arms, not his legs, not even raise his head.

"They beat ya awful and gave ya a foul drink forced in ya." Suhd sounded as if she was in tears.

Rogaan's concern for Suhd's safety exploded, causing a stout determination to fill him. He did not know where he was or what of their predicament, but he had to keep her safe. With a growl he lifted his head, then his arms and shoulders, forcing himself into an upright sitting position.

Every fiber of his muscles ached and burned. His head throbbed fiercely and for a few moments he feared he was to pass out, evidently again. Once sitting upright, he kept still for a while until his head slowed its spinning. He tried opening his eyes again. A distant dim light was all he saw. He focused on it. It came closer. His head pains dulled. The light grew. A blurred view of his bloodstained charcoal pants and boots formed. After a time, his vision cleared well enough to see he sat in a fired brick jail cell with bars, a cell door in front of him, and bars to his right. The light was dim, maybe dawn or dusk, he was uncertain. Suhd sat in her dirty and torn green dress in the cell next to him with streaks of tears showing she had cried on her dirt-smudged face.

Rage welled up inside Rogaan at the sight of Suhd. *Who dared touch her . . . harm her?* He demanded in his mind. All his pain fled as he rose to his feet. At first he almost tumbled over, if not for the bars of the cell to hold him up. Fighting through his body's refusal to respond to his mind, he kneeled at the bars next to Suhd. Reaching through the bars he tenderly lifted her chin. Her radiant blue eyes, even reddened with so many tears, melted him. "Who harmed you?"

"The guards had intentions, but lost them when Trundiir and Kardul straightened them some," Suhd answered, then further explained with renewed tears flowing down her cheeks. "They threw me in here with ya the night before last. Ya got angry at the guards for throwing me and knocked two of them down before a bunch of them jumped on ya and beat ya. Then they poured some foul-smelling drink in ya, and ya didn't move since. I feared . . . thought ya *lightless*, Rogaan. I thought ya *lightless*."

Tears flowed down her beautiful cheeks. *How could anyone hurt Suhd?* Rogaan asked himself. He sat and held her through the bars for a long time before her crying slowed to sniffles. As he calmed, he started to feel bruises all about him. It seemed only his privates and left side were spared. Everything else hurt, even his hair. The cells grew brighter in the dawn light. He and Suhd occupied the only two cells where they were being held, each with their own iron door and only one cell, hers, had a barred window. That window was almost up four strides of the five-stride-tall wall. The walls were made of fired brick, all fitted with mortar. Not well made . . . likely

Baraan doing, but functional. An untouched tin pan with a slopped on pile of something Rogaan could not guess at what sat just inside of Suhd's cell. A dirty and torn blanket lay on cots in each cell. Chamber pots next to the cots completed the decor. Not the vision he had when thinking of places to be alone with Suhd. Rogaan's mouth felt parched, and his head pain returned, though now dull.

"How long?" Rogaan asked Suhd while he held her as close as he could.

"Two nights," she answered without looking up from his arm where her head rested.

"What of Pax?" Rogaan asked, trying to piece together their predicament.

"He ran when we be arrested." Suhd sounded happy and sad at the same time. "Don't know about him after that except for the guards grumbling about a squirt of a shadow that keeps slipping away from them."

Rogaan smiled at that. Pax was good at few things most would not call useful, but sneaking about was his best. Rogaan hoped his friend had a plan to get them out of these cells so they could still set their parents free. His stomach suddenly rumbled loudly, embarrassing him.

"Ya must be hungry after not eating for days," Suhd stated as she lifted her head a little. She pulled that pan of something toward her. "It's not too bad . . . if you close ya eyes and hold ya nose, but its food. Here . . ."

Rogaan looked at the pan she held with mixed thoughts. He was hungry, but not so certain hungry enough to eat the yellowish gruel. Suhd looked at him with eyes pleading. She was pragmatic beyond her years, and he did not know if he liked that at the moment. "You need your strength. It might be all we have if we are ta break free."

Suhd smiled at him as she tenderly brushed his cheek with her fingers. Despite the iron bars, cold, hard floor, and their dank surroundings, he felt warm . . . all over. He just wanted to sit there with her tender touch on his arm and cheek and not worry about the world. He closed his eyes, and they were sitting on the rocks overlooking the Tamarad River in Brigum watching the fish and snapjaws play. The breeze around Brigum was still in the morning dawn with Suhd's hair smelling of wildflowers. Suhd stirred and squeezed his arm. Rogaan opened his eyes to the dank cells and a beautiful Suhd brushing his cheek. Her eye shifted looking from him to the tin pan. Rogaan looked at the contents of the pan and reluctantly decided Suhd was right, but he also needed her strong enough to run when time came. He smiled at her, "Are we to share?"

The iron-strapped wood door to the jail cells swung open slamming against the brick inner wall, startling both Rogaan and Suhd. A large Baraan dressed in a dark charcoal tunic and pants held tight at the waist by a wide hide belt that matched his boots and with a belt sash of gray, stood with hands on hips in the doorway. The sash also carried the color red, telling Rogaan the short, brown-bearded Baraan was of Farratum . . . a jailer, or *Sake,* most likely. He fingered a whip that hung from his belt on one side and large sap from the other. The Baraan's eyes were as intense as his arms and chest were big and powerful. The *Sake* stepped into the room along with two others also in dark uniforms, except they were of smaller stature. The big *Sake* pointed to the door to Suhd's cell. The two smaller Baraans wasted no time in opening her cell and slapping the pan from her hands, sending the gruel across the floor and wall. Suhd reeled in fear as the men grabbed at her. Rogaan exploded in anger yelling at the dark-uniformed Baraans to leave her alone. The Baraans recoiled from his right hand as he reached through the bars trying to grab one of them. They dragged her wide-eyed with fear from the cell room leaving Rogaan and the big Baraan alone, staring at each other.

"You're as trouble as they said," the big Baraan declared. "I want no more of this. Behave yourself or I'll be hard on you . . . *and* her." He said that last with a malevolent grin.

Rogaan's blood chilled ice cold in fear for Suhd for a moment, then launched himself in a fury at the Baraan, crashing into the bars grasping at him. "Leave her alone. I'll tear anyone apart who harms her."

The big Baraan broke out in a satisfied smile. "You're fit for the arena, you are?"

"Shackle him," the big *Sake* order of another pair of Baraan entering the room. They too were bigger in chest and arms than most. "And if he causes more problems, beat him until he stops or is *lightless.*"

The three *Sakes* stepped back from the bars in an orderly way, allowing a slightly built companion in a black tunic and with graying hair to approach the cell with a slender hollow wood tube. A quick puff on the tube sent a cloud of dust into Rogaan's face. Immediately he felt on fire inside and out as he choked and spat trying to breathe. Tears poured from his eyes such he could not see clearly. His throat and nose felt as if lava flowed through them. He coughed and sneezed, trying to get out whatever the little fellow put in there, to little avail. He heard the cell door squeal open and made out vague dark figures approaching him. He swung at them again, and again. They avoided his punches, then split one to either side of him before he felt something slam against his head, sending him stumbling to the wall where he came to rest on one knee leaning against the rough brick. Everything was wrong, spinning around, and upside down. Rogaan felt about to fall over . . . whichever direction that was. They pounced on him as he came to lie on the floor, shackling his wrists and ankles before he knew what was happening.

"To my liking," the big *Sake* spoke with bravado. "Get him to the wagons. Keep him from the lass. This one gets his temper up when she's near."

Rogaan drifted on currents of air with the help of others he was only vaguely aware of. He felt his boots dragging along a hard surface, then a softer one. Voices called out all about him conversing between themselves in words he did not understand. The burning in his throat and eyes lessened, but now a painful head throbbing added to his misery. The squeaking of metal hinges rang loudly just before he found himself floating in air, completely. Sharp pain then racked his body as something slammed into his head and right shoulder. He no longer floated; instead, he painfully lay on his back on a hard surface he thought wood before plunging into a world of grays and vague, distant voices.

Chapter 5
Bitter Bonds

Searing pain kept at Rogaan as he lay semi-aware in a surreal world of deep grays. He tried opening his eyes countless times, but found them too heavy to obey. Voices, distant, some familiar and some not, swam in his head just beyond his ability to understand their words. He tried to concentrate, tried to focus, tried to understand their words, tried to forget his throbbing head and his aching back and the sharp stabs, like daggers, in his ribs that came with every breath. Agony. Time passed, how long Rogaan was unsure, before the voices started to get closer, clearer, as did the buzz of biters, bloodsuckers, and bitemes. The voices spoke with sorrow, with confusion, with anger, all worn out and defeated in tone. Rogaan tried opening his eyes again . . . and the deep gray gave way to blue hues striped with dark bars. Suddenly, the voices went quiet—his ears filled with the buzz of biters . . . some actually biting him. Rogaan's eyes focused on something . . . a white cloud against a deep blue, set behind iron bars. The stink of animal urine and other waste suddenly pummeled his nose. His eyes shot open at the assault, and he tried to sit up. Pain racked him everywhere, but most intensely in his ribs, causing him to collapse backward with a groan, his head aching as he rested it on wood planks. Rogaan gritted his teeth and suffered at all the pain for long moments until the pain lessened, allowing him to let go of his grimace and look up. A thin face with slate blue eyes framed by cropped black hair appeared in his view.

"About time," Pax spoke. "Ya had me worried again."

Rogaan's head throbbed, and it hurt to breathe. The burning in his nose and eyes was gone . . . He was relieved and grateful for that. As he raised himself up on his elbows, his head throbbed more fiercely and his ribs protested with spasms of pain. Rogaan grunted, "I swear to the Ancients, the next one that gives me a foul drink or puffs in my face or tries to bump my head . . . I will pound him senseless into the ground."

"They be afraid of ya," Pax stated matter-of-factly as he sat with his back against the bars.

"They gonna be more afraid of me," Rogaan promised in a flare of anger, then mumbled to himself about being tired of getting poison-drinks, all the while trying to shake off disorientation and pains. He realized they had him shackled at both the wrists and ankles. Rogaan assessed the metal to be of average quality and the links breakable if he could find a way to get some leverage. Looking about, he saw that it was midmorning by the rise of the sun. He sat as a prisoner in a jailer's wagon that was part of a caravan on a slow move eastward . . . likely to Farratum. He hoped he was at least in the caravan with his father. The wagon behind was pulled by a pair of dark muscular niisku driven by two Baraans dressed in gray tunics. Flanking both sides of the wagons, Farratum *Tusaa'Ner* guardsmen in their dark blue armor and uniforms marching with spears and short swords. A new handful of either *Kiuri'Ner* or *Sharurs* on sarigs flanked the *Tusaa'Ner*. They patrolled at the edge of the caravan and the forest for dangers . . . likely *Sharur* on the flanks and *Kiuri'Ner* scouting ahead as Rogaan had come to understand their ways in his learning of them in Brigum. Rogaan took note that the caravan traveled along a road through heavy forest. The hard-packed road was wide enough for two wagons. Wheels, hooves, and feet kicked up little dust, and the road showed few ruts. Surveying the cage he was in, Rogaan found that he and Pax were captive along with two others; half-clothed Baraans who looked beaten and smelled as if they messed themselves. Both men lay flat trying to sleep. Their cage . . . rusting bars formed into a cube enclosure, except for the wood planks he lay on and the forward part of the wagon where the drivers sat guiding their beasts of burden with reins and whips. Flanking the driver's seat were a pair of incense burners, likely filled with a purple flower concoction to keep the biters away. At the center of their cage, a hole cut in the wood planks, too small for a person to fit though, was closed off with a sliding wood door. The area around the hole and door was stained wet with urine and brown-green matter. His stomach turned sour at the sight of it as a small halo of biters and bitemes hovered around the foul mess.

Pax sat leaning against the bars at the rear of the cage with his knees drawn up toward his chest. Pax was someone not easily quieted, but there he sat looking somewhat defeated. New bruises on his face and the way he moved hinted at him suffering in pain.

"How did they catch you?" Rogaan asked his friend.

Pax did not acknowledge Rogaan's question for a time. He simply sat unmoving, staring blankly. Rogaan waited silently for his friend to reply, knowing that pushing him would get him little. Pax answered and did deeds when Pax wanted.

"Burn da *Tusaa'Ner*," Pax spoke in anger. He worked his jaws and his blank stare turned intense as if he was watching or reliving something unsettling. "Guards tried and tried ta catch me last night. Fools. When they could no catch me da daimons threatened me ma. Took her from da wagon and put a hand ta her. Ma screamed for me ta stay hidin'. Same of me father. I kept ta da shadows. Da rot worms hit Ma some more. Then da dung shovelers called out sayin' they'd do Ma worse. I gave meself up when dey ripped Ma's dress and roughed her up."

Tears flowed down Pax's dirty and bruised cheeks leaving lines. Rogaan's heart sank for his friend. Family was very important to him. He considered himself a protector of his ma and sister, helping his father who worked long shifts in the mine to keep clothes on them and food in their bellies. Rogaan came to understand that Pax took any attack on his family with the utmost seriousness.

"They beat you when you gave yourself up." Rogaan stated his conclusion.

"No," Pax replied. "I got beat when me ma slapped one of the guards for handling me rough. I got beat ta teach her a lesson. Her howls watching me get beat hurt me more dan anything da worms could do ta me."

"Pax, I am sorry you and your ma suffer—" Rogaan was cut off by him.

"I no want ya 'sorry.'" Pax looked possessed with hatred. "I want ya anger. I want ya poundin' da daimon guards into da dirt. Break 'em. Kill 'em. Make 'em suffer."

Pax looked away, his face furious and intense and unwavering. Rogaan did not know what to say to his friend to console him, or if he even could. Never had Pax shown so much resentment, so much hate. Thinking to change the subject, Rogaan realized he did not know where Suhd was. Panic prickled his skin. "Pax . . . Where is Suhd?"

Pax was slow to answer, but did though he continued staring off into the distance. "She be with Ma and Father in da wagon ahead of us. Ya father be with 'em."

"Keep quiet in there." Commanded a sky-blue-clad *Tusaa'Ner* walking alongside of the jailer wagon.

"Quiet yaself!" Pax shot back so fast Rogaan thought the response came from someone on the other side of the wagon.

The guardsman struck the cage bars with his spear. "Speak again and I'll see your tongue cut out."

Pax rose to his knees and made to bark at the guard again, but held his tongue when he saw Rogaan put up a hand signaling him to caution. Pax shot Rogaan a long, heated stare until it got uncomfortable for him. He then repositioned himself in the corner of the cage, all the time mumbling to himself loudly, as he sat down. "I be in a jail wagon . . . with a pair of smellies. They must of messed their pants. And we be on da road ta doom. But no . . . Ya want me ta be good and quiet."

"Who ya callin' smelly?" A gruff voice with a bit of a whine in it asked accusingly. Rogaan sought who spoke and found one of the other two prisoners looking at Pax with accusing eyes. The haggard, brown-haired Baraan was beyond his prime and not in the best physical condition. He had not washed in a long while from the looks of the rags he wore and the dirt and grime on his wrinkled face, exposed chest, and legs. The other Baraan had more teeth missing than not, though he looked in far better condition than the less-clothed, brooding Baraan next to him.

"Ya havin' a trouble with us?" Pax shot back.

"Stop talkin' to that Tellen," the half-clothed Baraan demanded of Pax with open disgust. His eyes looked *lightless* except for the hatred that now flared in them. "I not spend my days fightin' the likes of him to see yawl friendin' up to that animal."

Pax's eyes went wide with surprise. He recovered quickly, putting on his usual mask of self-assurance hinted with arrogance while readying an answer to the half-clothed Baraan's declaration of unfriendliness. Rogaan made to cut Pax off before his friend got his first words out, but was too late. Pax launched, "What ya talkin' about? Ya both be stinkin'; messed ya bottoms, ya have, and ya know it. Ya have no self-respect. And don't be talkin' about me friend like he be some kind of burnin' pile of dung. He be a good friend."

The two ill-tempered Baraans stared at Pax and Rogaan with murderous eyes. Pax gave their murderous stares right back and seemed about ready to leap at the two. Rogaan feared a fight was about to erupt over him, just for him being part Tellen blood. *Senseless. We're all prisoners in a jailer wagon, and they want a fight about me being a bit different than them*, Rogaan thought to himself in disbelief. Glares and tensions grew more intense with each passing moment. Just when Rogaan thought Pax and the two raggedly dressed Baraans were going to attack each other, a spear tip rattled across the wagon's iron bars, startling everyone and freezing all in their places. A tall, lean *Tusaa'Ner* officer, another *sakal* by his plumage, dressed in sky-blue and charcoal-colored hide armor, plated with burnished metal on shoulders and chest and topped with a burnished helm with face guard and red plume, worked his spear back and forth across the iron bars until everyone inside fell quiet and paid him full attention. "Keep quiet and no fighting! The *Seergal* doesn't want her prisoners injured . . . before time."

The caravan kept its steady pace, slow enough so guardsmen could match it on foot. From the fatigued looks of the guard ranks, Rogaan guessed they were not used to forced marches. The tall *Tusaa'Ner sakal* seemed in better condition than most, easily working his way around the cage closest to Pax while keeping pace with the wagon.

"You are the one with family in the other jailer?" The tall *Tusaa'Ner sakal* made conversation that felt like it had a point. Rogaan did not like where this talk was heading. Pax exchanged looks with the *sakal*, but said nothing. Rogaan was impressed and yet worried all at the same time at Pax's silence. "A father, mother, and sister. A sister that should clean up good. I'll wager she'll fetch good coin when we get to Farratum. Lawbreakers with a fresh face and healthy body such as hers always go good as *servants*."

At the guard's word, Rogaan sat up in a snap and a fume, staring at the tall *Tusaa'Ner sakal* with heated eyes. Pain racked him, worse in his ribs, but Rogaan refused to show his weakness to keep the *sakal* from using it against him. What Rogaan wanted more was for the Baraan *sakal* to renounce his words, to confirm that was not Suhd's fate . . . a bonded slave. He fumed, but realized he could do nothing so long as the *sakal* kept his distance.

Rogaan maintained his seething stare as a deliberate challenge to Farratum authority. Arrogantly, the tall *Tusaa'Ner sakal* stepped forward and stuck the spear through the bars at Rogaan's midsection, stopping the blade tip just short of pushing hard enough to run him through.

"Careful, *stoner*," the tall *Tusaa'Ner sakal* sneered. "I'd like nothin' more than to stick you and see you bleed out, but the *Seergal* would lose the coin you'll fetch."

Rogaan glared at the *sakal*. They all seemed to hate him for being Tellen and who knew what more. Rogaan looked down to the spear tip pressing against his charcoal-colored hide vest. Little good the vest will do against that spear tip. Rogaan, helpless as he was, decided to relax his glare.

"Many ways for you to go," the *Tusaa'Ner sakal* spoke with palpable arrogance. "As a worker in the mines or on the docks or even the decks, or a conscript porter for us in the *Tusaa'Ner*. No. Maybe as a consort for an ugly enough old Baraan who likin' your kind and looks. If you can understand what I'm meaning."

The haggard Baraans captive with Rogaan glared at the *sakal* and loudly spat at his words. Rogaan took their response to the *Tusaa'Ner* pronouncement as disapproval, but why would they act as if they were defending him . . . a *Tellen?* He was unsure, though suspected they wanted to see him run through, killed . . . and they were agitating the tall *Tusaa'Ner sakal* in the hope he would do their work for them. Rogaan decided he needed to keep a closer eye on them from now on. The *sakal* barked at and threatened the two Baraans into a silent brooding and averted their eyes from him. Instead, the two put their dark glares on Rogaan in some act trying to make Rogaan unsettled. They seemed to need to make him feel unsettled, unwanted. In Rogaan's experiences, such small-mindedness and hatred focused against Tellens wasn't typical of most in Brigum, especially those that liked his father's work, but a few, like Kantus and his band, always found some way to make his life miserable. Tired of such treatment, Rogaan returned their malicious glares that brought the spear tip press harder into his vest.

"Take care how you look at folks in Shuruppak, *stoner*," the *sakal* sneered. "Tellens aren't much favored. Me . . . I think you all need to be bound as servants or tossed into the arena for everyone's enjoyment."

Pax grunted at the *Tusaa'Ner sakal's* hate-filled words. Rogaan's anger swelled. He did not consider himself better than anyone else. His father taught him to respect others, despite differences, and to work toward something common, as much as possible given all folks will not agree on everything. There appeared nothing common to work toward here, except for one fact . . . They were all prisoners of the *Tusaa'Ner*. Strange they would not work with him against a common enemy.

The *Tusaa'Ner sakal* poked Rogaan with the spear tip again. It started annoying him, but he did his best not to show it. To Rogaan, the *sakal* seemed to be enjoying himself. Several more verbal insults and a couple of spear pokes gave Rogaan the impression the *sakal* wanted him to believe Tellens were inferior to Shuruppak peoples . . . and him. Arrogant . . . and small-minded. If not for Rogaan's consuming desire to strike the officer, drive his face into the dirt, he would have felt pity for the Baraan. The *sakal,* again, pushed the spear tip a little harder into Rogaan's vest. The pressure hurt his midsection and felt close to piercing him. Fearing the *sakal* would go too far, Rogaan grabbed hold of the wood shaft just below the metal spearhead to keep him from pushing too hard in making his point. The tall *Tusaa'Ner sakal* was surprised at Rogaan's boldness and when he tried to pull, then push, his spear free, his surprise grew at Rogaan's strength.

"You are no better than our niisku beasts," the *sakal* declared with a sneer as if repeating a learned and practiced belief. "Strong and stupid, *stoner.*"

Rogaan yanked the spear free of the *sakal's* grasp then shoved the butt of the spear shaft back into the Baraan's chest. The tall *sakal* staggered backward, grabbing at the shaft to keep from falling. With a reestablished hold on his spear, the *Tusaa'Ner sakal*, with teeth bared and a growl, shoved the weapon hard, trying to skewer Rogaan, but Rogaan's two-handed grip on the wood shaft denied the *sakal* success. They struggled for moments before Rogaan managed to wedge the spear shaft against the cage bars where he had leverage on the weapon. An angry strike from Rogaan's right palm splintered the spear shaft precisely where he intended, an arm's length below the spearhead.

"Stick him, Rogaan!" Pax growled.

Rogaan gawked at Pax uncertain of what he just heard or what to do.

Does Pax want for me to kill this one? He wondered of his friend. Rogaan just wanted the poking and spitting insults to stop. Ending the life of the backend anseis was something he had not considered doing. Looking at the spearhead in his hand, Rogaan made his way to the cage lock keeping them from their freedom. Finding ample rust on the mechanism, just like that on the iron bars of their traveling prison, he thought if he struck it just right it would break. Without another thought, he drove the spearhead into the lock, breaking it. At first, Rogaan stared surprised that breaking the lock was so easy. Then a smile came to his face in the satisfaction of doing so. With the lock no longer a hindrance to escaping, Rogaan head-nodded to Pax for him to follow, but before he could move, spear tips poked at him from all directions. A deep voice boomed, "Hold! Or suffer a run through."

Rogaan froze in a crouch with the broken spearhead held ready to strike back. He looked about, the afternoon sun shining brightly on the metal spear tips pointing at him by four *Tusaa'Ner* spread out around the iron cage. They all had determined eyes behind their helmed, face guards. They meant to end his life at a command. The wagon had stopped sometime during the confrontation. He had not noticed that before now.

"Drop the blade!" A big Baraan commanded with the expectation of being obeyed. The Baraan dressed in dark armor covering his chest and arms, wearing a charcoal-colored tunic underneath, a short red cape, and a red-plumed silver open-face helm. *This one is different*, Rogaan considered. From his father's teachings, Rogaan recognized him not as a *Tusaa'Ner*, but a *Sake*, an Enforcer . . . a *Sake zigaar,* at that. A group with a not-so-good reputation that were feared by most because of their authority to judge on the spot and being known to be quick to execute. This *Sake zigaar* was as big as Kardul, yet with heavier muscles, if Rogaan ever thought that was possible. "Drop it or everyone in the cage finds the *Darkness*."

Outnumbered and with the lives of the others entangled with his own, Rogaan dropped the spearhead with a thud on the wood planks. He did not know what to do except surrender. That did not sit well with him. In fact, it was distasteful to him, burning him at his core, but he saw no other paths to his and everyone's survival. Several more *Tusaa'Ner* soldiers nervously worked the temperamental cage door, eventually opening it. The four with spears on Rogaan were ready to strike at a command. The big *Sake zigaar* casually approached and reached into the cage to retrieve the spearhead. To Rogaan's surprise, Pax made a move toward the *Sake*, but stopped as soon as he started with a steely-eyed glare from the *Sake zigaar* fingering his sword pommel and just daring Pax to do more. The two haggard prisoners in the cage with them turned away and cowered in the opposite end of the cell trying to keep themselves apart from anything to come. For Rogaan, the moment hung on forever. He took notice of details of each of those engaging him, from the fear-filled eyes and trembling spear points of the *Tusaa'Ner* soldiers, to the cautious body language of the *Tusaa'Ner* leader with his broken spear and his focus on the *Sake zigaar*, to the beads of sweat falling from Pax and his friend's darting eyes trying to see a way out of the stand-off and escape, to the utter, unshakeable confidence of the *Sake zigaar* and what seemed his hope Pax would act brazenly. A long unbearable time the staring stand-off took to pass for Rogaan, but Pax eventually retreated to a place next to him.

"Keep extra guards on this *one*," the *Sake zigaar* ordered. The Baraan looked more inconvenienced than anything else as he made it a drawn out point to stare down both Rogaan and Pax before commanding the broken spear *Tusaa'Ner* leader to fetch another lock for their jail cell. "I can see trouble from these two. If they choose to cause anymore . . . take the female youngling from the other cell and do what you want with her, then kill her."

Rogaan could not believe what the *Sake zigaar* just ordered the *Tusaa'Ner* to do . . . commit unspeakable acts on Suhd, then murder her for acts of another. Almost as bad were the looks from the soldiers surrounding them seeming to *want* him and Pax to cause more trouble. Pax said nothing when Rogaan looked to him to confirm he heard the *Sake zigaar* right. His friend just ground his teeth.

The *Sake zigaar* turned and strode with unquestioned confidence to his kyda to remount, his red cape and helmet plume fluttering in the breeze as he made unhurried movements that his steed matched when they rode to the front of the caravan. The *Tusaa'Ner* leader Rogaan had disarmed stared at him maliciously while wearing the ill look of a Baraan plotting revenge. A shiver took Rogaan. *What have I done?*

Chapter 6

Road to Farratum

As the sun declined from its midday height in a cloud-speckled sky, the caravan creaked, and snaked, and rattled along the hard-packed dirt road connecting Farratum to the Wilds, Brigum, and the Tellen nation Turil far to the west. An ordered throng of dark blue uniforms with burnished metal chest plates and gleaming silver helms, some swaying red plumes, rode mature sarigs at the front of the jailer and supply wagons. A crest-bearer rode with the lead group, displaying pennant flags of sky-blue and gray background with moon atop a lightning bolt crest of Shuruppak and just below that a red background with crossed spears between a pair of towers, crest of Farratum. Just behind the lead group, that Baraan woman, the *Tusaa'Ner sakal* that ordered his taking and arrest, rode with a Baraan dressed in a dark tunic and rimless square hat. Behind them, the *Sake zigaar* rode alongside Kardul. Rogaan stared dumbfounded at that each time he laid his eyes on them, wondering what business Kardul had with the Farratum *Tusaa'Ner* and the *Sakes*. Kardul's *Sharur* were nowhere to be seen. Possibly, they were off into the forest providing protection to the caravan. The *Tusaa'Ner* soldiers did offer a degree of protection in Rogaan's mind, flanking on foot his rolling jail cell, watching him and the other prisoners just as leapers might look at prey. They would be the first meal for any fanged terrors striking out from the forest darkness. A shiver ripped through Rogaan that he took no joy in feeling.

Traffic on the road was light at first, a couple of lightly protected small caravans with covered and open-top wagons carrying goods behind worn-out sarigs looking to have seen better days. By midafternoon, more numerous and larger wagon trains carrying supplies and weapons westward passed them. Each of these were accompanied by shiners, mercenaries on foot with spears and armor of various types. They were known to only hold allegiances to the coin of their service. Rogaan found himself looking down on the lot of them, not only from his slightly elevated position in the jailer's cage, but also for their reputed ruthless, selfish motives.

As the jailer wagon rolled on, Rogaan settled into a melancholy matching Pax and the others in their cage. He started to doubt and second-guess his choices . . . Choices that had led to him and his friends' capture. Reflecting on each in turn, most, he concluded were rash; a headstrong charge to save his father, reckless, and disobedient. Had he heeded his father's wishes, things would be better. Not like this. Not that he could have kept Pax from making impulsive decisions that he was so legendary for doing. Rogaan's cheeks heated at the thought of him starting to act like Pax—the very reason his parents were so guarded concerning their friendship. Normally, Rogaan resisted Pax's impetuous nature, acting as the voice of caution, but with events unfolding as they had, swirling events to the point of being out of control, and Suhd's insistence to be helped, begging him to help rescue her parents, Rogaan realized he had tossed reason away in the hopes of gaining trust and love from her . . . in addition to his wanting to see his father free. A heavy price to pay his father would counsel him in that even, thought-filled tone he had. Still, he felt torn between chastising himself as foolish and that all this being worth it for her affections. He found himself longing to hold her and for her to hold him back. He settled in with his longing misery as the wagons rolled along.

No one in the moving cage spoke of what was to come once they reached Farratum. Pax seemed none too happy with him. To make matters worse, Rogaan managed to spot his father in the other jailer wagon ahead of them as the caravan negotiated a slight turn allowing them to exchange eye contact. Rogaan could see that his father was not pleased with him by the scowl and intense stare he received. Regretfully, Rogaan realized he could not have made things much worse as he fought back a swelling of tears and the urge to burst out with a howl . . . for a lot of things done wrong, but mostly at his father's disappointment in him. Rogaan slumped against the hard, cold bars feeling more the fool the longer he reflected on his choices and actions since his return from the hunt.

In the midafternoon, what sounded like ravers closing on the caravan spurred the *Kiuri'Ner* and *Sharurs* into action, assuming command over the placement and readiness of the guardsmen. The *Tusaa'Ner* commanders deferred to the *Kiuri'Ner* without argument, as if practiced until all became reflex. Kardul and Trundiir then disappeared into the forest as the caravan continued on at an increased pace with the *Sharurs* protecting their flanks. Roaring protests from beasts unseen in the forest turned to silence except for the featherwings above and the biters below pestering those in the caravan, with the biters paying Pax more attention than the others. A short time passed before the *Kiuri'Ner* and his *Sharur* companion emerged from the forest shadows to announce that the ravers were no longer a danger. After that, the *Kiuri'Ner* and guardsmen went back to following orders from the *Tusaa'Ner* commanders as the column assumed a looser formation for the march forward.

As the midafternoon turned to late day, some started to trudge along. Fatigue had taken hold of those marching without the benefit of steeds. Mounted guardsmen changed positions with some of the foot soldiers as orders and information passed up and down the lines of *Tusaa'Ner*. All appeared to be on edge, diligently keeping a sharp watch on the forest for more dangers. As long shadows started falling on everything, they came upon several large columns of troops heading west. Rogaan thought that odd, traveling so late and away from protective walls. The first column flew the colors of Farratum's *Tusaa'Ner*, the second the colors green and red that Rogaan recalled from his father's teachings as the *Anubda'Ner*, the regional guard. The *Tusaa'Ner* column was smaller, no more than sixty strong with heavily burdened sarigs and several trailing supply wagons. They looked to be heading some place with urgency and planned to be there awhile. The *Tusaa'Ner* column reluctantly gave way to their jailer wagons, showing practiced, if not ritualistic restraint at the side of the road while Rogaan's captors and their prisoners passed.

The *Anubda'Ner* column could not have been more different, with hundreds of soldiers, all dressed in stout green eur armor and armed with spear, ax, and sword. Their muscular sarigs and kydas looked just as intimidating with bristling spines protruding from plated hide armor added to the steeds. To a Baraan, the *Anubda'Ner* demonstrated complete disdain for everyone not part of their company, forcing the jailer wagons and *Tusaa'Ner* guardsmen into the softer dirt at the side of the road, but only after the two groups of commanding *sakals* engaged in an aggressive stare down with growling shouts. The *Tusaa'Ner* gave way to the higher-order soldiers. The *Anubda'Ner,* winning the challenge, passed, riding on the packed dirt road atop their powerful steeds, striding with puffed out chests, uppity chins, and openly hostile glares. Their unbridled arrogance and contempt was something his father never described or warned him of. Not all was in harmony in the land, Rogaan realized.

Pax had on a hopeful expression of rescue until the *Anubda'Ner* passed without the slightest hint they intended in intervening to free them. With that glimmer of hope gone from his eyes, Pax plunged back into his gloomy mood with arms crossed and legs tucked close. Rogaan followed his friend's example, into his own deep gloom, resigning himself to what the fates intended to do with him. The caravan continued on.

A short time later they came to a bridge, two wagons wide, made of thick timbers. A guard post, a small building no more than five or so strides long and topped with a gray slate gabled roof and the Shuruppak-Farratum flags flying above, was tended by five *Tusaa'Ner* guardsmen dressed and equipped as those escorting the caravan. They halted the caravan in an unassuming and nonthreatening manner before holding a short discussion with the *Tusaa'Ner sakal*. Soon enough, the caravan was moving across the bridge, passing the bridge's guardsmen who stood at ease watching the entourage make its way until several *Sakes*, on their steeds at the rear of the formation, passed. With a bark and glare from one of the *Sakes*, the bridge guardsmen snapped to attention so hard Rogaan thought they might break their own backs.

The bridge spanned a slow-moving small river four wagons wide. Stout timber pylons rising out of the flowing water near each end of the bridge and another in the center of the river looked strong enough to allow heavy loads across the span. The caravan traveled in single file as it made its way slowly to the other side of the waterway. Despite its sturdy construction, the bridge creaked and groaned in protest at the passing of the caravan heavy with its burdened wagons and large-bodied draft animals. They traveled less than five strides above the shallow waters that supported a congregation of snapjaws. Narrow, sandy beaches dominating both riverbanks were thick with snapjaws basking in the late-day sun. Rogaan, in awe of the scene below, started counting the predators, but quickly gave up at the futile effort. Instead, he kneeled at the bars looking at a pool of certain death, if they were to fall. With a start, Rogaan realized Pax had joined him at the bars. He too appeared mesmerized by the scene below, with words of awe and wonder slipping from his lips. The sight of so many flesh eaters, so concentrated, gave Rogaan a chill at the thought of ever entering the water again. A strange sense of relief washed over him as his wagon rolled onto solid ground, high above and far away from the pool of teeth below. The caravan continued on with the last wagon, and then *Tusaa'Ner* clearing the bridge when yells commanding all to stop was given. The command and those responding in acknowledgments rippled down the column. Rogaan tried looking ahead to discover what was happening, but found his vision blocked by everyone else doing the same.

Chapter 7

Fouling the Light

A head on the north side of the road, a low-walled timber structure, maybe five strides high in the shape of a rectangle, had several *Tusaa'Ner* guardsmen standing high on what had to be small ramparts, such that only their sky-blue hide armor above their waists were visible. Here too flew the Shuruppak-Farratum flag pair on a tall pole. A large door made of thick timbers as tall as the supporting walls stood open, allowing a group of workers, dressed in clothing looking more like rags, to haul out large wood troughs, placing them on both sides of the road and timber structure. The workers ran from the structure to the troughs, filling them with buckets upon buckets of water. A murmur then passed through the troupes. Rogaan wondered what this was and what was happening, then quickly figured out this to be a watering waystation, built over a well.

A rush of more workers, male younglings with short-cropped hair and dressed in rags for tunics with brown skin toned so light they could almost be mistaken for Tellens, swarmed about the caravan guardsmen carrying buckets of water. At first it appeared that the column was being attacked, a wishful thought Rogaan had, before he realized they were being offered damp cloths and ladles of water. Suddenly, Rogaan's thirst worsened to the point of distraction and his stomach protested with a growl at not eating or drinking water since . . . yesterday, he realized. Looking at Pax only made him suffer his pains more intensely as Pax stared after the younglings with their water buckets and ladles, all with his tongue hanging out.

The two older Baraans on the other side of Rogaan's traveling cell made no effort to look at the stir. Instead, they both lay still in their own waste that started to waft around the cage. Rogaan wrinkled his nose at the smell. At least it stopped his stomach from grumbling.

"What be da smell?" Pax demanded an answer as he looked about. His eyes quickly fell on the two Baraans. With an overly dramatic sniff that brought a fierce wrinkle to his nose and a sour expression on his face, Pax launched into a fit of complaints. "Guards! Guards! Guards! Dese two be smellin' like dead niisku. Folks no be meanin' ta smell like dem . . . no beasts neither. Do somethin' about dis."

A young, square-chinned, brown-haired guardsman reluctantly broke away from a youngling and his water bucket. The youngling could not have been older than ten summers, yet he stood meekly, patiently, holding his bucket with unstained cloths the guardsman used to wipe his face and hands. As he approached, the guardsman grunted and put on a hostile glare at Pax while glancing at the two old Baraan. Casually, he drew his short sword and jabbed it at a surprised Pax, who barely dodged the blade, before prodding the two Baraan. One of them squeaked out a groan barely loud enough to hear. The other remained silent.

"*Kunza!*" The young guardsman called out loud enough to be heard over the talk of the throng. He then patiently held his tongue until a grizzled gray-bearded guardsman, marked by more scars than most would care to count, approached. "We have an eater. And that other isn't too far from it from the smell of him."

The grizzled guardsman gave a cursory inspection of the two, grunted as if clearing his throat, then spoke. "Douse 'em both. If the kickin' one shows no sign, carry 'em both off."

The young guardsman grabbed the water bucket from the young boy, then tossed its contents on the two old Baraans in the wagon cell, splashing water on Rogaan. One of the Baraans groaned, then rolled over and curled up. The other did not flinch.

"Have one of these two carry away the dead one," the *kunza* ordered, pointing at Rogaan and Pax. "Toss him to the snapjaws. Don't want him stinkin' up the wagon and makin' everythin' within smellin' distance think a meal is here."

The young guardsman saluted the *kunza* with his right hand mimicking holding a sword hilt as he touched his chin. The grizzled guardsman grunted in disgust. "I told ya to hold such for the *sakal*; she likes it. I'm a workin' warrior. Do it again and I'll skin ya. Now get movin' or you'll be joinin' this filth."

Jumping to execute his orders, the young brown-haired guardsman called to a small band of *Tusaa'Ner* Rogaan had watched him associate with earlier. They paid him little heed until one of them caught the hard eyes of the *kunza*. After that, they too jumped to aid their comrade. The five guardsmen, including the young one with brown hair, all with hands on weapons, watched with unblinking eyes as a worker, dressed in a gray tunic, opened the iron-bar door to the cage holding Rogaan, Pax, and the two Baraans. The young guardsman gestured for Pax to drag the unmoving Baraan out and to wake the other. Rogaan looked at Pax, who shrugged his shoulders before grabbing the ankles of the unmoving body to take it from the cell.

"Dis one be what be stinkin'." Pax made a horrible face as he dragged the Baraan. "He be lookin' dead."

Rogaan made to wake the other Baraan, but was called off by the young guardsman. Rogaan froze in place, surprised to be rejected for the manual labor task. He remained unmoving for a few moments in case the young *Tusaa'Ner* changed his mind. The young guardsman did not; instead, he urgently motioned for Rogaan to sit back down.

"Have that *stoner* pull the other one out," ordered the tall *Tusaa'Ner sakal* that tussled with Rogaan earlier in the day.

Everyone looked at the officer with dumbfounded expressions, even Rogaan. Rogaan then shrugged his shoulders, just as Pax had, and tried to wake the remaining Baraan. He stirred, but ignored Rogaan otherwise. Rogaan tried to wake him again, but got swung at as the Baraan kept his eyes closed and in his curled up position. Frustrated at being swung at, Rogaan grabbed the Baraan by the leg and arm, then slung him out the cage door with a little grunt, his shackles and chains clinging as he made the toss. The Baraan hit the dirt in a sprawl, then came to a stop after rolling over sarig dung. Only a groan escaped the Baraan's mouth. He lay still otherwise.

Rogaan immediately felt ashamed of himself for treating the Baraan so badly. The Baraan obviously did not feel well, body and likely much more. Rogaan did not know if he was to get run through for now helping the unmoving Baraan, but he made up his mind he was going to. He crawled out of the cage and planted both of his shackled, booted feet solidly on the ground as a statement to all he was free of his jail.

Rogaan felt relieved being outside the wagon jail, though he intended to conceal his regretful feelings and desire to help the Baraan who still drew breath. One of the *Tusaa'Ner* guardsmen tossed a carry-cot at Pax's feet, then grunted orders to pile the bodies on it. Rogaan and Pax complied, though Rogaan wondered at the guardsmen's intent as they showed no sign of concern for the old and defenseless Baraan. Rogaan soon found himself at the front of the carry-cot weighted by the two Baraans piled one on top of the other, the one still alive on the bottom. Pax carried the other end of the cot, struggling with the load by the way the carry-cot jerked in Rogaan's hands. The shackles on Rogaan limited the size of his steps, making their pace to the bridge slow as he heard Pax starting to breathe hard halfway to the timber structure. Heavily armed guardsmen with spear and sword flanked them, three to a side, ensuring they could not flee; at least not too easily. They growled and barked commands at Pax mostly, but Rogaan too caught some of their attention that he'd rather not have gotten. With each bark, Rogaan found himself gritting his teeth harder and harder, to the point he thought his teeth might crack if he was to hold his tongue and fist. Worse, he felt as if Kantus taunted him and he was bound by his word to not respond. When Rogaan set foot on the bridge, he began wondering what the guardsmen planned.

"Halt!" The *sakal* commanded. Two spears dropped crossed in front of Rogaan so close he feared they were to hit him. The *sakal* continued barking orders, "Set the carry-cot down and toss the bodies off the bridge."

Rogaan gaped at the *sakal* guardsman in disbelief at what he demanded. One of the old Baraans on the carry-cot still drew breath and would die from the fall. If, by a cruel chance, he lived, the snapjaws below would certainly tear him apart. Either way, the helpless old Baraan would die by their hands . . . by his hands. Rogaan looked to Pax for agreement they would not be part of killing the old Baraan. Pax was not as strong in chest and shoulders as Rogaan and stood straining at the weight he held in his hands while staring back at Rogaan with sweat dripping down his reddening, straining face. Realizing his friend's condition, Rogaan motioned to Pax to set their burden down.

"Good, young one," the grizzled, gray-bearded guardsman said sarcastically, then taunted with his gruff voice repeating his *sakal's* command. "Now, toss 'em over and be quick of it."

Rogaan looked Pax directly in the eyes, letting him know he would not obey. Pax widened his eyes while shrugging, as if asking . . . "*Why?*" Surprised by Pax's reaction, Rogaan narrowed his eyes and wrinkled his brow, causing Pax to give him his "*Who . . . me?*" look. Rogaan wondered if Pax truly could be part of sending this helpless Baraan to his death as a bloom of anger and disappointment with Pax hit Rogaan. Not wanting Pax to have a chance at talking, Rogaan turned to the grizzled guardsman meeting his hard eyes with his own. "I will not kill this Baraan."

The grizzled guardsman stroked his gray beard with an amused grin, then gave a glance and nod at Pax. Immediately, a scuffle ensued between Pax and two guardsmen close to him, catching Rogaan stunned with surprise. Pax struggled against their grasps with no success and stopped only after daggers were pressed to his side and neck. Rogaan made to help his friend, but found the tips of three blades pressing at his gut, side, and neck before taking two steps. Silence filled the air as Pax shared an uncertain gaze with Rogaan.

"I'm thinkin' ya will," the grizzled guardsman sardonically blustered, "or yur friend will go over first."

Rogaan stared at gray-beard defiantly. The grizzled guardsman returned a confident smirk full of cruelty. Unsettled, Rogaan looked at Pax for support, but found an angry, brooding face staring back at him. Hopelessness crept into Rogaan's thoughts as the grizzled guardsman continued his threats while pointing to the *Tusaa'Ner* holding Pax. "And if ya still give trouble after that, I'll have them go see that pretty little thin' and teach her to be grown up."

"Rogaan, ya can no be doin' dis!" Pax scolded him with heated eyes. "How can ya even be thinkin' dis way? Dat old Baraan means nothin' ta ya. Why do ya care about him goin' over before he be dead? He be visiting the Ancients soon enough with da look of him, anyway."

Uncertain of what to do, Rogaan kept silent while his conflicting thoughts spun uncontrolled in his head and heart. Father and Mother taught him to respect the living and to protect it, especially those innocent, and even more so those helpless. "Very Tellen," his mother would put it to him, and "the best of Baraans," his father would say. The old Baraan drawing breath clearly was helpless, but Rogaan knew not how long he had to live or of his innocence. He could be anything . . . a thief, murderer, or worse. Or, he could be a hero or someone fighting Farratum just as he was, now. The other Baraan reeked of death . . . and of him messing himself before dying. His teaching told him the dead should be given proper ceremony and burned, though Rogaan was not so bothered with giving the body to the snapjaws. Pragmatic . . . or a sign of uncaring and disrespect. He fought with himself on that thought too. But, tossing the helpless to certain death tormented his sensibilities. They all were helpless and at the mercy of the *Tusaa'Ner* . . . and the *Sakes* . . . and he did not know what else. *How can these guardians, sworn to protect the folks of Farratum, threaten and treat folks so without judgments against them? Why are they so gleeful and wicked about what they want to do to Suhd because of me?* Anger swelled in Rogaan at that last thought. No. It boiled. Rogaan found his thoughts turning to him fighting for Suhd . . . before they can harm her, before they commit foul acts against her. These were not the protectors of his father's teachings. They were something else, but what . . . Rogaan was uncertain of.

"We can no let dem hurt her," Pax growled at Rogaan. He stopped his struggles against the guardsmen holding him and instead put his full focus on Rogaan. "Ya care for Suhd? How can ya no protect her? Toss 'em, Rogaan. Toss 'em both over, before dey toss me and hurt Suhd."

"Pax, I cannot." Rogaan found himself pleading with his friend as much as himself. "It goes against all my teachings."

His breath ran out while trying to explain and at the explosion of insanity he saw in Pax's face. Pax made violent struggles against the two guardsmen holding him, shouting and cursing at them . . . and Rogaan. One of the guardsmen maneuvered Pax into a choke hold. The guardsman's muscles bulged until Pax dropped to his knees. When the guardsman lessened his hold on Pax's neck, his friend looked up at him with heated eyes.

"Ya be some friend, ya be. Choose him over us." Pax spat venom at Rogaan and only at Rogaan. Pax suddenly leaned, then launched himself at Rogaan. "Some friend." His words turned to choking coughs by the guardsman harshly reapplying his hold on Pax's neck.

Rogaan stood stunned as the uncomfortable prickling gripping him, stomach to chest to head, sank in deep. He and Pax shared an intense stare for long moments, neither speaking, yet much passing between them. Many unspoken words Rogaan wished he had not seen or read in his friend. Pax's eyes displayed fully a deep wounding pain and flaring anger. Never had Rogaan seen Pax so angry, so . . . desperate. Yes, desperate. For Pax, that meant something terrible. Rogaan realized he too was desperate. *What do I do?* He fought with himself and his beliefs. His innards swirling and twisting from his inner conflict . . . raging. Was defending an old Baraan, a stranger with an unknown past, more important than Pax and Suhd? His father's teachings and philosophies rang loudly in his head at that. "Defend those unable to do so for themselves. Protect the weak from the unjust strong. That is honor's way." Searching his thoughts and feelings, Rogaan reluctantly concluded his father would choose the path of honor, but find another way to walk the choice of paths given him . . . make others *walk with him*. And that he too should change the rules given him . . . set by others, for their convenience and their pleasure. He needed something . . . unexpected. Rogaan searched for that new *walk*; looking at the bridge, the water, and each of the guardsmen in turn, hoping to find something he could use to change the *walk*.

Nothing.

Desperation bit deep and wrapped up Rogaan again.

"Sun a wastin'," the grizzled gray-beard announced with impatience and now with an annoyance. With a dismissive wave of his hand, the grizzled guardsman barked the order Rogaan feared, tried to avoid, delay. "Toss the youngone over, then the two stinkin' ones. We'll get that pretty little one—"

Pax howled and kicked in protest as the guardsmen half-carried, half-dragged him to the side of the bridge. His words unintelligible, but their meaning clear. Pax fought desperately for his life, but was no match for the guardsmen's strength. Rogaan took a step toward his friend, but sharp pains of blade points still on him brought him to a halt. The weight of the world pressed down on Rogaan. He could not let Pax be murdered . . . or the old Baraan . . . or Suhd.

"Rogaan! It be up ta ya ta protect Suhd," Pax yelled at him as the guardsmen grabbed at him ready to toss him from the bridge.

"Hold!" Rogaan bellowed with a sorrow so deep he felt his *Light* foul. His tongue felt of fire and his stomach sour and feared his guts would spill up. *Pax must not pay for my honor*, Rogaan resigned himself. Try as he did, Rogaan thought of no way out of this. All the guardsmen fell silent and stood motionless, looking at him, except for the pair struggling with Pax. The guardsmen lifted his friend from the wood timbers of the bridge. Pax still struggled, trying to gain his freedom, only to have a hand grip his throat choking him. Pax gasped for air as he was lifted high. All hope drained from Rogaan. His *Light* broke. He surrendered as he yelled, "I will do as you say."

The grizzled guardsman, their *kunza,* smiled broadly, as did the rest of the guardsmen . . . even that *sakal*. The *kunza* motioned for the guardsmen struggling with Pax to hold their place before turning his attention back to Rogaan. "Do as ya was told. Toss the old ones and don't yap a word."

Rogaan reluctantly approached the two old Baraans lying on the bridge timbers. Both were still, yet one still drew breath. He could see the slight stir of the live one as he took shallow breaths. Rogaan purposely moved slowly, hoping for something to happen allowing him to change the *walk* on this path. *Nothing*. Choosing the dead one to pick up first, Rogaan found himself hoping they were right when declaring him dead. He smelled it. Rogaan wrinkled his nose at the foul odors coming from him, as if he lost his bowels from rotting innards. *Nothing . . . still.*

"Toss 'em, *stoner*." The command and insult came from the tall *Tusaa'Ner sakal* standing with his hands on his belt and blade handle.

"Faster, Tellen," the grizzled *kunza* growled.

Rogaan found himself hoping for a pack of ravers or something else ready to eat them to burst from the forest. He looked to the forest around them. *Nothing*. He easily carried the Baraan's body to the bridge side. The stench wafting from it caused Rogaan to gag and cough and spit trying to get the foul taste carried on the air out of his mouth. He found the body in his arms fragile, as well as foul smelling. *He must have starved or died from sickness*, Rogaan guessed, trying to take his thoughts off of what he was doing. No life was evident in what he held. *Yes, this one has to be dead*. Rogaan's confirmation gave him a sense of relief.

With a look of disdain at the smugly smiling gray-bearded grizzled

Tusaa'Ner, Rogaan tossed the body off the bridge. It hit the water with a dull splash, almost floating on the surface for a brief moment before sinking into the brown, flowing waters. A few moments later, the body bobbed back up to the surface a few strides further downstream only to be crushed and dragged under in the jaws of a large snapjaw. Other snapjaws, more than he could count, rushed in on the monster and its kill causing a tugging and tearing fight to break out between the beasts ending in the once intact body being torn apart. With a pang of guilt, Rogaan found himself relieved of being rid of the stench and that it did not cling to him. The selfishness of his thoughts unsettled him.

Rogaan looked to Pax for help in what was to happen next, hoping somehow he would not have to do what he feared he must to keep his friend alive. When Rogaan saw his friend's eyes, he felt even more unsettled at the anticipation Pax carried in them and the lack of remorse on his face. Without a way out from submitting to the *Tusaa'Ner's* demands, and Pax appearing to be good with killing a defenseless Baraan, Rogaan slowly set off to finish what he must, repeating to himself all the while that he has no choice except to obey. Looking down at the carry-cot, he found the old Baraan with half-open eyes, mouthing unintelligible words. Rogaan's *Light* screamed, and his body shook. *The Baraan's alive.* With pleading eyes, Rogaan looked to the grizzled guardsman, then to the tall *Tusaa'Ner sakal*, then to the other *Tusaa'Ner*, then to Pax, hoping someone would change their mind . . . especially for that old Baraan who lived. A sadistic smirk under satisfied eyes reflected back to him from the grizzled guardsman. The *sakal's* expression was that of anticipation. The other *Tusaa'Ner* were no better. Rogaan realized for the first time these guardsmen were no such thing and found joy in this Baraan's death and the torment it reaped upon him. With immeasurable regret, Rogaan picked up the old Baraan, then made his way slowly to the side of the bridge. This Baraan too weighed far less than he should. *They must have been starved.* Rogaan pitied the old one for his suffering. Urine, feces, and spit-up wafted about him, yet Rogaan did not concern himself about it. All he could think of was that this Baraan's death would pay for his friends' lives . . . and that he had no choice. *No choice.* Looking to the waters below, several of the smaller snapjaws, maybe three strides in length each, fought over the last scraps of the body he threw over moments ago. Rogaan looked to Pax, but still saw only anticipation—no remorse, no sadness. Rogaan looked to the other guardsmen, but only found stolid stares and half-grins. Then he looked again to the grizzled guardsman, but found only what he expected—sadistic glee. Though Rogaan did not know if it was glee for the old one's death or his death, inside, for doing this.

"Get on with it, *stoner!*" The command and insult came from the *sakal*.

"Get on with it or let yur friend feeds the beasts," the grizzled guardsman added.

Pax struggled fiercely against the guardsmen holding him at gray-beard's threat. "Do it, Rogaan! Do it!"

Rogaan looked into the face of the old Baraan. His half-opened eyes seemed to be aware of him, but he no longer mumbled. Rogaan mustered the courage, if he could call it that, to speak to the old Baraan. "Forgive me?"

"Forgive . . . yourself," the old Baraan groaned out before closing his eyes. Rogaan looked again to the *Tusaa'Ner* and his friend. All anticipated his next doing. *Nothing. No help.* He looked to the forest and the sky hoping to see jaws of death coming at them. *Nothing.* Then he looked to the caravan hoping someone . . . anyone would stop him. *Nothing.*

"Toss 'em, ya . . ." the *kunza* demanded.

Rogaan released the old Baraan. He fell . . . for an eternity it seemed, into the waters and the waiting snapjaws below. *No choice.* The Baraan hit the water in a splash, disappearing into the brown waters almost immediately. A thrash of tails and the boil of water told Rogaan the old Baraan was indeed dead now. Rogaan's eyes welled up with tears, and he groaned deeply as his *Light* cried out in anguish . . . for the wickedness he did.

Chapter 8
A Light in the Darkness

A swirl and boil of waters, tails, and teeth. Rogaan stood staring into the horrific scene below, unable to look away. Forever it seemed the snapjaws tore apart the old Baraan, turning the muddy waters churning red. His screaming moralities would not allow him the reprieve to cast his eyes from the carnage. Profound guilt and regret forced him to watch every detail, burn it into his mind. By his hand the old Baraan died. It strangled him in ways he could not have feared. Without warning, a rough hand grabbed him at the shoulder, startling him before jerking him from his feet into a backward stumble. He caught himself, keeping his feet as nearby words praised him for the old one's death. Shocked at the praise . . . praise for ending the defenseless Baraan's life, Rogaan watched amazed and disgusted at the *kunza* full of smiles as the tall *Tusaa'Ner sakal* congratulated him on his success. Rogaan felt lost as he stood silent looking at the wood timbers under his booted feet and the chains between them. He focused on nothing. He felt empty. Words abounded around him without him understanding their meaning. How long he stood there . . . he did not know, did not care. Then, his thoughts slowly organized, forcing back the chaos in his head well enough to regain awareness of the *kunza* chortling satisfaction, even happiness, at his deed while asserting a new dawn would rise for Rogaan.

Anger flared inside of him filling that empty space as he woke from his nightmare to a living dread, with a fierce shake of his head. His anger swelled within for not being stronger, for allowing himself to be manipulated. He wanted relief from the pain of it, wanted absolution from that which there was none. That taste was foul and impossible to swallow. They enjoyed his pain! Rogaan exploded into a fit of rage. Lashing out in all directions, Rogaan struck at the *Tusaa'Ner*, not caring who he struck first—only that he struck and struck hard. He landed blow after blow on the blue and burnished as tumbling boulders crush rocks below. He swung and struck for a time he did not know how long, trying to rid himself of his regret, his pain. He howled at life itself. Somewhere in his fury, Rogaan grew an awareness of a great pain in his side. It then shattered his rage, bringing clarity back to his mind well enough that he saw what carnage he reaped. The bloody bodies of three *Tusaa'Ner* guardsmen lay on the bridge. Their helms and chest armor dented badly. One of the guardsmen's jaw lay clearly broken. The other two had broken arms . . . one the bone peeking out from his skin and clothing. He had bludgeoned them to death, he feared. *More blood on my hands.* His regret was not so distasteful as before. The *Tusaa'Ner kunza* and *sakal* somehow escaped his wrath. A pang of regret hit Rogaan at that realization.

Powerful arms enveloped Rogaan's chest and neck from somewhere unseen, threatening to choke off his air. The pain in his left side grew worse as arms tugged and pulled him from behind. Rogaan stop his resisting. His rage burned out at the sight of the broken bodies.

"Blast ya, stoner!" Gray-bearded *kunza* held his chest and throat from behind. The guardsman no longer sounded smug and superior. He was angry . . . afraid. With a jerk he tightened his hold on Rogaan, then yelled out, "Throw this one's friend over as a lesson."

Rogaan was uncertain he heard the *kunza* right. Then Pax started yelling at the two guardsmen dragging him to the edge of the bridge. Rogaan realized then he did hear it right enough. They had every intent to kill Pax. Toss him from the bridge. To teach a *lesson?*

No! The world stopped. Rogaan saw everyone and everything clearly, in vivid details. The tall *Tusaa'Ner sakal* stood nervously four strides away on the other side of the bridge timbers making to order others after him, two more guardsmen near the *sakal* stood looking at him . . . waiting for their orders, and the burly hands of the *kunza* gripping him from behind. Then, they started moving, in that strangely slow way. The scent of sweat and death and fear filled Rogaan's nose. Knowing how the *kunza* positioned his hands, with a twist of his own arms and body, Rogaan slipped gray-beard's grasp more easily than expected. The sharp pain in his side seemed duller than before. He did not understand why. He did not care. Turning, Rogaan came face-to-face with a surprised *kunza*, then a frightened and angry Pax fighting against the two guardsmen trying to throw him off the bridge. The *kunza* wore a frustrated face at trying, and yet not being able to follow Rogaan quickly enough. Rogaan's more important concerns were the guardsmen setting themselves to throw Pax off the bridge. He charged them. Like a master-crafted hammer striking a weak and brittle metal, Pax and the two guardsmen went flying like broken shards when Rogaan struck them with his whole body. Pax and a guardsmen went tumbling to the wood timbers slower than what Rogaan expected should happen naturally. It was as if time slowed somehow, for all except for him. On his right, Rogaan caught a glimpse of the second *Tusaa'Ner* guardsmen flying off the bridge toward the place they intended for Pax. He did not know why, his instinct drove him to react without thinking, reaching out and grabbing the guardsman by his hide wrist guard. Just then, the world returned to its normal pace with the weight of the falling guardsman wrenching Rogaan from his feet, slamming him face-first into the wood timbers at the edge of the bridge, the force dazing him. Somehow, Rogaan held onto the guardsman as he lay hanging half off the bridge, the guardsman dangling below.

"Come to order!" A sharp female voice commanded with firm measure. Rogaan tried, but failed to turn his head to look at the face behind the voice and the cause of a thud near him. Doing so might allow the guardsman to slip from his grasp. He feared the *kunza* might not like having been bested in the scuffle and poised himself to strike from above. Despite that possibility, Rogaan decided to focus on the guardsman, the Baraan dangling below, whose fate rested, quite literally, in his hand. The woman's voice snarled. "I said, come to order, *Kunza*!"

Rogaan heard a shuffle of sandal soles on wood and the scraping of metal . . . a blade returning to its scabbard, accompanied by a low, angry growl. He hoped the sounds meant he was safe from attack, but wondered, as he expected the *kunza* and the *sakal* to be angry, possibly billowing angry. He hoped neither stood close. He hoped. The guardsman dangling from his hand flailed with his legs as he looked down at the thrashing waters filled with awaiting jaws and death. Rogaan's left side seared with pain and felt wet. The guardsman started pleading for his life and to be pulled up. Then, the guardsman's words quickly became frantic. Rogaan felt him slipping from his grip as he adjusted to lessen the pain in his side. He was uncertain how much longer he could keep the Baraan from his death. Deciding the situation was not going to get any better, Rogaan fought through his pain, straining, pulling the hanging snapjaw meal up to the bridge. When the dangling guardsman's free hand was high enough to reach the bridge timbers, he helped pull himself up over the edge of the timbers, roughly scrambling over Rogaan. Dejected, Rogaan stared at nothing for a moment, unbelieving at how "unthankful" the guardsman was using him as a ladder. *I keep him from death, and I get his knees and feet on my back and neck*, Rogaan more thought than mumbled to himself. He rolled onto his back and found that the gray-bearded *kunza* indeed stood near, stiffly, with his weapons sheathed, angrily staring at a female dressed in *Tusaa'Ner* sky-blue armor and a wind-fluttering red cape. Rogaan wondered, *what did I miss?*

Red-blond hair flowed about the slender face of a *Tusaa'Ner* Baraan woman standing on the wood timbers of the bridge as a light breeze blew her hair and cape and the waning light of the day highlighting her in a glow as described sometimes in stories of the Ancients. She stood proudly tall, without helm, despite being several hands shorter than Rogaan. Balled fists on her hips and her tone in speaking with the *kunza* told Rogaan she was not pleased with the guardsman. Her slight build took away some of the threat of her hard bearing as Rogaan watched her stare with heated eyes at the gray-bearded *kunza*. This obviously was not the first time these two had crossed. More blue-clad guardsmen stood behind her at the approach to the bridge, all standing stiffly at attention with spears erect and unmoving. Rogaan wondered at her age. She could not be much older than he by the looks of her. Yet, she carried herself with an experience unlike the lasses near her age. Instead, Rogaan felt as if he watched his mother or Lady Friskla before a scolding. She methodically inspected the scene in front of her with a face of indifference, noting the guardsmen standing and lying about with a mix of a hard and sad eyes. How she managed to hold two such emotions at one time, Rogaan wondered at it. She seemed to be of two minds concerning the guardsmen, but it was clear she did not care for the *kunza*.

"On another task for who . . . the *Sake?*" She spit accusing words formed in a question. The *kunza* did not reply, but his jaws ground so hard Rogaan thought, and hoped, his teeth would break. When he did not answer, the *Tusaa'Ner* woman continued. "More guardsmen to tally against you, *Kunza*."

"They live, Dajil," the tall *Tusaa'Ner sakal* spoke from a crouch over one the guardsmen Rogaan pommeled to what he thought were their deaths.

Rogaan felt an enormous weight lift from him. *They live!* Then, the memory of the old Baraan's face as he fell to his horrific death placed the weight right back on him.

"You stay your place . . . , *second!*" The *Tusaa'Ner* woman, a *sakal* by her near identical adornments to the Baraan *sakal* she addressed. "The *kunza* needs to account for himself."

The *kunza's* anger was plain to see. Even his gray beard appeared to stand stiffly, but he kept control of his words while remaining at attention. He replied in a strained tone. "*Sakal*, the old-ones passed. Stinking up the wagon and the . . . youngones were our *kungas*. When they refused their duty, I . . . encouraged them."

The *sakal* stood listening to the *kunza* with an impassive face. The grizzled guardsman turned, pointing down at Rogaan lying prone on the bridge. "This one, after ridding us of the second biter-lure, found it better to rage in anger than serve, almost killing Otuuku and the others. He's a dangerous one, for sure. Best to chain him to the cage."

"He did all this while in manacles?" The commanding *sakal* asked with her eyes a bit wider with surprise. She looked at Rogaan as one might look considering a purchase of a racing sarig. Rogaan did not like that feeling. She turned her eyes back on the *kunza*, "Doesn't speak well of your waning skills. Load the lawbreakers back into their cage . . . and leave them be unless they cause more trouble. You've delayed us long enough. She'll be anxious to see what gifts we return with."

Chapter 9

Farratum

The caravan traveled on, the jailer's wagons creaking and stiffly bouncing in increasing numbers of ruts the further they traveled into the edge of the night. Despite the jarring ride, Rogaan fell into a stupor lying on his back with eyes half-closed and only a vague awareness of the happenings around him. He felt numb . . . wanted to feel numb, to spare himself from his recent decisions . . . many poor, some simply bad. In his vain attempt to not dwell on the near past, Rogaan kept on in his daze, but his thoughts always returning to his regrets.

"Ya want ta see dis," Pax announced, his voice piercing through Rogaan's stupor. Curious, but reluctant to join the world and feel again, Rogaan rolled from his back to his side, propping himself up on his left elbow with a winch from the pain of the cut on his left ribs. He looked east, into the darkening dusk sky to see what Pax was so excited about.

It was almost nightfall with the cloudy sky gloomy and unfriendly. The trees were pushed back from the road, opening up to ranch and farmlands and sparse structures on both sides of the travel way. Ahead, a flock of white featherwings swirled just above a tall wall of gray, cut-block stone taken over by thick green, leafy vines in a few places. A smaller number of leatherwings circling, soaring even higher than the featherwings, were bright and colorful with the last of the day's sunlight. The stone wall sat deep in shadows. Two triangle, obelisk-shaped towers of cut stone topped by watch posts with slanted red-tiled roofs stood astride the heavy timbered gate, each adorned with poles flying slightly fluttering flags. The towers stood more than three times the height of the armored guardsmen standing at the gate entrance. Gray walls extended in both directions away from the towers and gate until they were lost into the forest or dusky gloom. Large torches lit the main entrance that was open to travelers ahead of them. The throng at the gate, wagons both simple and ornamented and carts, all pulled by work animals, made a line more than a hundred strides long. Goods filled both wagons and carts as folks dressed in all manner sat atop their possessions, all seeking refuge within the protective walls of the city before darkness fell upon everything.

The pungent odors of animals and things he cared not to think of filled the air and his nose, and grew stronger as they approached the city. The air seemed cool otherwise, not the stifling heavy stuff he remembered from earlier in the day. Guardsmen on both sides escorting his wagon looked anxious to move forward and get through the gates. A troupe of guardsmen, dressed as those flanking his wagon, stood tall before the open gates with spears pointing upward, watching travelers and caravans pass at a steady pace through the towers marking the boundary of western Farratum. Passing through the double-door timber gate, they entered a corridor of stone. The narrowing corridor they traveled appeared to be built for protection from all that threatened from outside. A thick odor of dung hung heavy in the air inside the walled corridor they passed through. Rogaan's stomach turned and his nose wrinkled at the stench. The buzz of biters and now bloodsuckers grew worse the further they went. Without more of the purple flower rub, Rogaan fell prey to the pests and found himself frequently swatting the annoyances away to keep them from biting. Everyone—prisoners, workers, and guardsmen alike—appeared affected the same. Emerging from the corridor, the inside area opened up with a main street running straight.

Once inside the stone barbican, its flanking towers, and the channeling corridor, the road turned paved with large cobblestones leading to a bridge to the main city. Few people were about on the street here. Those that were mostly had on dirty tunics drenched in sweat and carried the look of folk wanting the day's chores to end. North of the street in this village on the western shore of the Ner River lay a half-dozen large wood and brick buildings spread over some eighty strides along the road. The buildings appeared to have living quarters and workplaces for artisans. Behind the buildings, ample stables and pens for steeds and smaller animals spread as far as Rogaan's eyes could see. Illuminating the buildings were lanterns lit within as the day was coming to an end. Wisps of smoke rose from the chimneys of several buildings, the ones made of brown brick, carried on the air the scents of taters, greens, and spices, but no roasting meats. Local folks standing around the buildings, dressed in everything from soiled tunics of the assumed poor to lived-in tunics, shirts, breaches, and sandaled feet of those with a few hard-sought coins, looked on at the flow of wagons and animals as if this was a daily ritual. As they passed the locals, Rogaan looked back at them all with uncaring eyes. His insides remained numb.

South of the road was much the same, with another stand of similar buildings edging the road, with the land behind falling away into pens, tall fences, and wooden shacks lit with lanterns, torches, and bonfires. Folks here too looked and behaved the same as those on the north side. The pens beyond held multitudes of snapjaws, both small and moderate in size. Skins from the animals hung splayed on poles between the shacks drying and being worked by tanners. A buildup of stone buildings and wood docks butted up to the southern side of the bridge where their caravan passed through another barbican with more timbered gate doors set between flanking triangle-shaped towers.

"Dis be a sight ta see." Pax wondered at the grand walls, wharf, and docks of the region's capital. Rogaan lost his melancholy, if only for a moment, sharing with his friend the awe of being at the outer walls of Shuruppak's guardian city. The guardian city . . . That is what Rogaan's father called Farratum in his teachings.

A large gray stone bridge ahead stood almost thirty strides wide. The caravan left the cobblestone road at the barbican for the stone paved way spanning a wide flow of brown flowing waters separating the village on the western shores of the Ner River from the eastern shore where even taller stone walls rose from the massive stone blocks of the wharf and docks. Burning braziers running the length of the bridge on both sides wafted a cloud of pungent flowery smells of incense of some sort. Rogaan wrinkled his nose at it. He guessed the cloud was meant to keep away biters, bloodsuckers, and more as their buzz stopped the moment they cleared the barbican. Ahead, the busy wharf completely surrounded Farratum's western and southern sides. The sight stirred a moment's interest in Rogaan before he forced himself to return, again, to his uncaring numbness. Small boats and a few ships sat moored at the torch-lit docks with workers, carts, and cargo bustling about with lanterns, and handheld torches now needed to replace the waning sunlight.

Approaching the wharf, Rogaan's nose was assaulted by a mix of odors; the pungent yet flowery incense, smoke, fish, garbage, and what seemed to be meats cooking for evening meals. He felt himself fighting to not sick up. *How can anyone live in such a place?* Rogaan questioned the sanity of city living. Nobody else appeared to suffer the odors as he; instead, they had their eyes fixed on the high walls of Farratum. Rogaan thought the walls ahead impressive, but still, they were just stone, like his father taught him to work.

Passing over the busy wharf, the jailer caravan entered Farratum through another barbican with flanking triangular-shaped towers grander than all before and through a gate with large doors made of great timbers bound by thick bronze bands of metal all surrounded by massive stones tightly fitted against each other without a sign of mortar. Rogaan recognized the style. It felt familiar, almost comforting . . . the same as his father used in building their home, just with much-larger stonework.

The inner city opened up as soon as the caravan cleared the towers and gate. A smoky smell hung in the air matching the haze visibly hovering over the buildings and streets. While the smell of animal dung and garbage still mixed with chimney smoke, Rogaan welcomed the lessening of the odors of the wharf, here. Despite his melancholy, he watched in fascination at Pax looking in wonder at their surroundings as their creaking jailer wagon rolled down the main street passing between mildew-stained brick and wood buildings that stood two and three floors tall. Along their way, lanterns lit the cobblestones of the street and walkways along the sides of the main corridor. Melodies from flutes and harps came and went as Rogaan's wagon moved down the street. Throngs of folks dressed in all manner of plain and bright colors crowded the sides of the street walking on wood planks and paved stones. Most slowed or stopped their strolling to watch the jailer caravan pass. Riding sarigs and pack animals unevenly peppered the wood hitching posts spaced at fixed intervals at the edge of the cobblestones. Most were still with saddles and packs, not yet prepared for a night's stay in the stables or here in the main travel way of the city. Most buildings projected awnings of slanted wood planks or simple canvas, covering the elevated walkways separating the store fronts from the wide street and offering merchants and buying folks shelter from the hot sun of the day and foul weather the region was known for. Incense burners mounted on the sides of buildings and hitching posts spewed more of that pungent smoke the biters and other nasties did not like, making the street tolerable to walk and do business in.

Roasting meats and simmering spices from cook fires lofted on smoky fingers filled the air and Rogaan's nose the further his wagon rolled eastward. Hunger pains started making his stomach grumble and his mouth parched dry with thirst. He realized with disappointment and a bit of frustration he only received a crust of bread and several cups of water today. He felt weak and tired. He felt hungry. His stomach grumbled again.

Rogaan's moving jail turned left onto a paved street even wider than what lay behind. The caravan followed the street gently curving back to the right. On his left, at the edge of blue paving stones, sat single-story buildings of wood construction topped with weather-worn clay shingles. Light-giving lanterns, hung from each of the buildings, pushed back the gloom of the encroaching darkness of the new night sky. Canvas awnings and makeshift walls of browns, deep reds, blues, and bright greens, hung separating individual store fronts. Fruits, vegetables, and salted meats of all kinds on half-filled tables and carts from the day's haggling. Merchants, mostly dressed in plain, dull-colored tunics, some with stains of blood and fruits, sat on stools resting or cleaning with brooms and hand whisks or were wrapping up their goods preparing to close for the night.

Loud, repeated commands brought the caravan to a squeaking halt. Sweat-drenched *Tusaa'Ner* guardsmen, not part of the escorting troupe, cleared the street around the jailer wagons, shooing curious passersby away or back to the edge of the paving stones where the merchants and the last of their customers stood watching what Rogaan took by their stares a common sight. A ruckus erupted behind Rogaan to the right of the wagons. Looking, Rogaan fell dumbstruck and gawking at the massive works of the famed Farratum Arena his father had taught him about. Large-cut granite blocks fit together with precision formed the oval-shaped foundation of the almost two-hundred-stride long structure. Many smaller-cut granite and limestone blocks built up the thirty-stride-tall walls. Ramps and walkways and insets with statues of warriors of what Rogaan thought were representations of the Ancients punctuated the walls at fifteen and twenty-five strides high on the second and top levels. Fiery bowls sat atop poles at the edge of the structure's foundation. Smaller bowls of flames evenly lining the ramps and walkways cast eerie shadows on the stone outer walls of the arena, causing Rogaan to suffer a shiver at an almost sinister atmosphere that engulfed the place.

A light breeze gently fluttered flags of many colors affixed atop wood poles about the arena's walls. Most displayed symbols Rogaan was unfamiliar with, though some teased at his learned memories. After a few moments of awestruck gawking, Rogaan managed to close his mouth and assess the structure, as his father taught him to do . . . as all good Tellens would do. It had three levels above ground and no guess of how many beneath. He knew they were there . . . his father told him of them, and that it was the Ebon Circle that had seen to the arena's construction before the Shuruppak civil war. Rogaan recalled more specifically from his teachings that Im'Kas and his master, the most powerful of the dark robes, paid for much of the arena's construction out of their personal fortunes, refurbishing it many years ago when this place was a field of friendly competition. Recalling more of his father's telling of the story, the dark robe and Im'Kas defended Farratum from foreign invaders that came from the river Ur. Much destruction had befallen the city, with those two seeing fit to return Farratum's streets and structures to their former grandeur once the invaders were defeated. This arena was to be a focus and inspiration to the folks in the rebuilding of the city and community. Feeling the place's sinister shadow, Rogaan doubted the tale now as he gawked at it while a shiver ran through him. So legends get born of terrible times and great deeds with truth somewhere in the telling of stories, though you never know just where. Rogaan felt uncertain what truth was, now, given the happenings of the past few days.

Chapter 10

Descent into Anguish

Y ells up and down the caravan broke out. Rogaan looked around, trying to see what was happening, what caused the stir. He was not familiar with the words being yelled and assumed they were *Tusaa'Ner* commands. *Sakes*, dressed in those charcoal-colored tunics and some also with like colored pants, all with wide hide belts, short gray and red belt sashes, and hide sandals, appeared from heavy wood beam doors swung open from the sides of the arena. That female *Tusaa'Ner sakal* spoke sternly at the *Sakes* in her high-pitched voice as she briskly walked from the front of the caravan toward the jailer wagons, digging her heels in hard on the paving stones as she went with intent. She walked, spouting commands for the *Sakes* to take the prisoners below and lock them away. As she approached the wagon Rogaan and Pax remained caged within, one of the *Sakes* nervously sought the troupe commander's attention with a half wave of his hand while slouching his shoulders in a slight scrunch. The Baraan was slight of build wearing both tunic and pants and carrying a clay tablet with a pen. He looked all the stature of a middle-aged scribe or administrator, recording all that happened and accounting for items. Rogaan guessed what this scribe held responsibilities for were new prisoners. The other *Sakes*, most heavily muscled and all soaked in sweat as if they just came from the flaming Pit of Kur, looked as if they wanted nothing to do with the exchange between the scribe and the commander. *Courage does not always rise from strength, though often out of necessity for those ready for the challenge.* Another saying of Father's that Rogaan found popping into his thoughts as he watched otherwise capable guardsmen and *Sakes* shy from the confidant swagger of the *Tusaa'Ner sakal*.

"My apologies, *Sakal*." The scribe almost sounded as if pleading with his shaky voice. "We have nowhere to put *these* prisoners."

The *sakal* stopped in front of the scribe with a frown. At fourteen strides, Rogaan saw her well and regretted his meeting her and she becoming the bother to his life at Hunter's Gate. He felt the regret despite her keeping the guardsmen from him and Pax on the bridge. Road dust and sweat stains mottled her sky-blue *Tusaa'Ner* uniform, her red cape now missing. She was much younger than he expected . . . around his age . . . maybe a touch older, but not by much. With her red-plumed helmet tucked under her left arm, her red-blond hair fell to her midback, framing her slender face and perky nose. Rogaan found himself staring at her before he realized it, and his cheeks warmed considerably with guilt.

"No cells at all, Gaalan?" The young *sakal* asked in a sharp, high-pitched tone. Gaalan took this moment to explore the wonders of his sandaled feet.

"Aah . . . ." Gaalan seemed to be searching for an answer.

"Out with it!" The young female *sakal* demanded with her stare firmly fixed on the clearly uncomfortable scribe. She was slightly shorter than the Baraan standing before her, a hand or more than Rogaan, but her physical stature did not intimidate or deter her.

"All the cells are full . . ." Gaalan started to answer, then trailed off, not wanting to complete his words, "except those in the questioning room . . . where Ganzer and his aide are with a prisoner . . . in an inquisition."

"See," the *sakal* replied with a snide arrogance. "There *are* cells for the prisoners."

"But Ganzer will not be pleased if disturbed, Dajil," Gaalan replied with a hint of anger . . . or fear, Rogaan was unsure. The Baraan then straightened his back to speak further.

"I think Mother will want these prisoners taken care of seeing that she sent me to fetch them," the *Tusaa'Ner sakal* replied with her own flare of anger and intent to intimidate, invoking her mother as if her name carried some significance with the *Sake*. With a wave of her free hand she invoked another directive for the Baraan and guardsmen to get moving as she continued on her walk down the caravan. "Get these prisoners below . . . to the questioning cells."

The *Tusaa'Ner* commander walked past Rogaan's cage minding all inside little attention except for when she caught Rogaan's stare. Rogaan's cheeks heated again, and he almost believed that he saw the faintest hint of a smile on her face as she pressed on to matters of not his concern. She spoke loudly in that high-pitched voice as she walked away, "Kardul, we have issues to conclude. You and your *Sharur*, follow me."

Rogaan and Pax both put their heads on swivels, looking about for Kardul and his *Sharur*. Pax spotted them first, but only by a blink or two. They stood stolidly as a group close to the clay-roofed buildings where the merchants were still putting their food wares away for the night. Kardul avoided meeting Rogaan's eye, though his *Sharur* stared back at him with blank emotions. Only Trundiir appeared to have shame-filled eyes for their betrayal.

The cage door squeaked open behind, startling Rogaan. He sat closest to the door and went to turn to see what was happening, but before he could twist to get a look, he felt a pair of strong hands grab him and yank him backward out of the cage. Airborne for a moment, he landed on his back with a thud, sprawled on the paving stones, the air knocked from his lungs. Pain racked him in waves while flashes of light peppered his vision of the almost dark sky above. He gasped for air, but his burning lungs would not fill. Moments after he hit the ground an unintelligible voice barked something before he suffered a kick to his ribs. Several more kicks to his arms now protecting his ribs did little to help him take a much-wanted gulp of air. Anger flashed within Rogaan, but he kept himself from lashing out at the memory of the old Baraan . . . falling. Pax let out a growl from the cage at someone Rogaan could not see. "Leave him be, ya muck shoveler!"

Strong hands grabbed at him again. Angry at the handling, Rogaan coiled up his legs, rolling his feet over his head, pushing through teeth gritting pain. When his shoulders rolled to the paving stones, Rogaan drove his legs upward in a push of arms and midsection and hips and legs launching his body up, striking something solid. When his body fully extended, he filled his lungs before thumping back down on the hard street. Those flashes in his vision disappeared as he took another pleasing breath. His sense of joy was short-lived, however, as three burly charcoal tunics descended on him. Several painful baton strikes to his prone chest, head, and protecting arms inflamed Rogaan all the more. Fighting off the *Sakes*, he rolled to his feet, readying himself to launch at his attackers.

"Stop!" A familiar voice pierced Rogaan's anger-clouded mind. He hesitated as his father's demand sank in. With a flush of shame, Rogaan complied with his father's wish, just as he had his entire life.

"Well, I'm not a stoppin'," announced one of the burly *Sakes* who wore more scars on his face and arms than could easily be counted. The mean-tempered brute hit Rogaan square in the mouth with his sizeable fist. The punishing impact on Rogaan's jaw shook all of his body. He thought his jaw broken until he worked it about. Like a breeze on a kindled flame, Rogaan's anger flared. He took in the dirty, charcoal-colored tunic in front of him. The Baraan had sweaty, heavy muscles rippling under scars on his arms and a dark beard. He had the blunted face of a brute. Angry eyes of the Baraan held a contrast of expressions, something between glee and surprise as the *Sake* seemed unsure of what to do now that his punch had not dropped Rogaan.

"You hit as a little one," Rogaan spit, intending to insult and inflame the Baraan, but kept to his father's wish, otherwise. "A *little* one."

The *Sake* lost his uncertainty and swung at Rogaan with all his anger in a growl. Rogaan had slowly backed up to the wagon before he spat the insult. Watching the *Sake* move as if in water, Rogaan easily dodged the punch, leaving the bars and iron plates of the cell in the path of the brute's fist. Rogaan heard the bones of the Baraan's hand shatter in a sickening, crunching ripple when his fist struck the iron. The *Sake* immediately doubled over in a howl of pain holding his deformed hand. Rogaan felt calm as he stood watching the Baraan dance about in pain with his companions looking on in what could only be described as astonishment. A sardonic smile touched Rogaan.

"I'll kill ya!" Declared the *Sake* holding his broken hand in between pained grunts and groans. "Ya be *lightless*! You hear me? I swear to da Ancients, ya be in *Darkness*!"

Rogaan made to spit another insult at the Baraan, but stopped when he felt the tips of two swords pressing at his neck, one on each side. He looked with his eyes to see who held the blades. On his left was a familiar figure, a big Baraan in dark chest and arm armor and a red-feathered silver, open-face helm. Cold dark eyes stared at him from under the helm. The *Sake zigaar*. Rogaan suddenly felt cold and alone.

On his right stood the female *sakal*, several hands shorter than he, but with eyes burning with as much anger as the *Sake* who broke his hand. For a moment Rogaan thought she would run him through.

"I see this one is much more trouble than you thought," the *Tusaa'Ner sakal's* tone was even and confident with a heavy hint of disdain.

"Lock him away," the *Sake zigaar* ordered to no one in particular. Four *Sakes* jumped at the Baraan's command, pressing knives into Rogaan from all angles before securing him in wrist bindings. They quickly pushed and half-dragged Rogaan through the doorway the *Sakes* had emerged from earlier. His captors led Rogaan to a long, stone-paved lamp-lit passageway that sloped downward before unkindly pushing him in front of them. The air smelled foul of feces, sweat, and burning oil. Wails of pain and despair echoed ahead. The walls and floor shook as a tremor worked its way about the massive building. It was brief, but definitely a tremor; Rogaan felt it through his feet as any Tellen would be expected to. *What am I descending into . . . Kur?* He wondered and feared the unknown ahead. Sweat started to drip from his brow at the pressing shadows. The situation suddenly weighed heavily on him. He may never see home again.

Chapter 11

Questions Entangle

A puzzle of dancing symbols flowed along a confusion of patterns. Throbbing pain came again with those symbols. It always did. The agony and torment of that unsolvable puzzle was almost too much for him, his suffering preventing sound thinking and the focus to reckon it out. He didn't know what it all meant, but the symbols and puzzle teased him, thrived in compelling him . . . daring him to solve it. He feared these surprising and awful attacks of jumbled symbols within his mind, but having survived it so far, he wanted to figure it out; to fix what he had broken, and regain the respect he lost in his father's saddened stare. A mess he made in his disobedience. Now, self-exiled and with no one to help him, he suffered his disobedience when he closed his eyes, and often when they were open. At first, the aid offered by his now-uppity captors gave him hope, but their goodwill quickly showed itself as selfish intent. The two were more concerned with tormenting him than anything else it seemed . . . and felt. Nobody cared to help him from his pain and anguish. They all stood . . . wanting him to suffer. He would need to rely upon himself to make it go away . . . to solve the blasted thing. Yes, he would *fix* things . . . and make them all pay a hundredfold for his pain.

A different pain, a physical one, racked and wrenched at his shoulders as the ropes wrapped around his upper arms tightened. He feared them pulled from their sockets. It hurt, terribly hurt, but not as much as his throbbing head pains. *Oh, they will pay for this!* He promised himself as another flash of symbols spun in his mind. Sweat stung his eyes and blurred his vision. The rope treatment started after a day of simple questioning by the *Sakes* that soon turned him belligerent. *Such stupid questions . . . dim-witted Baraans.* Then they happened on it. Dead *Sakes* were the surprising result with the rest blaming him for it. *They blamed me!* It wasn't long afterward these two dressed-wells showed up, asking all new questions.

One treating it like a fanged animal set to bite. The other as if an animal to tame. "Why do you have it? Where did you get it? Did you touch it? How did you feel when you touched it?" When his answers didn't satisfy them, they moved him down here under the arena grounds to this place where his screams would mingle and be lost with many others. Then, he learned just how painful ropes can be in the hands of the competent and sadistic. All this because he fell to the street when a flurry of symbols took him unexpectedly and he didn't know up from down. His fall drew the attention of the *Tusaa'Ner*. Now, exhaustion started to wear on him with his feet and legs cramping from him keeping on his toes to lessen the agony in his shoulders and back. *What do they want?*

He reluctantly opened his tear-filled eyes. *They're still here.* His hopes dashed away. There would be no reprieve . . . no respite from this interrogation. The closest of his questioners stood near in the light of a table lamp, a lean Baraan just about his own height and in his middle years. The Baraan's dark, squinty eyes deeply sat in his clean-shaven tan face. Neatly-combed light brown hair framed his slender features and almost covered ears that looked more Evendiir than Baraan, with ever so slight points to them. His tormentor wore loose-fitting black pants, a dark lavender shirt of large weave with silver buttons down the front, and a dark charcoal, short coat of fine, light weave with silver cable clasps. The other Baraan kept back in the shadows, leaning casually against the stone wall with arms folded. He appeared more bored than anything else. *Can I use that?* That Baraan was a mystery since he walked in the room hours ago, his words few and of no particular importance.

"Aren," the Baraan in front of him spoke in that even, calm tone that appeared to be well measured to set the fact of him being in absolute control. The middle-years Baraan held up a red gem the size of his palm, shaped as a double-sided ax enwrapped in flames. He was careful not to touch it directly and kept a hide wrap between the crystal-like surface and his hand. "Son of Larcan, you have obligations to speak of your theft and all that you have seen since."

A jumbling of symbols shadowing a whirling pattern filled his mind. Pain throbbed in his skull as the symbols and pattern teased him. They had meaning, but that meaning eluded him since they first came to be in his head on the dreadful day when he snuck a peek and held the double-ax-and-flame gem several moon rises ago. Aren feared something had happened to him when the gemstone he held in his hands flashed an eerie, radiating red. At that moment his head filled with those damnable symbols, patterns, and that unsolvable puzzle. He then woke well into the night lying on the floor of his father's study, the gem next to him without its glow and that torment dancing in his head. He managed somehow to put back the gem in its hiding spot without his father's knowing he touched it. For days following, Aren avoided his father, not wanting to speak wrongly and let him know he had defied explicit instructions not to touch that red Agni stone.

"Young one!" Aren's questioner sounded impatient and annoyed. A quick stinging hand on his left cheek left Aren working his jaw and blinking to clear his vision. "Waste my time no further. Give me your eyes."

The stinging slap brought Aren back to the here and now. He worked to focus past the spinning symbols in his mind and see what his questioner demanded. Aren's anger helped him focus, if only to show his questioner a defiant stare. His vision clearing, he found the scowling Baraan with those dark, squinty eyes boring into him in a way that made him unnerved. Aren's skin prickled. The middle-aged Baraan looked determined. Despite Aren's helpless situation, his anger slipped from his containing it. "I told you, idiot. I know nothing of a gemstone."

"You've *touched* it," the Baraan's voice went low and dangerous. He didn't respond to the insult as Aren expected, with an argument of who had the better mind and logical thinking . . . of which Aren felt certain he did. "It's touched you, and you've seen what it wanted you to see before it slumbered. Tell me of it."

"Slumbered?" Aren sneered back. His anger and now frustration boiled. Pain racked his arms, back, and head. The physical he contended with; it was a practiced matter of not thinking on it, but the pain of those spinning symbols were blinding. He barely grasped some understanding of what he saw in his own mind's eye and didn't understand what his questioner was digging at. *Any explanation of what he saw or its yet unknown meaning would be lost on him and his companion in the shadows,* Aren reassured himself. He decided telling them of his jumbled visions would do nothing to help him solve the tormenting puzzle or relieve him of the pain accompanying the symbols. *They're too stupid to understand.*

A frustrated groan echoed in the room. The other questioner broke his silence while stepping from the shadows. "I've indulged you for too long. This one has nothing to tell."

The other Baraan stood just at the edge of the lamplight, short in stature and pudgy with a double chin. Adding to the image his clean and kept wavy black hair, a clean, well-made red shirt, brown hide kilt, and glinting silver-harnessed ruby gemstone dangling from his right ear. *A soft person unfamiliar to hard work, but thinks he's an authority over others,* Aren concluded.

The taller Baraan put on an irritated face with rolling eyes while keeping his back to the annoyance. His expression turned dark for a few moments, then, with an effort, he collected himself before turning to address his companion. "I *recommend* further questioning. He has more to say."

"She isn't patient, Lucufaar," the wavy-haired Baraan impatiently explained. "You've been questioning this skinny thing for days without results. I've kept Irzal away and uncurious as long as I can. She wants us attending to her tasks."

"What this young one knows *is* important to Irzal's plans, Ganzer," Lucufaar argued. The Baraan looked like he was trying to keep control of himself and close to losing the battle.

"No," Ganzer's reply sounded final. "With her daughter to arrive tonight, you know she'll be making all sorts of demands."

Suddenly, Aren's head was clear. Those jumbling, spinning symbols and that puzzle pattern along with the pain left him. Aren almost started laughing at the relief. Then, the burning from the ropes on his upper arms and his strained shoulders ached terribly. His shoulders felt near dislocated, making Aren want to cry out at the pain, but instead, he fought down the urge with gritted teeth. He wasn't about to give his captors the satisfaction of him showing pain.

Lucufaar now wore his annoyance openly. Aren thought and hoped he might hit Ganzer. Then, a smirk formed on the tall Baraan's face as his eyes took on a look of practiced serenity. It happened almost in a blink of an eye. With a baleful smile, Lucufaar turned toward Ganzer just as the door to the cell area swung open. Standing in the doorway crowded a pair of big *Sakes* with a bound prisoner between them.

"Leave us!" Lucufaar demanded with a stiff chin and heated eyes.

"Following our orders." One of the *Sakes* countered in a business-as-usual tone.

"Leave before you're reported to Za-Irzal." Lucufaar threatened with a tone of venom in his voice.

"Invoking Mother's name again, Lucufaar?" Sharp words spoken with a high-pitched voice. It grated on Aren. For a moment, he considered it better to have those symbols in his head. Lucufaar and Ganzer looked surprised. Ganzer then took on a nervousness with darting eyes seeking an escape. Lucufaar's annoyance returned, then inflamed visibly. *Maybe I can use this,* Aren noted to himself.

"Get this lump out of my . . . in the room!" That high-pitched voice continued on, grating at Aren, allowing him to forget his burning ropes for a moment. The big *Sakes* grunted before hurriedly pushing their unhappy prisoner into the room. Their prisoner, a Tellen . . . a tall one with an uncharacteristically close beard, dressed in dark pants and boots, a blue shirt, and charcoal-colored vest. He snarled at his captors before giving in to being handled by the *Sakes*. *He's trouble,* Aren assessed and noted to himself.

The *Sakes* kept on arrogantly pushing the unhappy Tellen past Aren's fuming questioner. Lucufaar aired an atmosphere liking to a thunderhead about to let loose with angry lightning. Aren was happy not to be the focus of the tall Baraan's attention and wondered when he would lash out. Ganzer still looked like a scurrying furbearer wanting to flee, but uncertain which direction to go. Following the Tellen, a blue-clad woman, barely past her youngling years, confidently strode into the room with her reddish-blond hair whipping about. She spared a quick glance at Lucufaar showing her casual disregard for him before turning her gaze on Ganzer.

"You need to do better keeping a tether on your helper, Ganzer," the Baraan woman was direct staring down Ganzer. Despite her young age, she displayed considerable confidence and authority over Aren's tormentors. It was difficult for Aren to suppress a satisfying smile at her boldness and her bullying them. He got a glance at Lucufaar when she called him Ganzer's "helper." The Baraan just about lost all control of himself.

"You petulant—" Lucufaar started before cutting himself off. His expression twisted for a moment before he put on another serene face.

The young woman, shorter than Lucufaar by a head, turned her heated stare on him. When Lucufaar didn't flinch, uncertainty flashed in her eyes until she launched into another chastising of him. "Know your place, Lucufaar. You serve and advise Ganzer, not Mother, and not me. Ganzer advises the *Za* as I do. Your place is where she and we say it is. Now be gone!"

"Our work is done here, Lucufaar," Ganzer squeaked out, interrupting what Lucufaar was about to say. The nervous Baraan wasted no time squeezing past the *Sakes* that were pushing more prisoners into the room. "Come along, Lucufaar, before you get yourself in trouble with the *sakal* again."

The blue-dressed, reddish-blond-haired woman waited as Lucufaar reluctantly withdrew himself from the room, all the while palming a cloth-wrapped object. She gave a long exhale and appeared relieved when the middle-aged Baraan finally left the room. *She fears Lucufaar*, Aren noted that for future use. More *Sakes* entered the room with prisoners stumbling before them. All were quickly dispatched into cells to Aren's right. In all, eight prisoners crowded into two of the three small cells. A family of three or four, parents and a youngling daughter and maybe a youngling son, in the cell furthest away. All Baraans. In the center cell next to Aren's vacant one, two Baraans and two Tellens, including that unhappy one, were crowded in together. It was difficult for Aren to tell if the blue-dressed woman seemed more satisfied or relieved when the prisoners were finally locked behind bars. As soon as the cell doors clicked locked, she turned her attention on him.

"What did you do to earn Lucufaar's wrath?" The blue-clad woman asked. She gave Aren a sympathetic look before it vanished almost as quickly as it was offered. She then whispered so only Aren could hear, "He has a bad side. Best to give him what he wants before you're seriously hurt."

"Release this one from the rack and put him in the empty cell," the woman commanded Aren's release. The *Sakes* complied, but not quickly. She stood in the middle of the room with arms crossed, a scowl on her face, and her right boot impatiently tapping the stone floor. Aren waited silently for the jailers to release him from his questioning ropes. When they lowered him, a burning agony washed through him in waves at each lessening of the strain on his arms and loosening of the ropes. The pain took his breath away. He fought hard to keep from passing out before he could get his feet under him, but instead, went straight to his knees and almost toppled over. The painful impact of his knees on stones further bloodied his dirty gray tunic. With no ceremony or sympathy, the *Sakes* roughly yanked him to his feet, then half carried him to the empty cell before pushing him in a tumble to the unclean floor. Aren lay where he fell for a long while . . . how long, he didn't know or care. His shoulders and arms were on fire, but free, and the cool stones were comforting. He thought to sleep and felt as if he could do so for days, but curiosity tugged at him and his worry at what the newcomers could do to him as he slept forced his eyes open. Aren didn't trust them, not one bit. They could be working for this Ganzer and Lucufaar. *Who are these newcomers? What are they about? Who do they want? Who's the woman that has sway over my tormentors?* Aren felt compelled to find the answer to his questions to see who and how they meant him harm. So his eyes stayed open, and he watched them.

Chapter 12

Newcomers

Aren painfully raised himself off the stones, propping himself up against the wall opposite the cell door. Looking around assessing his situation, he found the blue-clad woman gone. Left behind were two darkly dressed *Sakes* standing guard at each of the two doors of the room beyond his bars. The cell doors were locked and unguarded, but watched closely by the *Sakes*. Aren then corrected himself. The *Sakes* weren't just watching the cell doors. Several of them pretended not to be looking, but they were all either watching or stealing looks at the light brown-skinned Baraan woman-child in the far cell. Her green dress, though dirty, did little to hide her slender figure as she paced nervously about the cell. Her long black hair flowed over her shoulders and small breasts and down her back to her waist, framing her slender face and body. Even at her young age, she was plenty for eyes to take in—*for a Baraan, that is*—Aren caught himself. And the *Sakes* certainly had their eyes on her. They appeared to agree with Aren's assessment of her by the way their hungry eyes followed her everywhere. Leapers watching their next meal . . . that is what Aren's view of the *Sakes* reminded him of. *Poor thing*, Aren caught himself in a moment of compassion for the Baraan. She was in trouble if left in the care of these four . . . guardsmen. *Not my problem.*

The woman-child's mother, a handsome woman for a Baraan, in a torn, dirty yellow dress and with disheveled dark hair falling to her shoulders, tried to comfort her daughter with reassurances—*wishful lies, all of them*— that their predicament was a mistake and that they would be freed. Aren almost chuckled at the absurdities the woman spoke. *Thinking they'll be freed?* A dark-haired male Baraan, tall and lean and covered in sweat-streaked grime on both skin and clothes, stood next to the woman. Aren assumed the male Baraan was the girl's father. His flame-stoked eyes watched the *Sakes* watching them, watching his daughter with gazes of hunger. The father looked ready to do just about anything to defend his daughter, but he also wore a frustrated scowl at not understanding what was happening or how he could get himself and his family to freedom. *A pathetic sight*, Aren concluded. The young Baraan male dressed in a too large green shirt and black pants and boots wore a disdainful look at the *Sakes*. By the looks of him, Aren guessed he was the woman-child's sibling.

Four others in the cell closest to him seemed a mismatch. A muscular tan-skinned Tellen with a short beard and the height of a Baraan wearing a dark blue long-sleeved shirt and a charcoal vest that had seen better days, dark pants, and hide boots paced his cell as if a caged leaper. Aren believed he could wear a hole in the stone floor if allowed to keep at it. *This one is angry and not fond of being captive.* An older Tellen sat with his back against the cell's stone wall. He showed signs of middle age with wrinkles, shoulder-length black hair that was graying at the temples, and a long, braided, black beard with gray margins. Despite his age, the older Tellen looked fit with a broad chest and thick arms under a charcoal-colored shirt, dark pants, black boots, and a finely crafted silver belt buckle with symbols Aren couldn't make out. Aren guessed him to be a laborer or a smith, but the well-tailored clothing and high quality belt left him wondering who he was. Unlike his younger kin, this Tellen sat with a calmness speaking of patience and wisdom. The remaining two in the cell were Baraan males of middle age, battered badly from the few glimpses Aren had of them. Both sat withdrawn with legs tucked under arms and heads down, sitting in their corner of the cell beyond the older Tellen.

Despite the newcomers being Baraans and Tellens, Aren was half glad for them and half nervous at how they would treat him. Their arrival did manage to drive away his questioners and bring to a stop the pleasure they were having at his expense. Aren grimaced at having reminded himself of his aching body. His arms and shoulders shook with pain when he moved them . . . even when he breathed. Two days of suffering torment and the only thing they were able to liberate from him was the Agni stone they took . . . that red double-bladed-ax-and-flame-shaped gemstone that appeared as a ruby, but wasn't. It shone with a vibrant inner glow in Aren's hands, but appeared *lightless* and dead in the hands of Lucufaar. "*Slumbering?*" The stone *slumbered* . . . came to Aren's mind for reasons unknown to him, nor did he understand what it meant. He even thought the thing spoke to him a few times. *Impossible!*

Under the question for days, Aren felt pride in not having betrayed either his father or those *Kabiri* of the Circle who gave his father the thing to study and Aren . . . *borrowed*. Aren's tormentors seemed obsessed about the Agni stone, especially that older one. Try as they did, they didn't break him. With a half-smile, Aren settled down with his foul-smelling rag of a blanket that kept him warm enough to sleep the past few nights.

Aren tried his best to sleep, but those blasted newcomers just wouldn't shut up. At first they, the Baraans, yapped about their travels here and the hardships they endured. Only an occasional grunt from the young Tellen reminded Aren he was in the next cell. Aren noted the older Tellen kept silent throughout. The Baraans continued with arguing over whose fault it was for their sufferings. They reached no conclusion. Next, some of them started scheming how to gain their freedom. It all would have been interesting to listen to if Aren wasn't trying to sleep. He felt weary and in pain and, now, irritated. *Enough is enough!*

"Quiet!" Aren exploded from under his blanket, then continued in a grumble. "Idiots . . . all of you." Silence filled the chastised room except for the snickering from the *Sakes*.

"Quiet yourself. Go back to your sleep and be silent," the young Tellen spat as he paced.

Aren's sensibilities burned at the arrogance and insolence of that young Tellen. Aren, unhappy with being awake, wanted to dismiss all of their rudeness and go back to sleep, but the presumed superiority of that Tellen heated his temper. The heat within Aren quickly became too much. He kicked off his blanket and sat up, then locked his flaming eyes with the young Tellen. They stared at each other for a long time without either of them flinching. Aren meant to intimidate the Tellen and the others into silence so he could be left alone to the sleep he wanted. The Tellen wasn't cooperating, returning Aren's stare with what looked to be his own internal flames. The Tellen was bigger in bulk than Aren, he realized, and could likely pound him into the dirt. But Aren's hot anger kept him from backing down as many would to avoid a confrontation. Instead, Aren exploded.

"Such a pompous tail!" Aren stood launching his verbal attack from a slightly taller height. "Silence yourself. You arrive with your anger and expect me to bow to you? I haven't a care of you or your wants."

The young Tellen gripped the bars between their cells, turning his knuckles white. Aren immediately reconsidered his approach. *This one is really angry*, he realized. Aren consciously stopped himself from stepping back. *I can't demonstrate that I'm weak. Besides, there are bars between us.*

"Who do you think you are . . . ?" The young Tellen started. Aren immediately composed a response in his head to answer the challenge and more as he ignored the rest of what the young Tellen spoke. He felt certain his answer would make the Tellen's head spin and make him feel a hand tall. Pride filled Aren for it . . . and for not backing down from this hotheaded bully.

"My son," the older Tellen spoke calmly, controlled from where he sat.

The flames in the young Tellen's eyes quelled and flickered, then burst back to full intensity. His arms rippled, and his knuckles whitened on the bars all the more. He looked as if he was straining. Then the metal bars flexed. A spike of fear bolted through Aren.

"Rogaan," the older Tellen continued in his even tone, "hold your anger and contain it. More is happening than you know. You must keep from losing yourself."

Aren feared the old Tellen's attempt to get his son under control wasn't going to be enough. This . . . Rogaan . . . still gripped the iron bars with white knuckles and his eyes remained as angry flames. The bars Aren thought a safe barrier between them bent as the young Tellen strained. Panic swelled in Aren, growing stronger as the bars bent further and further. Then those flames cooled . . . some, as Rogaan's clenched teeth relaxed a little. Aren let out his breath realizing he had been holding it. He then sighed in relief as quietly as he could manage. *I must be more careful.*

"Let me arm go!" The protest came from beyond the Tellens in the far cell. A *Sake* had his big hands on the Baraan woman-child's right arm, dragging her fighting and screaming from the cell. The father, sitting in the far corner of the cell with his head in his hands a moment before, appearing to have just nodded off, now looked awake and shocked and caught off guard. The mother stood stunned with a horror-filled expression. The young Baraan male rushed the *Sake*, but found the darkly clad guard's left hand engulfing his throat in a grip that must have been as iron by the way the Baraan's eyes bulged red. The *Sake* then heaved the young Baraan back into the cell, thumping him on the floor before rolling onto his father with a groan of pain.

"Don't take me little one," the mother screamed her pleas. The *Sake* ignored her as he continued dragging her "little one" away. The father growled, demanding his youngling be unhanded as he rushed the *Sake*. They collided at the cell doorway with sharp exhales loud in the room, the momentum of the father pushing them all, *Sake*, father, and daughter, out of the cell. Aren watched dispassionately as the father struggled to free his daughter from the guard's grip. The woman-child screamed and cried pleas for her father to help her get free. He fought fiercely for several moments as his wife and the young Tellen both yelled for her to be let go. A crushing hammer of a fist from a second *Sake* sent the father back against the cell bars with wobbly legs and what Aren assumed were glassed-over eyes. Silence fell upon the room. The second *Sake*, the biggest and most muscled of the four, grabbed the Baraan father and shoved him back into the cell, adding a kick to his lower back that sent him flying and sounding as if something broke inside him. He landed on his son who was just trying to raise himself off the floor. Both went down in a heap. The groaning mother screamed her despair as the door to their cell shut and locked, keeping her from helping her daughter. The woman-child stood with wide eyes now that she was at the mercy of the *Sakes*. Aren was pretty sure she would get no mercy.

Aren struggled to keep his dispassionate air. He found it next to impossible when his eyes locked with the woman-child's just for a moment. She was terrified but silent, with shock visible in her wide tear-filled eyes. She had a horrified expression that Aren hoped he would never see again. It was haunting. She understood what was about to happen to her, it appeared. Her helplessness and the way she kept control of herself struck Aren, causing him to fight back a swelling urge to yell at the *Sakes* himself for them to leave her be. The *Sakes* pulled the helpless woman-child to the only table in the room, bending her over on it and holding her down with several hands pressing on her back, all the while they lewdly and boastfully made remarks about how they and she were going to enjoy what was about to happen. Her wet eyes pleaded for help. She didn't scream. Instead, a whisper escaped her lips. Aren heard it despite the din and the howls of her mother.

"Rogaan . . . help me." The woman-child pleaded.

"No!" The deep voice of the old Tellen sharply punctuated the din. Then, his tone turned more as a plea, "Rogaan, no."

Aren turned to see the young Tellen almost sideways suspended above the floor with his hands in a death-grip on the cell bars and his feet pressed against the locking plate of the cell door. His face was red and in a fury. His eyes gave clue to his inner state that Aren assessed could only describe as a complete bloodlust. Metal cracking rang like a dull bell throughout the room. The *Sakes* took pause at pulling up the woman-child's green dress, instead looking to discover the source of the noise. Rogaan strained even harder, if that was possible, and let out a deep growl that sounded like nothing Aren ever remembered hearing. The metal lock to the cell door snapped under its tremendous strain with a deafening crack that hurt Aren's ears, causing him to wince. The door flew open, slamming against cell bars in a reverberating clang.

Rogaan righted himself to his feet when the metal gave way. The young Tellen immediately launched himself at the *Sakes* with a quickness that surprised Aren. Rogaan ran full on into the biggest *Sake* holding the woman-child. Wrapping his arms around the guard, he drove him backward, slamming him into the stone wall hard enough to jar loose the bricks with a loud clunk. The *Sake* stood motionless, pressed into the wall as dirt and mortar both fell free from the wall and ceiling above. When Rogaan pushed himself off the wall, the big *Sake's* body went limp, collapsing to the floor where he lay unmoving. The other three *Sakes* stood in stunned surprise for a moment before one of them decided to draw his short blade and swing at the young Tellen. Rogaan ducked the blade and smashed his fist into the *Sake's* jaw with a crunch. Aren winched as he guessed the Baraan's jaw broke at the sound of it and by the way it now hung as he fell backward to the stone floor. His unflinching body hit with a sickening thud that reminded Aren of a melon being smashed on stone. The two remaining guards both drew their blades, but backed away, close to the door near the questioning rack. How Aren hated that thing. The guards appeared uncertain of what to do. Aren smiled. These block-headed jailers were not accustomed to someone able to fight back. Rogaan stood between the *Sakes* and the woman-child with heated eyes. But he didn't advance; instead, held his place, protecting the woman-child.

Shaken and unsteady, she dragged herself off the table before pulling down her torn dress to cover her exposed body. Tears flowed from her eyes as she steadied herself before timidly looking about the room. Her stunned gaze stared off into walls for a few long moments before speaking. "No more, Rogaan. No more."

The young Tellen's eyes questioned what he heard, then cooled, "softening" better described what Aren saw. Rogaan was still visibly angry, but when he spoke to her his voice was soft for a Tellen. "Are you all right?"

"No . . ." She started crying, weeping uncontrollably.

Rogaan appeared torn between tending to her and launching himself at the *Sakes*.

"My son," the old Tellen spoke in a deep calm voice. He stood at the broken cell door. "Suhd is wise. Do no more. Put away your fire. I never wanted this for you."

The door behind the *Sakes* burst open, knocking one of the guards to the floor. Filling the doorway stood a dark-haired bulk of a Baraan in dark chest armor. He ducked to enter the room, then stood surveying the chaos with measured, dark eyes. Aren had heard of this one from the *Sakes*. They feared and revered him all at the same time. He must be the *Sake zigaar*. The judge . . . and executioner when beyond the walls of Farratum, where laws still mattered and needed enforcing, but where few in the service of the law chose to go willingly.

"You four are worthless," the *Sake zigaar* growled. He stood assessing the situation of the room as if the entire world was his and revolved around him.

The *Sake* still standing had forgotten the young Tellen and woman-child completely, turning his back to them, so he could pay respect with a bowed head to the *Sake zigaar*. "Your forgiveness, *Zigaar*?"

The *Sake zigaar* didn't waste his breath on the jailer-guard. Instead, he assessed the room again. He walked to the broken cell door, ignoring the old Tellen who stepped back with a measured confidence into the cell, allowing the *Sake zigaar* access to the door. Four new *Sakes*, all dressed in armor similar to the *Sake zigaar's*, but less well made, filled the room taking up strategic positions at both doors keeping anyone from running off or from attacking their master. They appeared to pay little attention to Rogaan, but Aren guessed they were well practiced in not giving away what they considered important. The big Baraan didn't appear to need their protection as he continued his inspection of the cell door and bars. The *Sake zigaar* surveyed everything; the door, the cells, where everyone and everything was, the looks in the eyes of the prisoners, and their body-talk. One of his guards checked the two unconscious *Sakes*.

"This one lives," a dark-clad *Sake* announced after checking the biggest of the guards lying unconscious against the broken wall. "He took a hard knock. He still has breath."

"The other . . . is without his *Light*," another of the *Sakes* added. "His jaw is broken and his noggin looks as a dropped melon."

"Bind this one," the *Sake zigaar* pointed to Rogaan. He looked over the young Tellen as Rogaan stood between the woman-child . . . Suhd, and everyone else. "Do so and keep him from using his arms. He's too dangerous for any of you."

Two of his *Sakes* immediately moved to do their master's bidding, but Rogaan stood and moved to keep them from completing their task . . . and keep them away from the Suhd. After several failed attempts, the *Sakes* hesitated while considering how to fulfill their duty.

"Stand down, Tellen," the *Sake zigaar* addressed Rogaan. "I'll *punish* that young thing you cherish so much if you don't submit."

Suhd's hands took gentle hold of Rogaan's left arm. He visibly softened at her touch. She then spoke to him in a companion's tone, "Please. I be all right. I dare believe what he speaks, he'll do it."

"You have kept Suhd from harm, Rogaan," the old Tellen spoke from his cell in a fatherly manner. "It is time to show strength in other ways than by your brawn."

Rogaan seemed uncertain and torn between unfavorable acts. He looked to his father, then to Suhd. Then, after the woman-child hugged herself to his arm, he took a nonthreatening posture with a resigned sigh. Suhd kissed his cheek, causing him to blush. At the *Sake zigaar's* command, the dark-clad *Sakes* wasted no time binding him in metal shackles at the wrists and just above the elbows before escorting him back into the cell where his father quietly stood.

"Take the youngling female," the *Sake zigaar* commanded. "She has looks, too much for all of you and your weak natures. She's an unwanted temptation, here. Trouble."

Suhd's family and Rogaan verbally protested from their cells. Suhd's mother started weeping, again, and her father and brother were rattling the cell bars as they yelled threats of retributions. With his father's hand trying to restrain him, Rogaan protested growling with determined venom in his voice while holding the *Sake zigaar's* hard eyes with his own. "Harm her, and I will kill you."

Aren found himself split in opinion between feeling sorry for the family and finding their protests and threats ridiculous, if not useless . . . even amusing. The young Tellen looked and sounded serious and determined. Aren decided those two, Rogaan and the *Sake zigaar*, going at each other would be good for the sheer entertainment of it, but he wasn't certain who would be the victor . . . though he would wager coin on the *Sake zigaar*.

Appearing to ignore the Tellen, the *Sake zigaar* looked at the two guards lying on the stone floor. "I'm certain you'll try. Fear for nothing. She isn't to be harmed or abused by any hand under my command. That's my word. My bond. My duty."

Suhd was ushered out of the room by several *Sakes* before anyone could make any more protests or threats. She wore a frightened expression, and her eyes spoke of terror almost enough for Aren to feel sorry for her. Otherwise, she held herself controlled despite her helplessness. She locked eyes with Rogaan just before she disappeared from the room. Aren caught their unspoken exchange and realized she held as much affection for him as he had for her. *A tragic story, these two.*

More darkly clad *Sakes* filled the room, replacing the ones that took the woman-child away. They impressed and intimidated Aren with their discipline and efficiency. The failed *Sakes* that survived the young Tellen's rage were ordered to remove their *lightless* companion. As they dragged the body from the room, the *Sake zigaar* ordered for them to atone for their failures and be disciplined before retesting. Aren didn't know what they were to be retested for, but the tone of the *Sake zigaar* and the unsettled looks all the *Sakes* gave to each other at his order told him the experience would be an unpleasant one.

"Put the Tellens with that Evendiir." The *Sake zigaar* continued giving orders. Pointing at the pair of Baraans cowering in the back of the cell, "And toss those two decrepit things into the pit."

Aren watched as the Tellens complied, the young one begrudgingly, with the *Sakes* prompting them to their new cell. The young one offered little resistance after his father whispered something to him even Aren was unable to hear. The young Tellen made a clinched-jaw grimace, then settled himself. As for the two shaken Baraans, they cowered under the rough handling of the *Sakes* as they were extracted from the room. Aren briefly wondered what their fates were to be in the "pit," but then dismissed it all. *Not my concern.* What was of his concern was the pungent smell of the Tellens. Now that they were in his cell, Aren couldn't get far enough away from them to avoid their undesired scent. *They must not have bathed for days—if ever,* Aren guessed. And, well, Tellens just smelled . . . His parents had always instructed him. *What more must I endure?*

Chapter 13
Subar

Why am I floating? Aren felt weightless. He just didn't understand how or why. The sensation was pleasant except for the slight pinching of his upper arms. Then he felt his toes burning, but his unresponsive legs kept him from drawing them close, away from the heat. The pain was dull . . . tolerable, but a little uncomfortable. He struggled to understand why the flames didn't hurt him as they should. Aren tried opening his eyes, but they didn't feel like his. *Whose?* A surreal sensation of changing light levels experienced through his closed eyes left his head disoriented. *Maybe I dream?* Aren thought trying to understand his condition. *No.* He hadn't dreamt of anything but those damnable torments of spinning symbols for many nights. *Why are they not in my head? What's happening to me?* His eyes opened a little. Blurred cobblestones passed under him. Aren tried to clear his vision by blinking. No change. He felt anxious and started struggling to breathe. His toes burned. He wanted to see what was happening to him, but everything remained a blur. Now, he felt as if supported by his upper arms. The pinching sensation started to hurt . . . burn. Aren glanced sideways finding two big jailers, blurred, who were dragging him through corridors, some of which felt familiar. *Where . . . the prison under the arena?* He felt a pang of panic grip his throat. *What's happening?* Struggling to become fully aware, Aren felt as if waking from a deep slumber. The more he woke, the more he felt the burning pain on his arms and in his toes.

"Let go of me, you louts!" Aren angrily demanded as he found himself finally able to pull his legs up underneath him and set them at pace with the jailers. Pain spiked through his feet and a sinking feeling grabbed at him for a moment when he saw the tops of his bloodied feet. They stung painfully. Aren aggressively pulled his arms free of the *Sake* jailers at his sides, managing to keep pace with them after a stumble. They made to grab him again. "Unhand me . . . You slow-witted, smelly idiots!"

A fist struck Aren's head sideways, sending him into the wall of the stone corridor they walked. Holding onto the wall to stay upright, Aren shook off the dizzy feeling the jailer had just given him. Anger at his indignant treatment sped up his recovery, allowing him to stand without aid and glare at the lout who struck him.

"Silence, Evendiir." The *Sake* spit his words at Aren. "Speak another word and ya be having troubles eating with no teeth."

Aren wanted badly to insult the low-minded jailer but feared having his teeth knocked from him. He kept his contemptuous glare a blaze, but decided holding his tongue would do him better for the moment. The *Sake* motioned for him to get walking. Aren reluctantly complied as his jailers dispassionately continued their escort seeming satisfied he walked without them needing to prod him along. Aren feared where they led him, and he didn't know how long they dragged him before he woke. He realized he hadn't slept so soundly in a long time. He felt refreshed and relieved despite his sore jaw and burning, bloodied toe tops. Looking again at his stinging bloody feet made them hurt all the more so he decided not to think of them, keeping his eyes high as his escorts ushered him through unfamiliar corridors. The prison seemed larger than Aren thought, causing him some concern he may be made lost down here. *It must extend beyond the foundation of the arena above, into the surrounding streets*, he concluded. *Remember the halls . . . for future use.* Aren noted markings and significant aspects of his surroundings as the jailers led him deeper into the prison. Turning a corner, they started down another long corridor, this one lined by cells filled with all sorts of the unwanted. All but a few of the imprisoned wore filthy clothes and were offensive to Aren's sensitive nose. More than some were dressed in what once looked to be well-to-do clothes. Many slept on makeshift beds of various reeds and fronds and other things while others slept on the cold stone floor. Of those who were awake, only a few dared more than a glance at their passing. Aren noted the fear in many of their eyes and how they held themselves. He also noted that all the prisoners looked to be Baraan . . . not an Evendiir, Tellen, or even the foul-tempered Skurst. Strange, given the street talk of the Baraan hating other races, particularly Tellens with their plots, schemes, and secret societies within every corner of the city planning the overthrow of Farratum and Shuruppak. Aren expected more cells to look as his, with a mix of races. Crime on the streets was said to be much of the doing of low Baraans and unseen Skurst, supposedly the poorest and least able to fit into the fabric of civilized life. Observing what was before his eyes, the numbers and economic status of the Baraans jailed was surprising. *Why mostly Baraans . . . and of those, most of them looked to have had some coin?*

At the end of the long cell-lined corridor, his escorts led him into a foul-smelling large octagon-shaped chamber with a high domed ceiling and an open pit in the center of the room. Questioning racks were anchored solidly on each of eight walls. Fear froze Aren's feet in place at the sight of them. The smell of tormented pain and dried blood filled his nose. *What's happening here? What's going to happen to me?* His arms began to ache as he took ahold of himself to keep from shaking. A lone person in shadows almost half the room away on Aren's left stood near an open door that led to a dark void. Aren guessed the person to be a Baraan male by the size of him. He stood stolidly with hands clasped in front as if patiently waiting. An atmosphere of gloominess surrounded the Baraan, causing Aren to shiver . . . His feet still anchored to the stone where he stood. The Baraan was as tall as Aren, but more heavily muscled. His dark, shoulder-length hair was pulled back tight, allowing his angular features to be accentuated in the shadows cast by torchlight. In those shadows, his eyes seemed voids. Aren shivered again. *Am I to be tormented more? Is he my tormentor? Am I to be killed . . . or worse?* Dressed in clean charcoal-colored pants and a sleeveless shirt with wide shoulders and a belt sash of black and red, Aren concluded the Baraan to be in a uniform of some sort, though he was unfamiliar with the significance of the livery.

Hued symbols started spinning about in Aren's head again. *What? Why? Why have they returned?* The symbols danced, forming that damnable puzzle with a complexity that seemed greater than he remembered. It made his head throb and ache, the pain forcing Aren to shut his eyes trying to endure it and bringing to an end his wishful illusion. *I'm not cured.*

"Leave us," a voice commanded. The voice was calm, steady, and confident.

Aren opened his eyes to a squint to confirm the words came from the Baraan standing in the gloomy air. He caught the last of a hand wave from him dismissing his escorts. After a moment, Aren felt and heard the movement of the armed pair leaving the chamber . . . of *Questioning Racks*. Another shiver took Aren despite his best effort to suppress it.

"You're here to answer my questions," the calm voice told him.

Questions . . . Aren felt his knees weaken as a throng the hued symbols spun violently in his mind's eye. His stomach felt sour, not just from the crumbs they had fed him last night, but in expectation of what was to come.

"I see you've been properly introduced to the Cords of Truth?" The calm voice continued with a slight hand motion to one of the questioning racks. "Demonstrate your value to me and you'll be spared further sessions. Reject my offer at your own endangerment."

Aren's legs buckled a bit more, and the rumblings in his belly brought his unsettled stomach to his throat. And those symbols spun even faster and *hotter* somehow. Even the room seemed to move awkwardly with the colored symbols. Aren struggled to keep to his feet. He stumbled forward. He felt desperate to get his orientation back. Suddenly, he felt violently pulled in a direction opposite his spinning, then felt himself floating. It felt good . . . in that moment. *Thud!* Dull numbing pain shuddered through his whole body. He hurt everywhere.

"I'll not have you flop into the pit." The calm voice punched through Aren's dazed awareness. "At least until I determine if you have something of use for me."

Pain ran the length of Aren's aching back, and his head felt as if hit with a stone. His thoughts remained fuzzy and filled with symbols. Slowly and with much concentration, Aren's aching head cleared. The spinning symbols also slowed, but would not stop, would not offer him relief. Aren's fingers and palms felt the flagstones beneath him. *I'm on the floor? How?* He opened his eyes . . . slowly, afraid that he would see the Baraan above him. The blurred dome above the room glowed dully and danced with colors from torchlight. A heavy wood framing structure firmly anchored in stone at the top of the dome appeared to be sized just right for passage of a wood platform suspended just beneath the frame from four stout chains originating further above. Aren couldn't make out what was above the platform with his vision blurred as it was. The silhouette of an intimidating figure suddenly stood hovering over him. Fear seized Aren as bile rose in his throat. He fought to not sick up. With an effort and much blinking, Aren's vision started clearing a little, allowing him to see the dark features of the . . . Baraan. More shivers swept through him, charging every fiber of his body, causing pain to rack him for a moment before it settled into something manageable . . . endurable. Aren decided to lie still while looking up to watch the Baraan, reluctantly letting him know Aren recognized he was there. *Maybe a show of confidence will help me with him.* He was at the Baraan's mercy. How Aren detested being so.

"Are you firm enough to answer inquiries or do I return you to the cell?" The Baraan put on a smile with a menacing curl. "Maybe after a time hanging . . . your tongue with let loose the truth."

Aren winced at the words. Considering his alternatives in a flash of thought, pragmatism took hold of him. He could remain stewing in the anger he felt toward Ganzer and his strong-hand Lucufaar, or he could cooperate with this Baraan and maybe find or create leverage against the others. Maybe even find a way out of all this. The hued symbols spinning in their puzzle pattern slowed to almost a stop. Aren noted the behavior of the symbols. *Yes. I'll cooperate with and use this one.*

"Your inquiries?" Aren asked sincerely, with an unwanted hint of a quiver in his voice.

The Baraan smiled, not in triumph, but satisfaction. "What questions did Ganzer have his man-servant put to you?"

Aren considered how to answer. He didn't want to take too long or this one might think he wasn't serious with his cooperation or truthful. *So he's untrusting of my tormentors . . . How do I use this?* Aren quickly decided to stay away from telling him of the now slumbering Agni stone, instead, keeping his answers to the believable, the materialistic. "They asked of gems in my possession."

"Continue," the Baraan prompted with a flat, confident tone.

Aren panicked a moment with his heart pounding before gathering his thoughts and answering. Bluffing wasn't something he considered himself good at. While still lying on the hard stone floor, he answered, "They wanted to know where I stole them from."

"Ganzer isn't one motivated by wealth," the Baraan laid out, insinuating Aren was lying or at least holding back. "There is more to your *explanation*."

"I'm speaking truth!" Aren shot back with more heat than he intended, causing him to winch a little in trepidation after the words escaped his lips. He peeked up at the Baraan hoping not to see harm coming his way. To Aren's relief, the sharp-featured Baraan remained still and stolid. He took advantage of the moment to roll away and scramble to his feet, all the while looking for a way to escape the room, if the situation allowed it . . . and Aren wanted to escape. As he regained his feet, he caught sight of the *Sake* guards. They stood deep into each hallway Aren spied down. Far enough away to see, but not hear.

The Baraan grunted. When Aren returned his eyes to him, he motioned Aren to a stool near the entrance to that unlit room. This Baraan made him uneasy, at best. He was different from the others wanting knowledge from him. His tactics were not so brutish, but practiced manipulation. Long moments passed with Aren considering his options again. None would result in his freedom except taking a chance with this one. With reluctance, he submitted to the invitation and took the seat after making his way slowly to it, half-expecting to be bitten along the way. The Baraan carried an air of confidence and of being in total control. *Is he putting on a ruse, or is this one filled with that much confidence?* Aren didn't know which, but it made a difference to any plans he might work to gain his freedom. He dared say the Baraan acted with arrogance, smugness, and with a certain confidence that made Aren wonder of the authority that he carried. He concluded he must proceed carefully. Very carefully.

"Now . . ." the Baraan continued as if their conversation was not interrupted, "tell me of these gems."

Aren glanced to the dark inner room now at his back to see what was to jump out at him. The darkness mingled with the odor of suffering, both past and recent, setting his mind in a place he didn't want it to be. His skin crawled, and his stomach soured. He couldn't suppress a shiver that was visible to the Baraan. Aren needed to weave a believable story, but one with only enough truth to hide the truth. "I took them from a merchant passing through Windsong."

"Why would you take such things . . . when it's obvious to anyone's eye you didn't need them?" Aren could barely make out the wry smile the Baraan gave as he inquired. He too now sat on a stool of his own he pulled from the shadows. The Baraan's eyes looked black with a shine reminding Aren of metal, difficult to see . . . difficult to read.

"I have needs!" Aren shot back almost playfully, hoping to insinuate he needed coin and would use the gems to that end. *Be careful . . . This one is reading much more than my words.*

The Baraan smiled openly. "And what *needs* could an Evendiir of your youth have?"

Yes . . . what needs? Aren gave the Baraan a puzzled look meant to throw him off and give him time to fabricate the next piece of his tale. A half-truth came to him. "I wish to travel to Padusan and learn the ways of the sages."

"And what domain of sage do you wish to be?" The Baraan asked with half of that smile now, but let Aren know with his question he was knowledgeable of the sages.

"I wish to study in the ways of the Ancients." Another half-truth. Aren only wanted to be studied enough in the ways of the Ancients to rid himself of these damnable colored symbols . . . and get rid of that voice that sometimes talks to him in whispers.

"The Ancients?" The Baraan mused with a rub of his bearded chin. "They're long *lightless.* What could be so interesting of them for you to decide on thieving so you could become a respected Evendiir?"

Aren didn't have a quick answer. He needed a bit of time to figure out how to respond. *How do I answer? How close to the truth do I get?*

"What of the gems?" the Baraan asked simply.

"Lucufaar wants to know why it no longer shines . . ." Aren broke off his answer. Tricked. *You idiot*, he chastised himself. *Got me thinking of something else, but not far enough away from the truth I wouldn't answer him in my distraction.*

"Care to tell me more of this gem that no longer shines?" the Baraan politely asked.

"That's not my first thought," Aren replied with the realization he had been caught in his fabrication . . . and so quickly. That latter thought angered Aren more than causing him fear at being discovered in a lie. He felt an uncontrolled urge to be defiant. "Or my second."

The Baraan's playful demeanor turned dark. "Where did you get this *gem* from?"

When Aren didn't answer immediately, the Baraan continued with some heat in his voice. "No matter. I'll find answers in Windsong and those that find playing with such shiny things in defiance of the law."

Aren felt his blood freeze. *No . . . Father did nothing wrong. How do I keep this one from family? No . . . not my father.*

"What will you give me . . . do for me to keep my feet out of Windsong?" The Baraan asked in an even voice with clearly spoken words so Aren would understand his meaning.

Aren felt trapped. Those damnable symbols started flying and twirling about fast in his head making it difficult for him to think things through . . . figure a way out of this without involving his father. Guilt washed over him. *I've done enough to Father. No more. His disappointment will be the least of my worries if this one hunts him down.*

"What do you want of me?" Aren replied in a voice hinting of defeat. The thought of being bested by this one . . . bested by anyone, caused bile to rise in his throat.

The Baraan kept a serious face and his calm tone returned. "Simple. Keep your ears listening concerning your new prison mates. I want to know who they are, and what meaning they hold for their captors. Keep silent of our chewing this hide."

Aren didn't like how this session of chewing worked out. *Those ropes would have been better. At least it would be over when the questioning ended.*

"Are we at an understanding, young Aren?" The Baraan asked, using his name for the first time. Aren's response was to nod his agreement. The Baraan smiled broadly as he rose from his stool. "When you have information, ask your jailers for the *Subar*."

The *Subar* called the waiting *Sake* jailers, instructing them to feed Aren, then return him to his cell. Aren rose from his stool not fully understanding the "arrangement" thrust upon him and now was part of. He did understand his situation was a dangerous thing, and he needed to keep his head about him and watch his tongue. His world was changing by the moment with no way to determine where it was going, but at least he would get to eat. His stomach growled.

Chapter 14

As an Ear and Eye

A ren's belly felt full and his attitude much improved, even for being held prisoner without reason and the questioning and those symbols continuing to taunt him. His jailers fed him from their servings of pleasant-smelling tanniyn and beans instead of the unappealing gruel left-overs given to the jailed. Whatever the *"Subar"* is, the *Sake* jailer-guards and *Tusaa'Ner* guardsmen either respected or feared the authority he carried. *Maybe I can use this*, Aren thought. His jailers even allowed him to wash his feet with clean rags and clean, bloodherb-treated water. Though the stinging remained and his scraped toes looked bad, Aren no longer feared a raging infection and walked with an improved gait. Still, he didn't see the need in his captors taking his sandals when they locked him in. *The jailers aren't intelligent enough to know what I could make from them.* As he walked the corridors, Aren noticed all those jailed were barefoot. *Maybe these jailers are more experienced than intelligent.*

Aren winched in pain at those damnable symbols spinning in his head, staggering a step before catching himself at the flood of images hitting all at once. They made no sense to him. The colorful symbols had been there since he woke and upon occasions during the day, they roared large in his mind before settling back to an intensity he was able to put into the back of his head. His jailers only glanced at him as they escorted him back to his cell. When they turned him down a long hallway leading back to his prison bed they dragged him from earlier, Aren heard voices . . . arguing. *What's going on in that room?* He wondered. Surprising to him and much to his relief, those symbols faded as he approached the door to the cell room. *Strange . . .* Upon his jailers opening the door, a strong odor of sweat and unwashed bodies and a scene of anger struck him. Not between the *Sakes* and the prisoners, but between the prisoners themselves.

The Baraan elders were standing at the bars between the cells with pale-knuckled hands gripping iron berating the young Tellen about somehow getting them all involved in unclean Tellen affairs. The young Tellen was sitting with his back to the stone wall of his cell, the cell door evidently repaired and now locked. Rogaan was doing little to defend himself except for an occasional useless attempt in trying to correct something accused. The youngling Baraan was more involved in defending the Tellen from his own parents, but found himself verbally put down each time he tried to defend who Aren surmised was his friend. The two jailers standing next to the doors to the room wore amused smiles at the spectacle. They seemed to take pleasure in the sufferings of their prisoners. Aren wasn't amused. This bunch was going to ruin what little he had of a good mood with all their bickering. Aren noted the older Tellen, Mithraam, was absent. *Where did they take the old one?*

A firm hand in his back caused Aren to stumble halfway across the room. When he glared back at his jailers, he found contemptuous glares and satisfied sneers staring back at him.

"Put yur eyes to the floor, pointy ears," his jailer escort demanded.

"Pointy ears?" Aren's anger exploded without a warning as he cast a burning glare at the jailers. "Telling me to cast my eyes down, you half-witted dung-shoveler—"

Suddenly, Aren found himself on the floor with a throbbing head and numb left arm. He looked up from his sprawled position to find the jailer standing at the door glaring down at him with a mix of anger and disgust.

"Keep your tongue or I'll cut it out," the jailer threatened while imposing himself over Aren.

"You half-witted idiot." Aren started another insulting rebuke with the intent to involve invoking of the *Subar* to get them to back off. The jailer was having none of it, however, sending a sandaled foot into Aren's ribs. "Oomph . . ."

Silence fell over the room as Aren curled up in pain holding his ribs. After several moments, he took in a breath that allowed him to clear his head of the exploding sparks of lights. A click and a squeal from somewhere left him wondering what was happening. He felt himself hauled up with unkind hands and tossed. Before he could get his feet under him, he slammed onto floor stones. "Oomph . . ."

Aren lay in a dazed pain where he landed, trying to recover. He lay suffering with what he considered a silent dignity as throbbing waves of pain shot through his ribs, shoulders, and foggy head. He wished his physical strength greater to keep brutes like these idiots from dominating him, or that he could teach them a lesson in never touching him again. Aren's frustration burned. He hated being defenseless, helpless . . . not in control of his own being. Unexpectedly, he felt hands pulling at him. Fear shot through him anticipating what he was to suffer. He held his breath waiting to be struck on his head, back, or other places, or to be tossed to the floor again. Instead, Aren felt himself being propped up against the back wall of the cell. When he opened his eyes, he found the young Tellen hovering over him, making sure he would not flop over. When he appeared satisfied, this Rogaan sat down with his back to the wall next to Aren.

Aren tasted blood in his mouth. A quick inspection with his finger told him his lower lip bled. His frustration turned to anger, yet he kept it within himself. His jailers wouldn't care if he lost his composure in an explosion of anger. They may even see such a display as their victory. He admitted there was nothing he could do to them . . . now. *There will come a time when they regret their treatment of me this day.*

"Why did ya have her follower ya?" The mother of the young Baraan woman-child asked. At first, Aren thought she was just bereaved and asked the question without truly seeking an answer, but when he looked up at her he found a shaken and distressed woman tightly gripping the bars between their cells and eyes aflame with anger. She bore all of her focus on the young Tellen. The woman's husband clearly wore anger on his face as he slowly paced the far side of their cell. The young Baraan cautiously watched his mother as if afraid of what she might say or do. "She be innocent until she laid eyes ta ya."

"I have not dishonored, Suhd," the young Tellen replied with a hint of restrained anger in his tone. "Never would I."

"Den why did dey take me little one away?" The Baraan woman had tears streaming down her dirt-stained tan cheeks. "Why? Why . . . Rogaan . . . son ta da Mithraam da forger or whatever he supposes ta call himself dese days."

"Ma—" the young Baraan made to say something before being cut off by the combined glares from both his parents. For a moment, Aren thought the young dark-haired Baraan was going to defend the Tellen . . . his friend, before getting those scornful looks that shut him up.

"Dis be all ya fault . . . Tellen." The Baraan spoke at the young Tellen . . . Rogaan. "Suhd had no need ta follow off after ya. Ya should have pushed her away. Now she be gone with dem doin' da unthinkable ta her."

Rogaan gritted his teeth as they continued to accuse him of doing everything to destroy their daughter's life. He had the look of one seeing things in his head and not liking it. The Baraan woman quit her accusations and went back to just weeping. Their black-haired son stood leaning against the stone wall of their cell brooding with arms folded across his chest. Rogaan brooded as well, but something more than just the woman-child being taken or her parents blaming him seemed to be gnawing at him. His fuming anger appeared to be inwardly focused instead of at the woman-child's parents. *He blames himself.* Aren didn't know how he could use this, so he put it away in his memory for maybe a future use.

Aren shook off his concern for the others after he realized he was getting drawn into their troubles. He had his own troubles and needed to think of a way out. He pondered his situation and options for some time, running multiple future events through his head to see . . . think through, where they would lead. All led back to giving the *Subar* what he wanted. He had to play along with his assigned task as eyes and ears, observant to what these Tellens and Baraans were about and convey that to him. If he could get the *Subar* to remove him from this cell, he would have a chance to flee, but Aren couldn't figure out an excuse as yet for being liberated that he would find believable.

In the midst of his deep thoughts, the Baraan parents went at the young Tellen again, this time with plenty of words speaking to their unhappiness with the young-one's smithing father. This time, the young Baraan made better attempts at defending his Tellen friend, but in the end, was berated back by his parents into a brooding silence. Aren learned much from the exchange. The parents spared few accusations concerning the older Tellen . . . Mithraam. They spoke of his meddling in town affairs as an outsider and of his defiant acts against the town and of his secretive and sinister associations with the dark robes. *The Ebon Circle . . . What do they have to do with this Mithraam?* That last accusation provoked the young Tellen to the defense of his father before the Baraan parents turned the argument back to the young woman-child now in the hands of the *Sakes*. The young Tellen was silenced at the insinuation of Suhd being mishandled and that . . . Rogaan was the cause of it. Aren's attention piqued at the talk of associations with the "dark robes." Could this be the Ebon Circle whose temple looms in the lands south of Brigum? The same Ebon Circle his father had associations with and from where Aren suspected came the Agni stone that touched his mind and was now in the hands of his questioners. An anxious flush of worry swept over Aren. *Whispering to the Subar of Tellen associations with the Ebon Circle might well lead to discovering those of my father's and me.*

More accusing words poured at the Tellen. Hurtful words spoken in anger by the parents worried for their young woman-child. They had no way to take out their angst on those truly responsible, so Rogaan took the brunt of their emotions. The young Tellen kept surprisingly silent, sitting, staring at the floor in front of him. *I'd not take that abuse from anyone*, Aren admitted to himself. No new revelings were forthcoming in the continuous berating they gave Rogaan. With no new information, their rants became irritating to Aren, and . . . they still kept at it. Aren grew more irritated the longer it went on; even the guards who had been grinning earlier were now showing signs of annoyance. Aren's irritation was not so much that the Tellen just took the verbal pummeling without responding, but they were repeating themselves such that they were now interrupting his thinking. *Intolerable!* Aren couldn't take it any longer.

"Silence!" Aren repeated himself when the Baraan parents didn't comply with his first command to shut up. "Silence, all of you fools. How can anyone think with you jabbering on about things beyond your reach?"

The room went silent. Aren looked around, wanting them all to understand he would tolerate no more. The guards kept silent, but wore surprised, yet pleased expressions. Rogaan looked at Aren from under raised eyebrows with thankful eyes and a relieved half smile. The young Baraan . . . Pax, from the back of his cell mouthed with rolled eyes what Aren thought was "thank the Ancients." The mother stared at Aren shocked, as if she was seeing him for the first time. The father responded differently than the rest. He carried anger all about him and looked as someone about to do foolishness to satisfy his emotions.

"Ya pointy-ear judger," the Baraan father started with venom thick on his tongue. "Ya no tell me or me family ta be silent. It be ya kind dat causes troubles. Holdin' ya selves above all and dinkin' ya have a right ta judge us. Ya kind has no rights ta question us."

Pointy-ear? . . . The insult burned at Aren until he heard little else. First, his captors insulted his kind and him, more importantly, and now this low-witted lout. Without thinking things through, Aren leapt to his feet and grabbed through the bars at the older Baraan with the intent to painfully flick his head with sharp fingernails as a warning to stop insulting him. Despite the Baraan's surprise at the Evendiir's boldness, he side-slipped Aren's swipe and caught his arm with heavily calloused hands. *Oops* was all Aren could think of in that moment. He was not so careless, normally, but everything . . . the cryptic symbols, the burning ropes, the teasing puzzles, the painful torments, the spinning colors, and the insults all got to him. The angry Baraan then twisted the arm he had a strong grip on, causing Aren to cry out in pain. Aren tried, but couldn't pull free. Yanking and further twisting, the Baraan painfully slammed Aren's face into the bars while snarling as if he meant to pull Aren's arm out of socket. Aren realized he was in serious trouble and cursed himself for losing control so easily, but now . . . how to get out of this predicament . . . with his arm still attached? Frantically, Aren sought to pull his arm free of the Baraan's powerful grip, but failed with every try.

"Release me!" Aren angrily demanded.

Bracing himself with his body close to the bars to improve his leverage, the Baraan readied his whole body to pull on Aren's arm. Panic welled up in the pit of Aren's stomach, making it difficult for him to concentrate and think his way out of this predicament. Aren wasn't a match for the Baraan, physically. Intellectually, Aren knew he was more than able to put this low-wit in his place. *What was I thinking when I stuck my arm through the bars?* Aren admonished himself. He thought to beg for his arm. *No! I've done nothing wrong.* His thoughts then turned to pleading. *Yes. But I must take care not to sound as a beggar. This lout owes me an apology.* Aren felt a strong pull on his arm. He realized it was too late to speak words to secure his freedom. He held his breath and closed his eyes and braced and grimaced, ready to feel his arm and shoulder separate. He waited. And he waited. Those powerful calloused hands still held him fast, but didn't pull hard. Aren peeked open an eye. The Baraan gripped him with his body pressed against the bars, straining with a pained expression, trying to pull with all his might, but a tanned hand extended by a thick forearm gripped the Baraan's wrist keeping him from his intended work. Aren looked to his right and found the young Tellen, his arm stretched to the shoulder through the bars and his hand around the older Baraan's wrist, stalemating him. Shocked and relieved, Aren exhaled, then breathed in deeply and with tears welling up in his eyes he commented. "Uhhgggg . . . you all smell horrible. When did you last bathe?"

Ignoring Aren, the young Tellen grunted and pulled the gritted teeth Baraan to the bars. A genuine shocked expression took over the Baraan's face. Suddenly, arms of the young Baraan wrapped around his father's shoulders. The younger one's eyes were filled with concern and sadness . . . yes, sadness, Aren noted.

"Da," the young Baraan spoke with an unexpected stern kindness. "Ya can no do this. He's done nothin'. And I be seein' dat look in Rogaan's eyes. He not be lettin' ya go until ya let go of dis one."

Moments passed; long, painful moments for Aren. The older Baraan's face softened as he released his grip on Aren. Rogaan slowly released his hold on his elder. The Baraan immediately took hold of his wrist, wincing at his own touch on bruised skin.

"Stay away from me and me family, Pointy-ears," the older Baraan warned with a spat to punctuate his words. "And da same for ya, Rogaan. Ya be no longer welcomed in our family."

Aren backed away from the bars to ensure he wasn't caught up in another squabble between the Baraans and Rogaan. Rubbing his stinging wrist, Aren went to his spot and sat down with knees drawn up to his chest and his back against the brick wall. *I've got to keep myself from being careless. No more grabbing others, even if they're idiots. Use your tongue, Aren . . . Use your tongue.*

The Baraan father and Rogaan stared at each other for a long while, each wearing a determined air more than hinting of their unwillingness to give in to each other. Rogaan broke their silent standoff with a dismissive shrug, then sat down an arm's length from Aren. The Tellen looked in a brood . . . no, in an anger, Aren assessed, but wasn't sure who he was angry at.

The Baraans quieted down with only the occasional sniffle and sob coming from the mother. They kept to themselves for a time with only an occasional whisper between them. That young Baraan stood leaning against the back wall, looking fouled as if he swallowed a pond jumper. The guards too were quiet . . . finally . . . Aren felt happy at that. No noise coming from the cells or surroundings, and no spinning symbols or puzzles in his head. He leaned back against the wall, relaxing for the first time in a long while since he could recall.

He rested his eyes, closing them for a time while enjoying the quiet. Relieved of the pain and chaos in his mind, he started realizing just how badly he had felt. *What rid me of those symbols?* His mind calmed as his thoughts returned to the moment those spinning symbols left him. *Strange that the puzzle symbols left me when these new prisoners arrived.* The symbols had tormented his mind since he first touched the double-ax enwrapped, flame-shaped red gemstone. Aren then chastised himself for touching the thing when he took it from his father's study hideaway. The gemstone, truly an aged Agni stone, a gem of power likened to the kind used in temples of old by *Kabiris* and, if legend spoke truth, the Ancients themselves. Aren suspected the stone to be something like what it turned out to be when he found his father handling it so carefully, never touching it with his naked hands. Aren's uncontrollable curiosity at things unknown made him careless, blinding him to ancient dangers and bestowing upon him the pain and torment of those symbols spinning in his head ever since he woke from the flagstone floor of the study almost a full moon ago. Fearing his father's wrath, and worse, his disappointment in him, Aren snuck from their home with the gemstone carefully wrapped in a cloth seeking undisturbed time to figure out how to undo what he had done. Tucked away in his favorite hiding spot, Aren had only a brief opportunity to investigate the thing before a tall cloaked Evendiir he had seen engaged in discussions with his father earlier approached him speaking a tongue he didn't understand. Aren recalled a painful flash, then no memory of things until he found himself staggering at the northern gate of Farratum . . . a long way from his home in Windsong and his father.

Since the day Aren stepped foot into Farratum, he sought help, but no one offered beyond the occasional soup or bread meal. The streets had been his home with him doing little better than surviving. Aren's reluctant attempts to journey home and offer himself and his misdeeds to his father all failed. Usually, he found himself recovering in a dark place after blacking out. And, each time the painful intensity of those tormenting spinning symbols worsened, sometimes leaving him incapacitated. The last time he awoke, he found himself picked up by the street watch who brought him to this prison after they discovered his Agni stone. They were convinced Aren stole a rather expensive jewel, but when they handled the gemstone, bad things happened to them. After several incidents where guards were left with only half a mind, those questioners paid him the first of a handful of unpleasant visits seeking knowledge of the how, what, and where of the Agni stone he possessed. Aren was convinced the taller of his questioners knew or suspected the jewel more than its simple description. That questioner spent too much focus and time asking of it. He was persistent, if not relentless. And then, there were those cursed spinning symbols traveling along patterns in his head, seeming to tease, dare him to solve a riddle he didn't know existed . . . until recently, just before his capture. *What has rid me of the symbols? The answer is here; it has to be.*

Aren looked about his cell, the adjacent cells, and the room. *What is it about this place . . . ?* He looked for anything out of place or unique. Nothing. Even the material the room and cells were made of looked commonplace, if not well made. He looked over the guards. These four in the room were new, but dressed in dark uniforms near identical to those they replaced . . . more *Sakes*. Aren found nothing about them different than when he was first hauled into prison and thrown into this cell. He had suffered the symbols then. Painfully. It wasn't until these newcomers were thrown into the cells with him that he felt relief from the symbols for the first time. And this morning, the symbols returned as the distance between him and the newcomers grew. His return to this cell resulted in the opposite . . . the spinning, throbbing symbols retreated from him the closer he came back to the cells and the newcomers. The older Tellen was absent, and so were the symbols, so nothing about him, Aren concluded. Aren focused on the younger Tellen and the Baraans. *What about them?*

Aren silently studied the Baraans for a while, looking for anything. They seemed just a typical family thrust into a very bad situation and not knowing what to do about it. Aren surveyed everything about them; clothing, mannerisms, interactions with each other, even scars and skin paintings. Nothing stood out of them except that the skin paintings of swimming animals, sails, and entwined ropes on the father looked similar to those he observed on riverfolk down at Farratum's wharfs. Yet, the Baraan and his family were from Brigum from what Aren learned from listening to them so far . . . and it's landlocked. *No river to speak of there. There's something more to him, though.* Aren dismissed that thought, then took interest in the others. Nothing else appeared out of the ordinary concerning the Baraan or his family. Turning his scrutiny on Rogaan, Aren quickly saw that he was Tellen, but of mixed blood. Taller, slightly leaner of body, lighter skin, less thick of a beard than that proudly worn by Tellens he knew of. His hair was typical Tellen in color . . . dark, but not as coarse . . . more of a Baraan's hair. His muscles and strength displayed in defense of that young woman-child was Tellen and more. *This one is strong, maybe stronger than most I know except maybe the smiths in Sital. Yet, he doesn't braggingly toss his strength in the face of others as most Tellens would.* Aren observed the young Tellen . . . the mixed blood . . . Rogaan . . . looking all wounded in head or heart or both, but Aren noted that he appeared aware of everything around him, alert and watching and thinking.

"Wish you would stop looking at me in that way." Rogaan spoke in a low voice that sounded like a light rock slide.

Aren felt warm as a nervous surge rippled through him, causing his arms and fingers to twitch. The Tellen . . . Rogaan . . . had been watching him. Recovering quickly and not wanting to sound as if in the wrong, Aren asked a question. "How so?"

"As if I am a caged animal," Rogaan continued. "Like the strange ones merchants bring to town in their caravans and demand coin to see. You know, the ones they never let out of their cages."

"I meant nothing of it," Aren attempted a halfhearted apology. *This one thinks. And with strength . . . a dangerous combination.* He decided to try sounding as if befriending him, to find out more of him and the others, and use what he learned to help himself escape this place. "My name is Aren."

Rogaan looked at him as if considering how he should respond. A moment passed that left Aren uncertain of the young Tellen . . . Rogaan was considering to be civil or hit him. The young Tellen finally replied, "I am Rogaan, son of Mithraam."

Aren quietly exhaled with relief. No fist to the head. He followed this opening by engaging Rogaan in small talk for some time, learning a little of what brought him and the Baraans to Farratum and jail. Aren did so, he thought, without revealing much of himself except where he came from and what his captors did to him. For as insightful and intelligent as Rogaan unknowingly showed himself to be, Aren still considered him a Tellen and not as so capable as himself in reasoning and thought. Aren skillfully guided their talk. He discovered Rogaan's home was Brigum. His father a rather capable smith with an interest in the affairs of others . . . *Good to be aware the older Tellen has a penchant for putting his nose where it doesn't belong.* And that Rogaan's mother was an Isin. A mixed coupling of Tellen and Baraan. *That must be an interesting family gathering.* Isin, the friendlier of the Houses in the western reaches of Shuruppak and one at odds with House Lagash, as Aren recalled from secretly listening in on his father's conversations. Aren had no liking of Lagash. Many troubles in Windsong and Farratum were said to lie at the door of that House. He had no direct interaction with Lagash and hoped he never would. Still . . . being in good with House Isin could prove advantageous, Aren mused. *But what would they want of me?* Aren also unveiled Rogaan's liking of the bow . . . and if the Tellen was anything close in the truth of his word, a very good shot with one. More information the young Tellen freely spoke . . . Rogaan's friend in the other cell, Pax, has known Rogaan for years, but Pax and his family came from another place his friend and family have never shared. *They must be lawbreakers hoping not to be discovered. Too late for that.* And that the young woman-child, Suhd, is sister to Pax and a weakness for Rogaan and, from their behaviors, the rest of them. Rogaan's enthrallment with her got him in much trouble . . . even killed a guard. *That won't go well for him. And her family will likely suffer over her as well.* Rogaan was less easy with specifics of how they got themselves into tangles with Farratum law, finding themselves here with Aren. It had something to do with Rogaan's father . . . that story the young Tellen left unclear. *That'll teach the old Tellen and his nose a thing and some.*

For all his guiding of their talk, Aren discovered little to help him unravel the mystery of his taunting symbols or gain his freedom. He worked the discussion with Rogaan keeping him engaged in less intrusive subjects while slowly probing for anything that would lead to information Aren could use. The two talked on and off for what seemed to be hours, much to the concerned and jealous eye of his friend Pax. The young Baraan never spoke or tried to join them . . . likely out of fear he would provoke another tirade from his parents. But that one had signs of being both intelligent and cunning, if not protectively respectful of his family. Try he did, but Aren uncovered little else from Rogaan that he thought could help him. When Rogaan asked of Aren's past, he answered in vague images, never giving specifics on his life in Windsong.

Four *Sake* guards entered the room relieving the ones watching them with a short exchange of talk. A telling of the time passing quicker than Aren expected. *If my interrogation was in the morning, as I suspect, then it should be near the supper hour with this changing of the guards.* The new guards came in fresh and mean, prodding in front of them what Aren suspected were other prisoners dressed in dirty tunics carrying buckets and rough cloth sacks. With all four guards pointing weapons at Rogaan, the cells were opened and cleaned after they were carefully ushered out. Chamber pots, wafting stink, were emptied into larger buckets the fouled prisoners dragged into the cell room. It was neat and orderly. Once the cells were cleaned, Aren and the others were shoved back into the cells before all left except for two guards who stolidly took up positions watching over them. Aren observed a change in demeanor of the Baraans. They had become docile. Had they succumbed and given up? The young Tellen still looked as if a fire burned just underneath his controlled mannerisms. When Aren returned he took his spot leaning against the back wall, then started asking questions of Rogaan again.

"Why didn't you use this guard change and cell cleaning to your advantage?" Aren asked in a curious tone. "You're more than able enough to overpower one, maybe more of the guards and gain your freedom. With the help of your Baraan friend and his father, I would think your chances good . . . given how easy these *Sakes* break when you hit them."

Rogaan looked at Aren assessing him with intelligent eyes awhile before answering in a matter-of-fact tone, "Suhd and my father are in unknown hands. It would do me no good getting free to find myself in the streets and outside this place where I might be unable to learn of their fates."

Aren smiled to himself. This one sounds confident and determined in his unwillingness to leave his family and love behind. *There's more to him than at first sight . . . He's loyal or at least thinking on how to solve his problems.*

"Silence!" One of the darkly armored guards demanded in an unfriendly tone.

Aren felt the urge to strike at the idiot with some quick-tongued insults . . . that the Baraan would likely not understand, but Rogaan's eyes caught his with a look of "Do not press them." Aren thought for a moment before settling back against the wall, agreeing with Rogaan that his tongue might make things worse. Prudence considered, Aren still felt the nagging urge to give out that tongue-lashing.

Not long after Aren and Rogaan were commanded into silence, footfalls and ringing chains approached from the hallway. The metal-bound wood door on his left opened. A stumbling Tellen entered the room in a ruckus of metal clanging. It was Rogaan's father . . . Mithraam, looking a bit worked over by his exhausted face and new bruising on his arms that Aren saw through the Tellen's soiled and gray torn tunic. Rogaan jumped to his feet, grabbing the cell bars so hard that Aren thought he bent them a little. Rogaan's father wearily held up his hands in a palms-exposed manner that held fast his son. Two more darkly armored guards followed the old Tellen in the room escorting him into their cell. Mithraam said nothing as he plopped himself down against the cell's bars near the door with the help of his son. After Rogaan received a reassuring yet weary squeeze on his forearm from his sitting father, the young Tellen snapped up in a fume, stepping into the point of a long dagger held out between the door bars by the biggest of the guards.

"Not smart, stoner," the guard sneered while pushing the dagger tip a little firmer into Rogaan's chest. "Yur next when I come back."

Rogaan held his tongue as the guard finished locking the door before turning and walking away without a seeming care. Aren expected Rogaan to be more hotheaded and to do something dumb, but understood better his self-restraint when he saw his father's bloodied hand grasping his son's boot.

"All things need to reveal themselves." Mithraam spoke weakly before falling unconscious. Aren noted Rogaan's confused look. *So, the old Tellen is keeping secrets even from his son.*

Chapter 15

Voices in the Shadows

Ribbons of fog crawled across the roots of creepers, laurels, and oaks blanketing the soggy bottom of the low pass. Misty tendrils reached for him as if they had sentient intent. Confused, Aren looked about and asked aloud, "What is this place? How did I get here?"

Advancing misty tendrils were almost upon him, forcing him to back away . . . away from this living fog. His sandaled feet squished in soft moist soil. Aren's skin crawled. The air felt thick and wet, and smelled stale. Tendrils reaching out from the living fog moved in every direction, though the ones moving forward behaved as if seeking him. Aren couldn't explain how he knew they sought him, but he did. He just knew it. He retreated southward down the pass with the misty tendrils relentlessly in pursuit. Aren's foot caught something, a rock or a root, sending him tumbling down the pass. When he stopped rolling, he didn't feel injured, just vulnerable lying on the ground. His heart quickened. *What is chasing me?* He rose and slipped on the moist earth, falling to the ground again. Panic grabbed him as he mentally calculated the mist to almost be upon him. Looking up from his prone position, Aren caught sight of the first tendril slithering its way over a large raised oak root not more than a few strides away. His heart skipped a beat. His arms and legs betrayed him as he commanded his body to rise and run. Nothing. He remained lying on the ground watching the vaporous tendrils reach out to him. They were close, almost on him. Symbols suddenly blazed from within the vapors. Those spinning tormentors formed in the tips of now a dozen vaporous tendrils an arm's length away, calling to him, craving to touch him. Aren felt helpless as he rose to his knees just as the first vaporous tendril touched him. A shiver rippled through him at the slimy cold feel of the tendril wrapping itself around his right arm. Another took him on his left arm. Another around his waist. The slimy sensation turned to a painful burning of his flesh. Aren grunted in pain as he saw and felt those

symbols being burnt into the flesh on both his arms. More tendrils advanced
. . . many more. Aren realized his doom had arrived from the Pit of Kur
itself. He made to scream for someone—anyone—to help him as his world
plunged into a freezing darkness.

"What did you do to him?" A familiar deep voice asked out of the
darkness.

"I quieted his thoughts," an unfamiliar voice, equally as deep, answered.

"How can I be sure he is untouched by *darkness*?" Aren recognized the
voice as Rogaan's.

"Rogaan—" Another deep voice, familiar to Aren, sounded disappointed
and chastising.

"He has much to learn," the unfamiliar voice interrupted in a matter-
of-fact tone.

Aren struggled trying to open his eyes, but his body wasn't doing what
he wanted. A swell of panic rose within him. *What's wrong with me?*

"This one I know," the unfamiliar voice said. "He's Larcan's young one.
Aren is his name, as I recall."

He knows me? I don't know his voice. I'm at a disadvantage. Panic swelled
again in Aren. This time it gripped his innards and wouldn't let go. Aren felt
at the voice's complete mercy . . . at the mercy of everyone. It unnerved
him. He grunted in another attempt to open his eyes. He found his arm
responding, moving, but awkwardly. He raised his hand to his face expecting
to use his fingers to help open his eye, but found them open when he felt
the sting of his touch to his right eye. *I'm blind!* Panic swept through Aren.
"I can't see! I'm blind!"

"You made him blind?" Rogaan spoke with a trepid anger.

"Speak with respect, Rogaan." Aren recognized the older Tellen's voice
. . . Mithraam. "You have debt to him through me. If you had followed my
guidance, you would be safe and away from here."

"It's only for a short time," the unfamiliar deep voice reassured. "It
happens when a mind needs calming and fights against it. Especially a
troubled mind . . . as I feel he has."

Silence filled the air for a long moment. Aren feared somehow they all
vanished . . . or worse, planned to harm him in his weakness. Maybe this

new voice took them . . . maybe killed them or worse. *Am I next? What's to become of me? I can't see.* Anxiety at being totally helpless, sightless, rapidly grew into a storm. Fear gripped his innards in a way he never felt before. Aren reached out at the only one he thought might give him aid. He found the strong forearm of the young Tellen and grabbed it with all his strength. "Help me . . . Rogaan."

"Do fix him," Rogaan demanded with a still trepid voice.

Aren heard what could have been a low growl, but from nothing he knew of. His skin prickled as he felt his sweat wet his chest and neck. Then, with an angry tone, he heard Rogaan speak more forcefully, "He's helpless and looks to have suffered much already. Cure what you did to him."

"Rogaan . . ." Mithraam spoke with a hint of anger and a lot of disappointment. "Speak carefully."

"His sight will return without another touch of the stone," the deep voice spoke with authority. "I hold Rogaan in no debt, my friend. At least none, yet. Besides, it's refreshing to hear bold words make demands of me these days instead of the usual cowering and groveling displayed by those who speak with me."

A ripple of fear shot up Aren's spine, almost as if from a bolt of lightning. Sweat now soaked his chest, arms, neck, and brow. *"Touch of the stone". . . no . . . He couldn't have meant he used Agni powers on me! Cowering . . . groveling . . . Who is this one, and what did he do to me?* A fog appeared to Aren's eyes. He no longer lived in pitch blackness. The fog grew into a hazy light . . . no, two. They blurred, along with multiple dark-moving shadows. The lights came into focus and for a moment hurt his eyes, causing him to blink tears away. The shadows too came into focus. One was Rogaan who Aren strangely felt thankful to see. The other two were Mithraam and . . . no! Fear overwhelmed Aren, shaking him head to toes as his breath escaped him. Moments passed before Aren could think. *Am I still alive?* He asked himself. He remained unmoving as he stared at the living legend kneeling in front of him . . . "*the one who cannot die*" . . . the "*Right-hand of Darkness.*"

"See what I speak of, ol' friend . . ." The "*Right-hand of Darkness*" talked with an off-sense of humor as he inspected Aren as if prey he wished to ensure was *lightless*. "Cowering. He'll be himself in a little time."

The dangerous warrior gracefully turned his attention back to Mithraam. Relief rolled over Aren that his eyes were no longer on him. The Baraan was big, though lean with muscles rippling under a heavily scarred tan-colored skin. His strong jaw was accentuated by a short, trimmed beard under his combed short black hair. He wore dark clothing; boots to short-sleeved shirt, making him difficult to see with any detail in the poor light of the underworld of the arena prison. Aren looked for, but wasn't able to see, any weapons the warrior carried. Stories of him told by his father always had him with weapons . . . lots of them. *Where are they?* The warrior's gaze, with those piercing green eyes, seemed to take in everything, periodically sweeping over him, giving Aren a deep chill, making him wish those eyes looked somewhere else.

"Are you able to sit up?" Rogaan's question intruded on Aren's doom-filled world, annoying him for some reason. Aren fought the urge to lash out at Rogaan for breaking into his terror. Aren then realized the thought to lash out was driven by his fear of the Dark Ax. Aren swallowed hard, then took in a small breath, then a chest full of air before exhaling long. His wits were returning to him, if only a little at a time. *I'm still alive.*

"Yes." Aren almost whispered, not wanting anyone else to hear him speak. He raised himself up with Rogaan's help. Aren found himself with his back leaning against the stone wall of the prison cell.

"You look terrible." Rogaan half smiled at Aren. He wasn't sure how to read the Tellen, but he seemed friendly. "Dark dreams had you tussling as you slept. You spoke of fog, arms reaching at you, and the mark of the *Evil One.*"

"Mark of the *Evil One?*" Aren repeated not wanting to believe he spoke His name. He nervously looked about the cell waiting for ill to befall him for simply speaking the name . . . twice. *Why would I speak of His mark? For that matter, what mark?*

"You look worse now than when you woke," Rogaan said in a kind and concerned way. "Are you ill?"

Aren didn't understand why Rogaan attended to him. *Why would a Tellen care anything of an Evendiir . . . me?* Aren's experience with Tellens left him with a suffering image of them being overconfident, boasting of their own deeds, and denigrating others, especially Evendiir. And they smelled bad. "I'm not ill, but I should be."

"Drink this then." Rogaan held up a cup of water to Aren's lips after he took it from a bucket that wasn't present in their cell earlier. "He brought us water after he put the guards to sleep. He never touched them. They just fell over."

Aren froze. More Agni powers. He felt his skin crawl at the thought of the power touching him. He shivered visibly, and he spilled some of the water from his cup before taking a drink. The ground shook as well. At first, Aren thought it was the power, but soon realized it was the ground itself. Another earth-shaking. Ignoring the tremor, Rogaan gave Aren a skeptical look, then waited for him to finish his water before motioning for another. Aren waved away another cup. His stomach did feel ill after all. He rested his head back against the wall, then fell into deep thoughts. *Agni powers . . . My father studies them, others use them . . . some to do good . . . some for their ends. Dangerous . . . no matter what the intent. Dangerous to everyone around, and more so to oneself.* Aren recalled his father's teaching concerning the Spirit of the Stone overtaking a person touching an Agni stone, overtaking . . . replacing the *Light* in their own body with that from the stone . . . Their *Light* never to be heard from again. The new "person" would look like the old person while suffering mannerisms both new and old. Most go crazy, and they either run off or are dealt with by locals . . . getting imprisoned or killed. *No . . . no Agni stone for me.* Spinning symbols flashed in Aren's mind, then disappeared a moment later. He felt disoriented and sick in the stomach.

Aren felt himself getting shook. He looked up to see Rogaan again, now with a deepening crinkled brow and with concern in his eyes. His lips moved, but Aren couldn't hear him at first. Rogaan's lips moved again. "Wake up."

The Tellen turned to his father and the "right hand of death" after another failed attempt to get Aren to respond. Aren could hear him, but his body felt unable to respond. Rogaan spoke again to the others. "I said he is not well. Can you heal him . . . undo what you did to him?"

A dark figure entered Aren's blurred vision, looking him over for what he didn't know. Is this the "right hand of death" . . . the dark warrior . . . Dark Ax? Fear swelled up inside of Aren. The dark warrior then laid his left hand on Aren's chest. A chill streamed through Aren touching him everywhere. It turned to a tingle, then to a burning of his flesh. Aren felt himself shake uncontrollably, then go limp. Whatever was done to him was painful and left him exhausted. Through it all, Aren's mind kept awareness of what was happening to him, but he couldn't get his arms or legs or anything else to move as he wanted. His frustration grew into panic, without any way to express it.

"Nothing wrong with him physically that some good sleep and a few meals won't fix," the dark warrior spoke to the others from somewhere above Aren.

Another chill racked Aren. This one cold instead of painful. A euphoric sensation passed over him, leaving Aren unsettled, mostly that his body wouldn't listen to his mind. The dark warrior's blurred image looked to be focusing, concentrating. Aren felt another touch to his chest. Pain seared his mind and his body worse. He convulsed as he struggled for breath. Nothing. Aren tried to inhale again, uncertain if air entered his lungs. He felt light-headed. *The "right hand of death" touched me with Agni powers again . . . I'm doomed.* Aren's blurred sight suddenly went dark. He could still hear voices as if listening to dull echoes. Now, his chest stung. *What's happening to me?* Air burst into his lungs taking the sting away, giving him much relief. His eyesight started to return, the darkness pushed back by the dim lantern light of the cell room.

"Something is troubling his thoughts I have little experience with," the dark warrior stated with a hint of concern, or maybe curiosity. "It has a firm hold on his mind."

"Would *he* be able to help this young one?" Mithraam asked.

"Possible," the dark warrior replied flatly. "It will be some time before *he's* able to give Aren aid."

Aren lay still on the floor with his eyes open looking upward. *How did I get on my back?* He could barely lift a hand off the floor. Exhaustion touched every part of him, and his head ached. *Never again will I disobey Father.* Aren noted for the first time the ceiling was solid rock with the metal pillars of the walls touching the ceiling, but only so to support the bars of their cage. Compacted wood boards filled the space between the ceiling and the metal frame of the cells. *Why is this important? It isn't you, idiot . . . focus your thoughts.* Aren tried to raise his head, but felt it weighing more than the whole world. Exhaustion bathed him. He decided to allow his strength to return some before trying that again. Aren turned his attention to listening to the spirited banter of the others.

"I disagree," the dark warrior's voice grumbled. "You and your son are not safe here. A Baraan of considerable skills . . . and powers is about. Someone unknown to us was following . . . . You all need to be away from this place."

Aren opened his eyes at the word "powers." He caught the dark warrior nodding toward Rogaan, though the young Tellen missed the reference to him as he was engaged in a heated whisper through the cell bars with the young Baraan. Dizziness and a mild urge to be sick forced Aren to close his eyes to concentrate on controlling his body.

Aren heard a gruff huff, from who he couldn't tell. Scuffling noise from the adjacent cell preceded a chorus of voices, all demanding to be freed. They sounded angry, desperate, accusing. Wanting to understand them and figure out what was going on, Aren focused to separate the individual voices and what they were saying, while peeking a little.

"Dis be ya doin', ya ol' Tellen," the Baraan father stated as fact and accusation.

"Our Suhd be taken from us cause of ya and ya youngling," the Baraan mother added.

"We be givin' an offer ta take us from dis place," the Baraan father half-explained, half-stated with a heated tone. His tone then turned kinder, softer, and almost apologetic as he looked to the dark warrior. "Can ya find our young one . . . our Suhd and free her?"

"Can ya?" The young Baraan asked. "Can ya find Suhd and take her ta be safe somewhere?"

"Suhd's freedom is what is important," Rogaan added to the pleas. "Will you save her?"

"I'll stay here if ya can see me young one free." The Baraan father offered himself in trade for the dark warrior to free his daughter.

Im'Kas and Mithraam exchanged unreadable glances without speaking.

An unbearable silence built every moment they did not respond in favor of liberating Suhd. Im'Kas briefly looked as if torn between wants and duties, then resumed his unreadable mask.

"She will have need to endure for the present," Mithraam stated simply as if telling them the sun had just risen in the morning. "I say this with a heavy heart, my son, but to free her is to raise attentions on everyone."

"No!" Rogaan and the Baraans spoke almost in unison.

"If what you have spoken of Suhd is true," Mithraam broke into their protests before they started, "she is strong and will endure any sufferings they can impose on her. They have limits under Shuruppak law."

"Is what they did to Suhd on that table their limits under the law?" Rogaan growled pointing to the wood table beyond the iron bars. "I will see Suhd free."

"No!" The young Baraan protested. "Ya be comin' with us. All of us gettin' from here."

"No one is to come or go," Mithraam spoke with authority, crushing everyone's hopes and mood. "There is more at stake than any of you are aware of."

"Dat no be for ya ta decide," the Baraan father declared.

"I beg ya, Master Protector," the Baraan mother pleaded with sniffles. "My little one be so precious. I can no think of her ruined by this bunch."

A long silence filled the air. It begged for Aren to sit up well enough to see what was happening. Everyone wore dark faces, their expressions gloomy, desperate, and troubled. Suhd's parents and brother looked to the dark warrior, hoping for a decision to help them. With his reputation of carnage, Aren was uncertain how they could ask him what they did, but desperate people do desperate things. Rogaan looked at the dark warrior with what seemed an anticipation that he'd agree to go after the woman-child. For some reason, he seemed confident the dark warrior would. The older Tellen . . . Mithraam . . . stood stolid. Aren couldn't read him. *He's well practiced at stifled emotions in such engagements. A disciplined one he is.* Unexpected by Aren, the dark warrior wore a troubled expression. *He does feel for others. Maybe there is more to him than his living legend reputation in the stories they tell of him.* The big Baraan stood motionless for a long time, appearing to weigh options, formulating plans, evaluating them, throwing them down when the thought through outcome turned less than desired, and starting all over thinking through near countless other actions. Aren understood the look of someone thinking a problem through, having already done the thinking he was now working through. There were no good options if motivations were for anything other than gaining freedom for everyone. The dark warrior made to speak after his expression turned determined. The old Tellen preempted him.

"Im'Kas . . . no, my friend." Mithraam spoke confident, unwavering, but kind with a hint of sympathy. "Some would use our escape to claim you as lawless. That cannot be so."

"My choice . . ." Im'Kas replied flatly.

"It is not, ol' friend," Mithraam corrected him. "It is *his*. We all agreed and gave our word. We are on a path of greater purpose that I will leave unspoken. Rogaan and I will survive. My son is strong."

Aren glanced at Rogaan straightening his back with what looked to be a rise of pride. He immediately felt jealous of Rogaan as Mithraam's words, meant as fact and not a boast, spoke of a father's confidence in his son. Loss then filled Aren's heart as he struggled to recall praise by his father. It was rare.

"The others . . . ," Im'Kas made to make an argument for them while not hiding his dissatisfaction at having his hands bound in this matter. "They're innocent."

"Yes . . . they are," Mithraam replied with sadness in his voice, but solid in his convictions. "They will have to endure, as well."

"Talk for ya own self," the Baraan father spit. "We be takin' da woodsman's offer ta get us out of here."

There was an uncomfortable silence as Mithraam exchanged uneasy glances with Im'Kas. With all things said and observed, Aren concluded the old Tellen and the dark warrior's relationship was complex. *Very unexpected. What could these two have in common? So much to discover, to understand.*

"You must leave us," Mithraam spoke quietly, too low for the Baraans to hear, but not so low that Evendiir ears would miss his words, "before you draw attention."

Im'Kas reluctantly nodded before exchanging unspoken words with Mithraam. Aren grew concerned as Im'Kas scanned the cells. *What did they just agree to?* Aren dared not blink. He felt certain something was about to happen . . . and he wanted nothing of it. The Baraans noticed the silent exchange too. A flurry of questions and accusations of betrayal erupted from the parents. Their son pleaded with Rogaan and Mithraam for the dark warrior to rescue his sister and take her and his parents from this place. With a look of resignation, the dark warrior raised his hand to his chest, to a chain holding a . . . . A chill ripped through Aren. *No! He's invoking the power.* Aren's skin crawled, and he felt it difficult to breathe. He spotted the gemstone . . . the Agni stone under the dark warrior's fingers when he pulled it from under his shirt. A shallow breath was all Aren could muster. A blue-violet flash under Im'Kas's hand, followed by a faint glow all about the room that slowly faded away hung over collapsed Baraans and Tellens. All fell. Aren wondered if they were now *lightless.* His chest grew tight and burned. He felt unable to breathe. Sweat streamed down his temples as he felt his chest grow damp. *Im'Kas is a Kiuri'Ner. How is it he wields the Agni, the Powers?*

"The manifestation is useful on all except long-ears," Im'Kas explained to no one, though Aren thought his tone more instructional than defensive. Aren looked about to see only he and the dark warrior were awake. Another shiver took hold of Aren. "They'll sleep for a time and will remember little of what's happened."

Aren kept silent while keeping his eyes fixed on the dark warrior. Fear swelled in him. He swallowed hard, afraid the power was to be used on him and uncertain of what was to come by its use. Agni powers . . . "manifestations" hung in the air. Aren could see them, their dissipating glow all about the room, though mostly in the cells. Briefly they illuminated the entire chamber, then dimmed.

"Then there's you," Im'Kas continued in an even, confident tone. "You'll remember. You'll remember me. That's the Evendiir mind. So . . . What am I to do with you?"

Aren feared to answer. His mind raced in all directions. Panic! He struggled to form a thought . . . answer the dark warrior's question. *What to do? What to say?* Im'Kas appeared to glide up to the bars closest to Aren. The dark warrior crouched bringing his eyes closer to Aren's. Aren felt near to losing his bowels.

"Son of Larcan," the dark warrior held Aren's eyes with his own as he spoke in a low voice, "can I trust you?"

Aren stared back blankly at the dark warrior, his thoughts still unable to organize. Aren just knew he was going to be harmed by the dark warrior and his Agni power. It terrified him. His muscles froze him in his sitting position, and his tongue felt as if it filled his whole mouth. Sweat poured down his face. The dark warrior touched his Agni stone. Aren felt as if a great hand clenched his heart, stopping it from beating. His vision blurred. *I'm fading.* Strange words from the dark warrior were spoken, whispered in truth. A chill washed over Aren. *Agni! No!* Aren's mind screamed, but no sound issued from his mouth. Gloom engulfed Aren. His thoughts dissipated. Darkness took him.

Chapter 16
Masks of Corruption

"Wake ya, skinny, pointy-eared crawler!" A distant and unfriendly voice demanded.

The words and the unkind tone carrying them preceded a rolling sensation. Confusion wrapped itself around Aren, but only until he opened one of his eyes. He woke to Ugly. A wrinkled and scarred face hidden behind unkempt gray whiskers. It held a satisfied smile.

"Sleepy?" Rotten teeth and a breathy stink instantly brought Aren fully awake.

Gagging, he scrambled into the corner of the cell, away from the old smelly Baraan. Looking up, Aren realized the wrinkly-face Baraan was the same dirty prisoner that cleaned their cells daily. He stood with a hunched posture in his filthy tunic, smiling. Aren felt unclean just looking at him. The fog of slumber still clouded his head, but started clearing some with that unsavory waking. Beyond, Aren found lightly armored guards snickering as they held Mithraam between them. The door to the cell opened. He caught a glimpse of a bound Rogaan being escorted from the chambers and down the hall Aren walked yesterday. *Or was it the day before? I'm having trouble separating the days.* The Baraans were awake, but strangely quiet as they sat clustered in their cell whispering to one another. Aren looked past the guards flanking Mithraam to find the familiar dark-armored guards at the doors to their larger room. *Did that really happen, or did I dream it?* Aren felt uncertain.

"Git him up," one of the new *Sakes* commanded.

"Ya meanin' me?" The filthy Baraan asked nervously.

"Yes . . . you old one," another of the guards confirmed gruffly. "And keep that piss pot from slopping. These two are goin' to the Hall."

Disoriented and shocked with his abrupt waking, Aren found himself being guided to his feet by the smelly old Baraan. Ripping his arm away Aren barked, "Remove your hands from me!"

The Baraan cowered from Aren as if expecting the prisoner to strike him. A pang of guilt hit Aren for causing the old Baraan to react so, then another inhale removed all his guilt as he wrinkled his nose at the offense wafting around him. An unintelligible whisper to Aren's right drew his attention. Looking for the whisperer, he found the Baraan family still sitting and keeping quiet. Aren dismissed the whisper as just a noise sounding like a voice.

A *Sake* guard pushed the old Baraan out of his way to take hold of Aren, then looked as if he wished he hadn't touched the creature. Wiping his hands on his lower tunic with a disgusted face, the guard then took hold of Aren before shoving him out of the cell. He and Mithraam were unceremoniously escorted into the hall Aren last saw Rogaan walking. They were taken to an alcove cut into the rock some two or three strides directly off the hallway. A raised rim on the floor separated the hallway from the inset alcove. The wet alcove floor looked uneven and had a grate in the center. Aren and Mithraam were shoved into the alcove together by their snickering escorts. They were stripped naked, then smacked in the face with ice-cold water when they turned around. The cold wetness shocked Aren's whole body and stole his breath. More cold water hit him, the guards openly laughed now. Aren managed a breath and some unflattering dancing and a lot of shaking in between three more buckets. He was soaked, cold, shivering, and angry. Looking to see how Mithraam fared, he found the wet Tellen an unreadable stone. *How's it the old Tellen isn't angry? And . . . not shivering? That's just not right.*

"Don't worry yurselves," one of the guards taunted, tossing to the floor a pair of gray tunics for them. "Yul dry out some on yur little walk."

Sakes ushered them down underground halls, many new to Aren. While walking side-by-side, Aren glanced at the Tellen. Mithraam showed no emotion. He remained unreadable. Aren wondered at his unbreakable self control, even after being ill-treated and soaked with ice water. Aren's anger still had hold of him at the mistreatment. A spinning symbol flashed in his head. *No! Not again.* A fist slammed into Aren's back, sending him stumbling forward before he got his feet under him. His back ached. A strong hand from behind then pushed him forward in the hall. Aren felt confused. Mithraam somehow now walked ahead of him. One of the guards cursed at him to get moving. Aren realized he must have lost a moment, stopping at the sight of the symbol. Another colored symbol spun in his mind's eye. More followed. *Please don't return,* Aren pleaded to no one in particular. *Why have they returned?*

The *Sakes* turned them down a long, high-arched tunnel of cut-stone walls. Lanterns lit the left wall as iron bars lined the right. Prison cells. Guards prodded Aren and Mithraam to walk past the jailed cells full of folk, more than Aren could count. Almost all were Baraan, and by the looks of them, locals. Wrinkling his nose, a pungent smell hung thick in the air telling Aren these cells were ripe with waste. Most of the jailed appeared harmless, except for some coughing. Aren covered his mouth and nose while passing those sick. As he and his escorts walked the cobblestones, prisoners begged for water and food . . . many for their freedom. The worst pleas . . . wails, in truth, came from mothers begging for their children to be freed or simply fed. Aren ignored it all. At least he tried to. Their imprisonment wasn't his problem to solve, though the mothers and crying children weighed on him, tore at him before he could push his feelings down. A sick sensation in the pit of his stomach made Aren wish he had never seen this rabble. *Why are they here? The streets are not so unruly for so many to be jailed.*

Aren and Mithraam cleared the cells after what felt to Aren an eternity of one foot in front of the other. Many desperate pleas for food and freedom got at him, making him feel more miserable about his circumstances with each step. Passing through an open cut-stone doorway with a thick iron door held by two young blue-clad guardsmen, Aren, Mithraam, and their escorts found themselves in a large well-lit arched-ceiling chamber of plain stone blocks. A single arched opening opposite where they stood was the only exit from the area, other than the doorway behind them. Two more blue-clad *Tusaa'Ner* guardsmen, one with a red plume signifying him as the one in command, entered the area from that opposite doorway. They crossed the chamber without ceremony, stopping just short of running over Aren. The image of symbols spinning in Aren's head left him disoriented. With a look of disdain directed at the *Sakes*, the guardsmen bound Aren's and Mithraam's wrists with hide lashes, then led them through the opposite doorway while commanding the Baraans who had brought them from the arena underworld to set a rear guard, then join the escort. Aren felt relieved for the fading pleas as the six of them entered into another long passageway. The stone tunnel was minimally lit with lanterns, causing deep shadows to swallow the tunnel at regular intervals. The place was damp with water seeping in spots overhead. Only their echoed footfalls and the occasional heavy breath broke the silence.

More spinning symbols forced their way into Aren's head. He tried to dismiss them, but found them spinning faster for his efforts. Aren wasn't certain how far they had walked as they emerged from the passageway into a well lit room almost identical to the one at the other end of the tunnel. Two blue-clad guardsmen with sheathed short swords stood at a closed iron door at the opposite side of the room. A hand signal from the taller of their two escorts put in action the guardsmen unlocking and opening the door with an echoing chorus of creaking and grinding. Aren felt the noise rumble through him. It irritated him and caused him to work his jaws hard from side to side to relieve his nerves. The two blue-clad guardsmen resumed their positions of semi-attention on either side of the door just before he and Mithraam were shoved through the doorway into a chamber with a rising rail-less stone stairwell shaped in a rectangle. A red-caped guardsman made his way up the stairs without hesitation. Aren and Mithraam were both poked at from behind to follow and keep up. They climbed and climbed, to Aren's disbelief. He found himself fighting his mind to keep his vision uncluttered from those damnable symbols while stepping carefully to keep from tripping and falling off the stairs. Trying to keep his mind focused on things not of the symbols, Aren guessed they climbed more than twenty strides up, maybe more. Two more blue-uniformed *Tusaa'Ner* guardsmen armed with short swords flanked a stout wood door at the top of the stairwell on a platform large enough to accommodate the eight of them. Looking down, Aren felt queasy and a bit disorientated as those symbols kept spinning all the while he peered into the gloomy depths.

"Do not do that, my Evendiir friend." Mithraam spoke hushed . . . if Aren could call his voice hushed.

Aren looked at Mithraam quizzically, not understanding what he was speaking at. Not wanting to show subordination to a Tellen, especially in front of a crowd, Aren smartly responded to Mithraam's cautioning. "I'm well and capable without your help."

"You are unsteady as things be." Mithraam continued in his hushed tone, speaking as if Aren had not spoken. "Poor light and heights and your *distraction* will only make for a fall off this platform. I have no wish to see that."

Aren made to give a snappy and snide answer to the old Tellen so others would know him not a child, but he was shoved through the door by one of the guardsmen before words left his mouth. Immediately, he stood on marble stone under bare feet. Aren looked up to find he was at one end of a wide doorless hallway with a gleaming marble floor. The walls were of large dark gray stone and brick. Oil lamps lit the hallway well enough so no dark places loomed. The guardsmen barked at him and the Tellen to get moving before giving each of them another hard shove. They walked the hallway with the annoyance of being prodded continually. At the end of the corridor they turned a corner into another hallway of more marble and stone, but with heavy doors of polished wood at regular intervals. A bustle of folks dressed in clean tunics and richer clothes hurried about this passageway. Without ceremony, the guardsmen ushered Aren and Mithraam into a chamber midway down the hall.

Inside, Aren found himself in an aromatic, well lit room large enough to sit twenty or more on benches before a large rune-rich, carved stone seat that sat upon a raised dais. Standing braziers with flaming oil stood to either side of the dais, giving light to the chamber. Nobody except for himself, Mithraam, and their escorts were in the room. More prodding forced Aren and the Tellen forward. A guardsman ordered them to sit on a wood bench closest to the elevated stone seat. When they were satisfied at Aren's and Mithraam's compliance, the guardsmen silently took up standing positions behind them. There they waited . . . and waited . . . and waited. Aren wondered why he was made part of this and in these chambers in-between shooing away those spinning puzzle symbols in his head. He started questioning his grasp of what was real and what wasn't. Then, he wondered if last night truly happened. Were they visited by the dark warrior himself? It had seemed so real, but now . . . Aren thought it maybe his imagination, a dream while he slept since the old Tellen acted as if it had not happened. They waited some more . . . and more. His struggle with those symbols spinning and tormenting him reached new heights. Rich hues streaked across his mind's eye as increasing numbers of spinning symbols filled his head. At first they kept him from boredom, but quickly came to be overwhelming. He tried and failed, several times, to will the symbols away. Growing frustrated at his vain efforts, Aren made a serious mental effort to focus at having the symbols leave him. His head started aching and mental fatigue gripped him firmly. In desperation, Aren yelled at his tormentors . . . those symbols. He wanted the symbols to go away, but in doing so, he took the expressions of all of those around him who heard his outburst that they thought him losing his mind. *Maybe they're right.*

A group of the well-dressed emerged from a stout wood door in the far corner of the room off to Aren's right. At first, he thought them more trickery by his mind, but realized they were indeed flesh and blood when a short, almost plump woman entered the room. She appeared with yellow and lavender flowers set in her shoulder-length blond hair, eyes outlined in black, and cheeks of rose and lips of ruby. She wore a clean white, below-knee-length dress held tight to her waist by a wide red cloth belt and high-calf sandals of fine hide. She walked commandingly to the carved stone tall-back chair where she promptly sat. She carried on with an air of that chair being her throne and the room her hall. Flanking her right was a young woman with red-brown hair complete with blond streaks and eyes also outlined in black. She wore light sky-blue armor, a red cape, and a long knife of a *Tusaa'Ner* junior commander. Aren recalled her face from the jail several days ago. *Was it that long ago?* The seated woman shot unapprovingly glances at the young woman to her right as if expecting something of her, Aren noted in between chasing away spinning symbols in his head. On the seated woman's left were familiar faces to him; Lucufaar, dressed in a wrinkle-free blue shirt and pants and black polished hide boots, and Ganzer, dressed in a gray tunic over baggy black pants and boots, and carrying a black-hide haversack. They accompanied her closely. Behind them, Aren noticed two youngling girls, each carrying a bouquet of flowers, one with yellow petals and the other lavender. To Ganzer's left stood two *Tusaa'Ner* guardsmen clad in their sky-blue armor, though of heavier make than the young woman commander. Each carried a sheathed short sword, though neither donned a red cape, marking them as the muscle of the troupe.

"Dismiss them," the almost-plump woman spoke at the *Tusaa'Ner* commander with expectations her words would be acted upon immediately.

The *Tusaa'Ner* commander wore a passive face as her eyes fell upon Aren and those surrounding him. By the way she looked at him, Aren wondered if she was to unceremoniously send him back to the underworld of the arena.

"*Kunza*," her radiant green eyes held one of the *Tusaa'Ner* behind Aren as she spoke sternly in that irritating, high-pitched voice, "remove yourself and your *aguas* to the hallway. I will send for you when these two need further escort."

Aren heard the creaking of leather and the rapid movement of what he assumed was an arm in salute. The woman *Tusaa'Ner* gave a quick return salute of fist over heart that was followed by boots and sandaled feet behind Aren departing the chamber. At the echoed closing of the door, silence fell over the room. In the silence, those hued symbols still spinning wildly in Aren's head couldn't be ignored. He felt dizzy and tilted far sideways before catching himself. When he looked up, only Mithraam showed any sense of concern.

"Are you steady enough to sit without aid?" Mithraam asked in a serious tone.

"Of course, he is," the almost-plump woman seated upon the dais sneered dismissively. "My question to you, Mithraam of *Brigum* . . . Are you to give us the confession required of your ill behavior?"

Mithraam held a stolid demeanor as he stared back at the woman. Aren tried, but honestly couldn't read the old Tellen. Then, in a calm and even tone, he asked his own questions. "No, *Gal*, no, *Areli*, and no, *Kurdi* . . . *Za Irzal*? Am I to believe this to be a contestation to prove my innocence? A fair contestation?"

"You dare question me?" Irzal hotly rose from the stone chair. She realized immediately that she had lost control of herself and made to straighten her dress, tugging it down on both sides before reseating herself in a painfully slow movement. The woman *Tusaa'Ner* looked at her with concern while Ganzer wore an expression of surprised frustration, Lucufaar . . . disdain.

"You have no right to question me, especially here, *Mithraam Metalsmith. I* will ask questions. *You* will answer."

Mithraam returned a simple nod, but Aren saw in the old Tellen more than a prisoner being questioned. The old Tellen wasn't fearful of this *Za* and those she commanded. He wanted something and was willing to do what he needed to get it. This appearance here was just part of that necessary to achieve his ends. Aren shivered. A hail of colored spinning symbols blinded him for a moment before he could focus and see past them. *This Tellen is going to get me in much trouble.*

"As you say, *Zu* Irzal," Mithraam spoke in a calm tone.

"Then answer my question," Irzal demanded.

"No," Mithraam replied devoid of emotion. Aren nearly jumped out of his skin. *He's going to get me questioned again, before getting me killed!*

"No?" Irzal started to rise from her chair again, but caught herself and her temper and settled back down on the stone seat. She thought for a moment before turning to her aides. "Ganzer, read the transgressions Mithraam has committed against Shuruppak."

Ganzer pulled a clay writing tablet from his haversack, then cleared his throat. "It is announced that Mithraam of Brigum, metalsmith in trade, has committed transgressions against the State of Farratum and the greater Shuruppak Nation by withholding of proper taxes concerning valuables identified by Shuruppak as treasures. Further transgressions against the State of Farratum include the following: conspiring to keep treasures unknown, attempted bribery of Farratum officials, bribery of Brigum officials, insulting officials collecting taxes, insulting officials of the Low Court, insulting officials of the High Court, and failure to pay rightful taxes to Farratum and the greater Shuruppak as the appointed levy."

Irzal displayed a wicked smile that Aren took as satisfaction. He concluded the struggle between her and the old Tellen was personal by their exchange. Yet, Mithraam remained calm, too calm by Aren's expectation. Another pair of spinning symbols passed before his eyes. *Go away!*

"What do you say of these transgressions, Metalsmith?" Irzal sounded triumphant.

"You are no *Gal*," Mithraam countered. "I see no authority in this room to give my words. No one impartial to hear my words . . . as the law is very clear."

"I'm of the *Zas* . . . a *Za* . . . I *make* the laws, Metalsmith." Irzal nearly lost control of her anger again as she spat her words at Mithraam. "I am best to understand the laws I see ushered in and judge if they are broken. Not some *Gal*."

"You are not a judging authority," Mithraam continued in his calm tone, though Aren could sense a hint of anger in his words. At the old Tellen's display of self-control, the almost plump face of Irzal set in a simmer appearing close to boiling over. "I was there when the laws were first crafted . . . a best merger of the old Shuruppak Empire and Turil laws before they were proclaimed for this land."

"*You* . . . ?" Irzal sarcastically asked. "A metalsmith, and a *Tellen* at that . . ."

"Yes," Mithraam replied evenly. "You are no *Gal* and hold no authority here."

I thought I was in trouble, Aren quipped to himself as another several spinning symbols taunted him. *Go away!*

Looking about nervously in the odd silence after that unfriendly exchange, Aren felt certain he would be put to questioning soon after this old Tellen. *Is there a way out of here?* Mithraam would be hanged or worse, Aren was certain of that. Challenging a *Za* as he did . . . Mithraam was dead as he walked. *Za* Irzal's red face confirmed Aren's conclusions. She looked as if she was about to jump from her stone throne at Mithraam. *I'm doomed by this old Tellen by the way he's angering the Za. Even the Ancients won't be able to save me from this insanity.* Another pair of spinning symbols passed before Aren's eyes. They more than annoyed him; they angered him. *Be gone!*

"You're the one without authority here . . . Mithraam, metalsmith of Brigum." Irzal spoke with venom and measured frustration at Mithraam's challenge to her authority. It appeared she regained some of her self-control as a wave of her hand at the *Tusaa'Ner* guardsmen on her left set them in motion. One of the guardsmen returned to the door she had emerged from, opened it, and then waved his hand to someone beyond. A moment later, a rounded Baraan dressed in white robes secured at the waist with a red cloth, entered the room. "I have a *Gal* to inform you of new laws and to hear you confess. You've kept riches from Farratum, Metalsmith. I say you have more than the trinkets we've found. Where's the rest of it?"

Before Mithraam could respond, the *Gal* nervously stepped closer to her dais, clearing his throat as he stumbled before making a proclamation to the room. "Yesterday, at the authority of Farratum's *Anbuda'Za* and at the council from the Farratum *Saar*, all *Zas* of the Farratum region are granted status of *Utu'Me*. At this proclamation, *Zas* now possess authority to make and judge all laws."

Aren began to sweat fiercely at Irzal's triumphant and angry demeanor after the proclamation of her new authority over them. This new law granted her power to make laws and judge them against others. Aren looked around the room. *I don't understand why I'm here, but it can't be a good sign. I'm doomed.* Looking to Mithraam for any indication he would become humble before the *Za* at this new proclamation and beg for his life, what Aren found was a face of contemplation instead of one bathed in fear. The old Tellen sat trying to work something out in his head. *Did he not hear the proclamation?* Aren stared at him, amazed. *I'm SO doomed.*

"Who lies speaking of my keeping unknown wealth?" Mithraam spoke while keeping his narrowed eyes scrutinizing Irzal and those surrounding her. Irzal glanced to her left at Mithraam's challenge. It was quick, but authentic enough to make Aren suspect she unconsciously identified to the metalsmith her aide, Ganzer. *The old Tellen's crafty and relentless . . . and a fool to think he'll survive this. To Kur with him . . . What about me?* Mithraam continued on with an accusation the moment Irzal's eyes returned to him. "This new law of yours will not stand, Irzal. It is against Shuruppak law and will be thrown down when reviewed."

"Maybe . . . but until then . . . It's the law of Farratum." Irzal sounded triumphant and cold.

Silence filled the room at Irzal's reply. The implications of her open intent to misuse authority and power so brazenly astounded him. Even Mithraam looked unprepared for her attitude as he wore a perplexed expression. Aren caught surprised faces on Ganzer and Lucufaar at Irzal's openness, though Lucufaar's expression turned angry almost as fast. The woman *Tusaa'Ner* wore an astonished expression that turned to disappointment as the moments passed.

"Mother . . ." the *Tusaa'Ner* woman started with an irritating high pitch to her voice.

"None of that, Dajil," Irzal scolded.

Aren caught Lucufaar whispering a brief something to Ganzer followed by Ganzer nodding in agreement. The aide spoke directly at the Tellen, but with eyes glancing to Irzal for approval, "Tellen, you've not answered the *Za* . . . the *Utu'Me* question. Where's your remaining wealth kept? Where is the gold, the silver, the guidebook, and the stones?"

Mithraam reacted to Ganzer's question by cocking his head in a slight tilt . . . as if he wasn't sure he heard something he was sure he heard. The Tellen's braided beard looked odd twisting away from his face. A distant look appeared on Mithraam's face as if looking distantly for answers in trying to sort things out. After a few moments, his stolid demeanor returned.

"We are done here." Mithraam stood and stretched as best he could with his wrists still bound.

"You have naddles to spare." Dajil's high-pitched voice grated on Aren. "*Utu'Me* Irzal has not dismissed you."

"Irrelevant," Mithraam replied in an explanatory manner. "You continue to ask of that which does not exist. *Za* Irzal . . . *Utu'Me* Irzal will make judgment concerning my fate based on falsehoods. I need not be present to have these false judgments levied against me."

"What of your son?" Irzal asked.

Mithraam made to turn away, but stopped cold at Irzal's words. Dajil looked at her mother with that astonished face again. Ganzer stood impassive, though nodded in approval. Lucufaar simply smiled. The escorting *Tusaa'Ner* guardsmen and the flower-carrying younglings clearly did not understand Irzal's implied threat or its implications that the exercise of raw, lawless power was on display.

"It would be unfortunate for him to be found guilty of taking life without good cause," Irzal clarified her threat.

"All his actions had justifications the law recognizes." Mithraam spoke in a manner hinting threat. "Leave him from this, Irzal."

"Speak carefully, Tellen," Dajil warned. Her astonished face turned angry. She made a threat to draw her long knife as her two guardsmen put their hands on the pommels of their short swords.

"You speak as if you have some authority, Metalsmith," Irzal scoffed. "I see an old Tellen, jailed, and beholden to his transgressions against Farratum's laws."

"Try me not," Mithraam warned. "I do not have a secret treasure for your taking. What you have taken is my *Imur'gisa*, my family's crest . . . no more. It does have value both in material and to our family. It is not yours or Shuruppak's. It never was nor will be. To Rogaan . . . He is innocent of killing without cause. Your guardsmen meant to have their way with a youngling woman-child. They intended to brutalize her. Rogaan stopped their wickedness before she was gravely harmed."

"Interesting choice of words. I *will* try you, Metalsmith," Irzal responded with venom. "I find you guilty of your transgressions. You're to remain jailed until you provide us that which you've hidden from Farratum and that your '*Imur'gisa*' is declared property of the city. Your son is also found guilty of his transgressions and is to be jailed for the remainder of his days or until his status is reviewed after you provide what is demanded of you this day."

Mithraam glared at Irzal with the heated eyes of a father whose son had just been wronged. Aren felt pity for Mithraam and his son, Rogaan. *He's innocent of committing this "transgression". . . only guilty of having the wrong father and family*. Aren looked at the others surrounding Irzal. Dajil and Ganzer looked surprised and nervous at Irzal's declaration. Lucufaar appeared to be smiling to himself. *He's a strange one*, Aren concluded. With the exception of the sweating and nervous-looking *Gal*, the rest appeared oblivious to what was happening. A series of colorful spinning symbols blurred past Aren's eyes. His head no longer hurt, but these continuous distractions made it difficult for him to focus and catch small details he felt crucial to determining his future and what actions he needed to make it a favorable one.

"A mistake, Irzal," Mithraam warned. "No seeing in the court before a *Gal* for my son? No *Speaker of the Accused* to levy the transgressions? No *Speaker of the Rebut* to challenge the accusations?"

"So you declare," Irzal scoffed Mithraam. She dismissed him with a limp-wristed backhanded wave. "What other tasks do we have before us that we need to attend to, Ganzer?"

"There's the matter of stolen property," Ganzer spoke up. "This young Evendiir had in his possession a gemstone necklace of considerable value . . . an item well beyond his means."

Lucufaar unwrapped and held up a necklace with a large gem for all in the room to see. The necklace was gold metal with a large encrusted circular ruby as its centerpiece. Seven smaller rubies flanked the center gem on both sides, all encrusted in their own swinging mounts.

"That isn't the pendant!" Aren barked before realizing he spoke out. He wished for his words back, but it was too late.

"I know this necklace," Irzal stated with certainty and a sense of surprise. With raised brows, Irzal directly asked of Aren, "So, you admit to your guilt in taking it? The lady of the House of Laggash will favor its return, and you as her bonded servant so she can punish you all the days of your judgment. This will make for a quick ruling."

Aren's head spun. He felt off balanced and unnerved. He wasn't prepared for lies. *Why did he show this pendant and not the true one?* Symbols in many colors spun violently in his head, distracting him, confusing him. Aren cursed to himself.

"What are you wishing to say, Evendiir?" Irzal asked.

Aren looked up to the *Utu'Me* with a blank expression. He couldn't focus well enough to think, to speak clearly, let alone form what he would say.

"This one is clearly not in his right head," Mithraam defended Aren. "Look at him. His eyes are distant. He is confused and does not understand what you spoke at him."

"Ganzer, is this one well of mind?" Irzal asked impassionate. ". . . or is he acting the part of a fool to avoid the consequences of his transgressions?"

"He's as well minded . . . and as obstinate as the rest, *Utu'Me* Irzal," Ganzer answered.

"He suffers in fits with a calm head in between," Mithraam explained. "He has been this way for days . . . since you broke him on the questioning rack, Aide Ganzer."

"His mind wandered before we put him on . . ." Ganzer countered Mithraam's accusation, then caught himself short of completing his thought. Ganzer's face went from indignantly defensive to furious in an instant. A smirk made its way to Mithraam's face. Ganzer's heated eyes turned on Mithraam. "You manipulative stoner . . ."

"I've heard enough." Irzal tried to suppress her own smile at Mithraam's easy handling of Ganzer. She regained her composure before continuing. "There isn't sound proof of transgression if his confession was given while on the rack. His wellness of mind is in question and prevents me from declaring the judgment at this time. Do you agree, *Gal* Suundi?"

The rounded Baraan in white robes looked surprised at being asked anything. His thoughts were evidently somewhere else. He recovered quickly after a glance from the *Utu'Me*. "Yes, *Za* Irzal . . . I meant to say *Utu'Me* Irzal."

Irzal's frustrated and disgusted expression smoothed before she continued. "Ganzer, *Gal* Suundi is to judge this Evendiir's transgressions . . . when his mind is made well. Now, remove this scraggy thing from my eyes."

"The *Utu'Me* has spoken." Dajil looked directly to her two *Tusaa'Ner* guardsmen. "See the Evendiir to his escorts in the hallway."

Chapter 17

Quandary

Colors spun wildly in Aren's head as a distorted-looking blue-clad Baraan led him through a door. The vivid colors and wildly spinning symbols tormented and confused Aren, making him unable to focus. His head felt as if kicked . . . many times . . . by some big brute. He understood what happened in the judgment room and was relieved at Mithraam's help, but Aren felt helpless at his being slow forming rational thoughts and his inability at expressing them. *What's happening to me? Go away! Be gone!* Now, in the hands of his *Tusaa'Ner* escorts, being dragged along back to where he assumed dim and musty cells waited for him and the pleasant company of those whining Baraans.

They made a sharp turn down a long hallway of gleaming marble floors and dark stone walls. Aren remembered this hallway. *This leads to the stairwell to the arena underworld.* Near the far door to the stairwell, a Baraan as stoutly built as Aren's biggest escort stood stolidly with his hands clasped in front, patiently waiting. Aren felt an atmosphere of gloominess surrounding the waiting Baraan when he looked at him. Dark, shoulder-length hair pulled back in a tight tail provided a good look at the Baraan's angular features, accentuated in the light cast by a nearby wall lantern. The Baraan's eyes seemed strange, though Aren couldn't describe why. He shivered. *Not him again.* The *Subar* dressed as Aren remembered, in well-kept charcoal-colored pants and a sleeveless shirt with protruding shoulders, and with a belt sash of black and red. *The Subar . . .* Aren still didn't understand what that title meant, most importantly to himself.

Without the onslaught of questioning from the *Za*, Lucufaar's displaying of the wrong pendant, and the screeching words of that *Tusaa'Ner* woman, Aren's head cleared a bit. The symbols remained, but spun slower, and the colors seemed not so vibrant. He could focus, some. The *Subar* stood perfectly still at their approach, blocking the door to the stairwell. Aren noticed his escorts becoming agitated or nervous . . . maybe both as they closed the distance with the gloomy Baraan.

"By command of the *Tusaa'Ner sakal*, stand aside," Aren's blue-armored and red-caped escort demanded. When the gloomy figure didn't move in compliance, the young red-caped *Tusaa'Ner* became tense and fingered his weapon. His escorts stopped two strides short of the dark-featured Baraan. Not a flinch of his hair. Not even a flinch from the Baraan's dark eyes. Aren shivered.

"You are relieved on the authority of the Shuruppak *Subar*." The darkly dressed Baraan spoke so calmly and with such confidence Aren felt a need to comply by his presentation alone. An awkward silence filled the air for a long moment before Aren felt the hands of his escorts tighten around his arms. They shook slightly. *They fear this one.* His *Tusaa'Ner* escorts exchanged glances. The red-caped junior *sakal* hesitated in relinquishing Aren. He stood uncertain as what to do.

"Shoo." The *Subar* waved his hand dismissively.

The junior *sakal* begrudgingly relinquished Aren with an awkward command to his *aguas*. Aren felt their quivering hands leave him as they stepped behind him. Looking over his shoulder, he found the echoes of their brisk footfalls matching the speed in which they fled the *Subar*. Aren suddenly found himself wishing they hadn't gone. *What is a Subar?*

He returned his attention to the dark Baraan in front of him. Those colorful spinning symbols in his head remained constant. Aren didn't know what that meant. Aren and the *Subar* looked at each other for a short span with Aren growing increasingly uncomfortable. The *Subar* remained silent and unflinching. Aren started to wonder if he should be saying something, a missed formality he was not familiar with. The silent, dark stare from the *Subar* was just unnerving. It felt as if it penetrated Aren in ways that were unnatural. Aren shivered a bit before he managed to get his body under control.

"Walk with me," the *Subar* ordered, then stepped through the door into the stairwell.

Aren followed. He didn't know why . . . He just did. On the stairwell top platform, dark-uniformed *Sakes* replaced the blue-uniformed *Tusaa'Ner*. The

Subar barely gave them notice as he slowly stepped down the stone stairs. Aren followed at an extraordinarily slow pace. The symbols spinning in his head seemed to match their pace.

"What have you discovered?" The *Subar* asked.

Aren sorted through all he had learned of his captors and cell mates of the past few days. A blue spinning symbol passed before his eyes. Then a green, then a brown. *Go away!* He was uncertain of what he should share. This *Subar* seemed not to be so benevolent a being. He clearly had an agenda that Aren wasn't privy to. He just didn't know what it was. Too much information could get the Tellens in trouble. *They have been kind to me. They must want something of him too.* Aren suddenly found himself wanting to give the *Subar* information, even if it meant making it up . . . maybe of the Baraans to make them seem more important than they truly were so the *Subar* might take them away. Aren mused on that thought for a moment before a hail of spinning symbols streaked past his eyes in a yellow blur. *Be gone!* The *Subar* appeared patient, waiting for his answer as they made it to the first landing, the walls and walkway forcing them to turn left in their descent. Aren grew increasingly nervous at holding back too much from this one. The *Subar's* threat to visit Windsong combined with Aren not fully understanding what a *Subar* is and is capable of doing, he felt this one would spare little of his authority in finding what he sought. Aren resigned himself to open up, but only enough . . . if that was possible.

"The Baraans are a simple family . . . father, mother, son, and daughter," Aren started. "The daughter, an attractive lass for a Baraan, is now in the hands of someone given by the *Sake zigaar* . . . to keep her safe from the jailers and guardsmen."

"Why tell me things I already know?" The *Subar* asked flatly.

"Well, huh, the parents are not with good feelings concerning the Tellens," Aren tried to satisfy the *Subar's* want of new details a report might not mention. "They blame the old Tellen for their jailing and the loss of their daughter. They don't care much for the younger Tellen, as well. He is stricken with the Baraan lass and cares for her a great amount. Enough to not realize his own strength and kill another. The Baraan male youngling is fond of the young Tellen. I think them friends. Friends enough for the Baraan to argue with his parents over their treating the Tellen with harsh manners or blaming him for their predicament. His parents want to hear none of it."

"Are the Baraans of any importance?" The *Subar* asked directly.

"I can't be sure . . . I don't think so," Aren answered honestly. Another group of spinning blue symbols whizzed past his eyes, right to left, sending Aren stumbling down the steps. He found himself looking over the edge into darkness when he felt the *Subar* catch his arm and pull him back.

"What is illing you, Evendiir?" The *Subar* asked in a tone of frustration. "I've never before observed an Evendiir so unsteady or with so little focus."

The *Subar's* strong grip pulled Aren solidly to his feet. It took a moment for him to feel steady enough to stand on his own, in spite of those damnable spinning symbols in his head. Not wanting this *Subar* to know of his "problem," Aren deflected his question, he lied . . . a little. "The questioning Ganzer and Lucufaar gave left me unwell."

"Then, tell me of the Tellens." The *Subar* redirected the conversation along, not seeming to care about Aren's "condition." *I'm only a means to knowledge for him*. Aren wasn't certain if that was favorable or unfavorable for him.

"Rogaan, the young Tellen, is of no importance," Aren went on as they restarted their slow descent. Aren questioned himself concerning just how much to reveal about Rogaan. Rogaan treated him better than any other since he left home and somehow, when he was in eye or ear distance, it helped Aren control those cursed spinning symbols. "He knows little, though he seems able to get the guardsmen worked up."

Aren peeked over the edge of the stairs again . . . This time more cautiously. The symbols in his head had settled some, allowing him better concentration and focus . . . and balance. He and the *Subar* were almost halfway down. Aren was now able to make out dark-uniformed figures below. *Sakes or someone else?* He needed to complete his telling to the *Subar* more quickly. There was much to tell of the old Tellen. Too much, Aren feared. He had to give this *Subar* something . . . enough to benefit himself . . . and maybe Rogaan, but not so much as to bring harm to Mithraam and his son.

"The old Tellen is more than he allows others to know," Aren thought this knowledge was obvious to all involved with him by now. *But how much more to reveal? What can I say to take some focus off of Mithraam?* "Mithraam is at odds with *Za* Irzal . . . Who has her own sordid story. Irzal is not what I expected of a lawmaker. She's more concerned wielding as much authority as she can and concerns herself not for the good of Farratum, but herself. She thinks Mithraam has valuables he's hidden from Farratum authorities. She wants them. Mithraam denies he has any more valuables than . . . what they already took from him. What did he call it? His . . . *Imur'gisa*. I have no knowledge of what that is."

He and the *Subar* descended silently for a flight of stairs. They were almost to the bottom. Aren didn't know if the *Subar* wanted him to speak more or if the Baraan was contemplating on what was already told to him. The *Subar* remained silent. Aren's nervousness grew as the moments lengthened to a height that he felt near need to confess everything he knew.

"What of last night?" The *Subar* asked.

"Last night?" Aren stalled in answering by acting dumb.

"Yes. *Sake* reports speak of a stranger in the underground." The *Subar* was baiting Aren to tell more with a simple truth. "What do you know of this?"

Aren felt his chest tighten. *What am I going to tell him?* Again, he struggled with how much to tell. He had to speak of the dark warrior . . . the *Subar* knew of the stranger who seemed be able to come and go as he pleased, but too much would see him in much trouble, along with the Tellens. His mind raced, seeking a means to tell a half-truth. "I was woke by talk between what I thought were guardsmen. I saw a big Baraan in dark clothing leave the room who looked a *Sake,* maybe the *Sake zigaar*. After that annoyance, I rolled over and went back to sleep."

The *Subar* carefully watched Aren's face and eyes intently as he answered. Seeming satisfied with this truth of what Aren spoke, he praised him in an even and calm voice. "Well done, young Aren. Speak nothing of my inquiry or that you've imparted this knowledge to me."

"Yes, *Subar*." Aren acknowledge his compliance to him, though continued to wonder . . . *What is a Subar? How important and how much authority has he? Everyone seems afraid of this one. Most important . . . Can he see me freed?*

Aren set foot on the stone floor at the bottom of the stairwell without the *Subar*. The Baraan had left Aren a flight of steps above, returning to the top of the stairs. The dark-uniformed guards at the bottom of the stairs, *Sakes*, while complaining of *Tusaa'Ner* incompetence, rebound Aren's wrists and ushered him back into the arena underworld without ceremony.

Chapter 18

Unveiling

V isions of Suhd being mishandled by unknown guards tormented Rogaan every time he closed his eyes. Her beautiful face twisted in screams pleading to be saved from those wanting from her more than she willingly would give plagued his thoughts. Dwelling on that moment was not good for him, but he just could not help himself. Rogaan worried for Suhd and of her being soiled by others. That last thought made him feel embarrassed and dirty at his selfishness. Still, his feelings lingered. Unwisely, Pax teased him of being heartsick for his sister earlier when his parents were sleeping. He could always count on Pax to say the wrong thing at the worst times to gloom over his mood. Rogaan snarled at his friend's words. *That was unfair of me*, Rogaan chastised himself. *Pax was trying to cheer me up, and all I did was growl at him.*

His father allowed him his space, both physically and emotionally. They talked little over the past several days, in-between "questioning" sessions by the *Sakes* and others he did not know. The questions asked were all focused on his father and his father's associations. Rogaan endured both physical pains from the experienced use of ropes and mind games at the hands of Farratum's tyrants for not answering the way they wanted. He gave them little useful information, and that was only after they tricked him into saying something Rogaan wished he had not.

Rogaan's visions of saving his father and Pax's parents were now turned on their head . . . upside down. *Nothing like I thought it would be.* And, matters were worse. They had Suhd and were doing unspeakable things to her. A wave of anger and despair ripped through him like a dull knife cutting flesh at that last thought. Worse, the embarrassment he felt at his selfish feelings at them soiling her. *Do I hurt for her pain or my own?* Rogaan did not know the answer to that question, and it made his despair all the more terrible. And then there were Pax and Suhd's parents. They were relentless at breaking into conversations between him and Pax, spitting venomous accusations at both him and his father . . . mostly at his father. Their mood seemed to worsen with each passing hour. Pax's too. His friend had turned quieter since they took him and his father for their latest "questioning," and soon after that, Pax's father returning to the cell more bruised and limping than from previous sessions. The older Baraan, once almost considered family by Rogaan, fed off his own pain as he took liberties in yelling at Rogaan and his father, telling them what he thought of Tellens and their schemes. Adding to Rogaan's pain, the memory of that old Baraan he had tossed from the bridge to save Pax and Suhd returned often, haunting his waking thoughts. Rogaan despaired at it all, a mix of regrets and shame that made him feel less than should be allowed to live.

All sat quietly after Pax's father exhausted himself yelling. Pax now just curled up into a small ball and appeared to sleep. His mother wept as she tossed hate-filled glares at Rogaan as often as she could—all a cycle that repeated itself several times each day for the past several days. *They hate me. Once, I was welcomed at their table and laughed with them as family. No more.* Rogaan's heart sank further. He fought to keep tears from falling.

In the uneasy silence of the cells, the offending odors of their own sweat and waste wafting from chamber pots made worse Rogaan's mood. He hated using the things in front of others. He preferred privacy, especially where the females were concerned. The wafting pots got emptied at what Rogaan guessed was the start of each day by an older fellow . . . a Baraan as unpleasing to the eye as could be. Rogaan nicknamed him "Ugly" to amuse himself, but then he felt badly for it. Farthing Rogaan's dislike for himself, the old Baraan was harmlessly friendly . . . except to the Evendiir. The Baraan just did not like Aren for some reason. His exchanges with the Evendiir made for greater tensions, such that it almost felt a relief to be taken from the cells for questioning by the *Sakes*. Their clothes smelled too, despite having been washed every other day with buckets of cold water thrown on them. The *Sakes* seemed to be pleased by it all. *I've decided I do not like Sakes. Once, I regarded them as people of honor doing what must be done to keep the streets safe. Now, I know many of them as small folk with little honor and a propensity for self-amusement at the expense of others.* Rogaan reflected how his idealized world had changed for the worse . . . as he experienced it. It continued to bare ugly truths. *Honor is fleeting in these folks, and civilization, and maybe no more in them . . . or in me.*

A door to the larger room opened, allowing in a barefoot, dark-haired youngling wearing dirty rags for clothes. He struggled with a water-filled bucket almost too heavy for him to carry. *It must be nearing the nightly quiet time for the arena's underworld*, Rogaan guessed at the time of day as he felt completely lost down in this place. The youngling did as he did every night, just before the *Sakes* retreated from guarding and abusing the jailed. The youngling checked with each dismissive *Sake*, then the thankful folks in each cell to see who wanted water. The two darkly uniformed *Sakes*, as usual, refused drink from the same source the jailed drank from. Pax and his parents eagerly drank as the youngling poured water into their cups with a ladle. As the youngling poured water for Rogaan's father, he spoke a few hushed words in his ear. His father reciprocated speaking hushed words only the youngling could hear. Aren rose to take water in his cup after checking to see if Rogaan moved to take a drink. When Rogaan just kept his place, Aren encouraged the youngling to fill, then refill his cup several more times. Then the Evendiir quietly sat back down against the stone wall. Rogaan's father picked up his cup and had it filled again before offering it to Rogaan. Rogaan slowly drank two full cups so the youngling had more time to whisper into his father's ear. They quietly chatted. The skinny youngling was a go-between, and a poised one at that. The guards either did not realize the youngling's role or did not care as neither made to stop this daily ritual. Rogaan wondered who his father was communicating to through this go-between. When no one asked for more water, the youngling disappeared from the room without ceremony as quickly as he appeared.

Aren went back to keeping to himself and sleeping with his half-filled cup near. He wrapped himself in one of the thin blankets given to them. Rogaan's father stood and stretched, then sat down near him with his back on the bars so the guards could not see his face. He stared into his full cup for a time contemplating something. Pax and his parents went back to wrapping themselves in their own blankets. Pax looked unsettled and fitful, but his light snoring told Rogaan he found some peace in sleep. A little time passed with them sitting in total silence, except for some rude noises escaping from the bored guards. To keep from nodding off earlier, they resorted to tossing stones before the youngling disturbed them. Now, after a short while with no talking and little other noise, even the guards struggled to keep awake with their heads nodding and bodies unsteady. Rogaan too felt tired, but something about the way his father looked into that cup told him to stay awake.

"The path ahead will be very difficult for both of us, my son." His father's words were spoken in low tone and volume, and slowly. The guards seemed unaware that he spoke with their continued unsteadiness while leaning against the walls. "Your preparations are not complete. In truth, I was just getting started with you when . . . all of this took us."

Rogaan felt confused . . . What did "preparations" mean? "I do not understand."

"Expected," Mithraam replied as he reflected on something for a short time. "You have been thrust into a struggle as old as humanity's place on this world. I cannot reveal much in this place—too many ears, but I need you to keep strong your trust in me and what I am to tell you. Can you do this, my son?"

Rogaan had a sudden chill ripple through him. "Yes, Father."

"You will be tested and harm will likely find you . . . You will need to endure." Mithraam's eyes saddened as a frown filled his face. "Because of what I cannot give them."

Uneasy chills swept through Rogaan. *Fathers protect . . . It is the Tellen way, and the way of my mother's family.* Alarmed at his father putting something before him, Rogaan's confusion piqued. *And I will be tested and . . . harmed?* He opened his mouth to protest and ask a question to understand why, but was cut off by his father.

"The Shuruppak civil war came to an end . . ." Mithraam spoke with his teaching tone while glancing about, taking notice of the guards, Pax and his family, and Aren to be sure they were not paying him any attention. "The Houses made one last attempt to assert their authority over the people and lands of Shuruppak. We stopped them . . . the Ebon Circle with my aid . . . to answer your question who 'we' were. In the void of sovereign rule, the Ebon Circle battled the Houses to keep the people of Shuruppak from subjugation. Helped by a show of force by the Tellen Nation from Turil, the Shuruppak people and the Ebon Circle fought the self-proclaimed masters of these lands. We put together an alliance with some of the small Houses who broke ranks from those greater. These small Houses chose to see the people free from tyrannical hands. The cabal of remaining great Houses fell apart as they could not work together . . . Their ambitions for control, power, and authority over each other led to distrust and subterfuge. Their sought-after iron grip on the people and lands collapsed as much from their own failings as from our alliance. The once-great Houses withdrew back to their patchwork of lands and holdings within Shuruppak and were forced to become more focused on protecting what they had instead of expanding their influence. A negotiated peace was achieved . . . Houses great and small, the Ebon Circle, the Tellen Nation, and the representatives of the commoners of Shuruppak all signed. A compact was established where all would be ruled by laws . . . not by another's hand. All would have say in the laws through the lawmakers of Shuruppak; the *Ksatra'Za* in Ur and the *Anubda'Zas* in the regional cities were to have seats filled from the chosen of the people . . . the *Bartam'Eadda*, the noble Houses both great and small . . . the *Niral'Eadda*, and Guilds . . . the *Dagas*. It was a difficult beginning, but it held together . . . now for almost thirty years. A Shuruppak ruled by laws, just as Turil has been since the dawn of the Tellen Nation. Yes, the compact was fashioned after the Tellen Nation with allowances for the nature of the Houses instead of clans. The councils of each city, town, and village chose those to represent them in the lawmaking . . . the *Zas*. The original *Zas* established new laws forming what is known as Shuruppak's Servants of the People . . . the *Kiuri'Ner*, *Tusaa'Ner*, and *Sakes*. Their duties defined in the laws. They were to be limited in number, so they would serve and protect the people . . . no more. Lawmakers and Servants of the Law, the courts, were to be independent to thwart any attempt at consolidating power. They were beholden to the people and received their coin from the people. Their small numbers loyally served the laws and people of the nation. Until recently, the last few *Roden'ars*, their numbers remained small, then suddenly rapidly grew. With their expansion, a corruption crept in, tainting the Servants of the People and the lawmakers. Our safeguard . . . the courts, our Servants of the Law, with their mandatory review of new laws to stand against tyranny trying to oppose the freedom of the people, appears to be failing. It is not known why the courts are failing. Those elected into positions of trust are now disregarding our laws. The *Zas*, our lawmakers, are growing their own authority. In seeking truth and with intent to correct what has gone wrong, we discovered the corrupting influence is in these lands with a weakening influence as one travels eastward. That does not mean Padusan and Ur are not without troubles. They too feel it, but not yet so gravely as we do here. This *corruption* must be uncovered and defeated before it completes its plan and asserts itself everywhere. If we fail . . . all our freedoms can be lost. The people will be subjugated again, some willingly . . . the rest at the point of a blade."

Rogaan sat with a hollow feeling in the pit of his stomach. *Matters are far worse than I ever thought them to be.* He understood his father's words, but had difficulty thinking of him as more than a sought-after metalsmith. Rogaan had not an inkling of his father's secret doings . . . working with the Dark Temple . . . the Ebon Circle . . . and that Im'Kas, the Dark Ax. Rogaan felt himself in stories told to younglings to teach them of principles, of good and virtues . . . and that which fills the void when absent. He shuddered at the meaning, the implications, and the consequences of it all.

"How will I come to harm?" Rogaan asked with a calmness that surprised himself. He felt the fear of the unknown and the answer to his question. He wanted to know how he would be punished for the old Baraan, and for letting Suhd be taken, and for not rescuing his father, and getting Pax and his parents involved, and . . . so much more.

"A guard died by your hands." His father sounded sad.

"He was going to hurt Suhd . . ." Rogaan defended.

"Your motives were pure . . . noble, my son." Mithraam quickly settled down their voices. He spoke in that low tone again. "You did what any Tellen would do protecting those he cares for. I have pride in your act, but a guard is dead and those who want what I cannot give them are to use you to make me reveal things they wish to know."

"Do you have knowledge of what they seek?" Rogaan asked, then immediately felt regretful and embarrassed for doing so. His father's gaze on him was even . . . measured. A gaze Rogaan had experienced many times before when someone asked a question of his father that had an obvious answer. An epiphany struck Rogaan like a forge hammer to his chest. All of his father's teachings, his tests . . . his lessons on honor, virtue, integrity, goodness, and more principles told Rogaan his father was living his convictions, his self-accepted responsibilities that carried with it a great suffering of consequences. *Which of Father's teachings speaks to this . . . yes . . . "Evil prevails when Good does not challenge it"?* Rogaan realized he knew the answer to his question. *This is what it means to live with honor. I am not certain I like this path.*

"Are you at an understanding, my son?" Mithraam asked solemnly.

"I think I am, Father," Rogaan replied in an uncertain tone. He surprised himself at feeling no anger toward his father. *Mother knew this of him. That is what she was trying to tell me.*

They sat quietly for a time, father and son possibly understanding each other. A first for Rogaan as he relived and recounted his father's teachings in his mind. Many made sense to him, now, but a few remained beyond his grasp in understanding.

"What do I expect at the hands of Farratum?" Rogaan asked in a shaky voice.

His father did not answer. Instead, he put on that contemplative look without returning his gaze. Rogaan suspected he knew, but did not want to tell him of his fate.

"I am not certain," Mithraam started. "Either you will be tried properly, found guilty, and then jailed for a time that is unknown or made a servant to a well-off House until your jailing time is fulfilled. That is . . . if the *Za* does not get her way. She will use you to force my tongue and hand. She will try. She will rule without the justly concurrence of the Servants of the Laws. She will be involved in some manner in determining your jailing time. It will be . . . lengthy and . . . unpleasant."

"What of Suhd?" Rogaan asked, now trying to take his mind off the answer he decided he really did not want to know.

"I have little insight as to where she is," Mithraam replied. "She has done nothing that would keep her in bondage according to the laws. I suspect she is in the servitude of someone, if the corruption is as I think it is. She may be kept as a means to harm you, and me through you. Corruption has many forms."

"Will they take her innocence from her?" Rogaan felt his throat tighten. He almost did not ask the question fearing his father's honesty in answer.

Mithraam was slow to reply which told Rogaan what he hoped would not be. "There are Houses and others in authority that will not abuse servants in that manner. Let us hope they have placed her with one of them."

Rogaan was uncertain why Suhd's plight bothered him as it did. Was it for the pain she felt or his? He held her close in his heart and she held him in hers, it seemed and he hoped. That last thought brought a smile to his face. It felt good knowing she cared for him. Then his smile went sour as his thoughts turned to unknown guards taking her innocence. Rogaan's blood started to boil. He felt anger.

"I decided to accept your quest to become *Kiuri'Ner*." Mithraam broke into Rogaan's thoughts and growing foul mood. "I arranged for you to be trained at the Ebon Circle . . . if you managed to pass their tests."

Rogaan stared at his father with his mouth agape. It took him some time to shake off his shock. His father had been adamant he not learn or walk the path of the *Protectors of the Ways*. Instead, he was to become a well-taught smith of metals and a mason of stone. Now, his father was telling him not only had he decided to allow him his aspiration, but that he made arrangements to grant him learning from what rumored whispers say are the most revered *Kiuri'Ners* in Shuruppak.

"Why?" Rogaan asked. He knew his father had a reason . . . He always had a well-thought-out reason for every decision he made.

"Your heart is set to it," Mithraam replied matter-of-factly. "If you are to follow this path, then you need to learn from the most capable, not some group of wall-watchers from town."

The jail room door opened without warning. Three alert *Sake* guards, dressed in their dark armor, entered with stolid expressions. They relieved the two guards fighting off sleep, but held them from leaving. One of the guards opened the metal barred door to the cell holding Pax and his parents, waking them. They protested the intrusion which resulted in a backhanded strike to the face of Pax's father, sending him into the bars. Pax made to step between the guard and his father, but was instead grabbed by another dark-armored Baraan, bound, and hauled out of the cell. His father suffered the same fate. The guards growled words to each other, then barked commands at their two restrained prisoners before telling Pax's mother to quiet her weeping.

"He's ready for them now." The announcement came from what Rogaan took as the most senior guard. The Baraan wore a sadistic smile. "You Tellens go next . . . when he be done with 'em."

"Where are you taking them?" Rogaan demanded with his anger flaring at the treatment of Pax and father.

"Soon enough, Tellen . . . soon enough," the guard taunted as Pax and his father were unkindly shoved from the room.

"Where are they being taken?" Rogaan was on his feet asking of his father, his voice filled with confusion and anger.

Mithraam made to speak, but his answer was cut off with the reverberating metallic ringing of a guard's sword sweeping over the bars. "Keep quiet!"

Mithraam's eyes caught Rogaan's, telling him to let it be. Rogaan did not like "letting it be," but with his newfound knowledge of things, he decided to comply, keeping silent. He calmed himself well enough to sit. As he did, Rogaan's heated eyes met Aren's. The Evendiir looked as if contemplating on what was happening, but then decided all was well enough for him to return to his sleep. In a moment, the Evendiir was again wrapped in his blanket and oblivious to his surroundings. Wanting answers, Rogaan looked to his father. His father's eyes continued to caution against rash actions, meaning for Rogaan to not make an issue of things. Frustrated at keeping quiet, Rogaan reluctantly wrapped himself in the musty-smelling blanket. He stewed for a time waiting for Pax and his father to be returned. The weeping of Pax's mother quieted after a time, though she remained awake with a face filled with painful horror and streaks of tears. Not able to look at her any longer without feeling her pain, Rogaan's thoughts wandered. He tried to stay awake, but sleep took him sometime before his friend returned.

Chapter 19

Assay

S uhd smiled at him as they walked hand in hand on paved streets close to the water's edge. She wore one of her yellow dresses, one that showed more leg than he hoped for an outing. A matching yellow sun hat shaded her radiant blue eyes except for the times she looked up into his own eyes. He was happy that she looked up at him often. The high sun made the day warm, though pleasant, with a slight breeze and plenty of "ancient sun rays" streaking through a mat of scattered clouds. The water flowed lazily here with the deep creek almost as wide as a river. It was a good place to fish for hookfins and blue-scaled jumpers. Even the scent on the breeze smelled of pleasant flowers. Rogaan felt content with a happy heart. A happy heart he had given to Suhd.

A ruckus ahead begrudgingly drew Rogaan's attention from her. A group of five Baraans, barely older than himself dressed in gray and green tunics, hide pants and boots, approached them with anger and ill will in their eyes. Another group of guardsmen in blue poured onto the street from several stone and brick buildings. Their eyes too were filled with ill will as they made their way straight for him and Suhd. Some gazed upon Suhd with animalistic lust, as if she were a toy they wanted to play with.

Rogaan stepped between Suhd and most of those closing on them. They would have to go through him to play with their toy. He and Suhd shuffled rearward as the closer of the two groups pressed in on them. Suhd squeaked a warning that they had no more street. Their backs were at the water's edge. Suhd had to be protected. Rogaan would die for her to keep her from harm. He planted both of his boots firmly on the paving stones readying for the fight of his life. The street rabble and guardsmen closed . . . all wearing serious grins and eyes telling him they thought victory easy and certain. The guardsmen drew swords as the street rabble waved small clubs and knives. They raised their weapons to strike just a handful of strides from his Suhd.

They all halted suddenly with expressions of surprise and horror replacing those that they wore a moment ago. Rogaan heard a splash, a big one that signaled the pushing of large amounts of water. He felt sizable drops of water pelt him as he spun toward Suhd. Terror consumed Suhd's face as massive jaws filled with finger-sized spikes closed around her chest and pelvis in a horrifying crunching snap. The huge snapjaw whipped its head backward, then plunged into the creek with a great upheaval of water soaking Rogaan and everyone near. Suhd's scream silenced when she hit the water.

"No!" Rogaan shouted in shocked pain as he coiled to jump after Suhd. He needed to save her, free her from death's jaws. A massive weight pressing down on him kept Rogaan from launching after her. So much weight he collapsed under it, dropping to the cobblestones. He had to get free to save Suhd. Rogaan twisted with a strain rolling onto his back. He needed leverage. A shadow of a face appeared in front of him. Rogaan struck it with his fist in a half-jabbing motion. The bearded face went backward, body and all slamming against metal bars. Rogaan paused. *Where did the bars come from? Suhd . . . ?*

"I'd say . . . He's ready to see him," a deep voice spoke with amusement.

"By the Ancients," another voice with a drawl exclaimed. "He hit his own blood. A mean one, that one."

"Bind him and get him on his feet." The deep voice commanded.

Rogaan's head cleared some. He found himself still in his jail cell, lying on his back and shaken. *Suhd. I was dreaming . . . so real.* Rogaan looked about. Aren crouched off to his left with wary eyes, and two dark-armored guards stood above Rogaan. Each of them wore an amused smile as they reached for him. *Where's Father?* As his wrists were being bound with rope, Rogaan looked around the cell. He found his father sitting up against the bars working and rubbing his jaw. *I did not? No. I did hit Father?*

"Father, my regrets . . . striking you," Rogaan sincerely asked for forgiveness for his act. His chest felt as if it would seize motionless as his skin prickled all over. Never had physically fighting with this father entered his thoughts. Never. *How can I ever make amend for striking him?* His father shook his head several times trying to clear it of the punch before using the bars to slide up to a standing position.

"Bind the other Tellen and the Evendiir." The deep-voiced *Sake* commanded. "They go too."

Another *Sake* entered the cell and bound Rogaan's father about the wrists with shackles, then moved to do the same with Aren. *What is happening?* Rogaan looked to see if Pax was getting bound as well. The battered and bloody sight of his friend and father shocked Rogaan. *What happened to them?* They looked like punching sacks for Gygaens. Rogaan was hauled up to his feet as he gawked at his friend. The *Sakes* led him from the cell along with his stumbling father. Aren was prodded out of the cell, followed close by a dark-armored guard behind him.

The three of them were marshaled into an under area of the arena Rogaan was unfamiliar with. They walked a total of ninety-seven strides with two changes of direction, placing them in a thirty-four-stride-long hallway without cells. They were somewhere on the southeast side of the underground and about fifty strides from the center of the arena . . . if Rogaan's sense of movement and orientation was correct. On their walk they passed by numerous cells, most with prisoners, many of them battered and bloodied. Strangely, most looked to be wearing rags of clothes that once looked fit for the wealthy. He dismissed such thoughts, instead, keeping focus on his surroundings.

Rogaan walked with his father a few strides in front and Aren a few behind. Their three *Sake* escorts walked a stride behind and a stride left of each of them, with two more dark-armored guards following a short distance behind them all. Ahead, the hallway ended in a bright light coming from a large open doorway. The light was almost blinding . . . not something cast from lanterns or torches. The bright light forced Rogaan to shield his eyes as best he could with his bound hands. His father's *Sake* escort stopped just short of the doorway without bringing to a halt his charge. Rogaan looked left and saw his *Sake* do the same as Rogaan stepped through the doorway. *Something is wrong.* A stench of sweat and blood filled his nose as a heavy flat surface struck Rogaan, sending him airborne. For a moment, Rogaan felt weightless and physically numb all over. Pain then racked his body as he slammed into the stone floor, bouncing his way to a sliding stop up against a stone wall. He opened his eyes wanting to see what hit him, but found a bright blur with shadowy figures. He heard Aren yelling almost hysterically while moving . . . running around the room. Echoes of Aren's voice as he ran about allowed Rogaan to determine the room to be large.

"Have ah runner," a snarling voice stated somewhere to Rogaan's right.

"Dee's tu be like little rocks," a deep rumble of a voice remarked on Rogaan's left.

Rogaan blinked his burning eyes trying to see the room and who spoke. Foul air close to the floor penetrated his nose causing him to cringe and sit up gagging. After a few moments, his eyes adjusted to the bright room enough to see what he faced. Seven melon-sized orbs lit the room. All protruded a stride from the walls almost six strides high in hooded mounts resembling outstretched arms and hands. They radiated white light at equally spaced intervals around the circular-shaped room of large cut-stone making. The ceiling rose almost ten strides forming a dome. Glass wedge-shaped portals just over eight strides up spanning the entire circumference had moving shadows in them. *A watching room*. Rogaan's eyes returned to the floor where Aren stood with his back to the stone wall shaking his head as if trying to rid himself of something only he could see. When not looking at the empty air, the Evendiir kept his eyes on a looming big, brown-skinned brute dressed only in a loin cloth. The wide and muscular brute had a clean-shaven head topping just over two and a half strides tall. Rogaan guessed it to outweigh him by three times or more. Another figure, a Baraan . . . no, something else . . . lean and muscular with almost wine-black skin and sunset sun-colored top-hairs, beard, and fur down the center of his chest, stood a little taller than Pax at one side of the room. The dark, wine-skinned creature positioned himself over Rogaan's prone father who was trying to shake off what Rogaan assumed was a coward's punch just like the one that hammered him when he entered the room.

Somewhat recovered, Rogaan rose to his feet, then stepped toward his father to help. He stopped immediately, freezing in place when the creature drew two blades and held one just over his unaware father's head, the other pointed directly at Rogaan. The creature dressed in high-calf sandals and what looked to be the skirt part of brown eur armor and a hide harness with wide straps crisscrossing across his chest. Where he stowed the long knives prior to drawing them, Rogaan could only guess. The creature was fast and precise with intense green eyes, widely set level about his nose under a heavy brow. Watching Rogaan's every move, the creature's curved ears twitched at every noise. Its deep cheeks framed a mouth of thin lips and fanged teeth. Rogaan recalled seeing drawings in books of ancient warfare of warriors looking as this one, but could not remember its name. *An ancient Evendiir? No, it is something else.*

"What are you?" The dark, wine-skinned creature demanded of Rogaan looking at him down his left arm and blade.

Rogaan looked back at him, not knowing what he asked or how to answer. They stared at each other for a long moment before Rogaan felt uncomfortable and shrugged with open hands, "I do not know."

"Asra'Tellen . . . fighter, runner, or a coward to be made *lightless?*" The creature clarified the meaning of his demand.

Rogaan's skin prickled and his chest tightened at the unknown of the creature's words. He did not like that "to be made *lightless*" part . . . nor the "coward" reference or "runner," either. All sounded at the wrong end of the sword. What remained? Rogaan answered. "Fighter."

The creature flicked his left wrist tossing the blade twirling in the air toward Rogaan. Watching the long knife's blade and pommel rotating at him, Rogaan considered catching it in air so as to impress. Then he thought better of the consequences to anything but a great success at that, allowing the blade to fall to the bloodstained stone floor, clinking and clattering to the wall. Rogaan's eyes fixed on the stone floor beneath him for the first time. Blood, both dried and fresh, stained the floor everywhere with only spots here and there allowing him to see stone beneath the *Waters of Life*. As he looked on in shock and with growing horror, Rogaan saw his bloodstained clothes, arms, and hands. *Is this blood mine?*

"Asra'Tellen . . . take blade," the creature demanded in a matter-of-fact demeanor.

Rogaan looked at the blade, then the creature. *I will have to fight him if I pick that up.* The creature stood as a statue when Aren ran by him making a hysterical groan, the brutish big one chasing him close. Rogaan assessed the chamber large enough for two or three pairs of combatants not to interfere with each other as he watched Aren run for the doorway they entered the chamber from, only to veer away and run right following the wall. An escape was not possible as the *Sakes* crowded the entrance arch wanting to watch this exciting spectacle. Even if there was room for Aren to squeeze through, the *Sakes* would not let him escape. Turning his attention back to the dark, wine-skinned creature, Rogaan found him standing, unmoving, still above his father.

"Help me you, idiot!" Aren with desperate anger demanded of Rogaan as he ran by him right to left.

Rogaan glimpsed Aren running the curve of the wall after he passed. A quick look back at the creature to make sure he kept where he remembered . . . *crunch!* Rogaan went flying again . . . his face and right side of his head in pain. He hit the bloodstained floor hard, jarring his teeth before bouncing and striking the floor a second time.

"Little rock. Ha, ha, ha . . ." The big, brown-skinned brute loomed over Rogaan. The massive . . . *whatever he is* . . . seemed pleased with himself, wearing what Rogaan took as a grin for a moment before taking off after Aren again.

The taste of blood in his mouth gave Rogaan concern. *These two are serious about whatever it is they do . . . hurting, maybe killing.* His head ached, and his jaw felt numb from that shot. *That is twice since I have entered this room.* Anger started to boil within him. The scent of all the blood and sweat staining the floor filled his nose, causing him to gag and sit up to get away from it.

"Asra'Tellen . . . a strong one," the dark, wine-skinned creature snarled. "Most never rise after two thumps."

Rogaan spit to clear his mouth of the taste of blood, then stood up. Anger pushed him, giving him reason to rise. He stepped forward again, with the intent to aid his father despite the threatening glare facing him. He pushed on. Rogaan stopped short of the long knife-wielding creature, now two steps removed from Father. Rogaan then carefully made to help his father to his feet. The creature stood motionless except for his eyes that followed Rogaan's every move and those twitching ears. As Rogaan assisted his father up, Aren approached in a run, still irritably demanding help with the big brute chasing him. Fortunately, Aren was a bit faster than his brown-skinned pursuer.

"You going to help me with this Nephiliim?" Aren yelled as he passed, off and running and sounding panicked, but no longer hysterical.

As the Nephiliim closed, Rogaan pulled his father down into a crouch as that club of a fist passed just over their heads with a whoosh. They immediately stood back up looking at a thick brown backside waddle away after Aren. Baffled, Rogaan asked his father, "Nephiliim?"

"Asra'Tellen . . . a smart rock you are," the creature snarled with what Rogaan took as a confident grin. "Good with a blade?"

"He is not," Mithraam answered before Rogaan could. His father stepped closer to the wine-black-skinned adversary. "I am skilled, *Mornor skurst*. Test me, not the youngling."

Rogaan gave his father a stunned stare. His father had skills with hammers and chisels, but not blades! The only blades he ever recalled observing his father swing were those he tested . . . at still targets to ensure they cut and retained their edge as expected.

"Father—" Rogaan started to protest, but was cut off by his father's empty raised hand signaling for his silence. Rogaan mused at his father somehow managing to put a long knife in his other hand. *Where did he get it?* Footfalls pattered behind him accompanied by labored breathing. It was gone almost as soon as it came. Rogaan feared for his father playing blades with this "Mornor-skurst." *So that is what a Mornor-skurst looks like.* I've never seen one before . . . *Thud.*

Rogaan felt a tremendous impact to his head and the sensation of being weightless, again. The pain felt something terrible, but the weightlessness had a serene feel that somehow traded off with the pain . . . until Rogaan slammed into the bloodstained floor stones . . . again. This time, the wind knocked from him as his head spun in a daze. His face stung. Rogaan feared his cheekbones broken.

"Little rock no learn. Ha-ha." The brown-skinned Nephiliim loomed over Rogaan, again taunting him. He stood with his massive foot now pressing down on Rogaan's chest. Rogaan gasped for air, trying to fill his burning lungs, but failing. The weight on him made it impossible to take a breath. Flashing spots filled his vision. He hurt everywhere and felt himself slipping from this world. Then the pressure on his chest disappeared without warning, allowing him to gulp in a lungful of air, and then another. The flashing spots diminished, though his lungs still had a sting to them. A ruckus echoed in the cylinder-shaped room drawing his attention. He found his father standing between the Nephiliim and him. Somehow his father had forced the brown-skinned bully back as he kept waving that long knife in front of him to ward off his massive opponent. His father moved the blade in short, controlled slashes keeping his angry intimidator at bay . . . at least for a short time before an overhand hammer of a punch sent his father to the stone floor where he lay unmoving. A long, stunned moment passed for Rogaan as he stared at his still father, hoping he would rise but fearing him *lightless*. Not a twitch. Panic gripped him. *Is Father lightless?*

"Dat'll teach him tu cut me," the brutish Nephiliim declared, then chuckled.

Rogaan feared the worst and started crawling frantically to his father, hoping all he had suffered was a bump on the head. Rogaan found himself unable to stop from visibly shaking at the horrific thought his father was gone from this world . . . and from him. With painful realization, Rogaan, for the first time in his life, saw his father as mortal and that he, Rogaan, was not ready for his father to meet the Ancients, leaving his family behind. His throat ached and tightened as he crawled. Tears welled up in his eyes as he fought for a shred of self-control. *What am I to do with him gone? How can I tell Mother Father died protecting me?* Rogaan felt to howl in his pain, but did not. His captors would know his pain and weakness.

Powerful hands grabbed Rogaan by his shoulder and belt, then heaved him into the air. That weightless feeling took him again, though Rogaan allowed no comfort in it as the cut-stone wall rushed at him. He struck hard, bouncing off the wall, then slamming to the floor. Terrible pain rattled through him at each impact. Stunned and numb, Rogaan lay on the bloodstained floor, but only for a moment. Anger swept through him like a fire upon a dry field on a windy day. He exploded to his feet, propelled by his arms. With his booted feet firmly set to the crimson-stained floor, Rogaan quickly surveyed the room and everything in it. His attackers moved with that familiar slowness. The stench of the blood, sweat, and other body odors ravaged his senses. He chose to ignore his nose and what was filling it. Instead of being unnerved by it all as he had been before, Rogaan chose to use this thing, this *wild, raging surge* within. He, for the first time, welcomed it. He took in many details with a single quick scan. Father lay unconscious or *lightless* two strides to his right. The big brown Nephiliim stood growling at him three and a half strides to Rogaan's front. Aren panted heavily, leaning against the wall on the opposite side of the room. And the Mornor-skurst held a casual stance while sneering with arms folded seven strides to his left. The rancid odor of the room was powerful and tried to test him, but Rogaan chose to ignore it still. *That brute is to pay for his cruelty against Father.*

The Nephiliim started to raise his right arm and shift his weight in an attack on Rogaan. Rogaan saw each detail of the brown-skinned Nephiliim's moves and decided to avoid and counterpunch. He stepped to his left and twisted, allowing the brute's hammer of a fist to miss him as it swept in front of his face by less than his own hand's width. The Nephiliim's head with a growing look of surprise hung in front of Rogaan . . . an easy target.

With all his anger, all his fury, all his pent-up rage, Rogaan unleashed a righted-handed hooking punch propelled from his firmly set feet through the exploding extension in his legs, the rotating of his hips and torso, his even faster rotating shoulders and arms, until his painfully clenched fist smashed into the Nephiliim's right cheek. Rogaan felt the brute's cheek flesh compress and his thick face bones break as they gave way to the impact. The big Nephiliim staggered backward and to his left, his arms flailing and his tree-trunk-sized legs spread apart to keep from falling over. Rogaan did not give the creature a chance to recover. With his exploding anger and hunger to avenge his father propelling him, Rogaan launched himself at the Nephiliim, striking his right knee at the side with his foot, the force of his bounding attack bending the knee in a manner it was never designed to. The ripping of his intimidator's flesh vibrated through Rogaan's foot. The brown brute collapsed to the floor in a howl of pain, but managed to keep from sprawling on his wounded face by extending his right arm and hand to stop his fall. His father's tormentor awkwardly knelt before him on damaged knee and outstretched hand. Rogaan, his anger and his lust for vengeance still not satisfied, made to strike the wounded beast until it was no more. *No one hurts my family. Not without payment. No more.* He grabbed the brute's right forearm, pulling it up and back, forcing the brute into a kneeling position while Rogaan rotated his own body and stepped under the arm he raised. With his back to the intimidator, Rogaan pulled down on the forearm with every muscle fiber in his body contracting in a rage. The Nephiliim's arm at first resisted, but with a renewed burst of determination from Rogaan, snapped at the elbow with a slow, resounding pop, rending the flesh and bone as Rogaan bent it in an unnatural way over his shoulder. The Nephiliim's howls reverberated throughout the chamber. To Rogaan, the howl was long and wailing . . . and the beginnings of his satisfaction. The flame of his anger still not quenched, Rogaan sought to deliver more punishment. He cocked his left arm forward, then drove his left elbow back as he did his whole body backward with his legs. Rogaan felt his elbow impact what he thought was the brute's face. He felt bones collapse as he drove backward. Then, the big body pressing against him went limp, sliding to the floor with a reverberating thud.

Justice and payment for harming Father. Rogaan turned, hoping to see his father stirring. His heart sank. Still, Mithraam lay unmoving a stride from the silent, hulking brown body now lying with him on the floor. Stepping toward his father, Rogaan caught the glint of something to his right. *A spinning knife coming at him.* It almost hung in the air as Rogaan jerked his head and upper body backward, the blade passing in front of his neck, cutting him skin-deep on his chest. The knife then rang dully as it bounced harmlessly off the wall to his left. Looking to see where it had come from, Rogaan found the Mornor-skurst take up a readying stance as he remembered seeing his uncle twice take up in Brigum when preparing for close fighting. *The Mornor-skurst is War Sworn . . . By the Ancients, could this get worse?*

Rogaan and the Mornor-skurst stood staring at each other. The assumed *War Sworn* had not seriously harmed either Rogaan or his father, as Rogaan saw it. *Except for that blade a moment ago, there is no justification to fight him.* In truth, Rogaan felt intimidated at the thought of fighting one dedicated to becoming a supreme warrior, preparing to fight at the side of the Ancients in the End Battle.

Three mouth-gaping *Sakes* stuffed in the doorway looking from the

Mornor-skurst to Rogaan and back several times, waiting . . . anticipating something to happen. Rogaan felt little fear when considering them. But he did feel that sickness in his stomach and a wave of dizziness sweep over him as everything within the room moved about too quickly. Even the noises returned to what Rogaan considered normal, but so fast now! He fought his guts to keep from sicking up. Not wanting to show weakness to this group of dangers, Rogaan forced himself to continue standing as he did the moments before things *changed*. The Mornor-skurst canted his head and said something to the *Sakes* that Rogaan missed. One of them quickly took off down the hallway, but not before the look of relief spread across the Mornor-skurst's face.

Father . . . . Rogaan needed to know if he was truly alone here in this prison, to see if his father was without *Light*. The blow his father had taken was brutal. In an attempt at controlling himself, Rogaan relaxed his body and stepped toward his father while carefully keeping watch of the Mornor-skurst. He hoped no attack would befall him. Thankfully, the Mornor-skurst stood simply watching him from his ready stance, blade in hand, impassive face and eyes unblinking. *This Mornor-skurst is unnerving.* Rogaan kneeled next to his father and placed a hand on his chest. *He breathes!* A flood of relief washed over him.

"Father!" Rogaan gently shook the limp body on the floor. "Wake, Father. Wake."

A groan escaped his father's lips. Rogaan helped him roll onto his back while supporting his head. The bloodstains on his father's face were from a mix of what was on the floor and from his nose. With another groan, his father struggled to open his eyes. What Rogaan saw in those eyes appeared distant, unfocused at first. After a few moments, they regained the sharp focus Rogaan had known all of his life. He smiled at his father.

"You live, my son?" Mithraam half-asked, half-stated with relief. Then with a slight smile from under his beard he added, "This is fortunate. I will not have to answer to your mother."

Rogaan felt uncertain how to take his father's humor. It was so seldom displayed and often at the oddest of times, as now. *Maybe his head is not yet clear.* Rogaan helped his father sit up. Once sitting, his father took several deep breaths, followed by a crinkling of his nose. He turned his head looking around the room. Obviously, he needed to reorient himself. Rogaan too looked up. He found Aren still standing against the wall. The Evendiir's eyes went from the fallen Nephiliim to Rogaan and back again. Wide-eyed disbelief and a long sigh of relief were the Evendiir's only emotions Rogaan could read.

"How . . .?" Mithraam started to ask a question, then looked at the fallen bulk of a body lying next to him, and then back to Rogaan with scrutinizing eyes. "You?"

Rogaan nodded. "I do not know how. My anger at him striking you and fear at losing you to the Ancients somehow gave me strength."

"And quickness," Aren added as he carefully shuffled closer.

"I see," Mithraam spoke as if concluding something that needed confirmation.

"How did you move so fast?" Aren asked Rogaan as he knelt near the Tellens while poking a finger at the unconscious bulk. "I barely followed your strikes. He lives, though his face looks broken. Good. He'll need help to eat."

"I do not know how," Rogaan answered honestly. "And I do not care if this one dies of hunger for what he did."

Rogaan's father started to his feet as a team of armored *Sakes* and blue-clad guardsmen poured into the room, all with swords and knives drawn. Disbelief wore heavy on each of their faces.

"*Sakes* . . . bind the Tellen with irons." Commanded the Mornor-skurst.

Sakes and *Tusaa'Ner* guardsmen exchanged uncertain glances before a heavily muscled and confident guard stepped forward with two others following his lead. They made their way carefully to the kneeling Mithraam while watching him with nervous eyes. Rogaan made to step between his father and them, but Mithraam stopped him with an outreached hand. Rogaan felt torn. He did not want his father suffering anymore, but he felt compelled to respect his father's wishes. Deciding to obey his father, Rogaan made no action against the guards or guardsmen as they reached for his father.

"*Sakes* . . . not that old one . . . that young one," the Mornor-skurst scolded as he redirected them. "Careful care with that one. He is dangerous. Double bind him."

After a brief pause with nobody moving, the *Sakes* carefully approached Rogaan as if his sweat was as poison. They bound him at the wrists and just above the elbows. Wrists in front and elbows behind him. Both bindings were of metal shackles. Uncomfortable, but bearable if for a short time back to his cell. Any longer, and they would cut through his skin, maybe to the bone. The *Sakes* appeared surprised at Rogaan's compliance. Aren and Mithraam were then bound with ropes, arms and wrists in front of them. The three of them were lined up as a heavy escort surrounded them with drawn weapons, readied to cut down trouble at the giving of the order. The *Sake zigaar* entered the room wearing only his dark chest armor, kilt, and sandals. He filled the doorway that others cleared to make way for him. The dark-haired Baraan's scarred arms spoke of much fighting. Scars on his face spoke of great experience gained through pain. He surveyed the room in a glance with his eyes setting on Rogaan when he was done.

"Sworn One, how did this happen?" The *Sake zigaar* demanded.

"*Zigaar* . . . this one." The Mornor-skurst pointed at Rogaan. "You spoke of him being a bother, though you made little of it. Nixdatt couldn't strike him when he is alert. This one even evaded my thrown blade, though only by a hair. He felled Nixdatt in four blows . . . all bone breakers. He's more than a bother. He's a danger. Why did you not give warning?"

"Trouble you are, young one." The *Sake zigaar* ignored the Mornor-skurst as he scowled at Rogaan. "Even unskilled you achieve this. The arena hasn't seen the likes of you in a long time. How do you mark them, Sworn One?"

The Mornor-skurst pointed in turn at Aren, then Mithraam, then Rogaan. "Runner. Runner. Fighter. I say, kill the young Tellen and be done with him. Too much unexpected happens around him. That's not my liking."

"*Sakes* and *Tusaa'Ner*." The *Sake zigaar* again ignored the Mornor-skurst as he spoke deep and loud. "The young Tellen is to remain in binds at all times. Double the watch over him. Kill him without mercy if he makes more trouble. Keep him alive otherwise. The *Zas* may have interest in him."

The *Sake zigaar* spun on his heels, then strode from the room with purpose as a gathering of guards, guardsmen, and others parted way for him in the hallway. The Mornor-skurst turned his attention back to the room, if he ever took his attention from it, waving his dark, wine-colored hand to the armed escorts, signally for them to take the prisoners away. By knife and sword tips, Rogaan, his father, and Aren were prodded down the hallway, escorted on both sides, leaving no room for anyone in the throng ahead of onlookers to suffer anything other than being pushed out of the way. While concerned about their unknown fates, Rogaan oddly felt a sense of satisfaction. His father lived . . . and so did he. Even the Evendiir survived this *testing . . . whatever it was meant to test.* A small victory. One not to gloat over. He still did not know how to invoke his *wild spirit*, as he decided to call it. *It seems to take me over when it wants*, he resigned to himself. *And what does "runner" and "fighter" mean?*

Chapter 20

Revelations

A night and a day passed slowly for Rogaan since his brawl with the Nephiliim. His mind kept reliving the fight and how he came to be in it, and the strange combination of events. Was this chance, or guided by an unseen hand? His life had the tone of a story, though Rogaan did not know if it was one to be great or cursed. The most painful part for Rogaan was Suhd being taken from him, despite the assurances of the *Sake zigaar* she would not suffer at unknown hands. To not know her fate seemed more painful than losing her to the Ancients. Then there were the two dead at his hand, one Rogaan felt justified as he was harming Suhd. The other, he carried with a growing guilt and sorrow. Rogaan's head remained in a swirl. So much had happened since his ignorance became enlightened by dark realities and his innocence was taken from him during the hunt. So many regrets for the dead and suffering living because of him. He brooded.

Several tremors shook the jail cell floors, walls, and ceiling in that night and day. The shaking happened briefly both times, all without bringing the place collapsing down on them. Rogaan noted this underground was constructed well. He wondered if Tellens had any hand in building it. He knew he would not be surprised if they did. Rogaan guessed it was late afternoon from the shift changes of *Sake* guards and *Tusaa'Ner* guardsmen through a mental exercise he developed himself. Their only meal of the day, a meager thing of dried meat and some kind of herbs and water, should arrive soon . . . if his figuring was right. His stomach grumbled at the thought of the poor-tasting meal. He was not certain if it meant he was hungry or if his stomach would reject it. The bindings shackling him, an iron bar between his iron-cuffed wrists were in front of him and another bar bent across his back had a pair of thick hide straps securing his arms just above each elbow. It was impossible for him to sleep soundly with it on, and the bars made it impossible to stand or sit without doing so awkwardly . . .

and painfully. Using the chamber pot also proved a challenge. *Embarrassing*. Rogaan dreaded the need to use the thing in the presence of others even without the shackles. With them on and everyone trying to steal a look to see how he fared . . . He groaned at the image in his head.

Rogaan talked with his father intermittently after their surviving the *Testing*. His father praised him for besting the Nephiliim's challenge. He seemed genuinely surprised at Rogaan's victory. Rogaan's pride at his father's words was all the more sweetened by his father's amazement. But as much as this made him feel better than he had in days, Rogaan's thoughts kept returning to Suhd and her suffering. Rogaan asked his father more than a few times if he thought Suhd was safe and unharmed. He wanted assurance she would remain unspoiled and unharmed. His father could give him neither. They discussed family, more to the point, Mother, and how her being of the House Isin gave her a shield from some of the *high games* being played among the Houses and *Zas*. Then, their discussions turned to Father's "lessons," with him talking of grand philosophies concerning righteousness; freedom versus tyranny, the selfless and selfish, and the law-abiding versus those who *want,* at any cost, or have no care of whom they hurt. He heard all of these "lessons" many times over the years. For Rogaan, his father's teachings had remained out of his grasp to fully understand and appreciate until his recent experiences. Here in the arena underground, Rogaan felt the direct hand of power seekers and tyrants. He did not understand how one person could treat another with such disregard.

Rogaan's father then took up quiet words with him so to keep others from listening. His father spoke of his plan for Rogaan to take up and carry his obligations and responsibilities once his *Light* traveled to the heavens and Rogaan being properly prepared. He gave apologies for not completing these preparations. At first, Rogaan felt confused at his father's revealing. *What obligations? What responsibilities?* His father then revealed long-kept secret plans for him, but why now with them locked away in a Farratum jail? Still, his father kept from speaking too much of it. *Why so little after revealing it at all?* Rogaan's confusion turned to frustration the more his father spoke of these responsibilities. Bits and pieces of this plan were revealed, but not in a coherent manner allowing Rogaan to make sense of it. Further frustrating him, his father's answers to direct questions were never simple. Deciding this line of talk hurt his head, Rogaan asked how he was to see Suhd free. It burned at him thinking of her being touched by others and in ways he had not, yet. His mood turned dark every time he thought of it . . . thought of her . . . which was often. His father's answer offered little that could be done, mortifying and angering Rogaan. *How can he give up at saving Suhd? Is a cause worth her freedom and her dignity, as well?* Rogaan silently brooded on that thought, but got nowhere in answering it. *Does Father truly expect me to give up on Suhd . . . to let her suffer at the hands of . . . others?* "NO!"

Rogaan looked around uneasily after his unexpected outburst. Everyone nervously eyed him with their breaths held tight. *They are afraid of me.* With a growing curiosity, Rogaan stood, then moved about the cell to test his conclusion, especially concerning the guardsmen. They appeared nervous to Rogaan. Even bound as he was, they feared what they saw in his eyes before averting theirs. *Good.* It made him feel powerful in an unexpected way. Even his father looked at him differently. He did not know if he liked that, so he returned to his cross-legged seated position where he continued to think on all he had recently learned.

When not allowing the discomfort of his bindings to get at him and occupy his mind, Rogaan's thoughts always found their way back to Suhd. He increasingly worried at her being handled and abused. It tormented him, burning him inside until he felt ready to scream and bite at the cell bars to get free and find her and take her away. Images of that terrible moment when the guardsmen attempted to have their way with her kept filling his head. Rogaan found it more and more difficult to remember her as she was in Brigum . . . innocent. Instead, he saw her pain, suffering from assaults by unclean and uncaring captors. Rogaan ached at wanting . . . needing to protect her honor, keep her safe, and take revenge on those harming her. That sizzling flame of internal pain grew into a blaze, then a raging fire. It felt as if it would consume him. He stopped caring if it would as he felt power in his rage.

"Thinkin' of me sister?" Pax asked quietly from the other side of the bars. Rogaan, so intensely focused on his own tormenting thoughts, did not recognize his friend's voice at first. He looked at Pax as if looking at an unwelcomed stranger before struggling to back away from his rage so he could acknowledge his friend. Rogaan realized his friend broke the silence his parents demanded of him. Their unapproving glares confirmed Pax's defiance. *Same old Pax.*

"Yes," Rogaan replied honestly, but kept his answer short so as not to elaborate on all that was swirling in his head and heart. Rogaan did not want to give up his pain as it gave him purpose, but those self-created visions of Suhd in his head made it difficult for him to keep his emotions under control. He felt a need to explode, but did all he could to keep from doing so. It would do no good, not here, not now.

"Ya think she be . . . safe?" Pax asked while looking at his boots.

"I hope she is . . . safe," Rogaan answered solemnly. In his mind, there were different kinds of "safe." The kind where she lived and the kind she did so without injury . . . mind and body whole.

"Suhd be . . ." Pax tried to be positive, but his shaky voice betrayed him. He sounded as if trying to convince himself or his parents that Baraans were not having their ways with her. He fell silent for a moment with a dull, pained expression before his face twisted into a wounded and angry brother. "She be smart and knows well enough ta keep hands from gettin' places havin' no matter bein'."

Rogaan gave Pax a sour sideways glare meant to tell him he had to do better at convincing him. Rogaan's innards twisted and roared at the images flashing in his mind. The images seemed to be getting worse, more brutal. Rogaan tried to keep his emotions suppressed, buried deep inside.

"We must avenge her, Rogaan," Pax stated with begrudging acceptance spoken through angry clinched teeth. "Before here, she be innocent in all ways. I be fearin' she be no more."

"Likely chance at that . . ." A new guard who must have just entered the room through the now-open door boldly dug at Pax and Rogaan. Laughter echoed throughout the room as the dark-clad guards seemed to find humor in their suffering exchange.

"She be servant to Hurrim'Tal, I hear." The tallest of the three guards spoke loud enough to ensure everyone heard him.

"An appetite he has . . ." the shortest of now four guards added with a thick tone of cruelty. He too was new. The new guards quietly relieved the two who had been watching them.

"An appetite for the young and pretty." The taller of the two dug the blade in deeply as he watched Rogaan with cruel eyes. "You killed my friend for nothin', stoner. It's righteous your youngling pretty is having pleasures as a woman at the hands of that fat lawmaker and his attendants."

They kept at him, driving mental blade after blade of painful torment into him. Unwanted images all. Rogaan's head filled with horrible visions of Suhd's suffering. Laughter and more cruel taunts from the guards intensified as Rogaan sat awkwardly against the cold bars grasping them tightly in his hands, his eyes shut tight and teeth clenched. A howling pain sliced through him, spinning into a tempest of uncontrollable rage. He gripped the bars hard; trying to keep his pain and rage from exploding on those nearest, all the while fearing nothing could contain what he felt. Thoughts of unbridled revenge at Suhd's attackers entered his mind's eye. When he thought it could be no worse, more images of her being harmed flooded his mind. His rage exploded inside, more than he ever felt in all of his life. Yet, somehow, he held on to his sanity. He did not know how he managed it . . . protecting those near from his daimon thoughts needing to inflict pain and suffering.

"Rogaan . . ." A distant voice called to him. It was almost imperceptible.

"Rogaan." The voice called him again, louder and now deep. The voice was filled with concern, yet calm and familiar. The raging pain swirling inside kept him from focusing on the voice or anything else. Images of Suhd attacked spun wildly in his head. The fragile control he had over himself slipped. He feared it would fail completely as his pain howled at him.

"My son . . ." His father's voice pierced through the pain. "Breathe. Breathe deep and long. Your breathing only matters . . . only your breathing."

Rogaan resisted his father's guidance. He wanted to feel his pain. Make it part of him so he could do what was needed to be done . . . take Suhd from them and make her safe . . . and make them all suffer. He needed his pain.

Calm words of guidance kept at him, telling him to breathe, to take a breath one by one. Rogaan fought against it. Then, without warning, his chest filled partly. His raging pain subsided, but only a little. He wanted his pain to remain, to renew it, and make it raging. His father's calm voice kept at him, "Breathe and release." He found his father's voice calming, soothing. Rogaan's pain and rage eased. "No!"

His father's calm and even voice continued on relentlessly. Rogaan's rage lessened further. Those painful images in his mind started to fade away. Father's voice led him to breathing deeply, then exhaling in a steady rhythm. The images faded into a blur no longer discernible. Rogaan opened his eyes.

Rogaan found everyone looking at him . . . their stares unnerving. His father's eyes found and held him from his kneeling position in front of Rogaan. "A relief you returned to us, my son. You chose the worst of occasions to suffer the drunkenness of a young lass."

"Curse da Ancients!" The taller of two darkly clad guards shouted.

The Evendiir stood stiffly on other side of the cell holding an uncertain look Rogaan could not tell if fear or something else. Pax and his parents held their breath in the other cell. They all had pressed themselves against the far stone walls. Their faces bore both surprise and fear. Rogaan felt a stinging numbness in his hands and wrists and his chest ached terribly. Looking down, the iron crossbar of the shackles that bound him had broken from his right wrist cuff and the leather strap restraining his arms above the elbow was torn, allowing his arms and hands their independence. The bars separating the cells were bent and twisted, enough for Pax or the Evendiir to pass through. *How is this possible?* With shock and a fearful wonder, Rogaan let go of the bars as he looked at his father.

"Look at what da Tellen did," the other guard added in disbelief.

"Father . . . What is happening to me?" Rogaan asked with a shaky voice. "What ills me?"

Confident and kind eyes, softer than Rogaan had seen in a long time, looked upon him. His father knelt unmoving for a few moments, thinking as he stroked his beard. Rogaan knew the sign of his father considering what to tell him. What Rogaan expected to follow would leave him with more questions from his father's carefully chosen words that would speak tomes, but only if you had a mind to understand. Rogaan needed answers. He wanted the truth without having to figure out the meaning. What he saw in his father's face when the thinking and considering was done was relief, stern in the way his father held his brow and jaw, but relief was clearly on his face for those who knew what to look for. *Is Father to speak all of it?* Rogaan dared to anticipate his father's words.

"Call the *Tusaa'Ner* guardsmen!" The taller guard ordered almost in a panic.

The disbelieving guard stared at his superior a moment before it struck him to call into the hallway for the city guardsmen. A clatter of metal and footfalls told Rogaan more than a few approached. Four blue-clad *Tusaa'Ner* entered the room taking up positions next to the *Sakes*.

"Account!" The biggest of the *Tusaa'Ner* demanded.

"Look . . ." The *Sake* guard who had called for reinforcements pointed at Rogaan.

"What?" The *Tusaa'Ner* leader asked with eyes wide. "By the Ancients, how'd that happen?"

"It be that young Tellen again," the shorter of the two *Sakes* answered.

The *Tusaa'Ner* leader looked at Rogaan, then through him as he spotted the bent bars, then back at Rogaan, then glanced around at the others in the room, and then his eyes returned to Rogaan. "You're too much trouble, stoner."

The *Tusaa'Ner* leader turned to one of his guardsmen speaking something Rogaan could not make out. The young *Tusaa'Ner* exited the room without hesitation. Wearing a hard scowl, the *Tusaa'Ner* leader returned his attention to Rogaan. "If I'd get my way, stoner, I'd see ya hang or fed to leapers."

Rogaan kept silent as he peeled off all but the iron cuffs of the ruined shackles, those remained solidly around his wrists. *These shackles were not made well*. It was all Rogaan could think that allowed him to break them. But the bars . . . that both troubled and gratified him. He knew he was stronger than many, but bending iron bars was something more than he thought possible.

"Rogaan, heed my words." Mithraam's tone brought Rogaan out of his self-reflection. His father glanced around the room to see if any paid them attention. The guardsmen were already involved in disbelieving talk with the *Sakes*. Mithraam continued in a low voice while pointing at the broken shackles. "In your drunkenness with Suhd, your actions have shown them you cannot be controlled. They fear you and have need to be rid of you and maybe even made an example of. Prepare yourself for . . . more suffering, I fear, my son."

Rogaan's head swirled with confusion. He looked at his father with questioning eyes trying to put the pieces of a broken puzzle-box together. Skepticism and frustration filled his voice, "How can this be? How can I be punished without judgment?"

"The *Zas* have assumed *Gal* authority to condemn," Rogaan's father announced with an exhale. "*Za* Irzal, as the *Utu' Me*, has pronounced you guilty and condemned before *Gal* Suundi. Suundi confirmed the pronouncement."

"I was not there . . . how . . .?" Rogaan half-stated, half-asked. "I was not given opportunity to challenge?"

"Their new laws appear to have given her this authority." His father answered Rogaan's question, then went on explaining. "The victory you had over the Nephiliim . . . that dark-skinned brute . . . We were being tested to determine the manner our *Lights* are to be taken from us. This is the old way. These games were abolished at the end of the civil war as being too barbaric. The punishments have been renewed . . . a tragedy for the people and what we were building."

"We . . . ?" Rogaan asked as he challenged his father's use of words. "Only I harmed a jailer. You committed no transgression."

"Games of power have little reason more than to rid that which is feared, perceived a threat, or is uncontrolled," Mithraam further explained. "By her actions, this *Za* I speak of has no care of the laws, except what she can wield. She ignores what does not serve her and uses the rest as weapons against all between her and her goals. It appears the other *Zas* are little better or they would have muted her. Corruption has grown and rooted itself very deep here. More than we suspected."

"We?" Rogaan asked confused by his father's words. "Who?"

"You are seen as a danger." Mithraam continued his explanation, but not of what Rogaan asked. "The ones who see the people of these lands in need of ruling, who covet authority and work influences over the masses in soft steps to keep rebellion from rising, all the while the *Zas* and their devotees enslave the people . . . small step by small step. Strangely, many willingly ask for enslavement caring to feel safe instead of free or to have their bellies filled without need of laboring instead of being productive and responsible. Then, it becomes too late to dissent, those having authority invoke their iron grasp of rules against the masses and anyone a challenge to them. This place is filled with those who pose such a challenge to the tyranny. You saw them in the cells even if you did not understand what you looked at. Now, the coveters see you threatening their plans with strength and resolve, as they see me with ideas and principles. They want us *removed*."

"You mean *lightless*?" Rogaan asked as his body shook at the seriousness of his father's words and the realization that this was no game.

"Yes," Mithraam answered solemnly.

"I thought the laws and the law-keepers would always be there to protect?" Rogaan both stated and asked seeking a better answer from his father.

"They have been corrupted so even the unknowing aid the coveters." Mithraam's clarification did not help Rogaan's sense of dread and despair. "Many without coin and those of coin and the privilege it can bring have discovered true tyrants rise from the governing . . . those with power to make and enforce laws."

". . . the selfish, the coveters of authority over others, without honor and righteousness to guide them." Rogaan finished reciting one of his father's teachings from years before. He did not understand it, until now.

"Tyrants reign when no challenge stands in check to the gathering of power and authority over people." Rogaan's father sounded the teacher of days past. Then, in a saddened tone he changed the focus of his words. "Before they come for you . . ."

"Who is coming for me?" Rogaan asked as his innards turned and tightened. "More *Sakes*, *Tusaa'Ner* . . . who?"

His father gave him that look to keep his thoughts focused on what *IS* important. "We do not have long. You ask me what is happening to you. You are experiencing the *Zagdu-i-Kuzu*."

"My Coming of Age?" Rogaan asked as if he heard wrong. His father's teachings taught him the *Zagdu-i-Kuzu* an event having both flesh and spirit qualities. Rogaan only believed it a ceremony of passage . . . no more.

"A poorly understood part of Tellen ways," Mithraam replied softly. "The ancient blood sometimes rises in Tellens, revealing itself during the *Zagdu-i-Kuzu*. Most never feel it. For those that do, it is a difficult time for them with their blood *raised* so. Some perish. Others suffer it for a short time . . . days, and then it is gone, never to return. Others are forever changed . . . some for the better, some not. You have felt this raising for some days now, haven't you? I suspected it. You have qualities unlike most with the gift, though some would call it a curse. Only you will see it for what it is. Your ancient Tellen blood, that of the ancient Sentii, mixes with that of your mother's, also of a distant line of Sentii."

Rogaan fell back against the bars stunned and in fearful awe at his father's revealing. *Ancient blood? Father's? Mother's? Both of them?* Rogaan understood history lessons that the Tellens were descendants of the bloodline of *Our Lady of Battles*. She was legend to be Sentii, but that was only legend. His father's telling meant she *was Sentii*. And mother's . . . ? *What does this mean for me . . . curses or something worse?*

"Why have you both kept silent of this?" Rogaan asked with stunned curiosity.

"It is not something one speaks of to younglings," Mithraam answered. "They are too free of tongue and too many elders are fearful of the ancient blood. A *raising* of the blood often sees younglings cast out into the wilds. I was not to take that chance with a careless word off your tongue."

"My blood has been *raised* for many days, Father," Rogaan nervously admitted. His innards churned at the possibility something terrible was happening to him. Rogaan's father put on a concerned, contemplating face.

"When did these '*raisings*' first take you?" His father asked.

Rogaan thought back to when he first felt . . . different. In his memories, he stepped back in time through moments when he experienced the world slowing, when he perceived things strangely . . . in vivid detail, when his ears rang painfully at every sound, when he felt sickened. "It was the night I completed my *shunir'ra*."

"You are certain?" Mithraam looked at him with intense and serious eyes.

"As best I can remember," Rogaan replied.

Rogaan's father sat back against the bars lost in deep thought. He remained so for moments that seemed much longer. He was working something in his head . . . assembling a puzzle, as he had explained thinking to Rogaan when younger and full of "what's" and "why's."

"Father?" Rogaan interrupted his father's thoughts, causing those distant eyes to see the here and now. Then, footfalls synchronized in cadence by a handful of *Tusaa'Ner* approaching at a brisk pace. Rogaan felt them vibrating through the floor, at first, then heard them just as his father did.

"They are coming," his father announced with recognition that Rogaan already knew. Mithraam looked to Rogaan with serious eyes before whispering, "My son, your blood is *raised* with the touch of the stone. It has awakened your blood. There is no direct telling of this in the books of old, only stories passed down by elder words. You must seek their knowledge, and you must retrieve your *shunir'ra*. It is more than of your simple making. Keep it safe from others. It holds the key . . ."

Six fully armored *Tusaa'Ner* entered the room, crowding in with the others and forming an almost semicircle of blue around Rogaan's cell, all standing behind a now-alert *Sake* guard engaged in talk with the *Tusaa'Ner* leader. All blue-clad guardsmen had hands to pommels of undrawn swords. Several more darkly clad *Sakes* followed the *Tusaa'Ner* into the room before positioning themselves on the far wall.

The *Sake* leader, with the *Tusaa'Ner* behind him, smiled in relief and a renewed confidence as he waved his long knife between himself and the cell. "Now, we see that head of yours to the noose, or better, the ax."

Chapter 21

The Pit

"**H**old your blades!" A demanding and confident voice of someone thinking he is in charge rang out from beyond the room with an irritating sharpness.

"We've been commanded to kill this one for anymore troubles," the *Sake* leader proclaimed boldly as he pointed at Rogaan. "I say he's trouble."

"Then why isn't he *lightless*, already?" A light-haired burly *Tusaa'Ner sakal* asked as he entered the cell room wearing irritation from eyes to toes. Adorned in lightweight, sky-blue armor, a red cape, and calf-high sandals, he looked upon the room with a crossed brow. "Don't bother with your excuses, Tuumai. I've listened to enough of them already."

The *Tusaa'Ner* guardsmen made a hole in their formation for the commanding officer. He strode through with a sharp, irritated gait, stopping in front of the jail cells with his angry eyes fixed on Rogaan. Rogaan tried to look as innocent as he could with eyes wide and with the best youngling-like "oops" expression he could put on. Behind him lay broken shackles and bent bars and all. The commander's eyes flashed wide for a moment once he focused on the damage Rogaan had done. Looking about the cells, eyeing Pax and his parents, Aren, and Mithraam, he gave a dismissive huff.

"How did you allow these prisoners to do this?" The *Tusaa'Ner sakal* demanded to no one in particular, though Rogaan guessed his question was directed at Tuumai, the *Sake* leader.

Tuumai put on a surprised look at the question. Then, his face turned indignant as he angrily pointed at Rogaan. "It was that *stoner*. No others. He was angry about somethin' and started growlin' just before doin' all this breakin' of things."

"Impossible," the *Tusaa'Ner sakal* dismissed Tuumai's explanation.

"I swear by the Ancients, Commander," Tuumai replied in a venomous tone.

"How?" The *Tusaa'Ner* officer asked with a touch of his anger gone.

"He's stronger than to look at," Tuumai answered with a growing heat. "He's killed Arguu and injured Ezanu. He put down big ol' slow-wit from what the whisperings say. Now, he's broken his shackles and bent those bars. He's too dangerous to keep. His *Light* needs to join the *Darkness*."

"Afraid, Tuumai?" The *Tusaa'Ner sakal* asked contemptuously.

"Never!" Tuumai replied with contempt just as deep and angry. The *sakal* smiled at his rushed reply. It appeared he intended to put him on his heels and thought he succeeded.

The blue-armored, red-caped *sakal* fell silent for a short time. He looked in thought and as if considering one or more decisions. None of his guardsmen nor the *Sakes* spoke or attempted to interrupt him. Rogaan was not certain if their silence was out of respect or fear, though all stood stolid, with hands to pommels, ready to act with their weapons. After the long pause, the officer nodded to no one, appearing to have made a decision.

"Trouble, you are." The *sakal* looked Rogaan in the eyes, then gave orders without even a glance at those behind him. "Rebind him."

The largest of the *Tusaa'Ner* guardsmen looked to the *Sakes* before nodding a head toward the cell. Two of the closest *Sakes* complied with apprehensive steps, entering into the cell with another set of iron shackles. They cautiously positioned themselves on either side of Rogaan before quickly reshackling him, and then carefully helping him to his feet.

Rogaan's instinct now was to resist the *Sakes* and *Tusaa'Ner* . . . They were the errand younglings of tyrants, but he decided against it. He had done enough to put others in jeopardy. *If I comply, maybe the others will be let free.* When satisfied with the *Sakes'* preparations of Rogaan, the burly *Tusaa'Ner sakal* announced his intent with an order along with a dismissive hand wave before making to leave. "Toss him in the pit."

"Do not do this." Mithraam spoke out to the *Tusaa'Ner* officer.

The blue and red figure stopped to face Mithraam, then held up his hand. Everyone quickly halted once they realized he had commanded so. Frozen in their positions, the *Sakes* and *Tusaa'Ner* guardsmen all looked at him expectantly. Anger followed by contempt washed over his face. "What, *stoner?*"

"Do not do this," Mithraam repeated, challenging him as he stared back at the commander. "He has done nothing to you."

"His hands are stained with the blood of several Baraans," the *sakal* countered sharply. "He's to pay for his transgressions. Interfere and you will join him."

"With no challenge before a *Gal*?" Mithraam countered in an even tone. "Your guardsmen were harming a defenseless youngling. She was—"

"No concern of mine," the *sakal* cut him off. "I have my orders and need not meddle where rulings of law are made."

"It is a concern to all who follow and serve our laws," Mithraam challenged and chastised.

The burly *Tusaa'Ner* officer angrily stepped toward Mithraam while holding him with his stinging glare and speaking with an angry voice. "You dare mock me?"

Mithraam softened his stance, expression, and tone. "I only wish to remind you of that you know and oathed."

The *Tusaa'Ner sakal* moved close to Mithraam before speaking in a low voice so to keep the guards and guardsmen from hearing. "It's not like that now. Farratum has changed . . . and not for the better. The pit is your son's only chance at keeping his *Light*."

The *sakal* whirled away in a swirl of blue-red, then walked briskly out of the room as he ushered another command. "Fulfill my orders."

Rogaan felt the guards tug at him. He resisted until he caught sight of father shaking his head ever so slightly, warning him not to fight, not here, not now. Rogaan resigned himself to being ushered out of the room and down the rough-walled halls. His thoughts fixated on puzzling out his father not wanting him to fight . . . his father's plan. *He always has a plan. Maybe he did not want me to look belligerent. Maybe he has something else planned.* He discarded that thought as being too cynical almost as soon as it entered his head. *Be serious.* He scolded himself. *Did he fear I would get the point of a blade?* Rogaan gave that some weight, but it seemed not likely since all attempts to harm him and those about him so far ended with guards and guardsmen faring poorly. *Maybe Father has an escape planned . . . with that Im'Kas or the dark robes.* Rogaan shuddered at that last thought. *Father in league with dark robes?* Despite his father's assurances,

Rogaan could not bring himself to trust those working for them, the dark robes of the Ebon Circle. Too many townsfolk feared and spoke ill of them. Rogaan shook his head. His father was once a simple metalsmith and father in his mind. Now, with the dark robes as allies plotting influence over the lands, Rogaan did not know how to think of his father.

Sakes and *Tusaa'Ner* and lessers filled the halls, ushering people to and from cells and hauling things about. The smell of the place was thick with sweat, blood, and the occasional rancid stench of chamber pots. Rogaan's nose wrinkled more than a few times while being escorted through the chaos. *How does anyone breathe, let alone know what they are to do?* He caught talk of what all the hurrying about was for . . . the Arena Games. Its opening show was soon and everyone looked on edge. As they escorted Rogaan down another hall he caught more talk of the games and how unorganized everyone felt. They looked it.

At the end of a hall constructed of well fitted stone blocks each an arm's length in width, the guards and guardsmen brought Rogaan to a halt behind another group of three darkly clad *Sakes* surrounding a staggering prisoner. The Baraan looked well fed with a soft gut, standing just a few fingers shorter than Rogaan with short, matted black hair. Red stains on the black of the Baraan's neck and shirt hinted at blood being the cause of the matting. The Baraan's once richly made yellow pants and orange shirt were grimy and torn in many places, and his right elbow length sleeve was completely torn away, allowing all to see rope burns on his upper arm. The Baraan looked in pain. *Mostly from being worked over*, Rogaan concluded.

"What do you have here?" That high-pitched voice ground on Rogaan's spine. *The Tusaa'Ner sakal . . . from the jailer's caravan?*

"*Sakal*," the *Sake* leader of the group in front of them spoke professionally, respectfully. "Another proud one paying the price for hording."

"No need to question him so harshly," the woman *sakal* disapprovingly commented while looking over the prisoner. Rogaan's spine quivered as her high-pitched voice echoed all about him. "This one can barely stand."

Despite her annoying voice, a desire to see her taunted Rogaan. He caught himself trying to glimpse her and chastised himself for it. *What is wrong with me?*

BRETT VONSIK

"He spoke words against the *Zas* and Shuruppak," the Baraan *Sake* leader answered as if that was enough reason to commit any punishment against a citizen and would put an end to any further questions. Then he respectfully added with a hint of forcing himself, "*Sakal*."

Rogaan could not see or hear what then transpired between them, but the *Sakes* soon ushered the wobbly Baraan to a rope at the edge of a circular opening in the floor spanning more than six strides. There they pushed the screaming Baraan into the pit. Shock gripped Rogaan, prickling his skin all over. *Is that to be my fate?* He tried to not think of it with hope they had other plans for him. *Not my concern if I can stay out of the pit*, Rogaan told himself.

"Next," that high-pitched voice barked in Rogaan's direction before changing tone to one of dejection. "Not you?"

"Yes, Dajil." The burley *Tusaa'Ner* officer pushed through his guardsmen and past Rogaan while playfully answering the blue-clad *Tusaa'Ner* woman. He stood almost squarely between Rogaan and the female *sakal*. Rogaan could see only the back of his red cape and his short cut light brown hair until he leaned left, allowing a clear sight of the woman *sakal* . . . Dajil. A flush of satisfaction and surprisingly what Rogaan realized was joy swept over him. Rogaan felt a pang of guilt at it as he averted his eyes to look at anything else but her. The male *sakal's* tone with Dajil gave hint they shared a history between them. He behaved as if they were equals in rank. "It is I."

"Why do you keep bothering me, Jaxtu?" The *sakal* spat back at her fellow *sakal* before turning her full attention on Rogaan. "Tellen. Couldn't keep yourself from trouble, could you?"

Rogaan looked into the face of the red-caped woman, the cape signifying her rank as a *sakal* commander above the guardsmen, just as Jaxtu. Her radiant green eyes under red-brown and blond-streaked hair that went to her midback captured Rogaan. He ceased hearing her voice despite her lips forming words and sounding while nodding her head in rhythm. Her face and eyes were all Rogaan saw as he was ushered before her by the guardsmen escorting him. She spoke more words directly at him, then grew visibly frustrated as she tilted her head back and rolled those beautiful green eyes. When they broke eye contact, Rogaan shook his head and somewhat managed to clear it. *What is in my head?* Suhd . . . a wave of guilt washed over him, giving him reason to be angry with himself.

"Trouble keeping his bindings on," Jaxtu answered.

"And he's a bar bender," one of the guardsmen offered, then fell silent at a hard glance from his commander.

The *sakal's* eyebrows raised at their words, then her eyes narrowed at Rogaan with suspicion as she spoke to Jaxtu. "Speak true words."

"Truly . . ." Jaxtu confirmed his guardsman spoke truth. The *sakal's* face turned wide-eyed before concern crinkled her brow. Jaxtu continued, "He's too dangerous for anywhere but the pit."

Dajil looked unconvinced that breaking shackles and bending bars justified the pit as punishment. "There's no stepping back once in the pit."

"*Sake zigaar's* command," Jaxtu added for all to hear, then lowered his voice to near a whisper. "We'll all get skinned for keeping the blade from this one. Everyone challenging this one gets bloodied . . . or worse."

"Courage escapes you . . . Jaxtu?" The *sakal* delivered her insult with a wry smile. She glanced at Rogaan with a look that he took as satisfaction. Rogaan felt himself flush warm at her glance before another pang of guilt hit him like a sobering bucket of cold water.

Jaxtu stood still for a long moment before responding to the smiling blue-armored *sakal* standing before him. "The stoner is in your charge, Dajil. The *Sake zigaar* is not one to disregard, if that's where your head is at."

The burley *Tusaa'Ner* commander stepped to the side, motioning with his left arm for his guardsmen to bring Rogaan forward. A sharp prod in the back urged Rogaan to take a step in her direction. Reluctantly, he found himself standing before those radiant green eyes as he caught himself again wanting to stare into them and feeling guilty for it. He forced himself to look away from her. He saw for the first time he stood in a large octagon-shaped chamber with a high domed ceiling and circular open pit in the center of the room, four strides beyond the woman *sakal*. Stoutly anchored and darkly stained questioning racks adorned each of the eight walls. Rogaan thanked the Ancients that all stood empty. Tightly fitted flagstones covered the chamber's floor. Many were stained dark with what Rogaan guessed was mostly dried blood that someone tried washing away. Almost ten strides above, a square wood beam structure was firmly anchored into the stone at the top of the dome. The sun's rays cast beams of light through a large opening above and around a circular wood platform suspended by four heavy chains just below. Floating dust within the chamber made the sun's rays seem almost solid. This placed looked and smelled of suffering and death that nobody seemed to notice except Rogaan. A bustle of servants dressed in dirty tunics and barefooted hurried about at the shouts and grunts of darkly clothed guards that Rogaan took as unarmored *Sakes*. Eighteen strides across the room, beyond the open pit, two copper-bound timbered doors separated by some ten strides stood open. Servants leaving this chamber and entering the rooms deeper into this place had arms full . . . of what Rogaan could not tell, only to return moments later empty-handed. Some servants stood at the edge of the pit, dumping reed baskets with what looked to be discarded food, some of it rotten. That gave hope to Rogaan that the once well-to-do Baraan the *Sakes* and *Tusaa'Ner* tossed into the pit still lived.

"I said you'd be trouble." The *sakal* spoke more to herself as she looked at a parchment with a list of names in her hands. Her high-pitched voice that irritated him so was absent when she spoke softly. She looked up at Jaxtu, and then annunciated in her high-pitched voice, "He's not on the list for this day."

The burley *Tusaa'Ner* just shrugged his shoulders as if her problem was no concern to him. "The *Sake zigaar* demanded he be placed in the pit, not me."

The *sakal* looked at Rogaan with those radiant green eyes of hers. Pain and sorrow shown in them when Rogaan looked her in the eyes. She whispered to him in a pleasant, quiet voice, "Make no more trouble, Tellen, or *they* will see to un-pleasantries for your friends."

A shiver rippled down Rogaan's back, and his skin prickled as his heart skipped a beat. *How long are they to hold my father, Pax, Suhd, and the others over me?* Rogaan nodded as his gaze swept over her red-brown and blond-streaked hair and the graceful lines of her face, neck, breast . . . He shook his head again, with more guilt churning inside. *What is wrong with me?* He gathered himself and forced an expected answer, "I understand. What is to happen to me?"

"You're for the games," the *sakal* answered sadly. "You'll have your chance at freedom, but you must fight for it and your life. If you survive, you are set free."

"*If* I survive?" Rogaan did not like the sound of that. For a moment he considered fighting his way out of the chamber but decided instead to do what he needed to do to keep his father and his friends untouched. He looked at the floor, considering the need to show a humble self to those in authority and submit. He had little choice for the moment. He nodded.

The *sakal* pointed to the edge of the pit where a chain hung down from the platform above. It hung close to the side of the pit as it descended into the unknown. Dajil's eyes and face held pain. "Your acts are of noble intent, Tellen. My regrets. To the pit."

Rogaan reluctantly stepped to the edge of darkness. That alone caused the hairs on his neck to stand and his skin to prickle. A foul smell struck him as he looked down. The pit was some six strides across and just as deep. The bottom was dark and littered with refuse from what Rogaan could make out. Several Baraans wearing soiled clothing were eating the scraps Rogaan assumed that were just tossed into the pit. His stomach turned. The once well-to-do Baraan lay motionless on top a pile of refuse. Rogaan now feared him dead. What sent another chill down his back was no one seemed to care.

"In the pit, *stoner*," the burley *Tusaa'Ner* commanded with too much glee.

Rogaan found the Baraan's snide speak angering. Not because of the name "stoner," but from the tone of disrespect it was delivered in. Rogaan stood silently for a moment, hoping not to be forced to climb into the pit. He considered his options again, nothing workable if everyone was to remain unharmed.

"I have my duty," the *Tusaa'Ner sakul*, Dajil, regretfully whispered to Rogaan. "Into the pit to keep those you care for untouched and to have a chance at keeping your *Light*."

Rogaan looked at Dajil with new eyes. She stood stiff-backed. A hand and some shorter than he, she made up for her stature with attitude, an unyielding set to her jaws and featherwing-like eyes that now stared at him waiting for an answer in action to her counsel. Guilt washed over Rogaan again as he caught himself taking her in. *She's easy to look at,* he admitted. *Enough*! Rogaan chastised himself once more before grabbing the chain. He gathered his courage, then resigned himself to a descent into the foul darkness.

Chapter 22

Through Another's Eyes

"We'll all be in bondage soon," Sinthrie passionately ranted. "No House or street wretch is beyond their reach now that many suckle them through their handouts. Our freedoms be in their palms, and they mean to take all that we have. There will be no one left to challenge them before long."

Rogaan sat in a squat with his back pressed to the damp and filthy stone wall. He found the floor even less inviting with things of all numbers of legs crawling about. The stench was horrible. Brooding kept him awake for almost a day. He felt tired and fought the sleep tugging at him. He also struggled to believe the Baraan's, Sinthrie's, conspiracies. The once well-to-do Baraan survived his fall yesterday by landing on a padded garbage pile of something foul smelling. He still reeked of it. Rogaan rolled his eyes as Sinthrie continued his nonstop talking about how he woke to the truth once he was pulled from his status of earned privilege. He claimed his fall came at the hand of the *Zas* and those workings for them. Rogaan doubted little that the Baraan's outspoken and opinionated ways played a part in his getting jailed and wished he would lose his incessant need to talk. Irritation grated at Rogaan as Sinthrie retold his plight for the umpteenth time. He had been a successful mineral merchant who was taken at blade point by the *Tusaa'Ner* and condemned by a corrupt *Gal* to the Farratum jails, all after he dared challenge new decrees, he considered tyrannical, pronounced by the *Zas*. Sinthrie claimed all was so. Rogaan had little to reason doubt him, given his own recent experiences, but suspected that Sinthrie embellished much. The Baraan's stained clothing of fine making and his manner of speak as one learned in subjects beyond rocks and gems helped Rogaan believe Sinthrie's assertions. What bothered Rogaan was, if true, Sinthrie's story meant corruption ran deep to the core within Farratum, and its representatives possessed self-serving intents not obvious to the people.

"They deceive the street with their twofold words." Sinthrie passionately continued his ranting. He wanted the world to know of the corruption within Farratum, and that meant even those in this pit. "The same for the lesser Houses . . . Farratum selling their lies of plight and poverty as something made so by those with more than others. That those who have coin, assumed to have gained it unjustly by Farratum, horde it. It is in this Farratum fosters and creates envy and anger in the streets at the lesser Houses and in the lesser Houses at the greater Houses . . . then the cry to make justice . . . to take from those who have more by those with less becomes deafening. It is only Farratum officials who gains in all of this, the *Zas* and their benefactors, as the street only sees enough of that taken to keep it envious and angry."

"Untrue!" Uril growled.

The badly wounded warrior sat on a dry patch across the pit from Rogaan . . . and unfortunately for Rogaan, Sinthrie. The warrior Baraan looked to have seen better days. Uril, past his prime in years and visibly unable to carry a battle worthy of his heart, was, in his day, a *War Sworn,* of the Order of the Mace. *What did Uncle tell me of the War Sworn and of the Mace?* That last thought brought deep regrets to Rogaan. His mother's brother, also *War Sworn*, died seeing himself and Pax to freedom. *Freedom in a Farratum jail pit. How I have honored Uncle's death*, Rogaan grumbled to himself. Forcing his self-pity down in a surge of disgust, Rogaan sought knowledge buried within him. As he recalled, *War Sworn* seek perfection in their battle skills to be prepared for the time when the Ancients return to reclaim these lands and the peoples. One of two main factions of the *War Sworn* intend to pledge their skills and honor to the Ancients, the other faction to reject the Ancients and their ways of tyrannical rule over all those opposing them.

This once dark-haired *War Sworn* now had more gray than anything else and sat broken in this jailer's pit waiting for an unworthy death. It took the better part of a day for Rogaan to piece together the warrior Baraan's story from tidbits he and the other two in the pit spoke of. The warrior Baraan had fresh wounds across his face, arms, and legs that were deep and festering with infections. Dried blood on the side of Uril's head and the way he slowly turned his head spoke of a broken skull. Rogaan suspected more wounds could be found, but the Baraan hid it well and complained little. *Why is Uril here?* Rogaan could only guess.

"It is true," Sinthrie shot back with his brown shoulder-length hair matted to his face. "You see only that they wish. They tell the Houses and street lies while dribbling out foods and rags for clothing and enough to ease their plights. Many receive Farratum's givings paid for with coin taken from those who earned it, the same coin taken from us at every turn . . . calling it 'street fees' or 'gifts.'"

"Your pockets did well," the *War Sworn* accused Sinthrie of holding his coin he thought better used on the poor and needy.

Sinthrie's face contorted with anger before continuing his debate points as he held his hands palms up. "I built my trade in minerals and gems with these hands . . . scratching and clawing for everything. No *Za* or anyone else helped. Instead, they took coin from me and my workers in all manner of ways . . . fees to store my stones, taxes to take my goods through gates and over bridges and on the streets, more fees to ensure my stones were true, and more taxes and more fees and more taxes on just about everything I needed to conduct my trade."

"It is your duty to pay coin so others have no need to suffer," Uril countered with a heavy hint of disgust.

"Did you not hear me, fellow?" Sinthrie's neck and face grew bold red with a mix of frustration and anger, but somehow he managed to keep his tone polite. "They took *everything* from me . . . *all* that I made, and called me gluttonous and hard-hearted. They claimed it to help those with less than me and my family. They left my family nothing and put me here when I spoke out of their tyrant deeds telling all who would listen. They made my family into their poor. My pockets are lightened and empty now my family is in the streets. My younglings now sleep in the mud . . . hungry, hoping to be at the front of the line when Farratum hands out scraps."

The *War Sworn* sniffed loudly at Sinthrie's speech. It was clear he thought little of the merchant's plight. Rogaan did not know what to believe. The *War Sworn* seemed not to believe or care of what Farratum did to Sinthrie . . . as if the merchant deserved his troubles.

"And why are you in this place, *War Sworn?*"Ahea'tu asked. Rogaan almost fell over from his crouched position against the wall when Ahea'tu spoke. The last of the Baraans in this pit with him boldly wore a great watchful eye above a straight, thick line in the middle of his forehead. Rogaan was not certain what it represented, but had not asked of the symbol as it seemed a part of the Baraan's persona. That and he was a bit of a rough fellow. Added to that, the Baraan spoke little in the time since Rogaan laid eyes on his almost gaunt face. When Uril met his question with silence, Ahea'tu answered for him. "Same reason we are . . . You are a trouble for those coveting dominion over all they can see."

Uril's face took on a mood of dark brooding. The *War Sworn* kept his silence, as if something in Ahea'tu's words struck a chord of truth. Rogaan grew more curious at understanding why Uril was in this pit. Why were Ahea'tu and Sinthrie also here? And why he now shared this place with them. *Why am I here?*

"In Farratum, we're all troubles, in some manner, to those in authority," Sinthrie added as if he just realized this for the first time.

"Just as well you find yourself here, Merchant, so your fingers keep from another forbidden stone or passing one on to another undeserving *Light*." Ahea'tu spoke down to Sinthrie, almost chastising him.

"Well told," Uril added. "No hand should touch those foul things. Better to die in deeds than trust your life to a *manifester* with a *stone*."

"Agnis are forbidden to all not Ancients." Ahea'tu almost sang the words. "The Edicts of Enlil forbid us. You, Merchant, have transgressed before the Ancients and must atone."

"Atone, he will," the *War Sworn* said with a smirk. "The games have been goin' for a full day. Listen to the crowd."

All fell silent as Rogaan strained to listen to what Uril spoke of. All he heard was a distant unintelligible chant and felt a rhythmic vibration in the floor and wall, now that he had his attention on it. The vibration was like many people stomping or marching together. Uril was right. A crowd was cheering at something above.

"The crowd shall revel at our deaths when we are delivered to the arena soon," Ahea'tu snapped at the wounded *War Sworn*. He spat, then continued in a more measured tone. "The merchant speaks truth. We are in this cursed pit to keep our tales from the lands . . . and the people. The merchant tells a tale of these *Zas* and their hands growing in greed for all things. Your tale is of a great champion no longer able to fulfill his duty to keep the crowds entertained and distracted."

"I'm Uril of—" the *War Sworn* started.

"*Uril of the Mace*," Ahea'tu interrupted and finished in a mocking tone. "*War Sworn* of the High Order . . . Entertainer to all who wish to see carnage from the safety of their seats. You are no longer of use to them so they have you rot here instead of spending coin keeping you in the people's eyes."

"That's not my tale!" Uril spat out before abruptly falling silent with a grimace on his face.

"That *is* your tale," Ahea'tu growled. "Accept it."

Uril's eyes blazed with anger, but he kept silent until he calmed enough speak. "And you, Ahea'tu? What is your tale? Why are you here?"

"My tale is of no concern to you, *War Sworn*," Ahea'tu coldly replied to Uril without looking at him. The marked Baraan looked off distantly as if pondering something. A long moment of silence passed before he turned his attention on Rogaan. "Though it is to this young Tellen."

Surprise and shock rippled through Rogaan. This marked Baraan he did not know, but somehow he knew of Rogaan. "How is it you know of me?"

"I am Ahea'tu of the *Keepers of the Way*," Ahea'tu announced. "Our purpose is to keep mankind on the path given us by the Ancients, the Edicts of Enlil. I am witness to one close to the *Zas* that possesses great skill with the Agni. He made to extinguish my *Light* before guardsmen found us. I can taste still the hold of the Agni on me. A foul taste and stronger than I've felt of any *manifester* I've silenced. Instead of sending my *Light* to the *Darkness*, he condemned me before the guardsmen and commanded them to place me here . . . for a grand death in the arena."

"How does this have meaning for me?" Rogaan asked.

"They speak of a Tellen who causes troubles," Ahea'tu replied. "This Hand of the *Zas* spoke of this to others while I waited to slip my blade into his heart."

"What did they speak of?" Rogaan asked in a careful tone, not wanting to anger this *Keeper* . . . this *Light-Taker*.

"I heard little except your name, if you are Rogaan, and their frustrations concerning you." Ahea'tu answered.

"They must have spoken more than that if my name was spoken." Rogaan grew frustrated.

"They're interested in keeping the old Tellen for a task." Ahea'tu paused as he contemplated his next words. ". . . and having the young one's *Light* sent to the *Darkness* for all eternity. I assume they meant your *Light* as you are here in this *Pit of the Condemned*."

A wave of relief washed over Rogaan. His father had purpose and for that they would keep him alive. Then a thought came to Rogaan, and he worried what would become of his father after the task is completed. *Nothing is right . . . or easy*, Rogaan lamented to himself. He looked up to the platform above and tried to envision what was above . . . the arena and how he was to be challenged there. That he might die and have his *Light* taken from him was frightening, but if it meant his father would be spared he would accept the challenge. A strange calmness fell over him for the first time in many days. He smiled to himself.

"Tell me of this '*Hand*' that spoke of me," Rogaan asked of Ahea'tu in a careful tone.

"He aides the female *Za*," Ahea'tu answered slowly. "Strangely, he speaks of her with contempt to some, and with respect to others."

"What . . . How does he appear?" Rogaan refocused his question hoping to get an idea what this "Hand" looks like.

Reverberating creaks and groans of great timbers overhead along with the clanking of chains accompanied with slight vibrations in the floor and wall deafened any chance Rogaan had to hear Ahea'tu's answer. Frustration filled him. He wanted . . . no, *needed* to know who the *Right-hand of Darkness* was in these shadows. Looking up, he watched the wood platform descend in a clatter of chains and creaking wood beams. The platform stopped at the top of the pit where Rogaan heard a commotion of voices followed by many boots and feet on stone and timbers. The platform filled with shadows of people he could see through small openings between planks. The pit then plunged into darkness as the platform continued down onto their heads. Rogaan fought off a panic at the sudden darkness. He was unprepared for it. Every hair on him stood on end as his heart pounded so hard he thought it was to burst from his chest. Sweat quickly drenched him. He felt unable to focus and out of breath as the stench of the pit overpowered him and made him want to sick up. Looking up again, Rogaan feared being crushed just as the platform clanged and creaked to a halt only an arm's length above his head. A door in the planks, offset from the center of the platform, opened. A rope ladder dropped.

"You are summoned, *Keeper*," a booming voice announced almost as an invitation before it continued in an unfriendly tone. "Climb the ladder or be cut down."

Ahea'tu stood and approached the ladder. He wore a solemn face, a thoughtful demeanor. He looked at Rogaan as he took hold of the ladder. "Not much for choices. When you enter the killing grounds above, dare not cower. Take from them more than they expect. May your *Light* find peace with the Ancients."

Ahea'tu ascended the rope ladder without further ceremony, up through the trap door. The trap door slammed shut as a scuffle broke out on the platform. From what Rogaan could make out of the yelling, clinking, and boots stamping on planks, Ahea'tu either tried to escape or fought his escorts. The platform ascended without him knowing what came of the scuffle or if Ahea'tu still lived.

"At least he has heart," the *War Sworn* growled with respect.

"Heart?" Sinthrie questioned. "We're to die this day. How is having heart mean anything when we're *lightless*?"

"We all see our *Light* leave us," Uril answered calmly and coldly. "It's a measure of the quality of your *Light* how you depart this world that matters to the *Great One*."

Sinthrie argued with Uril over his callousness and misplaced bravado. As the platform cleared the pit, light rays bathed them, bringing brightness to the filthy pit. Rogaan felt better with his anxiety now melting away. Somehow, it even smelled better. Looking up again, Rogaan found himself needing to swallow hard. As the platform locked into the roof with a loud clatter, Rogaan locked eyes with his father, who stood at the edge of the pit with his hands bound in front of him. Pax and his parents stood next to Rogaan's father, as did the Evendiir. All bound as his father was.

"What is this?" Rogaan asked no one, asked everyone in a disbelieving voice. He wanted answers. He did what they asked of him! *Father was . . . is to live!* Rogaan yelled, "What is this?"

Mithraam held his son's eyes with his own with the intent to keep Rogaan from taking rash actions. When Rogaan shook his head no to restraint, his father returned his own head shake of no while wearing stern conviction only one who deeply cared for another could muster. Rogaan's heart sank as a numb void filled it. He was at a loss at what to do. The walls were next to impossible to climb; there was no way to reach his father or his captors and reaffirm his commitment to take his father's place. A deep sense of loss enveloped him as he stood exchanging silent words with his father for a time. Rogaan wanted the moment to last forever as he understood that once gone, so too would be his father. Groaning timbers broke Rogaan's almost trance. The platform descended once again. The crowd's noise from the high opening was almost deafening. They sounded unhappy, unsettled. Rogaan gave it a moment's wonder before returning his attention to his father, to look him in the eyes one more time before the platform concealed him. As the timbers groaned again and the chains suspending the platform clattered it to a halt, Rogaan lost sight of his father. His heart sank deeper; it ached with loss. Footfalls on the platform followed by the groan of timbers and the clattering of chains saw the platform rise to his father's doom. Rogaan suddenly hoped his father would still be standing at the pit's edge. The moment passed with profound disappointment and a stunned realization . . . *I am never to see Father again.*

Chapter 23

Arena

Tears welled up in Rogaan's eyes, and he found it increasingly hard to breathe as he helplessly watched the platform take his father away from him. *What am I to do?* He asked himself. Rogaan looked around the refuse filling the pit floor for anything that might help him that he missed from one of his many previous surveys. Nothing caught his eye. He then looked at the wall again. *It has to have imperfections I can use as hand- and footholds.* The wall offered none. Rogaan's frustration grew, along with his desperation.

"I can see the fire in you, young one." Uril spoke with conviction. Rogaan gave him a heated sideways glance as his tears streaked his grimy cheeks. Uril wore a serious face. "Take all that you feel into battle. Make it favor you. Make them fear you and your rage."

Rogaan felt undeniable pain building into anger, and his anger into rage. It was unlike anything he felt in all of his life. He wanted all to pay for their *transgressions* . . . taking his father's *Light* and Father from him and his mother. His rage grew more by the moment. How much, Rogaan did not care as long as it was enough. He welcomed it. He wanted revenge and wanted the whole world to feel his pain. Feel the loss.

"What's this nonsense you're telling the youngling?" Sinthrie half-asked, half-accused the *War Sworn*.

"It's the warrior's way, Merchant," Uril scolded.

"He's to get himself and us killed before it's our time," Sinthrie continued his complaining.

"Keep your thoughts silent!" Rogaan growled at Sinthrie. He wanted to unleash his pain, even if on the arrogant and frightened merchant.

Rogaan started to pace the pit, kicking refuse out of his way as he went. *How to get out of this pit . . . up to the arena . . .* Nothing. The walls were smooth, made so to keep one from doing what was in his head. Rogaan growled at no one. His rage needed releasing. His head and chest felt about to explode with such force as to collapse this whole chamber. He looked up to howl at the world. He stopped. A rope dangled from the platform's open trap door. The end hung not more than three strides above his head. *How did that get there?* Rogaan leaped for it. It was out of his reach. He leaped again. Still, it remained beyond him.

"Come here." Rogaan growled at Sinthrie.

Sinthrie shook his head no as he stepped back. Rogaan felt his rage focus on Sinthrie and readied himself to unleash it when a hand pressed on his shoulder. Rogaan whirled about ready to unleash his rage at whoever dared touch him. He found the *War Sworn* standing in front of him.

"Make them fear you." Uril interwove his fingers and held his self-made stirrup just at knee height.

Rogaan nodded to the *War Sworn* before planting his right boot into Uril's hands, then together, they launched Rogaan upward. A loud snap below echoed in the pit as Rogaan grabbed the rope in his reaching left hand. Hanging by one arm and looking down, he found Uril on the floor withering in agony in the filth with his leg at an odd angle. Rogaan had no room in his heart for sentiment . . . only anger . . . rage. He climbed with everything he had, his rage willing him up the rope. Hand over hand he heaved himself upward without pause. *They must answer for their treachery.*

Rogaan firmly focused on the rope and only the rope. Hand over hand. Hand over hand. He neared the trap door when he heard shouting below. He looked down finding a handful of *Tusaa'Ner* readying crossbows as their commander pointed up to him. Hand over hand, Rogaan quickly heaved himself through the square wood channel to the trap door and into the blinding brightness of a midday sun.

Armored hands clamped onto his shoulders. Rogaan grabbed the gauntleted hands of a *Sake* guard, then, without thinking what to do, he pulled the armored Baraan off balance, then rolled him through the trap door, but did not let go. With a growl, Rogaan strained holding the guard in air, his full weight suspended by Rogaan's left arm. Despite his rage, Rogaan did not mean for the guard to fall to his death.

A thundering roar from an unseen crowd vibrated the timbers and planks Rogaan lay across. Blinking to clear his vision in the bright sunlight proved unsuccessful. He was blinded. The weight on his arm and shoulder threatened to pull his arm from its socket, so Rogaan grunted the guard into a swinging motion in the hope he would grab the nearby rope. A scrape of metal and rhythmic footfalls on wood planks drew Rogaan's now blurred vision to an approaching dark, blurry figure. A flash of sun off metal helm and blade alarmed Rogaan into heaving the swinging guard toward the spot he remembered the rope hanging. The weight on his shoulder lessened. He released the guard, then dismissed him from his thoughts as he rolled and slammed the trap door shut. He continued his roll to a kneeling position in front of another blurred form of a guard and the glint off a blade as its tip slammed into wood he lay on a moment ago.

Why are you not helping me? Rogaan asked and cursed his strange abilities to slow the world. The *Sake* guard pulled his blade free from the planks, then slashed at Rogaan, cutting him at the shoulder. Rogaan rolled away to put space between them, then started to rise when he realized the blurry figure of the *Sake* was upon him again, with blade making a level cut for his neck. Rogaan arched back and turned his face, dodging the blade whisking through his short beard before falling back onto the wood platform. The *Sake* recovered, then attacked again, stepping forward as he raised his blade above his head with both hands in a maneuver meaning to drive the metal through Rogaan's chest. Rogaan threw himself back against the timber as he drew his knees to his chest and anchored his hands on wood above his head. Everything instantly slowed around him. He rolled further onto his back with his legs in a tight ball, ready to spring at his foe. The *Sake* stepped and leaned forward as he started driving his blade point down at Rogaan. In that instant, Rogaan felt his muscles and tendons straining, wanting to be released. With all his strength and with a roaring growl, he drove his feet at the *Sake's* chest while pushing off the wood timber platform with his shoulders and hands. His boots struck his target square and as solid as he hoped, in the chest, while driving his feet, legs, and body upward. Rogaan's shoulders launched off the wood platform while extending himself fully before falling to the wood with a thud on his back. He watched the darkly armored *Sake* guard slowly arc through the air backward before landing in a heap almost eight strides away at the edge of the platform. The *Sake* lay unmoving under what looked to be a hangman's timber crossbar. The Baraan's body lay still. Rogaan's rage cooled. For a brief moment, Rogaan feared he took the *Light* from the guard, something he wanted to avoid. *I have enough troubles.*

A deep, rumbling roar jolted Rogaan into springing up to his hands and knees. He viewed the crowd for the first time. A field of bright and varying colors of cheering and jeering people filled most of the arena bench seats, all under streaming sky-blue pennants bearing the crossed spears and two towers of Farratum. Rogaan kneeled, dazed at the sight. The world quickened and the roar of the crowd turned higher-pitched, along with the vibrations Rogaan felt in the wood timbers below him. Never before had he seen so many people in one place as he took in the entire arena with awe, from the five-stride-high stone wall enclosing the massive oval-shaped dirt floor of the center grounds to the highest seats more than fifteen strides above the ground. The dirt floor of the arena spanned some seventy-five strides wide and twice that in length with a set of large timber double doors at each end of the arena. In the middle of the arena stood the elevated stone and wood stage platform Rogaan now kneeled upon. Four large wheels, one at each corner of the timber platform, supported large ropes and chains that were attached to the platform at one end and disappeared into an opening in the platform at the other end. Where the openings went to, Rogaan guessed somewhere below. A half-stride-tall stout wood rail ran the parameter of the stage except on two opposite sides where the railing had breaks allowing passage on stone steps to the arena's dirt floor. The guard lying under the hangman's crossbar at the other end of the stage stirred. Rogaan noted the stirring with a momentary flash of relief before looking about for his father as the crowd roared again, with more cheers and jeers.

He found his father with the others in a gaggle some sixteen strides from the stage to his right. They were all bound at the wrists. Pax and Aren were frantically chewing at their hide bindings. Pax's father was working at his wife's bindings while Rogaan's father stood yelling at the stage while waving his bound arms. His father's words were lost to the crowd roars, but Rogaan thought he understood the meaning of his urgent waving . . . *Leave this place.* He motioned his father to come to the stage so they could escape together through the trap door near his feet. His father yelled to the others. Again, Rogaan was unable to hear his words over the crowd. The others looked to his father who seemed to understand what he was telling them. They all took a step toward the stage when a deafening bellow shook the air, stopping them in stride and silencing the crowd. Rogaan looked behind him where the bellow came from. His blood turned frigid and his skin crawled painfully with fear. Two bulky ravers, red with thick black stripes, stomped at the ground just inside the partially opened timber double doors. The ravers were almost eighty strides away, but Rogaan knew the distance meant little for these menaces. Worse, the stories he heard of these beasts as a youngling he confirmed with his own eyes in his journey here. These animals were fast and always acted as if they had a thorn stinging them. Rogaan's skin rippled with a fearful chill.

"Run!" Rogaan heard his father yell out.

Looking to see who his father spoke to, Rogaan found chaos. Aren and Pax ran toward the stage while Rogaan's father looked perplexed at Pax's mother who ran in panic away from the beasts and stage with her husband chasing after her yelling to her to run his way. Rogaan's heart sank seeing her frightened out of reason. Aren approached the stage ahead of Pax screaming for Rogaan to open the door. The Evendiir too was panicked, but clearheaded enough to know running to the opposite side of the arena meant death would come only after others died. Rogaan tried to open the trap door, but found it locked or jammed. He dug his fingers into the edge of the door's wood frame, then braced himself to pull on it with all his might when another deafening bellow shook him. A second bellow joined the first, just as powerful and terrifying. Rogaan looked over his shoulder again to find the smaller of the two ravers readying a charge at the stage. Rogaan froze in fear and indecision. "Smaller" was a poor choice in thinking of the menace. This one was just as big as the golden ravers Im'Kas killed when he attempted to stop Kardul from delivering them into the hands of the *Tusaa'Ner* and *Sakes. A fool I am.*

"Open the door, you half-wit!" Aren's words bit into Rogaan's sensibilities, angering him. Of all the accusations made against him, no one ever seriously accused him of being unintelligent. Rogaan looked at the Evendiir with smoldering eyes before standing tall and defiant.

"It's locked or jammed from the inside," Rogaan barked back.

"Then smash it with your foot!" Aren sneeringly directed Rogaan as he grasped the wood rail to the stage, then made to leap onto the platform.

Another deafening roar shook the air, stopping Aren from jumping up and commanded the Evendiir's full attention. Rogaan felt a rhythmic vibration growing stronger. *No!* He looked back toward the beasts. The smaller of the two pounded the ground in a full charge right at them. Aren let out a squeal, then tore off toward the opposite end of the stage where the hangman's timbers stood. He kept to the dirt and crouched a little as if trying to hide behind the wood rail from the raver's sight. Rogaan caught movement to his right. Looking, he saw his father running as fast as he could toward him, somewhat bowlegged and plodding. *Is that how I look running? It's a wonder I am not slower.*

Rogaan realized with a shock Pax was not near the stage. He expected him to be at his side by now figuring out how to open this trap door. Rogaan found him running after his parents, who were almost at the other double-timbered doors opposite the ravers. He was thankful to the Ancients for the timber doors being closed and nothing else chasing after them all. Pax looked back at Rogaan, then veered hard left. Rogaan's confusion lasted only a few rhythmic footfalls he felt through his feet, footfalls that grew in strength with each step. Looking back, he found the charging raver aiming to the right of the stage. *Father!* Rogaan feared for his father's life. He was not running fast and was in the path of the closing menace, if not the sole focus of the bellowing beast. It roared again. *No! That roar came from the bigger one.* Glancing to the open timber doors, Rogaan found the bigger raver stomping its feet as it let out another bellow. The air shook, this time with deeper vibrations. Suddenly, the charging raver passed by the stage less than ten strides from Rogaan. The surprise to him was momentary as immense relief blew through him like a strong breeze that he was not the ravers' choice meal of the moment. His relief immediately turned to terror as he watched helplessly the raver snap its jaws shut, taking a few of his father's hairs as the stocky body of his father just slid behind the corner of the stage platform where the raver could not take a full bite at him. Instead of stopping, the raver continued its charge forward. Rogaan's confusion cleared as he caught sight of Pax running toward the stage where Aren now stood, the opposite corner of the stage from Rogaan's father near the hanging timbers. The raver paid him no attention. Instead, the beast kept straight toward Pax's parents. Pax stopped and looked after the beast, yelling at the creature. Rogaan stood on the stage awed and stunned at everything happening—all at the same time. His head swirled.

"Open that door before we're all *lightless*!" Aren yelled at Rogaan as he climbed up to the rail. Aren froze with eyes wide as Rogaan felt the vibrations in the stage, rhythmic, rapid, and growing in strength. Looking to his left, Rogaan found the bigger raver pounding its feet into the dirt at a fast run passing the opposite side of the stage from where the smaller raver passed.

Aren dropped back to the dirt, then scrambled around the corner of the stage grumbling babblings as the big raver shortened its strides trying to turn with the agile Evendiir. Rogaan caught sight of Pax now running toward his parents. The smaller raver stood over the two mauling them. He thought he heard screams from Pax's mother before the big raver surprised him, obscuring his sight in front of him as the beast stalked Aren. Rogaan momentarily struggled with his emotions. Pax's parents and likely his friend were dying and there was little he could do about it. Rogaan's father flushed from his no-longer-safe spot, now ran along the edge of the stage close to him. Rogaan decided to help the one he could.

"Hide, Rogaan!" Was all his father could say as he ran past Rogaan, then stumbled when he tried to turn sharply around the corner of the stage. Rogaan feared for his father. The raver was almost on him.

"This is madness!" Rogaan cursed at the whole situation and to himself as he ran at the corner where he intended to distract the big beast, hoping to give his father a moment to flee. Rogaan's stunned indecision was gone. Replacing it was raw determination and a returning rage. The big black and red body turned at the corner of the stage sharper and quicker than Rogaan expected with its jaws gaping at his father. With a yell, Rogaan leapt from the stage landing on the raver's hip and tail, further back than he intended. His chest painfully struck the solid muscular beast. Armored plates and stiff, slender black feathers running the spinal ridge of the raver cut into Rogaan's chest and arms as he tried to grasp the beast. Before he could get a firm hold, the raver lurched, bucking Rogaan into the air before slamming him onto the ground. Pain rattled through him in a wave as he hit the dirt, but the air in his lungs he kept. Rogaan rolled to his stomach wanting to see if his father escaped the jaws of the raver. The beast turned to face Rogaan instead of pursuing his father. Spitting dirt from his bloodied mouth, Rogaan let out a growl in satisfaction which was immediately drowned out by a reverberating roar from the angry black and red hulking figure when it swiveled its head sideward and found Rogaan lying on the ground. The raver fixed its gaze on Rogaan as it narrowed its eyes with fury. Frightened beyond anything of Rogaan's experience, he now realized his success likely meant his death. A strange chill sensation passed over him as he felt his hair stand on end. Unexpectedly, he felt somehow refreshed. He felt strong.

The raver lunged at him with its jaws open and head tilting. Rogaan rolled sideways, narrowly avoiding the beast's snapping bladelike teeth. The smell of the raver's maw was foul, making Rogaan gag as he finished his roll before gaining his feet under him. Again, the raver lunged at him. Rogaan dove under the raging beast toward its three clawed toes. He felt the raver's hot breath and heard the deafening snap of its maw catching the air less than a hand away as dirt and sand kicked up behind him. The beast snorted in frustration. Rogaan regained his footing under it before rising into a crouch. The raver bellowed with frustration as it spun about trying to find its prey. Rogaan danced erratically with the raver trying to keep from getting trampled. His wind felt good, allowing him to dodge the claws of the infuriated beast. Rogaan felt a great sense of satisfaction annoying the raver while giving his father time to flee. He did not know how he managed it and considered it somehow part of his "*wild spirit*." He did not care at the moment. All that mattered was that he could dance with the beast without getting eaten.

The beast turned away from Rogaan without warning, forcing Rogaan to dash out from underneath the raver to keep from getting stomped. He found himself at the cut-stone corner of the stage looking at the big raver closing on his father and Pax. Both looked confused and desperate. Beyond them, still close to the stage, the smaller raver lunged at a terrified Aren who was scrambling on the ground before holding his arms up in a feeble defense against the beast. A flash of brilliant light erupted in the air between the predator and its prey, causing the raver to reel back in surprise and pain. Aren appeared shocked and confused as well, looking around for something Rogaan could not see. Pax stumbled backward into Rogaan's sightline to Aren.

"No . . . no be doin' this!" Pax screamed desperately at his father as he fell back into the side of the stage. A quick glance found Pax's father in the path of the big raver. He had pushed his son away from the charging jaws. Those jaws chomped down over Pax's father's right shoulder and chest with a sickening crunch. The Baraan yelled out in pain as the raver lifted him from his feet shaking him violently. Pax's father screamed out in horrible pain as blood soaked most of his shirt, but he remained alive, striking at the raver's snout with his left hand. His swings grew weak and feeble when the second raver clamped its jaws on his arm and tore it from him. Both Pax and his father let out horrific screams. Rogaan stood stunned.

"No!" Pax's attitude changed in a blink from shocked, confused, and helpless to desperate, angry, and ready to launch himself at the big raver. He yelled out with anger, "Let me father be."

Rogaan stepped and grabbed Pax just as he took his first step at the beasts. Pax looked at Rogaan with surprised and angry eyes. He then tried to pull free from his friend while yelling, "Let me be!"

Rogaan had no intention of letting Pax go. Despite the *Light* still in Pax's father, the ravers had already killed him. Blood soaked most of the self-sacrificing father's clothing. More blood squirted from where his arm once connected to his shoulder as the big raver shook him again. The second raver had swallowed its trophy and made to strike again at Pax's feebly yelling father.

With tears streaming down his face and painful anger in his voice, Pax tried to pull free from Rogaan again, while watching the beasts tear his father apart, each raver then holding half of him in their maws. Pax let out a blood chilling scream as he slumped to his knees, "Nooo!"

"Rogaan, bring Pax to the platform door." Mithraam spoke urgently with a commanding voice. "We must leave here before they finish."

A wave of relief filled Rogaan seeing his own father alive after watching Pax lose his in a manner nobody should ever witness. Pax's slumped form was little trouble for Rogaan as he half-carried his friend to where his father stood. He stayed low along the cut stones and wood rail of the stage to keep from being seen by the ravers, morbidly hoping they were taking time eating his friend's father. A wave of guilt and disgust washed over Rogaan at that last thought. He knew he was being pragmatic and hopeful that some of them could keep their *Lights*, but his heart ached terribly for his friend. Rogaan realized Pax's mother was nowhere to be seen. A rush of panic struck him. *No. I hope not.* "Pax, where is your mother?"

Rogaan felt no change in his friend's semi-limp body having asked what he feared to hear the answer to. Concern filled him as he looked to see if Pax was conscious. His friend's eyes were open, but glazed over and staring off to some distant place. He did not want to leave her if there was a chance she lived. Painful regrets filled him as he asked again, "Where is your mother, Pax?"

His answer came swift as Pax exploded into a tense ball of anger, striking Rogaan just below his left eye. The stinging punch came as an unexpected surprise to him. Pax screamed with heated, tear-filled eyes and a fuming face. "She be dead! Just like me father. Ya should no hold me from him. Ya had no right. Ya had no right!"

Rogaan and Pax now stood facing each other. Pax looked in shock and pain and near uncontrolled anger. Rogaan felt deep pain for his friend, but feared they did not have a moment to mourn. Rogaan did not know how to speak to Pax, to get him thinking forward, to get them to a safe place away from these beasts and the screaming crowd. A thought of caution rippled through him. *What is the crowd screaming at?* An air shattering roar gave Rogaan his answer and made his head ring in pain. Looking over Pax's shoulder, Rogaan saw the smaller raver, if that mattered, staring right at them. Panic flushed through him, making his legs and arms momentarily unable to move.

"Get up here," Mithraam's voice boomed from the platform. For Rogaan, his father's voice was both comforting and instructive, giving him focus in the midst of chaos.

Before Rogaan could act, the smaller raver started a trot toward them. Pax broke free of Rogaan's hold and wheeled about, standing defiantly before the approaching beast. Rogaan realized Pax intended to fight it out with the raver here and now. *His Light will be taken.*

"Ya took everythin' . . . ya Spawn of Ninurta," Pax yelled in a rage at the approaching raver. "Come ta me. Take me, if ya can."

The raver approached warily, but approach it did. It looked at Pax and Rogaan with unease. It seemed almost intelligent, as if trying to figure them out, considering what to do next. At fifteen strides, Pax spat curses at it again daring it to charge him. A chill ran up Rogaan's back as internal trumpets sounded, warning him against antagonizing the beast. Pax continued yelling even worse curses at the beast. It responded with eyes turned bloodthirsty as it stopped and coiled itself, readying its body to spring at them. In a moment of alarm, Rogaan grabbed Pax by the shirt and neck, dragging him backward, away from those deadly jaws. Pax fought him, trying to get free of his grasp as Rogaan awkwardly withdrew him. The raver took on a mean air and launched into a charge. Positioned poorly due to Pax struggling against him, Rogaan had to pull Pax in a direction away from the stage in the hope to avoid the raver's charge. Rogaan's blood turned chill and his mouth went dry as he assessed their changing situation. *We are going to be lightless.*

"This way, you ugly beast!" Rogaan heard his father yelling in a deep voice he almost did not recognize. Rogaan looked over his shoulder while continuing to pull his protesting friend now toward the stage platform. At least Pax stopped his goading of the ravers. Looking to the stage, Rogaan's father was waving his arms and yelling at the ravers. He was drawing their attention to give them time to escape. Rogaan felt a mix of relief and concern. The raver approached dangerously close to his father . . . and the Evendiir, now on the stage, who was unsuccessfully trying to get the stubborn Iellen to stop seeking the beast's attention. Mithraam ignored Aren as he kept on after the beast. Rogaan felt his grip loosening on Pax who had decided to go limp and act as dead weight. Rogaan spun around, pulling Pax to his feet as he chastised his friend. "Do not do this, Pax. I need you if we are to survive this."

A scream of pain from the stage drew his attention away from Pax.

Rogaan felt his heart stop at the scene before him. Chaos! The Evendiir was on his hands and knees at the edge of the stage, completely vulnerable to the raver. Fortunately for Aren, it did not pay him any attention. Instead, the beast had its focus on a lump on the ground near its feet. *Father . . . No!* Rogaan's father somehow had been pulled from the platform by the black and red beast and now helplessly writhed in pain at its clawed feet. Blood soaked much of father's once light charcoal-colored tunic. Rogaan stood stunned staring at the scene, not knowing what to do. *Father!* The raver reared back, readying itself to put a killing bite on his father.

Rogaan let go of Pax as he broke into a hard run toward his father without a thought or hesitating. Aren slipped from the stage in his attempt to flee, landing hard on the ground with a cry of pain. The raver shifted its attention to the Evendiir and snapped at Aren. Rogaan's skin prickled and the hairs on his neck stood on end as a brilliant, soundless light grew and burst in a flash between the raver and Aren. The flash momentarily blinded Rogaan, forcing him to stop. He could hear the raver growl as he blinked until his sight partially returned. Aren was gone, and the stage railing behind the raver was smashed. Sharp edges of wood debris lay everywhere. The raver shifted its stance while vigorously shaking its head trying to clear its sight. Taking advantage of the raver's disorientation, Rogaan's father rose to his knees, then unsuccessfully tried to stand. Fear that his father could not flee the raver without help struck Rogaan. He again broke into a run to aid his father. As Rogaan approached the raver, the beast having recovered some of its sight and now holding a meaner disposition stepped forward and viciously clamped its jaws on his father's torso before lifting him high.

"No!" Rogaan desperately charged the beast as his father cried out in pain. Rogaan slammed his body into the raver's leg, the impact jarring his teeth and nearly knocking the wind from him. He started pounding his fists on the raver's leg, striking with all his might. The beast shuffled sideways, trying to avoid the pounding while keeping its jaws clamped on Rogaan's father, its head in an elevated position away from Rogaan. The beast appeared to be trying to keep its meal from being taken. Rogaan yelled at the raver as he struck the beast's leg another blow. The raver shuddered from the impact, then responded by taking quick steps forward with hips shifting sideways and its tail in full swing at Rogaan. With no time to move out of the way, Rogaan gritted his teeth in anticipation of the tail slap. *This is going to hurt.* The jarring impact shook Rogaan's entire body as the lighted arena vanished into a deep gray void. He felt himself floating and strangely weightless, then pain ripped and seared through his entire body as he felt the wind leave him, dirt kick up in his face, and the ground scraping at his exposed skin. He hurt everywhere as he struggled to breathe and cough up dirt at the same time. Pain inflamed his anger and made him more determined. *I must save Father. Curse my feeble chest . . . I need to breathe!* Every moment he lay on the ground allowed the raver a better chance at taking his father's *Light*. Several more painful tries at forcing in a breath found him filling his lungs. The world suddenly grew brighter with his lungs expanding as the burning in his chest subsided. Rogaan rolled to a crouch facing the stage as he drew in another full breath. He watched the raver drop his father's limp body to the ground, then looked ready to step on his unmoving meal to tear him apart.

"No!" Rogaan charged the beast with a growl, angry at his own ineptness and the beast's thirst to kill. He aimed his body at its slow-moving legs . . . the only part of the beast low enough to be certain he would strike. Rogaan slammed his shoulder into and wrapped his arms tightly around the raised lower leg of the raver, preventing it from stomping down and crushing his father. The impact jarred Rogaan, sending waves of pain through his body as flashes of light filled his head. He could not—would not—let go. *Father will die if I give up.* With his eyes shut tight, Rogaan pumped his feet and legs driving forward as his body felt near to snapping under the weight. He growled and strained with every fiber of his body driving his legs and the raver's leg forward. A chill washed over him as his skin prickled. He immediately felt stronger, able to drive forward the raver's leg with an unexpected ease. At any other time Rogaan's curiosity would get the better of him and look for who aided him, but now . . . He did not care. He had to keep driving . . . had to keep the raver from killing his father. Rogaan dug in his boots as he again drove forward with his straining body. The beast's leg tilted away from him. Rogaan kept driving his legs. The raver's leg rotated over his shoulder as an enormous weight pulled his upper body backward leaving his legs drive out from under him. He slammed to the ground on his back with the raver's leg on top of him. A great howl escaped the beast as its legs thrashed, knocking Rogaan from underneath it. Pain rippled through Rogaan's chest and arms from the beast's kick. He hurt everywhere. He painfully rolled up into a kneeling position. Looking at the thrashing raver, he watched it in its death throes before falling silent. The sharp tip of a bloodied wood stake pointed skyward from the raver's chest. A piece of the stage's railing felled the beast.

An air of silence fell over the arena as Rogaan kneeled in shock staring at the lifeless raver. A sense of awe rippled through him. *How did I . . . ?* A roar erupted filling and reverberating throughout the arena. Rogaan felt the roar of the crowd more than he heard it. With the stage at his back and the lifeless raver in front of him, Rogaan stood and looked about. The crowd was on its feet yelling with a mix of disapproval and encouragement, the latter losing to the former by a measure of volume. Pax stood off to his right sixteen strides from the stage. He looked stunned and confused . . . lost with wobbly legs staring into the distance beyond the far side of the stage where the big raver bobbed its head down, ripping apart what Rogaan could only guess was what was left of Pax's father. Intense sorrow gripped Rogaan. His eyes welled up with tears, and he suddenly found it difficult to breathe. A low, agonized moan on the opposite side of the stage from Pax sent a wave of horror and urgency through Rogaan. *Father!* Spinning, Rogaan found his father lying bloodied and struggling for breath as the Evendiir kneeled next to him with an uncertain and conflicted look. Rogaan did not know if Aren intended to run or aid his wounded father, who, a bloodied mess, reached out to the Evendiir with a crimson stained hand in a plea for help. Rogaan needed to save his father, bind his wounds, and get him to a safe place. To Rogaan, the moment lasted forever. He could not move his body fast enough to get to his father. Bolts of pain shot through his shoulder, chest, back, and legs as he commanded his body forward and over the raver. Frustration and anger filled him with each move as he climbed over the raver's stinking midsection. The beast suddenly breathed, drawing air into its lungs and launching Rogaan awkwardly, headfirst, onto the arena dirt. He landed hard with waves of pain shooting throughout his body. Rogaan strained his neck and torso to catch sight of his father, hoping not to see the beast take his

Light with a final bite. The raver snapped its jaws and growled in frustration as Aren dragged Rogaan's father just beyond the raver's teeth.

"Get off your rump and help me drag your father, you half-wit!" Aren growled as he struggled with the near *lightless* body of Mithraam. He was slowly dragging him to the corner of the stage. Rogaan realized Aren was not strong enough to lift his father onto the stone steps to the platform.

Excruciating pain rippled through Rogaan as he struggled to his feet. He took a step toward his father and Aren when the impaled raver let out a moaning roar, then fell still. Rogaan hoped it was the end of the beast this time. Another roar silenced the crowd. Pax screamed at the larger raver as he rushed it. *What is Pax thinking?* Rogaan stood dumbfounded for a moment as he watched the big raver, with the head and arm of Pax's father hanging from its jaws, walking behind the stage, away from Pax. *My friend's Light will be taken,* Rogaan feared.

Pax slammed into the leg of the big black and red raver, just as Rogaan had earlier, but bounced off it. Pax kept his feet somehow, but clearly wobbled dazed from the collision. The raver spun left, sweeping its tail at Pax, who barely ducked the wall of muscle, then staggered into the trail the tail made. Rogaan saw the raver drop what remained of Pax's father as it faced away from Pax, then continued its leftward spin, stopping when it faced his Baraan friend. The raver's eyes, snout, and jaws were hot with rage. *Not good!* Rogaan told himself as Pax took off in a sprint to his right around the far corner of the stage toward the struggling and unaware Aren . . . and Rogaan's father. The raver bellowed with anger and chased after Pax. *Not good!* Ignoring his injuries and pains, Rogaan broke into a run for his father, intending to get him to the stage and out of reach of the beast.

Pax rounded the corner of the stage much faster than Rogaan expected, yelling as he ran, the raver, with jaws agape, closing on him. Rogaan willed himself to move as fast as his body could, and then some. He cursed his slow feet. Ahead, Aren turned to the approaching noise. Death rushed at him. Without a flinch, the Evendiir let go of Rogaan's father and leaped to the stage with a scream. Rogaan tried to will himself even faster. He would not be in time to pull his father to safety. He desperately wished for his *wild spirit* to rise, giving him a slowed world . . . giving him time to save his father. *Nothing.* As

Pax approached Rogaan's fallen father, he suddenly, and expectantly, turned hard into the stage as the raver snapped at him, its jaws slamming shut at only air. The beast's eyes then found Rogaan's father struggling in a crawl toward the stage.

How to save Father? Rogaan's mind frantically searched for an answer. *Draw the beast from him.* It came to him in the heat of thought as his boots pounded the dirt, desperately trying to get to his father before the raver. Rogaan swung wide right of his father as he let out a desperate roar, a battle cry, trying to get the raver's attention. It seemed to work as the beast's eyes and head followed him. He saw the battle move he was about to attempt once, by Im'Kas. *It worked on those ravers.* Relief flashed in Rogaan as the raging raver fixed its sight on him and not his father. *Now, to keep me from Darkness.* Rogaan wished again for his *wild spirit*, making it possible to do what he was about to do. *Nothing.* He had no time to feel disappointment or anger at its absence. He and the raver were nearly upon each other. The beast opened its jaws to bite down on Rogaan like a hammer with dagger blades and its running body propelling them, a killing strategy honed over countless eons of its kind's existence. All he had to save himself was an insane move he watched made by a living legend . . . once. His skin prickled as he launched himself into the forward roll. He hoped his timing was good . . . or he would have his *Light* taken from him in an agony of crushing and rending pain. He felt and smelled the hot putrid breath of the beast wash his left side, shoulder to thigh as he curled his head, neck, and chest down. He feared his timing too late. Searing pain in his left calf confirmed his fear. The raver's teeth found him as his body continued forward into a roll, his neck and shoulders striking the ground as the rest of his body, except maybe his lower leg, rolled after with him. The air left his lungs as he hit the ground hard, then slid awkwardly to a stop as the heavy body and thundering footfalls of the raver passed by him.

I live! I have my Light. But he needed to know, *do I still have my leg?* He opened his eye fearing the worst. He looked at his left calf. It bled from a stinging slice just above the boot. He wiggled his toes. *I still have them. It worked!* Looking up, the bright sky forced him to squint and turn his head from the wispy and scattered clouds above. The crowd came into focus, a revelry of colors cheering support and yelling disappointments. Rogaan did not care of the crowd's fickleness. He felt contempt for them all. He and his family and Pax's family were not bothering anyone in Brigum. All of them in the crowd brought this upon them . . . the pain, the sorrow, the death, and the *Darkness*. And for what?—to entertain their unhappy lives, trinkets of wealth that belonged to his family and others items of comfort his parents worked their lives to achieve . . . to make a home for family and friends? No, Rogaan would hold them all in contempt . . . the crowds for wanting pleasure from his and other's pain, taking from others what was not deserved of them . . . the *Tusaa'Ner* and the *Sakes* for being willing hands of injustice for the *Zas*, the lawmakers, and all who served them and their selfishness in seeking power over others. A moment of clarity struck Rogaan in the midst of an insane and unneeded chaos. Anger filled him.

Rogaan felt vibrations in the ground from heavy footfalls. The raver still retreated. *It's at a distance . . . Maybe I have time to get Father safe to the stage.* With a powerful determination of purpose, Rogaan leapt to his feet, ignoring his pains. As he turned to find his father, he caught a commotion, the *Tusaa'Ner* struggling with some of the crowd at the top of the stone wall at the far western end of the arena, ninety-one strides distance, near where Pax's mother lay torn apart. A flash of sorrow burned hotter his anger, his rage. His father lay where he remembered, near the stage. Broken pieces of timber railing were scattered around him. His father's eyes fixed on him. *Thank the Ancients, he lives!* His father's eyes held a mix of relief, pride, and concern, a strange mix Rogaan did not expect from his father. Pax was pulling himself up to the side of the stage. He looked unsteady. Aren kneeled at the edge of the stage with a hold on Pax's torn green shirt. Aren helping Pax to his feet surprised Rogaan. *Is he helping out of self-preservation, or does the Evendiir dare commit a selfless act?* Still, Rogaan's father lay helpless and exposed. Nobody was aiding him. Rogaan's anger boiled at the edge of rage. It needed to be satisfied.

He hurried to his father with even, confident steps. Everything around him moved slowly. His *wild spirit* was upon him. *It feels good.* Rogaan kneeled at his father's side to get a better look at his wounds. He felt strangely calm. He did not understand, but welcomed it. His father's wounds were bad.

How he still lived, Rogaan wondered but was grateful for it. *He is stubborn.* The raver's teeth cut open his midsection in several palm-sized lines. He lost a lot of blood and looked to be in much pain. His father grabbed Rogaan's forearm with a grip surprisingly firm for one so close to *Darkness*.

"Flee . . ." Mithraam croaked out to his son in a drawn out manner Rogaan now understood as a result of his *wild spirit*. "My *Light* leaves me. Save yourself and protect your mother. Your *shunir'ra . . .*"

"No, Father." Rogaan calmly cut his father off while trying to talk slow. Mithraam's head settled back to the dirt, his breathing labored. Rogaan saw the rock-steady Tellen who gave him everything he was, made him what he was, losing his *Light* before him. Rogaan would not abandon his father. He wanted him to live. *Mother needs him, and there is much more he needs to teach me.*

No binding I have will fix this, Rogaan assessed. *Moving Father will end him.* Rogaan needed a kind hand from the Ancients to see his father live. He did not put much faith in such things, but he was willing to receive help from anyone at the moment.

A shuddering bellow from the big raver shook the air. Rogaan looked toward it with a calmness that even surprised himself. The beast stood forty-eight strides in the direction where it entered the arena. It stared directly at him with angry and malicious eyes while stomping the ground. It was challenging him, readying to charge if Rogaan did not retreat . . . maybe charge even if he *did* retreat. *How did such an animal ever come to be?* Rogaan wondered. He needed to stop the beast so he could find help for his father . . . maybe a *Kabir* or *Kabiri* from one of those temples in Farratum.

The raver stomped again and bellowed, louder and longer than before. *It will charge at any moment.* Rogaan needed a way to get the raver to leave them be. He needed to inflict enough pain on the beast to make it wary of him. *How?* The raver stomped again, impatiently, then took a mock step at him. Rogaan looked around and realized he had weapons . . . the broken railing. Selecting a thick pointed shard slightly longer than his forearm, he grabbed it, testing its weight and balance. *It will have to do.*

"Leave . . . Save yourself, my son." Mithraam coughed up blood before settling his head back to the dirt.

"I will not abandon you, Father," Rogaan answered him speaking slowly and with conviction. Rogaan stood and took a position between the death beast and his father, holding the shard firmly in his hands.

"What be ya doin', Rogaan?" Pax asked with a tone hinting of insanity.

"What I must," Rogaan answered without taking his eyes from the raver. With some concentration, Rogaan could make out fine details of the animal. Scars about its neck and snout told him the raver had experience fighting . . . and winning. The raver's head pitched up suddenly, snapping at a dark featherwing swooping at its head. Rogaan wondered at it a moment before dismissing it, just another strange happening for the day. The beast returned its attention back on Rogaan, stomping, then crouched, readying itself to launch at him.

"*Make them fear you and your rage.*" Rogaan heard the words of the *War Sworn* in his head. *I may die, but I will not let that animal at Father again.* "Let it and all of them fear my rage."

The raver dug its claws into the dirt, then launched at Rogaan and his father, Pax and Aren. Rogaan crouched and dug his boots into the dirt, readying himself to charge the beast, to strike at its eyes, wound it . . . blind it. Make the animal fear him. Rogaan watched the rhythm and length of the raver's strides . . . measuring them and the distance between them, waiting for it to lower its head further before he charged back at it. The wrath in the beast's eyes was unmistakable. The raver wanted Rogaan's *Light*. Then the animal dipped its head as it opened its teeth-filled maw. Rogaan tensed his body to spring into his charge as his skin prickled and his hair stood on end. He caught movement above and just to the left of his head. A spear tip and shaft flew past his head unnaturally fast. Despite the embrace of his *wild spirit*, the spear moved with the speed of an arrow, not as a heavy-shafted weapon from a *Tusaa'Ner* that it looked to be. With a thud and crack, the spear buried itself into the skull of the raver just left of square between the eyes. The beast's eyes lost their focus and anger before the raver stumbled, then collapsed to the ground, sliding toward Rogaan. The *lightless* eyes of the animal came to rest a stride from him, the spear shaft passing him on his left. The raver's last putrid breath left it a moment later.

Rogaan stood confused. *What happened . . . who?* He turned to see who threw the spear with such deadly accuracy and force. Rogaan took notice that the arena stood eerily silent. The crowd appeared to be shocked by the events. Scanning the crowd, Rogaan saw at the far end of the arena, almost one-hundred strides away, where the commotion he noted earlier, lay unconscious or dead a contingent of *Tusaa'Ner* guardsmen on the wall and on the arena ground. A lone darkly clad figure jumped from the wall landing and rolling with the grace of a leaper. His roll brought him to his feet and a run in one smooth movement. *Who is he?* Rogaan did not fear the approaching stranger. If he was the spear thrower, he just saved all their lives.

Rogaan felt his *wild spirit* leave him as the stranger approached, making it difficult to discern who the cloaked one was until he was almost upon them. The stranger dressed in a dark gray cloak, hide pants, and vest that had more sheathed knives, pockets, and places to put and attach things than could be counted. The stranger was familiar to Rogaan. His short cut black hair and a closely trimmed beard, solid build, and that dangerous, confident stride gave a wave of relief to Rogaan. Im'Kas. Rogaan cast his eyes to the heavens and thanked the Ancients.

Chapter 24
Righteous Purpose

Im'Kas ignored everyone and everything as he approached, his focus completely on Mithraam. He kneeled over Rogaan's father and placed his hands on Mithraam's mortal wounds. Rogaan's skin prickled, and his hair bristled. He backed away from Im'Kas a few steps. *What is he doing that makes my skin crawl so?* Mithraam convulsed and gasped violently. He looked to be in terrible pain, causing concern to sweep through Rogaan. The way his father's body convulsed gave him fear Im'Kas was doing something unhallowed. Rogaan held his tongue though. *Im'Kas and Father are friends*, Rogaan hoped. His father a mere breathe away from his *Light* leaving him made Rogaan no choice but to trust Im'Kas. His father did. That would have to be good enough for Rogaan.

"Open your eyes, my friend." Im'Kas spoke kindly to Mithraam while wearing a deeply concerned look. "I've done all I can. You must do the rest, if you're to live."

His father lay motionless, causing Rogaan to fear the worst. Tears filled his eyes, and his chest tightened. *Show mercy, great lords of the sky and world,* Rogaan prayed to the Ancients . . . something he seldom did. Im'Kas's face turned sad. The Dark Ax lowered his head and closed his eyes as if saying his own prayer. *Father's body remains still.* Rogaan's chest tightened so much he struggled to breathe. He just wanted his father back. Tears washed down his cheeks. Im'Kas looked to Rogaan with sorrow-filled eyes.

"My heart is heavy with regrets, young Rogaan," Im'Kas offered kindness with a pained voice. "I fear I'm too late. His wounds too—"

Breath filled Mithraam's lungs before he let out a painful groan. Rogaan watched, stunned as his father came back from the edge of oblivion. Mithraam's eyes opened and darted about, confused at where he was for a few moments before focusing on Im'Kas. Rogaan's father offered a slight grin to his friend.

"I thought you might . . ." Mithraam hoarsely coughed his words, "ignore my wishes."

"It appears I was just this side of too late," Im'Kas almost smiled back.

"I am . . ." Mithraam coughed more words, "joyed you disobeyed us. Rogaan . . ." Chills shook Rogaan at his father's reference to the Master Dark Robe.

"—is alive," Im'Kas interrupted.

"Lord Dark Ax." Pax spoke with a pained and unsteady voice. Rogaan looked to his friend and saw him visibly shaking from fear of Im'Kas or the loss of his parents, he did not know. "Could ya . . . would ya . . . do dat ta me ma and father. Brin' 'em back?"

Im'Kas did not speak. He appeared to be considering his words. He looked at Pax with those pained eyes. "It doesn't work in that manner."

"But ya saved Rogaan's da." Anger flared in Pax's voice as he pointed at Rogaan.

"Rogaan's father is whole of body," Im'Kas replied calmly, kindly.

Pax made to lash out at Im'Kas with his famously wicked tongue. Rogaan saw it in his friend's eyes and heard it in the tone of his voice. With his left hand, Rogaan reached out and gave Pax a firm grip on his right arm. Pax looked at him with anger oozing before pulling his arm away. Instead of lashing out at Im'Kas, Pax focused on Rogaan.

"Dat be me ma and da layin' out dere." Pax pointed to the bloody mess of bodies where his mother and father lay torn apart. Tears poured from his eyes. "He saved ya da. What about me . . . and Suhd? Don't we be needin' our parents? Why be it ya father and not dem dat he saves?"

"Pax . . ." Rogaan's father tried to comfort, reason with Pax by his tone . . . weak as he was.

"Ya no need ta be talkin'." Pax addressed Rogaan's father with a voice filled with pain and anger. "He saved ya . . . must mean somethin' ta him. Me parents just be nothin'!"

"Aaaah . . . we have more important troubles than crying over those *already lightless*," Aren broke in with impatience. Pax fumed at Aren's interruption, but Aren ignored him as he pointed to the wall. "Look!"

Scores of *Tusaa'Ner*, each armed with bow or crossbow, took up positions on the wall in front of the Seats of the Honored with its many streaming sky-blue pennants, half-bearing Farratum's gateway symbol, and the crossed spears between two towers. Five sky-blue, armor-clad guardsmen entered the arena grounds from a small door in the wall under the perch of the Announcer of Games. They approached with hurried strides.

"I care not of any of 'em," Pax growled at Aren.

"Be still." Im'Kas held Mithraam's eyes, but spoke to Pax and Aren. He lowered his voice such that only Rogaan and his father could hear his next words. "They come to demand my surrender."

"They cannot." Mithraam struggled to speak his words before coughing and settling his head back onto the dirt. He was weak and pale in color. Rogaan realized that whatever Im'Kas did for him was just enough to keep his father from slipping into *Darkness*, but might not be enough to keep him from that final slip after all.

"I know, ol' friend." Im'Kas calmed Mithraam, then stood facing the gathering guardsmen and archers filling the wall.

"Violator of laws." The lead *Tusaa'Ner* guardsman, a *sakal* in his red cap, spoke with confidence as he and his fellow guardsmen stopped some nineteen strides from Im'Kas. Despite the guardsman's display of command, a hint of nervousness carried in his voice as his words echoed throughout the arena. "Disarm and surrender yourself."

"Then disarm, and I'll accept your surrender," Im'Kas replied loudly and as if he meant it.

The *Tusaa'Ner* commander appeared confused at Im'Kas's response. He looked to his fellow guardsmen as if confirming he was not alone in misunderstanding. "Perhaps you misunderstood—"

"No misunderstanding, Commander," Im'Kas cut him off. "I'll not parlay with you as we have no quarrel."

Rogaan's skin prickled again, and his hairs ached as they bristled. Im'Kas stood tall as if about to address an audience.

"Is this your new justice?" Im'Kas's voice boomed throughout the arena. "Is *this* how we treat our citizens? I knew us better than this."

Rogaan did not know who Im'Kas addressed. His gaze was beyond the guardsmen and upward into the seats. A stir in the Seats of the Honored drew

Rogaan's attention. *Is he challenging the powerful?* Rogaan took a few small nervous steps backward away from Im'Kas. Im'Kas stood firmly waiting for a reply as the *Tusaa'Ner sakal* grew more confused. The wait was short. A trumpet from somewhere near the Seats of the Honor sounded, announcing a richly dressed Baraan male in blue robes speaking words from the Seats of the Honored. A white and blue-robed Baraan male of long years stepped up to the announcer's perch speaking on behalf of his masters in the seats above.

"Make their surrender or cut them down . . . by order of the First *Za*," the gray-haired announcer spoke, relaying orders from the lawmaker above, his words echoing loudly throughout the arena. The *Tusaa'Ner* commander standing before Im'Kas regained his composure before taking a step forward.

"By orders of the First *Za*, surrender yourselves," demanded the blue-clad, red-caped commander.

Im'Kas shook his head *no* in response, then replied, "*Zas* hold no such authority under the laws of the land. They make laws, not command their obedience, nor do they pronounce judgments."

"So be it."The *Tusaa'Ner* commander's voice hesitated, but was strong as he raised his right hand.

Scores of *Tusaa'Ner* archers lining the arena wall drew and aimed their weapons toward Im'Kas and all near him. Rogaan looked about for cover. He found Aren on the stage behind him wearing a doubfounded look. Pax was gone. A glance found him kneeling over what was left of his father's body beyond the edge of the stage. Rogaan felt great pain for his friend, having just been to the brink of that possibility himself.The only good of it was Pax hopefully was safely out of the way of all but a stray arrow. *Father!* Rogaan thought of his father lying helplessly under a storm of arrows unleashed upon them. *Father will certainly die.*

"What in Kur do you think you're about?"Aren got the words out before Rogaan could ask the same of Im'Kas. Im'Kas ignored him. "You'll see us all into the *Darkness*."

Rogaan rushed to his father's side, readying to offer his body as a shield. A hand grasped Rogaan's forearm. He forced a smile at his father.

"Do not think it, Rogaan," Mithraam coughed. "Get from me and take protection behind the fallen beast."

Rogaan shook his head no in reply. He would protect his father, shield his body with his own. *Maybe Im'Kas can give to me that healing, if I live.*

The *Tusaa'Ner* commander looked hesitant to give the signal to fire. Im'Kas merely stood waiting, saying and doing nothing except staring at the guardsmen. Rogaan was at a wonder. *What is he doing? He must be mad.*

"You've lost your head, now it'll be your *Light*, Tellen," Aren ranted from somewhere behind Rogaan. A scamper of sandals on wood told Rogaan Aren was on the move looking for a hiding place to protect himself from what was upon them.

"You don't have to do this," the *Tusaa'Ner* commander offered Im'Kas.

"Same of you," Im'Kas offered back. "This doesn't have to be."

Rogaan felt his skin prickle again, and his hair raised on end. Breathing became a struggle as the air felt heavier. He looked up at Im'Kas when the *Tusaa'Ner* commander lowered his arm down in a command to unleash Kur upon them. Rogaan held his breath as a volley of arrows from all directions filled the sky. His innards felt as if he was falling from a great height, making him dizzy. Realizing his father was still exposed, Rogaan fought through his disorientation enough to lay across his father's body, shielding him, he hoped, from a certain death. Rogaan closed his eyes and held his breath waiting for the onslaught of pain of arrowsheads ripping through his body. Again, he prayed to the Ancients for mercy and salvation. He made his peace with the coming *Darkness*, he hoped, then waited . . . and waited. The pain did not come; no arrows pierced him. He waited a few more moments with eyes closed tight. *Is it my wild spirit again?*

A resonating gasp filled the arena. Rogaan felt it as much as heard it. He looked up and stared in awe and wonder. Every metal-tipped blue arrow hung still in the air after having arced downward toward them. A wall of blue surrounded them, the closest white fletched shafts stopping less than two strides away. Im'Kas was deep in concentration and did not seem to notice the suspended projectiles of death. The dark-clad Im'Kas slowly raised his head as a murmur from the crowd turned into another gasp as the wall of blue and white fell to the dirt.

"It was never to be." Im'Kas spoke directly at the *Tusaa'Ner* guardsmen as the commander and his guardsmen backed away with fear-trembling strides.

Im'Kas stood taller as he addressed the Seats of the Honored in a booming voice. "This . . . is not of our laws. The dead were not judged before the courts, the *Gals*. These younglings were not proclaimed guilty . . . of any crimes before the court. This dying Tellen is accused only of hording wealth, a family heirloom, passed down father to son through the generations."

"That young Tellen made my guards *lightless!*" A tall, blue-robed Baraan proclaimed in a heated tone. His voice carried throughout the arena as he stood stiffly at the railing surrounding the Seats of the Honored. Two blue-tuniced escorts framed the robed Baraan.

"Put him before the *Gals*, First *Za*," Im'Kas countered without hesitation. "Let the law decide if his actions were righteous or not."

"Stealing the *Lights* of those serving the *Zas* is *never righteous!*" The First *Za* pronounced. One of his blue-tuniced escorts quickly got the First *Za's* attention, then exchanged unheard words with him. The First *Za* began waving off his blue-tuniced aide, seeming to not like what he was being counseled about.

"Are these accounts true?" Asked a blue and white-robed, white-haired Baraan of long years who now stood at the far left end of the Seats of the Honored. "I am disturbed by what I hear."

The First *Za* looked perplex at the interference of his exchange with Im'Kas. With an aggressive posture, the First *Za* made to speak something to the white-haired Baraan, but his aide stopped him. After a short and heated private exchange between the First *Za* and his shaking aide, the First *Za* asked of the white-haired elder, "*Gal* Nigina, what is your proclamation?"

"Yes," Rogaan's father wheezed from under Rogaan.

Realizing he still lay across his father as a protective shield, Rogaan lifted himself up, then sat down beside him. "What is this about, Father?"

"I feared Im'Kas . . . lacked strength to shield us." Mithraam struggled to explain, coughing up a little blood. "He again proves me short of faith in him. Im'Kas confronted the unruly *Zas* before the people . . . and *Gals*. First *Gal* . . . that white-haired Baraan, has . . . authority to proclaim . . . to rule . . . justice. Honoring the laws. Honoring . . . your life."

Trumpits sounded, drawing Rogaan's attention to the Seats of the Honored. The First *Gal* stood where the First *Za* stood moments ago. The First *Za* now was nowhere to be seen. The First *Gal* spoke his proclamation that echoed loudy about the arena. "By order of the *Mes*, justice must be served. I make the following proclamations seeking justice. I order the Tellens, the young Baraan, and the young Evendiir to the courts. The injured Tellen is to have healing. See that done immediately. Im'Kas, you have made quite a mess of things. Your reputation as one for disturbance remains unspoiled in this, but have managed once again not to have violated known laws if the guardsmen you . . . laid to ground live, as they stood between you and injustice. Your actions, unorthadox as you are famous for, were in defending the unproclaimed from judgments. You may go your way. Seeking truth and justice for the dead lying before us, I order *Truth-finding* to reveal lawbreakers."

The First *Gal* watched as several troops of *Tusaa'Ner* and *Sakes* entered the arena grounds from several different doors, then quickly made their way toward the stage.

"What is to happen to us, Father?" Rogaan asked, fearing the worst.

"The law . . ." Rogaan's father coughed up more blood.

"You are dying?" Rogaan asked with a trembling voice. He feared his father would not last much longer.

"I will live, my son," Mithraam comforted Rogaan as he coughed again. "Hear me."

Rogaan nodded to his father as Im'Kas approached them ahead of the *Tusaa'Ner* and *Sakes*. The Dark Ax then kneeled next to Mithraam and Rogaan. Rogaan felt more confused than ever and did not know what to make of things.

"Rogaan," Mithraam coughed. "Im'Kas kept us . . . from *Darkness* . . . this day. Tomorrow will see . . . the laws judge us. All but you . . . have little to account."

"What do I have to account?" Rogaan asked honestly.

"The blood and *Lights* of guards and an old Baraan," Im'Kas answered so that Mithraam need not have to. Mithraam looked weaker with each cough and word he spoke. "No telling how the Hall will judge you, but your words will be heard, unlike this abomination today."

"What does that mean?" Uneasiness rippled through Rogaan. "What is to happen to me?"

"That is not yet written, son of Mithraam," Im'Kas offered. He pointed to the *Tusaa'Ner* approaching. "Do not struggle against them. Allow judgment to flow its path. Your immediate days will likely be unpleasant, but long days to come will try you harsher."

"This is not how I envisioned saving Father." Rogaan spoke to himself more than the others.

"I would expect not," Im'Kas agreed with Rogaan. "Your father has been a fierce foe of tyrants and tyranny for many years. He achieves great things out of sight of most. This is one time our foes have spied us and sought open conflict to end our challenge. Your father hoped you would join us and take up his banner when his days come to an end."

Rogaan stood up looking at Im'Kas dumbfounded. "Take up his banner . . . of *this? Darkness* and suffering?"

"It's necessary to remain free," Im'Kas replied simply. "There are always those seeking power and authority over the weak and unaware, most often at the sufferings of those they subjugate. And the subjugated cry out against the tyranny only after they lose all they thought would last forever."

"You speak of this as if it is a simple thing to do," Rogaan challenged, still finding this all difficult to believe.

"Not simple." Im'Kas continued speaking as if he were conversing with Rogaan over an ale. "Not without charge, sometimes requiring all of that we have. I was once counseled, 'all tyranny and its evils require is for good fellows to watch and do nothing'. It took years for me to understand."

Rogaan thought he understood, but did not want to. It frightened him mightily of the implications this Baraan of legend was telling him. Then Rogaan recalled the words of the *War Sworn* and spoke them. "It is a measure . . . of the quality of your *Light* . . . how you depart this world . . . that matters to . . . the *Great One*."

Im'Kas looked quizzically at Rogaan. "Do you know what that of the '*Sworn*' means?"

"I think I do," Rogaan answered more timidly than he wanted.

"Seldom does one see clearly the path they ultimately walk." Im'Kas offered wisdom he appeared to be reflecting upon. "If done so with righteous purpose . . . honor, moral honesty, and knowledge you will do so with few regrets."

Rogaan felt confused by a great many things, an unknown future, and such strange happenings to him and those around him. He looked about and found Aren in the hands of several *Sakes*. It looked as if he made a try at escaping, but failed. *What is he about?* Pax too was in the hands of unkind *Sakes* who were dragging him screaming from his father's rended body. Rogaan's heart ached for his friend and Suhd as they lost everything except each other. Tears welled up in Rogaan's eyes. *It's my fault. They paid a heavy price for their friendship with me.* Tears flowed freely down his cheeks.

Two sky-blue armored guardsmen took hold of Rogaan's arms, leading him away from Im'Kas and his father. Struggling with himself to comply with Im'Kas's and his father's wishes, he found it in him not to resist the guardsmen. Looking back, he saw four more guardsmen placing his father on a poled hide carrier, all at Im'Kas's directions, the guardsmen all nervously following the Dark Ax's commmands. Carrying his unconscious father on the pole carrier with Im'Kas at his side, they quickly fell in line behind Rogaan and his armed escorts. Looking ahead, Rogaan feared the vast unknown and his uncertain future as the *Tusaa'Ner* escorted him from the arena. *What is to become of me and those I care about?*

Epilogue
Wind of the Ra'Sakti

D istant voices, mostly unintelligible and echoing, speaking of ship damage, being hunted, and worse—crew both wounded and dead taunted Nikki. She was unable to see . . . darkness remained all around, despite her opening her eyes. She grew anxious. *Am I blind?* "I can't see."

"Nikki?"The voice of Anders sounded distant, not real. "Nikki. Can you hear me?"

"Shawn . . ." Nikki started to cough, then stopped as her body was racked with pain. She hurt everywhere so badly that tears were flowing down her cheeks. *Pain . . . Make it stop!*

"Nikki . . ." Anders's voice was stronger, then it cracked and squeaked. He sounded ill with nausea again. "Don't talk. We're taking care of you. We'll fix you."

His words alarmed Nikki. *What's wrong with me?* Panic welled up inside her. She fought it, trying to maintain some element of control over her emotions. *Imagination is always worse than the real world,* she rationalized. But her body hurt all over. A painful migraine headache rapidly grew. She cried out, "What's wrong with me?"

"Nikki, this is Doctor Dunkle."The doctor used a calm tone. "I need you to lie still.You have injuries you will make worse if you move around. I'm giving you medication that will help with the pain."

Nikki felt the pinch of a needle, nothing compared to her other pains. Moments later, her thoughts grew fuzzy and her suffering eased. She lay there recalling . . . reliving the nightmare she dreamt, of the ship being attacked and of . . . Rogaan. She was free of his emotions she felt in her dream. *It was a dream . . . good.* Nikki found herself feeling disappointed. She wouldn't admit to herself why. A stench of something burning filled her nose causing her to involuntarily wrinkle it. The smell of burning flesh and something caustic sickened her. Nikki grew anxious. Still unable to see, she asked questions with a trembling voice, "What's that smell? What's happening?"

"Nothing to concern yourself with," came the even-toned reply from Doctor Dunkle.

"I can smell it, Doctor," Nikki shot back with slurred words. "What . . . who's burning?"

"Nikki," Anders's voice was a comfort as the doctor continued fussing over her. He spoke with gulps and gasps. "We are hit pretty hard. People . . . are dead. More are injured. The ship . . . back here, is . . . torn up. That awful smell is coming from a couple of . . . burning bodies . . . of the crew and one of those armored soldiers . . . and what was the weapons bay."

"Oh . . ." is all Nikki could think to say in her semi-surreal condition. Pain still throbbed in many places, but it felt almost as if it was somebody else's pain.

"Ouch!" Anders yelled. "Would you stop doing that?"

"The second injection will take care of the last of that nausea," Doctor Dunkle informed Anders in his matter-of-fact manner. "Can't have you falling over at the smell of the dead and dying."

A ruckus rose among the crew with yelling and footfalls and shuffling feet and clanking and handheld weapons being armed and readied for use. Then it fell eerily silent with only the wind and the ocean filling the silence.

"Stop walking and put your hands on your head!" An unknown voice demanded. A few moments passed with only murmurs among the crew.

"I said, stop walking and put your hands on your head!" The unknown voice demanded again with increased anxiousness.

From somewhere in front of Nikki, not far away, voices spoke. Nikki didn't know who was who and wanted to see what was happening. Either her head was clearing or she was getting used to the pain medication. She started concentrating on seeing for the first time since the explosion. Nothing. She tried again. Nothing. A voice with a mix of emotions entered her head. She hoped it was Rogaan. Quietly, she listened. Moments passed before she could better feel it . . . know it. The voice was troubled, confused, and a little angry. Nikki became alarmed. *This isn't Rogaan.* Nikki strained to see. She feared it was *him* . . . experiencing a new world without counsel, guidance. His volatility and tendencies would lead to conflict, or worse. Light danced at the edge of her vision. Then a little more. Blurs of light formed. Nikki blinked hard, trying to clear her vision. The blurs of light gave way to blurred shapes, then people standing on a mangled structure in front of her. They were all armed, anxious, and fearful. It was dusk just before the deep night. Lights from above cast a greenish glow on the superstructure and deck around her. She found seven crewmen all pointing rifles at a spot to her left and lower. That anger she sensed elevated.

"Put your hands on your head!" One of the senior crewmen who Nikki could not remember his name demanded again. "Comply or we'll fire."

"*Za gabaldu we!*" The voice speaking Antaalin was familiar to Nikki.

A wave of dread swept through her . . .

"You challenge me?" As if any of the crew were a challenge to him. That anger she felt flared. She knew what he was capable of doing when unrestrained and feared for them all. She looked to him on her left, just barely visible on the deck below.

"*Nagaah!*" He growled in Antaalin. The crew were fools challenging a danger they didn't even know.

"Aren. *Na!*" Nikki yelled in Antaalin as searing pain shot through her chest at the effort.

Arcs of directed lightning shot out from Aren striking each of the crewmen pointing weapons at him. It happened so fast that Nikki looked twice around the deck before she would believe her eyes. Each crewman went down without firing a shot. She feared them dead . . . Aren clearly intended it so. *No threat lives.* Nikki wondered where that thought came from.

Wanting a better look at Aren on the walkway below, Nikki tried to raise herself up. Pain wracked her all over as she slumped back to the metal deck. She looked down at herself wondering what was wrong. Horror met her eyes. Her legs were a bloody mess with her right shin and calf bones showing and the foot at an odd angle. A compound fracture sticking through her blood-soaked khaki pants. Her left leg was a little better. It was cut up badly with some of her pants and flesh torn away and some burnt. Her midsection and chest both bled in spots through her khaki button-down roll-sleeved field shirt. Nikki howled in misery as she realized just how badly she was injured before falling back against the superstructure staring at the aft deck in front of her. She felt numb all over, and it wasn't just the drugs. She feared she would not walk again, maybe not even live beyond the next few minutes. That mattered to her, she realized, as well. She wanted to know why this was happening to her. She asked with a groan to nobody in particular, "Why me? Why did this happen to me?"

"You have knowledge of us." Aren spoke in a half fact, half sardonic manner from the walkway below. "Clamor . . . chaos is our companion, and you have become part of the path."

Nikki stared at Aren as he rose from the walkway below. She was uncertain if he climbed the ladder or . . . somehow elevated to her. Now standing about ten feet to her left, he was still barefoot and dressed in his black sensor robe as he appeared to systematically survey the chaos around him. Doctor Dunkle and Anders hadn't moved from their crouching positions next to Nikki. They both appeared to be stunned or mesmerized by all that happened. Aren's gaze returned to Nikki.

"You understand our words." Aren spoke in English as if he had been raised with the language. Then he spoke in Antaalin, "*Za marr ima ga sagdu. Edei!*"

"I don't know how to get out of your head," Nikki replied honestly with a gurgling cough. Something wet was on her lips. She raised her right hand to her lips to wipe it away. More blood. She was bleeding internally. Hope to see another dawn slipped from her. Her vision became blurred with tears filling her eyes.

"*Resussun sha!*" Aren demanded of Dunkle and Anders in Antaalin. When they looked at him dumbfounded, Aren's expression changed from that of arrogance to one of eye-rolling exasperation. "Help her!"

"Her injuries are too great for me to do anything other than make her comfortable," Doctor Dunkle answered with a frustrated tone as he looked at Aren, then back to a flexi-display and hand scanner he held.

"*Tebu nizu!*" Aren demanded of Dunkle in Antaalin. When Dunkle didn't respond to his words, Aren took another deep exasperating sigh, then spoke in English. "Remove yourself!"

Dunkle and Anders both remained on one knee next to Nikki exchanging uncertain looks. Aren's expression turned from impatient to frustration, then, with a backhanded flick of his fingers, both of them flew several meters away from Nikki where they landed painfully. Nikki tried to suck in a breath at Aren's dismissal of the two, fearful he would toss them from the ship. Instead, she started another coughing fit with more blood spitting from her mouth. She looked up to Aren with unfocused eyes watching his blurry figure kneel next to her and touch her chest. An icy-cold wave rippled through her making her involuntarily convulse. Nikki hovered somewhere between pain and pleasure. It was a sensation unlike anything she ever felt. She was uncertain which sensation dominated, but when a breath filled her lungs free from fluids that were drowning her, she knew it was pleasure. Aren then placed his palms on her stomach. Another icy-cold wave rippled through her. Nikki felt something inside of her chest become . . . unbroken. She didn't even want to know what he healed. Aren repeated his mending of Nikki for each of her legs. With each touch, the black Agni gemstone he wore around his neck faintly flashed of dark vaporous light so briefly she would have dismissed it if it had not done so multiple times. He healed the burnt and torn flesh of her one leg, then fixed the compound fracture of the other, but became visibly tired when attempting to heal the flesh of her leg around the once-fractured bone.

"Mending takes much from the one healer," Aren offered in a weakened voice. His head slumped low with his hands on the deck holding himself up. Nikki thought Aren exhausted by the look of him. Then, Aren then looked up with tired eyes. "*Rogaan kalag za lutila.*"

Nikki looked down at her legs. Her left looked and felt healed despite the bloodstains. Her right leg no longer had the compound fracture and her foot was almost at a normal-looking angle. Her muscles were healed such they looked like they might hold her weight, but her skin remained torn and burnt away. Pain from her right leg started to work its way through the medication and whatever Aren did to her. Nikki did her best not to cry out from the deep stinging and burning sensation, but she couldn't keep from groaning as she futilely tried to move her leg into a pain-free position.

"Let me help," Doctor Dunkle half-demanded, half-asked for permission as he in a low-crouch shuffled back to Nikki's side.

"Aren says Rogaan can make me healthy," Nikki told Dunkle through gritted teeth.

"He's not here," Doctor Dunkle replied matter-of-factly as he searched his medical kit. "There it is."

Aren remained still watching the doctor administer a spray to her leg from his medical pack. Relief from the pain was immediate. Nikki sighed. The doctor told her in his rough bedside manner, "You're not walking on that leg without surgery, but it looks intact. Amazing."

"*Asar me Rogaan?*" Aren asked.

"How did you do this?" Doctor Dunkle excitedly asked Aren, ignoring the question.

Silence was all Aren provided. He still held his head low and his arms remained bracing his body up. At first, Nikki thought Aren about to collapse, but the heated emotion she felt from him told her to be less compassionate and more wary.

"*Nichole, asar me Rogaan?*" Aren asked again without looking up.

"I don't know," Nikki answered with a slight tremble in her voice. Aren frightened her, almost as much as the other one. Pointing aft to the poop deck and helipad, she continued. "Rogaan was thrown overboard when that ship out there shot us there."

Dunkle and Anders looked to the poop deck, then out into the darkening ocean. It was a futile effort. Aren slowly lifted his head allowing his eyes to scan the ocean. Nikki felt a deep concern coming from him.

"What is it?" Nikki asked Aren with her trembling voice.

"Rogaan hates to be submerged in water," Aren answered simply in English. "Puts him in terrible mood."

"Status, Doctor?" A familiar voice demanded, filled with confidence and being in charge.

Nikki saw the captain climbing the ladder on her left. He looked to be struggling, mostly when using his left side. His dark-colored uniform, complete with a black coat with insignia, was ripped in a number of places and bloodstained mostly on his left side from head to just above the knee. Drying blood on the left side of his head and dark hair covered him from ear to eye. Nikki wondered how he kept standing.

"Captain, you need medical attention," Doctor Dunkle voiced an obvious observation everyone likely agreed with.

"No time for it, Doctor." The captain waved him off with his right arm, his singsong inflections muted. "Get off the perch watching over our guests and tend to the wounded. More of the crew lay injured as you go forward. Hop to it!"

A young blond crewman dressed in khakis scrambled up the ladder as the captain surveyed the aft deck and damage the U.N. had caused his ship.

"Captain, we're hit badly," the young crewman reported in an American Southern accent.

"Doctor Dunkle, I said . . . *hop to it!*" The captain reemphasized the *hopping* part of his order. The doctor wore a look as if he heard the captain's order for the first time. Then he disappeared in a couple of bounds to the ladder.

"Go on, Mr. Miller," the captain ordered with a grimace of pain.

"Main power is down." Miller tried to sound official. "The fusion reactor is in working order, but the power conduits are ruptured. Its output has been set to minimum until repairs can be made. We're working to get backup power to the engines and command systems. Both aft mini-railguns are inoperative. So are the antiair weapons. The forward mini-railgun is fully operational as are the other assets below in their bays. We have the old shoulder-fire units available too. The bridge is destroyed and unusable. The auxiliary bridge is fully functional once we get power to it. The diesel engines and QDPS are also fully operational."

"Thank you, Mr. Miller." The captain spoke in an even, stoic tone of command, his rising and falling inflections purposely restrained.

"Also . . ." Miller added with a hint of his Southern drawl, "our UAVs have located the 'mother' and are now monitoring her from a safe distance. Her flags are flying black over blue."

"Next time . . . tactical situation first, Mr. Miller." The captain looked at the young man with a disappointed expression. "Black over blue. I would have preferred the Chinese. Distance?"

"Twenty-two thousand meters and closing," Miller replied with heated cheeks and his Southern drawl thicker. "Their attack and boarding craft, two Ghost Gliders, are half that distance. They'll catch up to us in ten minutes."

"Almost no time for it . . . ," the captain spoke to himself, then raised his eyes to the crew in full command. "Deploy four wave runners on remote. Two assigned to search and rescue of those overboard, the other two with ordinance."

"Yes sir!" Miller responded, then was off like a rocket to see the orders fulfilled.

Nikki watched Miller slide down the ladder to the starboard walkway, then run forward. The young bridge crewman had maybe a few years on Nikki, she guessed, but his responsibilities seemed enormous as a wave of embarrassment swept through her for not achieving more with her life as did this young man. He acted with purpose, where Nikki felt lost since her teen years and more so since her Bubba's death. Nikki suddenly felt uncomfortable.

"We'll at least give a good show at slowing the frigate down." The captain seemed to talk more to the air than to those around him. "Maybe we'll get lucky and sink her."

Nikki watched the captain give more orders as he looked the deck area over. His crewmen all immediately jumped at following them. A disciplined and loyal group of men. Anders still crouched by her side watching Aren, who stood at the railing on the port side of the deck looking southwest out into the dusk-time sea. The ship not only was at drift, it was turning into the wind from the southwest like a weathervane. Nikki tried to sense Aren's emotional state, but found nothing to listen to.

A hailing tone came from the captain's wrist PDA. A glance at the information display brought a grimace to his face. He spoke to the PDA. "I'll take the call. Route it to me."

The radio message was loud enough for Nikki to hear. "Vessel *Wind Runner*, you are again ordered to lie to and prepare to be boarded. All other actions will be considered hostile."

The captain spoke into his PDA. "Mr. Beckmire, do not reply to the call. As soon as you have the QDPS on line prepare for a max speed dash. Keep all ship systems as they are . . . play dead until told otherwise."

Nikki felt a flare of emotions from Aren at the mention of the ship's name. *He knew him too*, she realized. Aren now stood watching and listening to the captain instead of the sea. At the mention of making a high-speed dash, Aren's emotions further flared, troubled and in conflict. The Evendiir wanted someone or something to happen, and his instinct was to compel it, but he fought with himself as to . . . how to behave. *Is he stable . . . of a sound emotional state?* Nikki worried. An out of control Aren could be . . . She didn't want to think of it.

"I insist you find my companion before leaving this place," Aren demanded of the captain in an even tone that was unmistakably a threat— *do what I say or else* . . . . Aren stepped confidently toward the captain to emphasize his words. Surprisingly, the captain met him almost halfway and with an even stare, despite his painful injuries.

"Aren, please . . ." Nikki tried to interject herself in between them to stop an argument that would surely lead to the captain's death, but was cut off by both of them each raising a hand to signal to her to remain quiet and out of their discussion. Indignity swirled inside her at their casual dismissal.

"You will not leave Rogaan to this great water." Aren continued his demand with an unblinking stare at the captain, both of them standing only an arm's length apart.

"I have no intention of doing so," the captain replied with an emphasized singsong inflection returning Aren's steely stare. "If you both are what I've been briefed, the world is about to need you. Right now, I need your trust, Mr. Aren, to get you where I have orders to take you, *both* of you. Can you give that to me? Will you give me your trust, Mr. Aren?"

Nikki felt a whirlwind of emotions pummel Aren. Suspicion, betrayal . . . fear, to name a few. Aren wasn't a trusting one; in fact, Nikki sensed he distrusted everyone, even Rogaan, though to a much-lesser degree. It was almost painful for her to experience his erratic emotions as they spiked harshly before Aren could get them under control. He worked hard at self-control. She wondered how often he lost his battles.

"Trust . . . *nigina. Surim!*" Aren spat back to the captain. "*Za ina ula su . . . . You have nothing to satisfy me you are trustworthy.*"

The captain reached into his right coat pocket causing another spike of emotions to explode within Aren. It took Nikki's breath away at their intensity. Somehow, Aren fought to control his suspicions and distrust . . . his paranoia . . . but only barely. She felt bad for the Evendiir not being able to trust anyone fully, even Rogaan. Nikki suffered his internal conflict. *Is he going to attack the captain?* She worried. Aren stood ready if the captain should produce a weapon from his pocket. Instead, the captain revealed a small black cloth bag with a drawstring, one used to carry small objects.

"A mutual acquaintance gave me this . . ." the captain explained with a confident gaze that hinted hope. ". . . should I need it, to provide you confirmation I can be trusted."

Aren cautiously accepted the bag, then opened it, spilling its contents into his left palm . . . a single round and smooth gemstone with jade and pearl halves. A flood of emotions swept through Aren. Nikki quickly felt overwhelmed by them and gasped as she stared off into the darkening sky, unable to move. She lay there semi-aware of her surroundings as if in a surreal dream. A shadow entered her vision. It was unmoving as the storm of emotions raged. Then, the storm calmed, ordered itself, and became controlled. Nikki's vision cleared, finding Aren kneeling in front of her speaking to her in Antaalin, "*Za aste nu palahu we.*"

Nikki felt dizzy and sick. She wasn't sure what just happened, but she never wanted to feel like that—ever again. She heard Aren repeat himself in Antaalin as her dizziness let up. She swallowed hard, wondering if she should be honest in her response. She decided almost as soon as she raised the question to herself. Filled with fear, she took a chance at it. "How can you ask me that . . . not to fear you? You're a demigod . . . a god compared to the rest of us. You and Rogaan can do things we don't even know are possible. You're the most powerful people on earth . . . and you have a temper."

Aren looked down into his hand at the smooth jade and pearl stone. He smiled. *He smiled!* Nikki thought the stone flickered with a faint glow for an instant. She dismissed it as her imagination. Aren looked up, meeting her stare with calm eyes, then spoke in English. "No. There is one more powerful."

"Mr. Aren, I ask again for your trust." The captain calmly reiterated his request after breaking into their moment. He wore a serious expression.

"They're soon upon us. I . . . We need your help if we are to get out of this sticky wicket."

Aren kept his eyes on Nikki as he stood. His storm now calmed. Nikki felt it, Aren in control of his emotions instead of them controlling him. His mood now had a familiar feeling to that of Rogaan's . . . determined.

"I will ally myself with you, Captain," Aren answered. "And we will help with this 'sticky wicket' that is dangerous to your ship."

The captain made to clap his hands in relieved celebration, but instead, cringed in a wince of pain. His wounds were impossible to hide without carrying himself stoically. Aren placed his hands on the captain's left chest and ribs. That black Agni gemstone of his faintly flashed of light as the captain gasped. Nikki couldn't decide if the expression on the captain's face was pain or pleasure. *That's how I must have looked when Aren mended me*, she blushed. Aren left the captain, walking slowly aft toward the helicopter pad without speaking a word. Nikki felt Aren's weariness. Healing tired him. The captain look after the Evendiir with a confused look. It lasted a few moments before he regained his stoic composure.

"Mr. Beckmire . . ." the captain talked into his PDA with his singsong inflections. "Send me the Cuban . . . with those shoulder-launched missile units."

"What just happened?" Anders asked Nikki. He hadn't moved from his kneeling position or spoken during the entire exchange between Aren and the others. "My find of a lifetime that you say is from a time long ago making a deal with the captain of a modern ship I didn't know even existed before a few days ago and both of them having a mutual acquaintance?"

Nikki smiled at Anders. "Help me up and let's find out."

Anders supported Nikki as they made their way toward the helicopter pad, around the destroyed weapons, near the poop deck where the Evendiir stood alone. Her left leg felt well, but the right was painful and awkward to put weight on. She hoped Aren was telling her the truth about Rogaan being able to heal her completely. Rogaan . . . a sense of dread swept through Nikki. *Where is he? Is he alive?* She asked herself, fearful of the likely answers. She looked out into the sea now almost invisible except for the whitecaps reflecting the last of the sun's orange rays.

The crew Aren shocked with lightning were now recovering. Most were disoriented and confused. Some wanted to engage Aren again, but the captain called them off of committing that silliness a second time. The Cuban arrived with two long cases Nikki assumed were missiles. She smiled at herself and how casually she now thought of missiles as being part of a normal day. A pair of veiled UCAVs flew around and over the ship. They were invisible to her eyes, but their whining hums gave away roughly where they were. Nikki felt the ship lurch forward as the water stirred behind the *Wind Runner*. No engine noise. She wondered what the captain was doing.

"Your captain is ready to try his escape," Aren informed them without looking at either Nikki or Anders. His stare remained focused behind the ship into the sea where Nikki suspected Rogaan floated. She hoped he floated . . . and was still alive.

"The *amelnakru magan* . . . enemy ship is at distance place," Aren continued his announcing of their situation as he pointed. "*Sina adkuds* . . . two boats with *ursa* . . . warriors approach there . . . and there."

Nikki followed where Aren pointed, but could not see anything. *Are his eyes that much better than human eyes?* She wondered as she spoke, "I can't see anything."

A pair of roars from behind them startled Nikki and Anders, causing them to flinch and duck a little. Aren seemed to have expected them and remained unmoving. Glowing flames from the rear of the missiles passed over them out into the almost-dark sky. Their trails were faint, but something Nikki could follow. Seconds later, two explosions in the sky were followed by trails of falling smoking debris. Cheers erupted from the crew behind them.

"New assembly of *ishe santak* . . . sky wedges approach." Aren pointed to the sky off their stern. Again, Nikki couldn't see a thing in the dark expanse. Seconds later, the whining hums of four distinct flying craft passed by the *Wind Runner*.

"Get me more missiles!" The captain demanded from somewhere behind them.

"Hold, ally!" Aren shouted to the captain.

Aren focused his attention skyward and stood motionless for a short time. It seemed long to Nikki, but she knew it was only seconds. She felt him searching—then finding what he was looking for with a sense of satisfaction. His mood turned more focused just before he raised his hands to the sky. Nikki felt what seemed like an electrical current passing through her, causing her hair to stand on end. Anders looked at Nikki, fidgeting with a worried, yet annoyed expression, but said nothing. With hands raised to the sky, Aren spoke to himself words too low to be heard by others. Moments later, four wedge-shaped UCAVs fell out of the sky, swallowed by the dark waters just aft of the *Wind Runner*.

"They will trouble you no further," Aren told the captain with a shout.

"How did you do that?" Anders asked Aren, awed at his manifested wonders. Aren ignored him as he kept his eyes searching the waters behind the ship. When Anders realized his question would be unanswered, he complained to Nikki, "Looks like he only wants to talk to you and the captain."

Nikki barely heard Anders and decided responding to him would carry this line of discussion on, taking away from the task at hand. She continued watching Aren closely, without speaking, as she sought to sort out his emotions and try to read him. Aren proved evasive and frustrating. She noted the *Wind Runner* had picked up speed and now cruised at a meager clip with a totally silent means of propulsion. The ship kept revealing secrets about itself.

"Oh, *surim!*" Aren blurted out without warning.

Nikki felt a surge of electrical current flare intensely around her, prickling her skin and straightening her hair. She looked at Aren who held his left hand open and right arm with forearm positioned as if to block something unseen while facing the gloom off the stern of the ship. His expression grim and his emotions high . . . fear mixed with excitement saw his eyes fixed on the gloom. Nikki just had time to glance to the gloom before a brilliant flash not far off the ship's stern forced her to close her eyes and reflexively turn away. Moments later, the roar and shockwave of one of those high-speed railgun weapons passed over them, causing her to stumble from the pressure wave. An explosion forward on the ship sent another shockwave her direction, forcing her to stumble back toward Aren. The blast made it known it struck the ship. She looked forward finding flames and flying debris everywhere in smoking trails from the top of the superstructure to the decks and water below.

"What . . . ?" Anders started to ask, then fell silent.

"Did they shoot at us again?" Nikki asked Aren with shocked eyes and quivering voice. "They tried to kill us?"

"*Na. Inaa anbar bar su imhas kita sur*," Aren answered and sounding as if he was out of breath. "*Ni zagtag*."

"Flying heavenly metal . . . strike below us?" Nikki tried to piece together what Aren told her. "And you pushed it away?"

Aren's face went blank and eyes focused on something very distant as he looked straight through her and Anders. Nikki grew concerned. She spoke aloud before she realized it, "Is he having a seizure or something?"

"It would be a bad time for it," Anders told Nikki as he pointed off the stern of the ship.

Two angular-shaped Ghost Gliders almost undetectable to her eyes approached the *Wind Runner*. She guessed they were more than a hundred meters out as what caught her eye were the smooth flying, angled-shaped silhouettes of the boat hulls above the waves and the thin straight-line wakes their foils made on the low rolling sea.

"Feel the Wind, young Nikki?" Aren asked, deliberately speaking English.

Nikki looked at Aren who wore a smirk when he met her eyes. Confused by his words, she looked at Aren oddly wanting him to explain. Aren just stared back at her with his smirk. Frustrated, Nikki rephrased his question back at him, "Yes, I feel the wind. It's blowing my hair around."

It was Aren's turn to be confused. Her answer threw him off for a moment before he put on a look that he understood what the child was saying, but that the child was not yet understanding. He spoke again, slowly, in English, "The Wind rises out of the depths. Feel the Wind?"

Aren took her hands in his as Anders held her upright. Immediately, Nikki felt . . . something. It was unlike anything she felt before. His reference to the wind had nothing to do with the air above or around her. She felt a presence . . . intelligent and powerful. It had purpose. A purpose partly guided by . . . "Him!"

Aren smiled at his young apprentice and nodded her success at the lesson.

Nikki felt Aren's emotions, stronger than before . . . satisfaction and a touch of pride for her . . . and his weakened state. He didn't show it outwardly, but he was not far from collapsing in exhaustion. Aren suddenly broke away from her. He looked alarmed and with a growing anger or frustration. Nikki wasn't sure which. His eyes again fixed on the gloom to the stern of the *Wind Runner*.

"*Surim!*" Aren growled with gritted teeth as he held his hand open and forearm up. That familiar electrical charge filled the air, prickling Nikki's skin and giving rise to her hair. "*Surim . . . dung.*" Nikki smiled as she now understood. Aren was cursing when he spoke the word. A sense of pride blossomed in her at her discovery.

Anders pulled her close as the stern area of the ship flashed in a blinding brilliance. This time, Aren was knocked backward onto the deck as countless bluish-orange fragments flew in all directions—except theirs—from less than twenty meters from them. Nikki felt a little heat from the muted explosion though nothing she would expect from a weapon detonation in their faces. Very little pressure from the blast reached her and Anders, despite them standing only a few meters away. She then realized Aren shielded them and absorbed most of the energy of the explosion and deflected the shrapnel. They would all be dead if not for him.

Aren groaned as he struggled to regain his feet. He rolled about, raised himself up only to fall back to the deck. He seemed disoriented. *He's alive and awake! Good!* Nikki felt relieved. She and Anders helped him to his feet. When upright, Aren pulled away from Anders when he realized it was not Nikki touching him. There was an odd silence between the three of them for a few moments. Aren's emotions felt to Nikki somewhere between thankful and indignant.

The reports of mini-cannon gunfire from the sea and ricocheting bullets all around them forced the three to retreat back away from the stern edge of the helipad and to duck down.

"The Ghost Gliders." Anders said what was on all of their minds.

"*Sum!*" Aren angrily swore, then stood up stiffly.

The uncontrolled rage building in Aren made Nikki uncomfortable, then concerned for her and Anders. She didn't know who Aren intended to receive the swirling red-yellow glows of what looked like superheated plasma around each of his hands. She hoped Aren's declaration of "Enough!" was for the bad guys. Aren then deliberately stepped to the edge of the helicopter platform as a hail of bullets from the burp of a minigun somewhere astern vaporized several feet in front of him. Aren raised his right hand at the Ghost Gliders, striking one of the craft with a glowing ball of hot plasma. His right hand now looked normal. The craft still maneuvered as flames in several locations defied being extinguished. Aren raised his left hand at the same boat with the result being the craft erupting in flames, forcing its riders to abandon the craft by jumping into the water, most of them burning until they were completely submerged.

The second Ghost Glider fired a burp from its minigun at them. The bullets again vaporized in front of Aren, except for the last couple in the burst. They struck Aren with enough force to knock him down on the helipad. Nikki felt all of it . . . the glee of unrestrained use of his Agni powers and the pain of exhaustion and having been hit by bullets despite his desire to maintain the wall of energy he erected in front of himself to absorb the weapons' fire.

Nikki crawled over to Aren, afraid he might be dead. "Aren, Aren, are you alive?"

Aren lay unmoving. Two bullets struck him in his right thigh and shoulder. Both wounds bled and needed treatment, but neither looked lethal.

"*Marr zu zisagal?*" Nikki asked Aren again, this time in Antaalin, if he lived.

"I still don't understand how you know that language, Nikki," Anders stated as he applied pressure on Aren's shoulder wound.

"I told you, but you dismissed me," Nikki shot back. "It came to me when I was inside that broken travel gate. I somehow became aware or linked to Aren and Rogaan and . . ."

A groan came from Aren. Without opening his eyes, he spat words tenaciously at Anders in English. "Don't touch me!"

Anders held up his bloodstained hands in the air. "Okay—then bleed to death. I try to help you, and all you do is complain and give me that evil-eye thing."

Aren placed his hands on himself, right hand to right thigh and left hand to right shoulder. He took a deep breath, then his Agni stone glowed slightly as he trembled and gasped. "*Ul sum.*"

"What do you mean, 'not enough'?" Nikki asked, concerned what Aren meant by his words.

"I need to renew," Aren answered her in English. He looked exhausted, and he trembled with every move. "I'm without power to help if attacked again."

More burps of mini-gun fire erupted on the starboard side of the stern. Bullets riddled the walkway below them. The crew were yelling to each other trying to coordinate return fire at the attacking Ghost Glider.

"*Uzal,*" Aren commented as he lay on the helipad.

"What's a waste of time?" Nikki asked him.

"Your weapons against that boat," he answered in English. "Too much fortified."

Without warning, Aren grabbed Nikki and pulled her to the helipad deck with a thump of her head and a statement of protest. Her head throbbed in pain. Anders made to protest just as a deafening boom and pressure shock wave passed over them, knocking Anders off his feet and sent him tumbling forward on the helipad. The shipborne railgun round from the closing U.N. frigate ripped through the *Wind Runner*'s bridge superstructure, exploding on the other side, sending countless burning fragments of metal and other materials flying in all directions. Nikki instinctively rolled toward Aren to try to cover him and protect him from the shrapnel. They collided to both of their surprise as shrapnel rained down all around them, some burning, some not. After the metal rain ended, they inspected themselves for injuries. Neither was hurt from this latest attack.

Nikki looked for Anders. She found him lying at the edge of the helipad unmoving. She tried to stand up, but fell when she put weight on her right foot. She tried again. When she fell, tracer fire passed just over her head from a burp of bullets expelled by the minigun of the remaining boarding fast craft, that Ghost Glider.

"We're going to die, aren't we?" Nikki felt herself trembling as she remained still on her hands and knees, paralyzed with fear. This all was too much to take. She shouted out in anger and desperation, "Stop it! Stop it!"

A groan with Nikki's name in it came from the edge of the helipad. Nikki looked up to find Anders half-crawling, half-stumbling toward her in the dim light of the dusk. Most of the exterior lights of the ship were either destroyed or without power. The almost-full moon provided more illumination than the ship's lights now. Tracers ricocheted off the starboard side of the helipad as others flew just over Anders before he dropped back to the deck. He crawled to her the rest of the five meters.

"Are you okay?" Anders asked with a desperate tone.

"No!" she replied. "They're shooting at us, and we're going to die."

"Calm down——" Anders tried to instruct her how to control her emotions.

"Calm down?" Nikki cut him off as she glared at him. "The ship's been torn up. It's no match for whatever that ship is out there and its big gun, Ghost thingies and drones and Tyr soldiers. Aren's saved us a couple of times, but he's in no condition to fight, and Rogaan is lost to us."

Anders had nothing to counter her assessment of their situation. He opened his mouth a couple of times to refute her, but comforting words escaped him. "I have nothing."

Nikki looked over at Aren. He was smiling again, as he lay there on the helipad. His casual attitude was totally wrong for their situation, and it angered her. "What in the hell are you smiling at?"

"*Sud inaa Im, seher Nikki!*" Aren stated in Antaalin, no longer phrasing his words as a question. Aren sat up looking to the stern of the ship.

"What is he babbling about?" Anders asked.

"He wants me to feel the wind," she replied.

"That's stupid," Anders scoffed. "Feel the wind at a time like this? What's he thinking? He's lost his mind."

Nikki did feel . . . something. It was that sensation of a presence both intelligent and powerful. She could feel it without Aren having to help her. *Where is it coming from?* She looked off the stern of the ship. A light below the surface of the water approached fast. Her heart sank. Another weapon from the U.N. frigate?

Nikki feared she was really going to die in this attack. A strange sense of urgency struck her. She thought to speak to God in her last moments . . .

pray to Him and ask Him for forgiveness . . . for not going to church . . . and not praying to Him, and not being a good, loving person her Bubba asked her to be. Tears welled up in her eyes. And Nikki wanted to thank God for taking her Bubba into heaven. She missed her so much and hoped she was in a better place. She had regrets too deep for one simple prayer to wash away. It was too late for more prayers Nikki realized, as the submerged light was about to strike them . . . end their lives. No! She wanted to fix the things wrong in her life. She wasn't ready to accept her death.

The white light burst from the water a rock throw from the stern of the ship. A splash of water soaked them as the light, now turning into a glowing elliptical disc with four or more white vaporous tendrils hanging from its underside, passed over them. The glowing disc banked and turned to the starboard side of the *Wind Runner*'s superstructure, then descended to just above the waves racing back to the ship's stern going head-on with the U.N. Ghost Glider as the craft's minigun blazed tracer fire directly on the white glowing disc. As the disc passed, Nikki saw the topside of it. It had a seat and console in front of that, all white from the glow coming from the disc surface below. The disc had a rider, a single rider, flying directly into the hail of tracers and bullets that were being vaporized orange-red as they touched the white glow.

"You've *got* to be kidding me . . ." Nikki looked at Aren. The Evendiir had a knowing smile along with his now casual stance on the helipad.

The rider of the glowing disc held in his right hand what looked to be a dark-hued sword. He held it out to the side as he passed to the left of the Ghost Glider . . . the tracers and bullets never-ending from the attack craft until the sword sliced through the craft's armored hull and gun mount. The Ghost Glider slowed as it came apart on its topside. Tyr soldiers emerged from the craft, all searching for, then firing on the white glowing disc as it turned back toward them. Again a hail of bullets along with mini-missiles rained on the disc, all vaporizing orange-red as soon as they touched the white glow. A single projectile with a glowing trailing tail emerged from the white glow as it closed rapidly on the damaged Ghost Glider. The projectile passed through the three Tyr soldiers standing on the craft before ripping through with electrical arcs of what Nikki took as the pilot compartment.

All three supersoldiers collapsed to the deck, then fell off the sides of the Ghost Glider into the roiling waters. The Ghost Glider suddenly jerked to the left before collapsing sideways into the waves and quickly started sinking. The glowing tail of the projectile continued on, allowing Nikki to follow it as it turned back toward the disc. It slowed as it closed on the approaching disc, then flew into the white glow.

"What just happened?" Anders asked Nikki.

"I don't know . . . a miracle maybe," she answered, still stunned from the turn of events.

The glowing disc slowed as it approached the *Wind Runner*'s stern. It took up a position a couple of meters astern of the ship just under the elevation of the helipad. Nikki urged Anders to help her quickly get to the edge of the helipad. He was apprehensive but unable to slow her encouragement. Aren was standing at the edge of the pad when they caught up to him.

"You waste time enough before arriving," Aren chastised him in Antaalin. Nikki understood every word. Anders stood watching, but wasn't demanding for her to translate word for word. "We endured the hammering work."

"Lacking my help, old friend?" Rogaan wore a smile as he stood on the disc surface straddling a seat that looked as if it was an extension of the disc surface below. He too spoke in Antaalin. Still in the white sensor gown with his bow case and sheathed blue sword strapped over his shoulders, he held his blue metal bow in his left hand while engulfed in the white glow coming from the disc surface under his feet. The disc hovered in the air, matching the speed of the ship that still cruised at its meager clip propelled by its noiseless propulsion system.

"Forget that!" Aren sounded cranky and in a hurry, still in Antaalin. "Place yourself three strides lower and face that other ship. Hurry!"

Rogaan had a confused look on him as he complied with Aren's instructions. Aren grabbed Nikki and had her kneel down on the helipad. Anders followed suit.

"What now?" Rogaan asked in his native tongue while keeping his eyes fixed on the gloom behind the *Wind Runner*.

"*Dung!*" Rogaan growled in Antaalin as blue metallic tendrils from his left forearm guard attached to his bow, reshaping it into an oval-shaped shield for Rogaan to brace himself behind.

"Crap!" Nikki saw it too . . . a flash from the U.N. frigate . . . its big gun or a missile. She understood what she was looking at now. *But Aren can't stop or deflect this one!* Nikki cringed as she held her breath and Anders even more tightly. An electric current surged around her making her feel as if insects crawled all over her. She shivered. It came quickly. She barely saw it before it struck. The entire stern of the ship exploded in a brilliant light, a blast of pressure and a deafening roar, a clang, a thud. An explosion somewhere behind her told her she was still alive and that somehow Rogaan defected the hypersonic projectile. *Probably into the superstructure again. This is the stuff of science fiction and myths and legends and fairy tales*, she thought to herself. Worried Rogaan was injured or likely dead, she looked for him on his disc as soon as her eyes recovered from the bold flash of light.

"I swear by the fire sands of Kur!" Rogaan jumped up from where he had been slammed into the seat from the impact of the railgun projectile when he deflected it with that shield of his. He started dancing about . . . in pain, his words flowing in his ancient language. Nikki couldn't keep up with his unsavory expletives as her cheeks reddened. Amazingly, he was still on the disc, though he was in a lot of pain and trying to shake his left arm as he groaned and growled and danced about. Nikki would have thought his display overdramatic if it hadn't been for him deflecting a weapon designed to sink a ship.

"Why not tell me . . . you work ass!" Rogaan yelled at Aren in Antaalin. Aren put on a simple smirk as he waited for Rogaan to finish his tirade, which Rogaan continued, "You bastard!"

"That is without politeness . . ." Aren wore his smirk proudly as he replied to his friend in English. "I *have* a father."

"Say something before it takes place," Rogaan scolded Aren while continuing his dance to shake off the pain. He also spoke in English, matching Aren's linguistic abilities. Nikki suspected they now spoke in English so she would not misunderstand, or maybe they were competing with each other by the way they were exchanging quips.

"They are getting ready more heavenly barbed arrows," Aren stated as calmly as if giving Rogaan direction to a bathroom.

Rogaan stopped his dancing and shaking his left arm. He stood unmoving, giving Aren a long look of disbelief, then a head shake in disgust, or *I cannot believe this*. He then took up a solid stance, left foot forward and right foot back, at the left side of the disc's seat as he stared into the dusky gloom, breathing with an even rhythm. The night hadn't fully engulfed them yet. The sun's rays still touched the superstructure of the distant *Watchman* making the ship visible through the gloom. The U.N. frigate had quickly closed on them and now was less than a mile away, if Nikki judged the distance right.

"Curse me with violence in Kur if that ship strikes us again," Rogaan vowed. Nikki didn't know to whom he vowed or was talking to. Rogaan then spoke loudly with a motion of his head meaning his comments were for her. "The ship is three thousand and six hundred strides from us."

"How can he know that so precisely?" She looked at Aren.

"He is superior at evaluating distant places," Aren spoke with amusement in his voice.

"Why are you not afraid, Aren?" Nikki found his mannerisms out of place. It worried and angered her. "What do you find so amusing?"

"Feel the Wind . . ." Aren said in a carefree manner as he raised his arms high. He looked around as if expecting something to happen, then dropped his hands. He shrugged his shoulders and raised his arms to the sky again as he spoke with a louder voice, "Feel the Wind."

Moments passed and nothing happened. Nikki tried to suppress a snicker at Aren's antics. He looked the part of an actor on stage . . . in a failing production. Aren's expression turned frustrated.

"Nothing?" Aren sounded a bit put out as he asked the sky.

Nikki watched Aren, not knowing what to think. She looked to Anders and agreed with his earlier assessment. "You're right. Aren has lost his mind."

Aren's cheeks turned crimson as his face soured. Again, in English, he barked at his friend, "Burn you, Rogaan. Make disappear that demon ship out there!"

Nikki felt Aren's frustration with Rogaan and his desire to play one-upsmanship with him. She saw Rogaan's serious face and determined eyes acknowledging his friend's impatience before he looked back to the *Watchman*. More so, Nikki felt Rogaan's determination and focus. So focused, that nothing else existed for him other than his bow and the *Watchman* . . . and that presence, its intelligence . . . its power. Nikki shivered. The blue metallic shield on Rogaan's left arm reshaped back into his bow. Nikki watched awed by the ancient artifacts and Rogaan's command of them. Rogaan raised his bow at the *Watchman*. When the fingers of his right hand touched the metallic bow string, an arrow formed from the flow of blue metal from Rogaan's right forearm guard. A faint glow engulfed the arrow. Rogaan released the arrow, so calmly and without moving any other muscles than his fingers. He held his position as if a statue while the arrow streaked in a slight arc toward the *Watchman*. The arrow flew far faster than any she ever saw . . . and she never heard of anyone making a more-than-three-kilometer shot . . . with a bow. She followed the arrow's faint glow to its target over a span of a handful of seconds. Nothing happened. *Did it hit? Where's the explosion?* Nikki waited a few more moments for something to happen. Rogaan lowered his bow, then stood with eyes fixed on the U.N. frigate. Nikki wanted badly to ask if the arrow was a dud, but was afraid of the answer and what it would mean for them. A flash from the *Watchman*'s deck told Nikki another railgun round was on its way to them. *We're doomed!* Nikki lost hope as she agreed that Rogaan was going to Kur.

In the storm of the battle, Rogaan stood unflinching as the hypersonic projectile streaked at them. Then, the ocean between the ships turned to vapor several hundred meters astern of the *Wind Runner*, right in the path of the projectile. A reddish-orange beam of energy blasted its way skyward from the roiling waters. The speeding projectile from the *Watchman* instantly vaporized as it passed through the energy beam. Nikki's jaw dropped, seemingly to the ship's deck as her hopes rose.

"Watch," Aren told Nikki. He was excited with anticipation. "*Feel the Wind.*"

The energy beam disappeared, but the ocean continued to roil, and it was now illuminated in a multitude of colors from below. An object appeared in the center of the swirling and bubbling waters. A pointed tip-shaped object of gleaming metal rose. No . . . a pyramid, as big as or bigger than the Great Pyramid of Giza rose. It appeared made of gleaming blue, red and black metals with large red semispherical crystalline structures adorning its side faces. The pyramid rose out of the water to hover a hundred meters above the waves, water pouring off the massive structure. A strong wind blew out from its underside and into the faces of those on the tail of the *Wind Runner*. Black swirls of vapor surrounded the underside and lower sides of the pyramid . . . the *Wind*. *That's what it's called and what Aren has been trying to tell me*. Nikki felt a surge of pride at that realization and her new understanding. It was then she fully felt its presence, its intelligence, and its power . . . ancient power . . . so much ancient power. It threatened to overwhelm her. She slumped a little on trembling legs before Anders caught her. He exchanged silent looks with Nikki, too afraid to speak and draw any attention to themselves.

Rogaan pointed at the *Watchman* with his bow and spoke with a determined calmness, "Burn."

Multiple-colored beams of energy emitted from the pyramid's crystalline structures striking the *Watchman* simultaneously. The ship disappeared in a cloud of vapors. It was gone in mere seconds. It was over. No more shooting. Nikki felt shocked, stunned, and relieved, all at the same time. Then she took in this flying pyramid hovering not far away. She swallowed hard.

Rogaan lowered his bow and looked up to the sky and the pyramid. An odd silence fell over everything. Only the blowing wind made a noise, a rumbling in Nikki's ears. She realized the pyramid made no sound otherwise. Its propulsion system silent. The disc Rogaan stood on rose until it was level with the helipad, then tucked in close to the ship. Rogaan jumped from it onto to the *Wind Runner* next to Aren. The white glowing disc, with its vaporous tendrils beneath, then accelerated away at high speed toward the pyramid. It flew directly into the pyramid without slowing down. Nikki didn't see a door or anything like an access portal open for it to enter. It was simply gone. A deep, resounding hum started, then grew louder, vibrating Nikki, the ship beneath her, the water, and the very air around her as the wind picked up to almost hurricane strength, forcing Nikki to rely on Anders to hold her upright as they both braced themselves while leaning into the powerful wind gusts.

Awesome and majestic, the pyramid started rising, then accelerated vertically through the aloft clouds of the dusk sky. The sun's rays high above gleaming from its metallic exterior before it disappeared to places beyond earth in several handfuls of seconds. The wind gusts in Nikki's face now settled to a light breeze.

They all silently stared at the sky for a time. "Wow" was all Nikki could think or say. She found it difficult to grasp all that just happened and struggled to think all of this was anything but a dream. Less than two weeks ago, she never could have imagined anything like this in her life. A calmness then filled her. It wasn't her, she realized. The feeling came from Rogaan and Aren. They shared similar emotions . . . calmness and . . . satisfaction. The two started bantering with each other in Antaalin. Nikki understood their every word as if she spoke Antaalin her entire life.

"How is it . . . that *Wind* finds us at the time it was needed?" Aren asked, still looking after the vaporous contrail left by the ship.

"Unknown, but I am pleased for it." Looking skyward still, Rogaan commented as if talking about his favorite possession or an event. "And I enjoy those *qufas*."

"You promised to instruct me to fly them . . ." Aren bantered with Rogaan as they started walking toward Nikki and Anders and the *Wind Runner*'s damaged island superstructure.

"It always seems a bad time when they appear," Rogaan offered rational for his tardiness in teaching his friend. "It is difficult to give instruction while others try to kill us."

"What did you do to goad these United Nations people?" Aren asked suspiciously.

"They attacked the ship before I woke," Rogaan answered. "The woman, Nikki, to be broken by one of the dark-armored warriors when I opened my eyes."

"You ended his life?" Aren asked knowingly, almost making more of a statement than a question.

"A tyrant is not difficult to see in his servants." Rogaan sounded like he quoted someone who gave him guidance in the ways of wisdom. "These servants showed their high-proud and oppressive ways. They were on the hunt to kill these people of this ship."

"I ponder these United Nations people wanted to capture us." Aren commented as if in a scholarly discussion.

"Then they wanted us without our *Lights* . . . when we acted not following their plan," Rogaan added.

"When *you* acted not following their plan to submit," Aren verbally jabbed at Rogaan, clarifying his statement. He did so with a half-smile. "Again you catch me in your acts of righteousness."

"I will not accept them murdering innocent ones," Rogaan countered with a wounded, indignant tone as he glanced Nikki's way. He then changed his tone to boastful. "Like . . . me . . . to submit?"

"Not since the backstreet quarreling in Padusan." Aren recalled a moment in their past that in part shaped Rogaan into who he is now. Rogaan momentarily put a regretful look on his face as he remembered a painful lesson. Aren continued, "You carry your righteousness in a manner that attracts trouble. It aids you well much of the time, but when it does not . . . affairs go badly."

"Talking of affairs . . . Are we on earth or have the gods taken us up to one of their worlds?" Rogaan asked Aren in a serious tone. ". . . if on earth, when are we?"

"I judge we continue on earth, old friend. As to when . . . the future." Aren fell silent for a few moments considering things he wasn't sharing. "If my judgments are perfection, an acquaintance from long ago may tell us that, and more."

Rogaan let the "acquaintance from long ago" hint pass without comment as he rubbed his stomach. "I'm starved. I'd like to know where there is something favorable to eat."

"Always the stomach leads your life after a battle," Aren bantered.

"Destroying evil and wickedness grows a voracious hunger," Rogaan boastfully bantered.

"Let us look for something to eat near where they held us on those painful beds." Aren set out a plan of action as they walked away, forgetting Anders and Nikki.

Nikki stood looking dumbfounded at the two, walking and talking like what they just went through was an everyday occurrence . . . "all in a day's work" or something like that.

"What in the name of all the gods and hells just happened?" Anders asked Nikki with an overwhelmed and disbelieving tone.

"I think we got a lot more than a set of bones on this dig." Nikki tried to make light of their situation. "I think we're smack-dab in the middle of some serious trouble."

"Biblical." Anders clarified. Nikki nodded in agreement.

"Help me catch up with them, Shawn," Nikki asked of Anders as she clung to him for support. Her foot remained at that odd angle, making her ill when she looked at it, and her right leg was starting to hurt again.

"Why?" Anders asked. "You need to lie down. Those two aren't going anywhere."

"You have that all wrong," Nikki corrected him as she intently watched Rogaan and Aren walk past the wreckage and carnage on the deck of the *Wind Runner* before disappearing under the island superstructure back the way of the medical lab.

"How so?" He sounded as if he didn't believe her.

"When the captain handed Aren that gemstone of jade and pearl and spoke of a 'mutual acquaintance' to prove to Aren he could be trusted . . ." Nikki explained with a seriousness born of unquenchable curiosity and a terrible trepidation. ". . . strong emotions ran through Aren. Enormous amounts of respect, but an even greater sense of fear. Aren thinks he knows what's behind all of this and is determined to find and confront it."

And the story continues . . .

Book 3 of the Primeval Origins Epic Saga
is anticipated for release in the winter of 2016/2017.
Follow the adventures of Nikki, Rogaan, Pax, Aren, and others
Beyond the Light of Honor.
Visit the Lexicon and Encyclopedia and
Explore the latest Primeval Origins News,
And much more at:
www.primevalorigins.com
www.facebook.com/primevalorigins